THE
HONEYMOON

The Honeymoon

DINITIA SMITH

Other Press

NEW YORK

First softcover edition 2017
ISBN 978-1-59051-888-5

Production editor: Yvonne E. Cárdenas
Text designer: Julie Fry
This book was set in Bell and New Caledonia
by Alpha Design & Composition of Pittsfield, NH.

1 3 5 7 9 10 8 6 4 2

Library of Congress Cataloging-in-Publication Data

Names: Smith, Dinitia, author.
Title: The honeymoon / Dinitia Smith.
Description: New York : Other Press, 2016.
Identifiers: LCCN 2015037067| ISBN 9781590517789 (hardcover) |
ISBN 9781590517796 (ebook)
Subjects: LCSH: Eliot, George, 1819-1880—Fiction. | Women
novelists—Fiction. | Man-woman relationships—Fiction. | BISAC: FICTION /
Biographical. | FICTION / Literary. | FICTION / Historical. | GSAFD:
Biographical fiction. | Historical fiction. | Love stories.
Classification: LCC PS3569.M526 H66 2016 | DDC 813/.54—dc23 LC record
available at http://lccn.loc.gov/2015037067

Publisher's Note:
This is a work of fiction. Names, characters, places, and incidents
either are the product of the author's imagination or are used fictitiously.

For David, as always & Peter, Daniel, and Layla

A Note to the Reader

This is a novel, a product of my imagination inspired by the life and writings of George Eliot. It is an effort to depict her inner world as she lived out her life. To write it, I have sometimes transposed phrases from Eliot's novels, letters, and journals. The rest, however, is my own creation.

For the sake of clarity, I have taken some dramatic license in the chronology, but there is nothing in this story that I know with certainty did not happen.

Most, but not all, of the letters quoted are Eliot's own, or those of her circle.

I have profited enormously from the biographies and scholarship on Eliot and her contemporaries. An essay on sources is appended at the end.

THE
HONEYMOON

May 26, 1857

My dear Brother

You will be surprized, I dare say, but I hope not sorry, to learn that I have changed my name, and have someone to take care of me in the world. The event is not at all a sudden one, though it may appear sudden in its announcement to you. My husband has been known to me for several years, and I am well acquainted with his mind and character...

Your affectionate Sister, Marian Lewes...

PART I

La Vita Nuova

Chapter 1

One late afternoon in June of 1880, a rather famous woman sat in a railroad carriage traveling toward Venice with her new husband, a handsome young man twenty years her junior. The journey from Padua had taken just over an hour, across the flat plain, through vineyards and olive groves, and now the train was approaching the iron bridge that led across the lagoon to the city. As the woman glimpsed the shimmering waters ahead, and in the distance, the misty domes and campaniles of the celestial place, the light in the sky over it just beginning to turn pink, she discovered she was unable to give herself over to the surge of excitement she'd experienced sixteen years earlier—to the day—when she caught sight of the city with her first husband, George Lewes, by her side.

The woman's face was partly hidden by a lace mantilla, as had been her custom for several years, white, not black now (she was no longer in mourning), and she wore a gray silk moiré dress that she'd bought for her trousseau. The mantilla served to prevent her from being recognized and set upon by tourists who begged for autographs. Though not completely hiding her face, it distracted from it, from her large nose and broad jaw, and she welcomed this because she believed that she was homely. She was sixty years old and her auburn hair, speckled with gray, hung in thick, heavy curves on either side of her face. Her skin was lined. Her gray-blue eyes were heavy and watchful. But her figure was still lovely, slender, almost serpentine—she'd never borne a child.

But now, as she watched her new young husband, it was as if he were drifting away from her, going farther and farther into his own world, and she didn't know why.

He was staring out the window of the compartment, his brow furrowed in the light. He was a tall, athletic-looking man with dark red, curly hair that peeked out from under the brim of his straw hat, vivid blue eyes that shone in the heat, and a small, neat beard. As always, he was wearing an elegantly cut suit, white linen, which had somehow preserved its freshness from the journey—Johnnie loved good clothes.

Yet he was still his same kind self, the way he had always been, tending to her every need. Ever since April, when she'd accepted his proposal, he'd been frantically rushing around, arranging the wedding and securing the new house, anxious to attend to her every comfort—that she have her shawl with her in case it was cool at night, and the best room in the hotel, that she not get tired, or have to stand waiting too long for their trains. He hadn't been sleeping, he'd hardly been eating. There were shadows under his eyes, his cheeks had hollowed out. "Darling," she would say, "slow down. You'll make yourself ill."

And he'd try to calm himself, like a child forced to sit still for a moment, but then he was up again, springing into action.

Perhaps Venice would make him better, restore him to his old self, and the romance of the city, its sensuousness and foreignness and hidden ways, the strangeness of it, would free him and bring him back to her.

The train had reached the bridge. A cinder from the track flew in through the open window and caught her in the eye. "Oh dear," she cried, and tried to get it out. Johnnie, awakened from his reverie, jumped up. "Here, let me," he said. He bent over her and gently managed to ease it out with his pocket handkerchief. "There you go," he said, and then he sat down again and resumed looking out the window.

After a few minutes they had crossed the bridge. The train pulled into the Santa Lucia station and they disembarked.

When they emerged onto the *fondamenta*, they were met by a scene of chaos, crowds of tourists and piles of baggage, porters and boatmen yelling and bustling about.

"You stay here, Marian," Johnnie said. "I'll go and find the boat."

She waited under her parasol. The air was filled with an anxious cacophony of French, Italian, English, German, as the tourists searched for the boatmen from the hotels who were supposed to meet them. A Gypsy girl was sitting on the pavement with an infant, begging, holding it out to the tourists and whining, *"Il bambino ha fame. Il bambino ha fame...,"* wearing a look of exaggerated suffering on her face.

At last, Johnnie returned to her. He'd found their boat, and he led her across the *fondamenta* to where it was tied. The gondolier was standing on the shore waiting. When he saw them coming, he threw his cigarette into the canal with a decisive gesture and began loading their luggage.

"This is Corradini," Johnnie said. "Madame Cross." The man was older, she noticed, in his fifties, weathered and thin and muscular, with close-cropped gray hair, very pale blue eyes—probably Dalmatian, a lot of the gondoliers were, or a remnant of the Crusaders that you saw sometimes among Venetians. He had a browned, seamed face and he wore a gold ring in one ear. The gondolier nodded at her cursorily, then extended a rough hand to help her into the boat. No bowing or scraping, no kissing of the hand, no false effusion. As she passed close to him to step into the boat, she smelled an unwashed odor, old tobacco and sweat, and something else, cologne meant to cover it.

He'd probably done this job for many years. The gondoliers held the tourists captive. They were their first contact with the city. Only the gondoliers knew how to navigate its labyrinthine ways.

All around them now, on the Grand Canal, the boats, full of people who'd gotten off the train from Padua, were crowded together and banging up against one another. The gondoliers were trying to separate them. "*Premi! Premi!*" they cried. "*Stali! Stali!*"

At last untangled, the gondolas spread out across the water. The journey to the hotels was under way.

It was suddenly quiet, as if everyone was too exhausted and stunned by the sights, and too busy absorbing the strangeness of the place, to speak. In the boat, Johnnie sat perpendicular to her, his long legs drawn up awkwardly in the small space, silent, absorbed in looking across at the shore.

To their right was San Simeone Piccolo—Ruskin called it a huge "gasometer," with its great, dark dome, like a

Greek temple oddly attached to a plain red-brick building. They passed silently among the columned palaces with their Moorish arches and red-and-white-striped mooring poles, their facades of marble and Istrian stone, their inlay of jasper and alabaster and porphyry, faded by sun and water; their foundations darkened and stained green with algae from the flux and retreat of the tides over the centuries. As always, she was surprised at their small scale, given the expectation of what Venice would be.

The gondolier stood erect in the stern, feathering the water with his oar, moving from one side to the other, swerving his hips. His skin looked as if it had been oiled. His striped shirt and black trousers fit tightly to his body, but there was a softness around his waist that betrayed his age.

Ahead of them loomed the humpbacked Rialto, its archways and shops packed with tourists. As they passed under it, in the confined space the smell of putrid effluence rose up and engulfed them. She could see brownish things bobbing in the water. She held her handkerchief to her nose to block the smell.

As they emerged again into the pink light, she breathed in the salty, brackish air with relief. When the real heat came, the smell would be insufferable. Well, she thought, along with everything glorious and holy, there had to exist its opposite: decay and death. For there to be light, there must be darkness, mystery.

The canal curved southwest, then bent again eastward. She glimpsed on the shore the white marble Hôtel de la Ville where once she and George had stayed. As they passed it, she glanced back, but said nothing to Johnnie.

At last they came to the sign for the Hotel Europa. It was in the old Palazzo Giustinian, an umber-colored brick building with white Gothic arches and balconies overlooking the canal. Just beyond it was the Piazza San Marco.

"There!" Johnnie called to the gondolier. They stopped, and a grizzled old *ganser* reached down from the *riva* with his pole and pulled them over to the steps.

The gondolier threw up his rope and the man tied it. Johnnie gripped her tightly under the arms and raised her up from her seat. She was dizzy from standing up too quickly, and tired from the journey. Johnnie held on to her a moment, then leapt to the shore, reached down and lifted her up onto ground. "We've made it!" he cried.

He handed the gondolier a coin. But the man didn't move. He stood there with his palm open, looking down ostentatiously at the coin, then up at Johnnie again. Flustered, Johnnie dug down again into his pocket and offered him more coins. At this, the gondolier clamped his hand shut and got back into his boat.

"Greedy swine!" Johnnie muttered, clenching his teeth, as they made their way to the *portego*.

Inside the hotel, they climbed the stairs into an immense, marble-columned lobby with a high, coffered ceiling, gilded and blue, and glass chandeliers and potted palms. At one end was a reception desk with a sign, TELEGRAFO. Other tourists, scattered about on chairs and settees, stared at them as they entered.

Johnnie led her to a settee and went to register. Was she imagining it, or did he welcome this bodily distance from her, being away from her for these few minutes?

After a brief period, he came back across the lobby followed by a man in a black morning coat. "This is Monsieur Marseille, the manager. He wanted to meet you. Madame Cross," Johnnie said.

"Madame...George Eliot!" said the manager, hesitating a moment as if puzzled by the man's name for a woman. He bowed. He was wearing a wig of flat black hair and he had a handlebar mustache, waxed and pointed at the tips.

"Of course, you know we have had many famous writers staying with us," he said. "Chateaubriand, Mr. Ruskin. Many famous people, Mr. Turner, and Wagner, also Verdi. You are in excellent company."

"How did you know who I was? she asked.

"The English lady over there." He indicated a woman sitting across the lobby on one of the settees, watching them. "She inform us of who you were. She say she recognize you. She tell us we have a great English authoress in our midst—"

Johnnie interrupted, "Mrs. Cross doesn't want to be bothered. She's on a private holiday. We'd appreciate it if you didn't tell anyone else she's here."

"Of course, Monsieur."

This had happened many times. George used to sign their hotel registers with false names to prevent them from being bothered. But people knew her, even though, after she became famous, she almost always refused to be painted or photographed. Still, when they went to the Pop Concerts at St. James's Hall, people sketched her. George would glare, but it didn't stop them. None other than Princess Louise once drew her likeness on the back of her program at a benefit concert for the Music School of the Blind. Truthfully, there were times when she didn't mind the attention. Sometimes the fame, being recognized, was like a match being struck, a temporary light, a moment of pleasure, forgetting all her doubts, the lack of confidence, the headaches and kidney pains. But now she dreaded it. At this very moment in London she imagined there was a new scandal unfolding.

As people read the wedding announcement in the *Times*, they were laughing and twittering over their morning coffee about the besotted old woman marrying the handsome man young enough to be her son.

To alleviate the manager's chagrin, she asked politely, "You are French?"

"My grandfather, Monsieur Arnold Marseille, bought this palazzo in 1817. This year, we install private baths. Very grand, very convenient."

A footman was hovering behind him. "The footman will show you to your room. We have here today six English families. There is the table d'hôte at five o'clock. Perhaps you and your son would care to join us?"

Her chest plunged. Johnnie's face reddened.

"Please!" Johnnie cried. "The signora is my wife!"

"Oh!" the manager said. *"Vous devez me pardonner!"* But his mortification only magnified the insult. He was mirroring back to them the truth. She did look like Johnnie's mother.

As they ascended the stairs to the *piano nobile* and their rooms, she said, "We knew this would happen sooner or later. Imagine what they're saying in London."

"We don't mind what they're saying," he said firmly, his jaw set, gripping her arm.

They came to the landing, and the footman threw open the gleaming mahogany doors to their *appartement.* It was hung with chandeliers, gilded mirrors, and oil paintings, and furnished with silk-covered *fauteuils.* There were great, mullioned windows which looked out directly over the canal and crimson velvet drapes fastened with braided silk ties and tassels.

On either side of the *sala* was a bedroom. Johnnie went to the door of each one and peeked inside. He pointed to the one on the right. "This is the best room," he told the footman. "The lady's trunk goes in there. The other trunk's mine. In there, please," he said, indicating the second bedroom across the way.

It was their usual ritual.

While the footman put their luggage away, Johnnie stepped out onto the balcony. She followed him. To their left was the landing of San Marco, the black gondolas parked in front of it swaying in the water. To their right was the view down the Grand Canal.

He began enumerating the sights, as if learning them himself. "There's the Dogana," he said, indicating the customhouse across the canal, its gold weathervane, the figure of the goddess Fortuna, moving faintly in the late afternoon sun. "The Salute," he said, sweeping his arm across to the imposing dome behind it. "And San Giorgio," he said, across the Bacino, the little island on their left.

He stopped and looked down at the canal, suddenly silent.

She touched his shoulder. "Please," she said, "don't mind the stupid manager. I'm perfectly all right. You shouldn't feel sad for me. We expected this. We knew it would happen.

I'm so happy to be here. Everything's going to be all right now, you'll see."

He continued staring down into the water as if he hadn't heard her.

"Johnnie, did you hear me?"

He nodded, still not looking at her.

"Please, Johnnie, smile for me," she begged. "Let me see you smile."

He looked around at her and forced his mouth into a thin smile.

"Shouldn't I be the one who's angry?" she asked. "Not you. It's not your fault, is it? It's I who look old!"

He didn't respond. He seemed to be looking right through her. She reached up and touched his red curls — she was allowed to do that, wasn't she? He was so tall. She loved the moments when she could touch him with impunity. His hair was so soft and silky, like a boy's.

Behind them there was a knock on the door. "*Chi è?*" he called out irritably.

"*Sono la cameriera,*" a woman's voice answered.

"*Entra!*" he commanded. He sighed. "They're always bothering you."

A maid entered. She was a girl of about sixteen, in a black dress, white cap, collar, and pinafore. She had a mass of dark blond curls tied behind her neck, green, heavy-lidded eyes, and a prominent aquiline nose. A Northern face.

"I unpack for Madame?" she asked in English.

"Yes, please. Thank you," Marian said. "That one." She pointed to her bedroom.

On the balcony, Johnnie said, "You can smell it from here. That smell of putrefaction underneath everything."

"You forget about it," she said. "You get used to it. When the wind shifts, we won't notice it at all. And when the tide comes in, the water's very clear."

The sky was darkening, burnished with gold. "Look at the light," she exclaimed. "The sun's going down. This is the glory of the place."

He put his arm around her waist and drew her to him, a protective gesture, warm and kind. She was acutely conscious of his touch. She looked up at his face. It was the familiar posture of a woman looking up at the man she loves, she thought, her life's companion, his face in profile, the face she possesses as her own, but the face of someone separate, unknowable. All men were mysterious to her, except George. She and George had been like one person. Johnnie's was a handsomer face than George's of course, an ideal of masculine beauty. Before she and George had come together, she'd heard people call him "the ugliest man in London"—not true! But Johnnie's face was troubled. His forehead was drawn in a frown.

By now George would have been animated with excitement. "Look, Polly!" he'd cry, calling her by her girlhood nickname. Always full of enthusiasm, rousing her from tiredness and worry and depression. "Can't wait till morning!" he'd say. And he'd awaken her into his own joy. He was irresistible. When he pulled her close, her body melded completely into his. No distance between them, the line of his wiry thigh against hers, he, who relished her body continually, her slenderness, always, with each new day and night as if he'd never known it before and it was a constant surprise to him, whatever it was he saw in it, distorted by blind love.

Now, behind them in the hotel room, there were sudden, soft bursts of light. The chambermaid was lighting the oil lamps, leaving the edges of the room in shadow.

"Let's have supper brought up," he said. "Someone else might recognize you and that would be a bother."

"Yes," she said. "Do let's. I can't bear to see anyone else tonight."

Chapter 2

The maid brought their supper up to the room on a cart, set the table with thick white linens, and lit the candles. As they ate and it grew dark out, the sounds of the canal began to quiet, except for the occasional raucous cries of the gondoliers intruding on the calm and the whisper of voices and footsteps on the *calle*.

Johnnie picked at his veal and cuttlefish. "You aren't eating anything," she said, like a mother.

"I'm just not hungry."

"But the fish is perfect. Very light."

"Yes."

"You've got to eat, Johnnie. You must."

"I know," he said, without interest.

"Tomorrow we should go in the morning to the Accademia," she said. "And visit Ruskin's man, Bunney." Ruskin had spotted their wedding announcement in the paper and sent a note congratulating her. People saw little of Ruskin these days. He was supposedly sequestered in a house in the Lake District where, Thomas Carlyle said, he'd gone mad. Hearing that they were going to Venice on their honeymoon, Ruskin had written to them, however, to say they *must* visit his employee, John Wharlton Bunney, a painter who worked for him in his St. George's Guild. Ruskin was on a campaign to stop the restoration of the ancient buildings of Venice, and he was paying Bunney to paint pictures of them before they were destroyed. He wanted to enlist Marian in his cause, and he had sent a letter to Bunney telling him that "Mr. and Mrs. Cross" would soon be calling.

"I'm looking forward to meeting any man called 'Bunney,'" Johnnie said now. "He must be a very industrious bunny." He smiled. She was glad for the smile.

Their meal finished, they went out on the balcony again and sat together on the bench. Their bodies didn't touch. His big, masculine hand rested on the velvet cushion, but he didn't reach for hers.

The sky was a great depth of smoky darkness. The waters of the canal were black, punctuated by the wavering reflection of the lights on the embankment. From behind them came the tactful clinking of dishes and silverware, the chambermaid clearing away supper.

The girl finished, then asked, *"Signora, le preparo il letto?"*

"Yes, I'm coming," Marian said, and rose. Johnnie was summoned out of his trance and he stood up and bent and kissed her hand. She brushed his cheek briefly with her fingertips.

"You'll sleep well tonight from the journey," she said. "It'll be quiet. You'll feel better in the morning." Freed from your new, mysterious, unnamed sorrow, she thought.

He looked downcast. "I hope so. I feel as if I'm incapable of sleep. It's an art lost to me. Something other people know how to do, but not me. Perhaps there's something wrong with my brain?" There was a tone of desperation in his voice. "Something physiological?"

"There's nothing wrong," she said. "You've just been overexcited. You've taken on too much. Now that it's all over, it's time for you to rest."

"I hope so."

"Perhaps you should take something?" she said.

"I've tried. It doesn't seem to help. I'll have a whiskey." She had noticed that he had been drinking more.

"But you mustn't have too much!"

"I'm careful."

The chambermaid was watching them with big round eyes. Marian hoped she didn't understand much English. She must have witnessed all forms of behavior from tourists in the intimacy of their hotel rooms—heated and romantic conversations, bouts of quarreling and coldness.

Johnnie kissed her hand again. She sensed he wanted her to leave. Because he was unhappy, she thought, and wanted to concentrate on his unhappiness, whatever it was, to try and survive it, focus all his energies on the effort.

She left him standing forlornly in the dim light.

In the bedchamber, the maid turned back the bed and helped Marian undress to her chemise and drawers, then lifted her nightgown down over her head.

"*Vorrebbe un po' d'acqua d'arancia, la mia donna?*" she asked.

"Thank you," Marian said. The girl poured the orange water from a silver pitcher by the bed. As she took the glass, the maid glanced at her hands. "*Le sue mani sono belle, la mia donna.*"

"Thank you, that's very sweet." She spread out her fingers. People always noticed her hands, her fingers were long and slender, good for the piano, the skin delicate, nearly transparent. Her hands and her feet were the only beautiful things about her. Whenever she complained to George about her looks, he'd just laugh at her. "Oh, stop, Polly. You're beautiful! And I know it even if you don't." He'd kept it up for all those years, not once through nearly a quarter century together slipping and giving in to her. "You don't look like a dolly," he said. "That's all. I know what it's like to love a little dolly," he said, "and it didn't please me at all." His wife, Agnes, he meant, who'd been so pretty in her youth, a fair, bright-complexioned girl when they'd married, but now a round, fat little thing, her body worn and stretched from giving birth to eight children.

"One hand's bigger than the other," she told the maid. "From churning butter when I was a girl. I'm a country girl," she said. "I grew up on a farm. What's your name, dear?"

"Gerita, Madame."

"'Gerita.' I don't think I've heard that name."

"From 'Margherita,'" she said.

"And how old are you?"

"*Diciassette.*"

"Seventeen," Marian repeated. "Where did you learn to take care of people so kindly?"

"*Mia madre.* She is ill. I look after her when I not here at the hotel."

"I'm so sorry," Marian said. "What is the matter with your mama?"

The girl touched her breast. "*È malate di cancro,*" she said.

"Cancer. My poor mother had that too."

The girl's eyes widened. "*Sua madre era malata?* Your mama also? Did she, your mama, die?"

"*Si, cara.*" She looked at the girl. "But your mama will be all right. I'm sure of it."

The girl crossed herself. "*O, mio dio...*" Then, "Would Madame like the mosquito net?"

"Yes, please." Fever was always a danger here.

She climbed into bed and the girl drew the netting around it, then curtsied and exited through the thick, paneled doors, closing them softly behind her.

She couldn't fall asleep. She watched the play of water reflected on the wall opposite. From below on the canal came the sounds of shouting and singing.

What was he doing in the next room? Had he gone to bed? Was he still out on the balcony, looking down at the water, beset by his worry? The manager's tactlessness had upset him so. She felt a sudden longing to put her arms around him, to comfort him, heal him with her love, make him better.

In the darkness and privacy, she remembered being with George in the Hôtel de la Ville. The seclusion and freedom of travel was liberating, the mosquito netting around them an added privacy. That night they'd made love not once, but twice. When it was over, he'd said to her, "Not bad for a man of forty-seven."

"To me, you'll always be young," she'd told him, placing her arm across his chest and resting her head on his shoulder.

Now, at last, came a wonderful sleep, as if she were on the gondola again, rocking and swaying gently in the water.

At midnight, she came to consciousness briefly when the bells of San Marco sounded, clanging and echoing off the empty Piazza next door, then she fell asleep again.

Somewhere in the premorning hours came the dream.

Chapter 3

She was a little girl and they'd sent her away to boarding school because her mother couldn't take care of her anymore. It was the depths of winter, she was so cold, the damp seeping into her very bones. She was trying to get to the fire, but a group of girls was standing in front of it. "I'm freezing," she cried. "Please—let me in!" But they were bigger than she was, and they'd gotten there first and they were hogging the warmth, and she was forced to hang back behind them, shivering so hard that her teeth were chattering and her bones were rattling in her skin.

Here in Venice, she woke up from the dream, and instinctively, half asleep, she moved as she always did when she had a bad dream, toward the other side of the bed, seeking him. Contact with his body magically soothed all her terrors and put her to sleep like a drug.

But now she grasped only air. Next to her the bed was empty, the wide mattress white in the moonlight.

She'd had this same dream again and again for more than fifty years, but in the past, George had been there to comfort her. Instead, the memories of her childhood came pouring back, the loneliness returned. She was unable to sleep.

The dream came from when she was at Miss Lathom's. She remembered it as vividly as if she were still five years old, the harshness of the place was imprinted forever upon her brain. She was the youngest girl in the school. That first night, after lights out, she'd lain in her iron cot amid the long rows of girls and the homesickness had spread through her body like a dull, wet ache. What had she done to make them send her there? Was she such a bad girl? Why had her mother made her go away? She'd tried so hard to be good and not to be any trouble.

Lying there in her cot, she started to cry. Her sobs and sniffles punctuated the darkness. "Shhh! Be quiet! *Do* shut up!" From up and down the aisles had come angry whispers. She tried to hold her sobs in, but they kept escaping from her.

Her sister, Chrissey, was asleep in the cot next to her. Chrissey was five years older than she was. She climbed out of her bed into Chrissey's, and she snuggled up against her bony body, and when Chrissey felt her there, she half woke up and sleepily took her in her arms and patted her. "It's all right, Polly," she whispered. "It's all right, dear...Hush now...don't cry..."

In the ensuing days, she'd held herself proudly, haughtily, apart from the rest of the girls. She followed Chrissey around and refused to look at anyone.

Her father had promised that he'd come on Friday afternoon at five o'clock, to take them home for the weekend. At four o'clock sharp, she went to the parlor so she could watch for him from the front window. She fixed her eyes on the driveway, willing him to come with all the force of her mind.

At last she caught sight of the gig and she dashed out the front door, breaking the rule that no pupil could leave the building without permission. She ran across the driveway to him and threw her arms around his legs. "Aye, little wench!" he said, and laughed. "You'll be knocking me over!" He picked her up and kissed her. The stubble on his face pricked her cheeks, and she smelled the reassuring smell of his old tobacco and the fleshy scent of his hair. She would keep that big, strong man from ever leaving her again.

She'd been sent away because her mother had given birth to twins. She was very young, but she remembered everything, every moment was burned on her memory. (George once said, "You never miss anything within the curl of your eyelash, do you?") She remembered the sounds of the birth, sitting at the foot of the stairs, listening to her mother's cries coming from behind the bedroom door, while Aunt Mary rushed past her carrying bowls of water and sheets. Her mother was suffering so, she wanted to help her, to save her from dying, to stop her pain. "You can't go in there," Aunt Mary told her. "You go downstairs now." She didn't, cowering in the shadows of the stairs, hoping no one would notice her there.

Then...a final, terrible scream. Aunt Mary emerged from the room. "There's two of 'em," she said briskly. "They'll not survive."

"I want to see Mama."

"Not now," she said. "Run along now."

The door to the room closed and opened, there was a momentary shaft of light from inside, then it closed again.

Downstairs, her mother's other sisters were seated by the fire. They had all come for the birth. Aunt Elizabeth, obsessed with illness, her own and those of other people, had been sitting through the cries from above, weeping and worrying and useless. Aunt Ann, thin and sallow-skinned, who had married the richest of the husbands, was useless too. She didn't want to dirty her elegant silk dress by helping out with the birth. Only Aunt Mary was of any help.

Her father was out on his rounds as manager of the Arbury Estate, and as usual Chrissey was a good girl, bringing Aunt Mary the tea for her mother, sitting quietly on her stool by the fire with her patchwork when she wasn't needed. Their brother, Isaac, kept away from the house, running wild, out fishing at Round Pool, or in the barn with his rabbits.

"I want to see Mama," she said again.

Aunt Mary let out a rough sigh. "One minute only," she said.

She entered the bedroom as quietly as she could, afraid to make a sound for fear of somehow hurting her. The air was stale and thick with smells, the only sound the crackling of the fire in the grate. On the high bed her mother lay, her face to the wall.

Near the fire stood a hooded cradle. She went up to it. Inside were two tiny creatures, smaller than her dolls, swaddled in white, with their eyes swollen closed. They looked barely human, but they were moving, their little faces scrunched up, panting, struggling for air. She could hear grunts and feeble mewlings coming from them.

She was terrified to touch them, repulsed, as she'd been at the runts of the litters of puppies born in the barn, ignored by their mothers because the mothers knew they were going to die, while the healthy ones suckled ravenously and kicked the runts out of the group.

"What's their names?" she asked Aunt Mary.

"Them's William and Thomas," Aunt Mary said crisply. "Don't trouble Mama now." But she couldn't stay away. She had to see her. She approached the bed and her mother, sensing the movement, winced and turned her face toward her. With difficulty, for she was still small, Marian climbed up onto the bed. Her mother's face, once lovely with its delicate features, was pale and yellowish now, and there was dried blood in her blond curls and on her nightcap. Her eyelashes were transparent, her lips were chapped. She looked at Marian foggily, as if she didn't recognize her, as if she were an intrusion, a stranger coming to bother her.

"I love you, Mama," she whispered.

She reached across the bed for her mother's hand and took it. Her mother's fingers were icy cold. She squeezed them gently so as not to hurt her.

"Do you love me, Mama?" she asked.

Her mother gave her a faint, pained smile, it was obviously an effort. She felt a pressure from her mother's hand on her own. She went to kiss her cheek, but then her mother turned her face to the wall again.

She was a child so filled with love, an overflowing river of it, a need to give love, a hunger to receive it, a need for someone to whom she could be all, who would focus only on her. Sensitive, easily moved to tears. Even as a little girl she was a jealous lover.

Ten days later, the babies were dead.

After two weeks her mother came down from her room, but she lay mostly on the divan, covered in her quilt, pale and weak. Before, she'd been such an energetic person, used to taking care of everything, seeing that the house was cleaned and scrubbed to perfection, supervising all, doing the sewing and mending, but now she couldn't accomplish the things she was accustomed to. She was tired and frustrated and sharp-tongued because she didn't feel well. Marian longed to lay her head upon her lap while her mother stroked her hair, but her caresses were fleeting and slight. "There, there," her mother said. "Be a good girl and go outside and play."

Aunt Mary came every day to help, bustling about, in charge of them all, her voice loud, the curls of her wig bobbing under her bonnet. Her mother's family, the Pearsons, were of a higher class than her father's, the Evanses. The Pearsons were yeomen farmers, their father a church-warden. The Pearsons knew their superiority, they did things the proper way, their way—bleaching the linens, brewing the cowslip wine, curing the hams. But Marian's father, Robert Evans, had started out as a humble carpenter with hardly any "eddication." Still, he was clever and ambitious, and a good worker who'd risen to be agent for the Newdigate family's Arbury Estate. The Newdigates gave him Griff House to live in, a big, warm, ivy-covered red-brick house, with lots of places to explore and hide.

Her mother had desperately wanted more boys, but after the death of the twins no more came. Isaac, the only boy now, three years older than Marian, was her favorite child. After that, her mother loved Chrissey, the oldest, best—Chrissey was named "Christiana" after her, pretty and well behaved and no trouble, and she looked just like their mother had, with her perfect blond curls, her button nose and rosebud lips. Marian was the youngest child, plain, with dark, sallow skin and the big Evans nose, her dull, auburn hair forever tangled. She was like some discombobulated bird, flapping about all the time, and always bursting into tears.

"That child looks like a mulatter," Aunt Mary said.

"Marian," her mother asked, "did you wash your face today?"

"Yes, I did!" she replied, affronted.

"That child's hair is a mess," her mother said to Aunt Mary. "Fetch me my wool from the bedroom, then," she told Marian.

Marian climbed the stairs, twisting her hand on the bannister, and soon became fascinated by the squeaking sound it made on the wood. At the top she called out, "What was it you wanted, Mama?"

"For goodness' sake," Aunt Mary said. "That child's head's always in the clouds. Come here and let me brush that hair. If your mama won't do it, I will."

Aunt Mary rose and came up after her. She grabbed her roughly and dragged her down the stairs. Then she took up the hairbrush and began pulling at the hated, tangled hair until sparks of agony emitted from Marian's tender child's scalp. "Ow! Ow! Ow!"

Her scalp was burning. She escaped Aunt Mary's grasp and fled, her mother calling out after her, "You come back here and let Aunt Mary brush that hair! You hear me, now? That child'll be the death of me."

She ran into her mother's room and snatched a pair of scissors from the bureau. Gulping down her tears, she began sawing off great chunks of her hair until it stuck out like a shorn cat's. Now she was *really* ugly. She would punish them.

Slowly, defiantly, holding her head high, she descended the stairs. They looked up and caught sight of her.

"Good God!" her mother said. "What've you gone and done now?"

"Come here till I give you a spanking," Aunt Mary cried. She leapt up and grabbed her roughly by the arm, pinching her, and there and then she tore down her knickers and walloped her hard until she screamed. She'd exposed her bare bottom to the world.

She escaped again, up to the attic this time and out of their reach. The attic was her refuge, quiet and smelling sweetly of woodworm and dust and cobwebs. She kept her old wooden doll there, naked and discarded, its painted-on face faded and washed away. It was her "Bad Doll," her "Naughty Girl Doll." Now she grabbed it and she began stabbing at it with a pencil. "Bad girl! You are a bad girl!" Again and again she stabbed it. "Will you never learn?" she cried.

Her mother was too tired and weak to love her anymore. She was a rebellious, difficult child, the youngest now, wanting attention, too much for her mother, but her father loved her.

In the morning, after the incident with the hair, her father came down and saw her cowering angrily in the corner, her face smeared with dried tears. He saw the catastrophe of her hair and sensed the irritation of the women in the room. "What's the matter, little wench?" he said, and picked her up. Her mother reported to him her misdeeds. "There, there," he said. "I'll take her with me today on my rounds." He patted her on the back, and she lay her head on his shoulder and glared at her mother. He carried her outside, lifted her up onto the gig, and off they went.

The Arbury Estate was her father's kingdom, it was thousands of acres, a country unto itself. They sped along in the gig in the sunny, spring-scented air, on the rutted lanes, wildflowers everywhere, speedwell and starflowers, the hedges filled with wild roses. Beyond was the Coventry Canal with its brown waters, the boats passing by, loaded with coal and timber from the estate, bound for the city.

Every now and then her father stopped to collect the rents from the tenants and to talk to the workers about repairs on the barns. All the while, she asked him questions. "What is 'measuring timber,' Papa?" "What is 'rotating crops'?"

"Questions! Questions!" He laughed. "Tha's a clever little 'un. Tha' shouldsta been born a boy."

They came to the colliery, which lay not far beyond the green meadows surrounding Griff House—all day and night you could hear the sound of the machines pumping water from the pits. There was the steam engine house and the water wheel, and a rail line connecting the colliery to the canal. The earth around the colliery was black with coal dust, and so were the miners, their knees permanently bent from crouching in the underground tunnels. Some of them were mere boys, just a bit older than she was. When they saw her father coming, they stopped work and stared sullenly at him. He spoke only to the foreman.

After a few minutes they took off again. "Can I drive the gig, Papa?" she entreated. "Can I?"

He moved her over between his legs and wound the reins around her little hands. "Pull 'er a little to the left," he commanded, and she did, and lo!, the horse moved to the left. It did what she told it to!

Holding the reins tight, she cried out in glee as they went and his strong legs gripped her tight and she was safe.

Ahead of them, they saw a tall, gray figure walking determinedly along the road. A group of boys was chasing after him, throwing stones. But the man ignored them, his eyes on the ground.

"Who is that man, Papa?" she asked.

"That's that poor old weaver. He's a hermit, lives over in Coventry Wood. Hey, youse!" he shouted at the boys. He slowed the gig. "Get thee away from here 'til I give you a beating with my own hands." The boys, caught, looked at him fearfully and slunk back. The weaver didn't acknowledge any of them, but just kept on his steady walk. Her father hated injustice. Once when he was riding in the stagecoach to Kent a sailor was behaving rudely to a fellow passenger, a woman, and her father grabbed the youth and with his huge hand held him down all the way through the rest of the journey.

After a mile or so, rising before them out of the flat fields like an apparition was a great Gothic mansion, with battlements and turrets. It was Arbury Hall, the Newdigate family seat. "I've got to stop and see Mr. Newdigate," he said. "Be a good gel and say not a word and I'll let you come in with me."

They pulled into the long driveway and drove through the park, passed a wide lake on their right, white swans drifting slowly across it, and drew up to the house.

A footman in livery came out to greet them. As they entered the great front door of the mansion she held tightly onto his hand, looking up all around her. The ceilings were high, vaulted like a cathedral, white with elaborate patterns traced all over the plaster like lace, speckled with gold. There were immense chandeliers and huge oriel windows looking out onto the park.

The footman escorted them to the study, their footsteps echoing in the great space. An old man with rheumy eyes and wobbly wet lips was sitting at a desk in the window. It was Mr. Newdigate.

She stood there with lips sealed while her father spoke to Mr. Newdigate about "disturbances with the colliers...dissatisfied...the price of corn," his tone anxious, assertive. "We're setting up petitions in every parish to continue the Corn Laws. As you know, the Radicals want to do away with the import duties to lower the price..."

There was turmoil in the land, and the baronet listened, frowning and cold, and shaking his head, as her father reported on it to him.

————

It was he who gave her her first book, when she was five. It was called *The Linnet's Life*, and she made him sit down at once and read it to her. The linnet was a homely little brown bird, just like her. *"None of its colours are splendid,"* her father read. *"Its want of gaudiness is well made up by the sweetness of its song, and its rich variety. Its manners are gentle and docile..."*

There were pictures of the linnet sitting in the tree, and of the mother linnet feeding her babies. But it was the picture of the little girl and her mother looking out the window when the bird flees its cage that gripped her. The girl in that picture had a dark complexion, just like her, and a big nose, and she was plain, not pretty at all. The little girl in *The Linnet's Life* was *her.*

Every night she made him read the book to her, sometimes twice over again. "But I jes' read the whole thing to you," he protested.

"Please!"

And he would comply.

How, then, let me well inquire,
Can I gain affection truly?
To the highest points aspire,
Then esteem will follow duly—

"You left out *'Useful virtues I'll acquire'*!" she cried.

"How'd you be knowing that then?" he asked.

She had memorized the entire thing. But she didn't tell him that because then she wouldn't be able to lie against his chest and listen to his deep, comforting voice as he read it to her, while her body relaxed and she drifted off into sleep, waking only when he picked her up and laid her down on her little bed and covered her with her quilt and kissed her good night.

Her father was her first love. But after him came Isaac. Isaac, sturdy and strong, rosy-cheeked, with the big Evans nose, only on Isaac it was good-looking. She trailed about after him like a puppy.

"Come on, Polly," he ordered her. "It's ten o'clock!" She couldn't yet tell time, of course. He ran toward the gate and she hurried to keep up with him.

They could hear the thrumming of horses' hooves in the distance, and there it was, the mail coach dashing by on its way to Coventry. You could tell the time by it, green and yellow, its gold crest flashing on the side, HIS MAJESTY'S MAIL, drawn by four grays, the pounding of their hooves fil-ing their ears, the coachman and the guard in scarlet uniforms with top hats, the guard stationed at the rear by the mailbox holding his blunderbuss, in winter the outside passengers bundled up in furs and blankets, their luggage and baskets of game tied to the back. Fast! So fast! The fastest thing you'd ever seen. It stopped for nothing. The coachman lifted his hand to wave to them. "He knows us!" cried Isaac, as if it was the same man each time, and he appreciated their waiting for him, their friendliness and loyalty, and he liked them.

She and Isaac played "house" for hours and hours on end under the yew tree. "You be the father," she told him. "And I'll be the mother and Dolly'll be our baby."

She held the doll out to him. "Kiss baby," she said, and he kissed it perfunctorily, shyly, like a boy. She pulled the doll back toward her. It was as if he were really kissing *her*, for in real life, of course, he never kissed her.

"Off to work," he said, like their father. And he went out from under the shelter of the tree, and a few moments later returned.

"Here's your supper," she said, and handed him a saucer from her tea set on which she mixed earth and water into mud for his "food." He pretended to eat it, smacking his lips. They played this game over and over again for hours, as if in a trance, hating to be interrupted in its rhythmic repetition, stalling when it began to grow dark and Aunt Mary called to them to come in for supper.

He let her go fishing with him. She carried the bait basket while he marched ahead to Round Pool bearing the line like a banner.

"Here, you can thread the worms," he said.

"But it'll hurt it!"

"They don't feel anything. Don't be a baby, Polly," he said. And gingerly, she pierced the slimy little thing with the hook, trying not to squash it to death between her fingers.

"Hold the line," he commanded, "while I go and look for more. Think you can do that, Polly?"

"Of course," she said. She sat dead still on the bank, afraid to scare away the fish from biting, holding the line rigid with both hands, staring fixedly at the glassy water while he disappeared among the willows.

All was quiet, but for the rustling of the trees and the reeds and the dripping sound as the fish rose and fell. Presently Isaac appeared again, carrying the basket.

Just then, the line began to tug violently. She sat back and gripped the rod with all her might. He saw what was happening and ran to her.

"You caught something, Polly! Good girl, Polly! Your first fish!" He took the rod from her and reeled it in.

It was a silver perch. Isaac pulled the hook from its mouth and it flopped about on the bank until finally it lay still on the grass, its mouth gaping, and the warmth of Isaac's praise flushed through her body.

———

After the twins died, they sent Chrissey away to Miss Lathom's first. Then Isaac was sent to the Foleshill School in Coventry. Before he left, Isaac put Marian in charge of his rabbits. "Don't forget to feed 'em, Polly, promise?"

"I promise I won't!"

As the gig rode away, there was an awful silence in the barnyard, the birds chirping and flying about, oblivious to her, someone so small. Beyond the barnyard, the fields stretched out beyond her. She was alone. There was no one to play with now, her mother was ill, and horrible Aunt Mary was beyond in the house.

She batted about the grounds, tried to play house with her dolls under the yew, but without Isaac the game was incomplete, there was no "father," no "family." She missed him unbearably and lolled about, dreaming of him, counting the days till he would return for the weekend.

"What's the matter with you, child?" Aunt Mary said.

"I'm bored."

"Idle hands are the devil's playthings. Go and look at those books of yours. Do something useful."

But what was "useful" when you were five years old?

———————

The first time he came home, she ran to meet him, her face full of joy.

He alighted from the gig, bent down to receive her kiss, then he ran past her, to the barn to see his rabbits.

Suddenly, she remembered. Her chest jumped to her mouth. She went after him to stop him going in there. But by the time she reached the barn door, he'd disappeared inside. She hung back outside, afraid to go in, paralyzed.

A minute later he came storming out, his face red. "They're all dead!" he cried. "They're dead! What did you do, Polly? You didn't look after them! You didn't feed them. You let them starve!"

He ran into the house to tell their father. "Look what she did, Papa! Look what Polly did! She killed my rabbits."

She'd forgotten to feed them. Standing there in the barnyard, she imagined the rabbits weakening, getting thinner and thinner by the day, starving and dragging themselves around the floor of the hutch. She was awful, awful, a murderer! She could never be a mother, she was too forgetful, too irresponsible.

Her father came out of the house. "Bad gel, Polly!" he said. "Them rabbits is good for a stew now!"

"No, Papa!" Isaac cried. "Don't say that. No!"

And for the rest of the holiday, Isaac refused to speak to her.

They bought him a piebald pony. He got up on it, trotted off, and he was gone all day in the fields, coming in only for his meals, gobbling down his food and barely answering her, only wanting to go out again. She had lost her one friend in the world. It was never again the same between them.

After that, they sent her to join Chrissey at Miss Lathom's.

One day, during the holidays, Mrs. Perry, their neighbor, lent Chrissey a copy of *Waverly*—Chrissey didn't touch it, so Marian took it up to the attic to read herself. Cleveland was in love with the enchanting Minna. *"She extricated herself from his grasp, (for he still endeavored to retain her), making an imperative sign to him to forbear from following her—"* But Mrs. Perry took the book back before she finished it. So she wrote her own ending to it. *"Clevelan got don on his hans and nees and beg Minna to marry him...she sayd yes and they livd hapili ever after..."*

When she was nine and Chrissey was fourteen, her father took them out of Miss Lathom's and put them in Mrs. Wallington's school in Nuneaton, a mile away. But again, the homesickness and the loneliness overtook her. The first morning after breakfast, before lessons started, with the day looming before her, she went back to the dormitory and just cried. Suddenly, she felt a pair of arms around her. She looked up and there was one of the teachers, Miss Lewis, a plump young woman with an ugly squint.

"Poor wee thing," Miss Lewis said in her thick Irish brogue. "What ere's the matter wid yew? Come on now," and she raised Marian up and held her against her big, soft breasts. "Here, here, donna yew cry," she said. "All right now."

Miss Lewis took her under her wing and became like a mother to her. She was always there ready to hold her against her warm body—she smelled of yeast—to offer consolation, to soften her loneliness and soothe her sensitive nature.

She was an Evangelist. Theirs was a simpler, more personal worship than the formal rituals of the Church of England. The Evangelists emphasized helping the poor, proselytizing, spreading the gospel.

She made Marian pray with her. She knelt and pulled Marian down beside her. *"I have heard thy prayer,"* she said, *"I have seen thy tears."*

Every night now, before lights out, Marian prayed passionately, for her mother and father, and for Chrissey and Isaac, and that God would make her be a good girl. She prayed that she would be loved: "Please God…Please make people love me…Make Mama love me, and Papa and Isaac love me…" As she prayed, she dug her knees into the stone floor as if somehow the pain of it would earn her an answer to her prayers.

Miss Lewis had nowhere to go for the holidays, so Marian pleaded with her mother and father to let her come home to Griff, and they allowed her to, though she urged Miss Lewis to be a little gentle with her Evangelism, as Mr. Evans had no tolerance for Evangelists or for Dissenters in general. He disdained "enthusiasms," and he was on a campaign against the Evangelical reforms that the new curate at the Chilvers Coton church, the Reverend Gwyther, was trying to institute. For one thing, the Reverend Gwyther favored Meeting House tunes, humble hymns sung without music over the grand old Sternhold and Hopkins Psalms accompanied by bugles and bassoon that everyone loved to sing.

The Reverend Gwyther was very ordinary-looking, always sniffing as if he had perpetual hay fever or a cold. "The man has no majesty," her father said, as they drove away from Sunday services.

There was also gossip in the village that the Reverend Gwyther had befriended a woman who called herself a countess and who was always in the company of a man she said was her father but was actually her lover. It was said that the Reverend Gwyther had become too close to the countess, even while his wife was pregnant.

Marian's father was a conservative through and through, ever loyal to the Tory Newdigates who'd given him his rise in the world. But all around her, amid the peaceable realms of Griff, she saw pockets of misery, the laborers' and miners' hovels, barely shelters, tiny structures of broken stone and wood, and their children so thin and dirty. And when she went with her father to the Abbey Street market in Nuneaton, there were the weavers with their pale, worn faces and their soot-covered cottages, the air filled with the rattle of their looms.

Now the workers and miners were demanding a better lot for themselves. In most places, people couldn't vote unless they owned land, and they wanted the franchise. There was a Reform Bill just introduced in Parliament which would give more people the vote, but the Tories opposed it. Her father sided with the Tories, of course. Uneducated workingmen were incapable of choosing for themselves, he said, and he held a breakfast for all the Newdigate tenants to try to persuade them to vote Tory in the coming election.

On election day, in December, she drove with him into the town. But at the entrance to Nuneaton, they came upon a mob of drunken navvies and pitmen rioting outside the Benefits Club, throwing raw potatoes and turnips at the Tory sympathizers and breaking windows. There was the stink of ale in the air. She saw a man staggering about holding his head, blood dripping from it, and a crowd jeering at him, "Bloomin' Tory bastard!" There were constables and magistrates on horseback riding through the crowd trying to quell them. The supporters of the Radical candidate had taken over the polls, and they wouldn't allow the followers of the Tory candidates to vote.

She'd never seen fighting like this before, men enraged, out of control. She shrank against her father and buried her face in his shoulder. "Are they going to hurt us?" she cried.

"Hold tight, there," he said grimly, and he clicked at the horse and turned the gig back toward Griff.

After a few minutes they were clear of the violence and on the road to home. "Scoundrels!" her father said. "If they can't read or write, how can they vote? They don't even know what they want, they're just parroting what other people tell them to say."

Later, the newspaper said that the rioters had beaten one of the Newdigates and the magistrates had called in the Scots Greys. The Greys had ridden through the mob, trampling on people. The next day, there was more violence, a crowd of laborers had set upon the Tories again. A man was killed, and two Scots Greys were beaten and stripped naked. The violence frightened her so much that she was terrified to go into Nuneaton again for months.

———————

That year, Mrs. Wallington told her father that she was too intelligent a girl to remain at the school, the teachers had taught her all they could. She suggested he send her to the Misses Franklin's school in Coventry, the best in the area, where she could learn French and music and arithmetic. But it was expensive.

Coming into the house one afternoon, she heard her mother and father in the kitchen debating the matter. "She's got a poor chance a' marryin', tha' one," her father said. "It's worth it. She'll go into service, be a governess. The French will help her." They didn't know she was there, near the door, listening. But it was a death sentence, for everything her father said was always right. She was too plain and awkward ever to marry. No man would ever want her.

Chrissey was eighteen and finished with school now, at home and helping their mother. She'd grown more lovely and was, as always, sweet, helpful, and obedient. She was being courted by a young man, Edward Clarke, from Leicestershire. Edward was tall, thin, and boyish-looking, quiet, studying to be a doctor. He said he wanted to help the poor and be a doctor in a workhouse.

Meanwhile, Isaac was struggling at the Foleshill School. He wasn't nearly as good at his letters as Marian was. "He shoulda had the little wench's brains," her father said. "They shoulda swapped places, the two of them." He wanted Isaac to take over his job as manager of the Arbury Estate one day, and he announced he was removing him from the Foleshill School and sending him to Mr. Docker in Birmingham, who would "get him straight with his letters and give him a good High Church education."

That September, Marian entered the door of the Misses Franklin's school on Warwick Row. There were pupils there from many other places too, from London, even a girl from India, and another one, a relative of one of the Franklins, from America. Miss Mary Franklin was a kindly, bustling sort who managed the school, while her younger sister, Miss Rebecca, was in charge of lessons. Miss Rebecca had spent a whole year in France, and she was very refined. She spoke in educated tones, carefully enunciating the beginnings and endings of all her words.

Marian excelled in her studies. Miss Davenport read her composition on "Affectation and Conceit" to the whole class as a model of its kind. In it, she'd condemned pretty women who *study no graces of mind or intellect. Their whole thoughts are how they shall best maintain their empire over their surrounding inferiors, and the right fit of a dress or bonnet will occupy their minds for hours together."* The first year she won the French prize, a copy of Pascal's *Pensées.*

Miss Franklin let them read novels, Edward Bulwer-Lytton, Sir Walter Scott, and G.P.R. James—some people thought that novels could lead young girls astray, but Miss Franklin was cosmopolitan. One day, Marian sat down and tried to write a novel of her own, *Edward Neville*, it was called, about the Roundheads and the Cavaliers. A mysterious stranger rides up to a castle on a black horse. *"The Rider must have been about six and twenty he was tall and well proportioned and bore in his very handsome countenance the marks of a determined and haughty character."* After six pages, she didn't know how to go on.

She became the teachers' favorite, and she basked in their praise and the glow of her achievement. Their praise was a form of love she'd never had, and she was ambitious for more, to be cherished by these women. She wanted to be the best at everything and she discovered in herself a hunger for everything they could teach her. Every new accumulation of knowledge set off a little burst of pleasure within her.

So good was she at the piano that Miss Rebecca asked her to play for guests in the parlor. One afternoon, she was making her way through "Für Elise" when she hit a wrong note. Nonetheless, the guests applauded. She managed to stand briefly and bow, and then she fled into the hallway weeping.

Miss Rebecca ran after her. "Marian, whatever is the matter?"

"I was so awful," she cried.

"But no one heard that, Marian. You were excellent," and Miss Rebecca hugged her and kissed the top of her head.

She wanted to be just like Miss Rebecca. Listening to her speak in her lofty tones, she became conscious of her "country" accent, the way she said "ayah" instead of "is not," and "What sort of books am them?" instead of "What sort of books are those?"

If she couldn't be beautiful, then at least she could make her voice beautiful. She began to imitate Miss Rebecca's speech and to speak in low, melodic tones, and she noticed that people leaned forward to listen to her, and it made them pay attention to her words.

The Misses Franklin were Baptists. Like the Evangelists, theirs was a more intimate religion than the Church of England that she'd known since childhood. Faith was a question of the relationship between a person and God. Salvation was the result of faith, and sometimes believers declared their faith aloud in front of the congregation. The Baptists didn't believe in christening babies, but only those people who'd declared their faith. They didn't sprinkle water on them the way people usually did, but totally immersed them.

All the pupils at the Misses Franklin's school attended the Cow Lane Chapel to hear the Misses Franklin's father, Francis, preach about suffering and penance and the hope of salvation.

As she listened to his sermons, Marian felt herself becoming even more pious, like Miss Rebecca. She began to feel a closer communication with God; she became like a little minister herself. One day, she came upon two girls fighting in the Common Room, pulling each other's hair. She grabbed them and forced them apart. "Stop that now," she commanded. They ceased, intimidated by her, she knew, because she was so holy and she was Miss Rebecca's favorite. "Come, let us clasp hands and pray," she ordered, and they stood there sniveling as she joined their hands and they prayed.

If she'd never marry, she'd become a saint. She would live the life of the mind, the spiritual life. The activity of the mind, that was eternal, something that could never be taken away from you. She started wearing a Quaker cap which covered her untidy hair, and to dress plainly in a gray gingham dress—if she couldn't be pretty, she would be plain then!

Meanwhile, Isaac had become a young buck, fond of dancing and ale and hunting. She disapproved of him, and he could sense it. When she came home from school and he saw her dingy new garb, he focused on her a moment and said, "Miss Holier Than Thou, is it now?"

Then, in December, when she was sixteen, it all ended. She was in mathematics class when Miss Rebecca appeared at the door and summoned her into the hallway. "You're to pack your things," she said. "Your papa's come for you. Your mama's ill and you're needed at home."

At Griff, she found her mother in bed again and suffering from great pain. She had cancer of the breast and it had spread to her bones.

As the weeks went by, the cancer filled her, her leg broke, she became paralyzed and couldn't walk. Her father fashioned a little trolley on wheels and covered it with cushions and pulled her around the house on it.

But as her mother declined, her grief-stricken father could only stare helplessly at her, and Marian took over her care. Marian tried to soothe her. She stroked her brow and softly sang to her: *"There is a land like Eden fair, But more than Eden blest..."* Her suffering became so great that both Marian and her father prayed for the end to come to bring her relief.

In February, with darkness everywhere and the snow deep on the ground, her mother died, and when the earth thawed, she was buried in the courtyard at Chilvers Coton. Her father stood over the grave, tears streaming down his face. She had never seen him cry. "Papa, I will take care of you now," she said, taking his hand, and he looked at her a moment, a faint smile coming through his tears.

The next spring, Chrissey married Edward Clarke. Edward was now a member of the Royal College of Surgeons and an apothecary, and he was setting up a practice in Meriden. Chrissey wore her best blue dress for the wedding, and a lace cap on her blond curls. Marian, her bridesmaid, wore the brown dress she always wore for church.

As Chrissey and Edward stood at the altar, Marian thought a light seemed to emanate from her sister. During the service, Edward bent over her tenderly and protectively, his eyes only on her, a smile of love and expectation on his face, as if she were the most delicate flower, the prize of his life.

No man would ever look at Marian that way. She was seventeen years old and no man would ever love her.

If she was not to marry, she must establish an independent self and do good works. So she started a clothing club in Nuneaton for unemployed ribbon weavers. And she dutifully attended church with her father.

Isaac had begun to court Sarah Rawlins, the daughter of Samuel Rawlins, a friend of their father's, a rich leather merchant from Rotton Park in Edgbaston, whom he'd met when he was staying in Birmingham at the house of his tutor, Mr. Docker. Sarah was ten years older than Isaac, thirty-five, really too old to marry, tall and gawky with a big round nose and thin lips, and even touches of gray in her hair. Marian didn't understand it.

She was mistress of the house now, in charge of everything. She supervised the meals and mended her father's clothes. In the evenings, she played the piano to entertain him and read aloud to him from his Walter Scott novels. She loved to hear him laugh again when she read the parts about the Baron of Bradwardine and the lawyer Clippurse and Sir Everard's attempts to win the heart of Lady Emily.

To keep herself occupied mentally, she decided to make a chart of ecclesiastical history. She drew long columns on a piece of paper and in tiny, neat handwriting wrote down all the great events of the Christian Church.

"What's that you're doing there, gel?" her father asked.

"It's my chart of the church. See, there are the names of the Roman emperors and their dates and what's happening to the Jews at the time. And here's the birth of Christ."

"My Lord, did you see here what she's doing, Isaac?" he said to her brother, who sat by the fireplace, his big shoulders bent over his gun, carefully cleaning and oiling it.

"Umm," Isaac said, not bothering to look up. "Clever, ain't she?" She heard the sarcasm in his voice, as if he were mocking her father's words about her.

The next day when he went to Arbury Hall, her father boasted of his daughter's piety to his employer, Mrs. Newdigate. Mrs. Newdigate was so impressed with her religiosity that she said that Marian could use the library at Arbury Hall for the research for her chart, and she was free to wander among the volumes as she pleased.

The first time Marian entered that big, dark room at Arbury Hall, it was as if she were in a holy place. There were stacks of volumes up to the ceiling, bound in red and green leather with gold stampings on the covers—all these treasures were hers now, nobody else ever came here.

Every afternoon, when her housework was finished, she rode over to Arbury Hall. In the quiet and privacy of the library, she read all five volumes of the Milners' *History of the Church of Christ,* and the Oxford tracts.

She came across a book called *An Inquiry Concerning the Origin of Christianity,* by a man called Charles Hennell. She'd never heard of him before. He was a junior clerk at a banking firm in London. The book had just been published. Hennell said that the Bible was full of inconsistencies. For instance, according to Matthew, Jesus entered Jerusalem on an ass and a colt. But Mark, Luke, and John mentioned only *one* animal, the colt. Moreover, Matthew said that during the Crucifixion they gave Jesus vinegar mixed with gall to drink. But Mark said it was wine *mingled with myrrh. "The discourses which allude to these miracles bear strong marks of fiction,"* Hennell wrote.

Hennell believed that Christ's miracles as presented in the Gospels were but mythological events, like those of other ancient religions. Christianity should be freed from its dependence on these myths; it couldn't rely on the uncertain events of two thousand years ago. Christ wasn't divine. He didn't perform miracles, and wasn't resurrected from the dead. He was simply a great teacher and reformer. There was indeed a profound truth at the core of Christianity, Hennell wrote, a mystery that would eventually be revealed; until then religion should rest on the best impulses of human beings themselves, on their efforts to help their fellow men, on their love for one another, and on the beauty of nature itself.

Hennell's words struck her with an almost physical force. All her life she'd been accustomed to listening to the stories of the Gospels as if they were the truth, engraved in stone. But Hennell was saying that these stories were but fables.

It set her into turmoil. She turned Hennell's assertions over and over in her mind. The house of her old faith was collapsing around her. She didn't know where to turn. As she sat beside her father in church and listened to the

Reverend Gwyther read from the Scriptures, she brooded on what Hennell said in a kind of anguish.

Yet her essential piety wasn't shaken. If anything, she felt a deepening of it, a greater immediacy in her connection to God, as if there was nothing now between her and the ineffable spirit within her which was a reflection, an embodiment of Him—her need to love, her compassion for the poor and sick, her urge to comfort them. It was as if the rules and rituals of the church were but decorations, barriers between oneself and the mysterious and indescribable true spirit that lay within everyone.

She ventured further, read books on science, physics, mathematics, and chemistry. Her father let her buy as many books as she wanted at Short's in Nuneaton, and for her twentieth birthday she bought a present for herself of Wordsworth's poems. Opening those pages for the first time, she read:

> *There was a time when meadow, grove, and stream,*
> *The earth, and every common sight,*
> *To me did seem*
> *Apparelled in celestial light,*
> *The glory and the freshness of a dream.*

For this man too, God existed, not in the myths of long ago, or in the doctrines of the church, but in everything around us; God was part of nature—He *was* nature.

How she loved the poet's words, the music of them, their plasticity, rolling off the tongue. And as she read his work, she marveled at the infinite variety of the English language, words in general, the rhythms of the English sentence, the sentences twisting and turning into themselves in a symphonic complexity. Words playing off one another, defining or evasive, their meaning sometimes clear, sometimes to be felt rather than discerned only through intellect. Words alone were abstractions, but when they were joined and linked, they could thrill and take possession of the soul. Words were the weapons and playthings of the mind.

She felt compelled to write a poem of her own, to feel the words being born in her own body: *"As o'er the fields by evening's light I stray, / I hear a still, small whisper—Come away,"* it began. It was a hymn to death, to giving up earthly things. She sent it to her old teacher at Miss Wallington's school, Maria Lewis—she was no longer "Miss Lewis," she was now a friend, they were only ten years apart. Maria urged her to submit it to the *Christian Observer.* Lo, it was accepted and published, signed "M.A.E."

Her father, ever mindful that she must one day earn a living, and proud of all her learning, said she best keep up on her lessons, and he hired a Signor Brezzi from Coventry to tutor her in Italian and German.

Signor Brezzi was in his early thirties, dark-haired, with black eyes. Sitting there gravely opposite her, he was so stiff and proper in his suit. But his eyes, mustn't they hide a passionate nature? She noticed the strong, muscular curve of his thighs under his trousers. He said he was from the Piedmont, but otherwise was reserved, conscious, no doubt, that her father had hired him to teach his daughter. She found herself drawn to him, wanting to break through his impenetrable propriety. Was he married? He didn't say. He didn't wear a wedding ring. *"Bene, signorina, ripeta,"* he urged.

And she did. Foreign languages came easily to her. Italian was similar to English and to Church Latin. She loved the sensual, staccato rhythms of it. And the sweet, liquid sounds of German, the way German words at first appeared to be long and complicated yet yielded to careful, logical pronunciation.

"*Bitte sprechen Sie mir nach— Ich bin— du bist— er ist...*"

"Very good," Signor Brezzi said.

She studied hard to please him. But he seemed to look right through her, as if she were but an object to him upon which he must focus. His eyes were penetrating, but he didn't see her. Whatever sensuality he had within him didn't apply to her. Or perhaps he didn't want to focus on her because she was plain. She was the negation of all that would ever find love and esteem, she thought. As the lessons continued, she decided to give herself a motto: Cease ye from man. She would live her life by it.

The more knowledge she gleaned from her studies, the lonelier she felt. There was no one around with whom she could discuss all that she was learning. There were no other women like her—not even her former teacher, Maria Lewis, who'd read all the books she had now, who knew the secrets of German verbs and the physics and philosophy she had discovered in the Arbury Hall library, who could understand her love of language. It was as if she had a secret life. She belonged to a different species from the good people of Nuneaton. Most women of her age were married or engaged to be married, and occupied themselves with housework. She was a stranger among them.

One evening, she went to a party at the house of their neighbor, Mrs. Bull. She sat against the wall and watched the dancing, the young men holding the women around their waists, waltzing to the music. A man with a lock of orange hair on his brow and friendly blue eyes approached her, smiling. She sat forward, expectantly. Her heart lifted—he was going to ask her to dance. But when he saw her, he said, "Oh, sorry, I was looking for Miss Adams," and he walked away.

The evening wore on and still no one asked her to dance, but she was too proud to get up and leave, everyone would see her. The music pounded in her head, seemed to grow louder and louder, the room was very hot. Everyone must be noticing her there, sitting alone and shamed. She pulled her chair back into the shadows. At midnight the music stopped, and she went home to her room and sobbed.

She began to have headaches, piercing pain coming from behind her eyes. Only darkness, and sleep, many hours of sleep, brought relief.

In June, Isaac married Sarah Rawlins. How could Isaac marry such a plain woman when he was so good-looking himself? She knew he was marrying Sarah partly because the Rawlins family was rich, and the marriage pleased their father, and it would pave Isaac's way in the world. Again, Marian was a bridesmaid, at the Edgbaston Parish Church, wearing the same plain brown dress that she'd worn at Chrissey's wedding and had patched and repaired so often since then. She was twenty-one, and the prospect of marriage seemed more remote than ever.

Chrissey was living in Meriden now with Edward Clarke. Edward was struggling to set up a practice, the new doctor in the town competing with the old doctor, Dr. Kittermeister, who'd been there for years. Soon they had three little babies to feed. Chrissey named her third child Mary Louisa after Marian, and sometimes she brought the baby over to Griff and let her sister keep her. At night, Marian would hold the warm little thing in her arms and sing and rock her to sleep.

Three months later, Mary Louisa was dead. Oh God, to lay the little creature in her tiny coffin in the merciless earth, the one she had warmed with her own body, whom she had loved so much.

Then her father announced that he was retiring. Isaac was taking over his job with the estate and he and Marian were moving to Coventry. She was being cast out of Griff, her childhood home, the magical countryside of her childhood, because Isaac wanted to live there.

———————

She lay now in the Hotel Europa in Venice, her memories of childhood dissipated, but the sadness was still there. There were no kind arms to embrace her, no soft breath to ruffle her ear.

A new wave of homesickness passed over her. In this, the most exquisite city in the world, she longed for Witley and the Heights, the bright, clean sunlight of the English summer and her old routines, for Brett and Mrs. Dowling, the servants, so totally devoted to her, and Charley, George's son, to care for her. To be at work again on the book that had been brewing inside her, completely absorbed as she summoned the words and tried to make sense of the universe. She hadn't brought any of the books for the research—one wasn't supposed to work on one's honeymoon. It would be insulting to Johnnie. Perhaps she could write to Charley and ask him to send some of them to Venice?

But on your honeymoon you weren't supposed to work, you were supposed to...

Chapter 4

I n the morning it was a lovely, sunny day. There was the murmur of voices in the *sala*. Johnnie was up, a servant was making an inquiry. She noticed for the first time the faded outlines of cherubs and garlands on the ceiling, the blue plaster on the walls stained and chipped and flaking from the perpetual damp. The paintings were copies of Titians and Raphaels. You could tell by the clumsy features of the people and the dull folds of their robes.

From beneath the window came the sounds of people talking and of banging. She rose and looked out at the canal, where tradesmen in their boats were delivering food and supplies to the hotels. Men were unloading wooden crates from the boats. Among them was the gray-haired gondolier, Corradini, in his striped shirt and black pants. She watched for a moment as he bent down to grip the crates with his sinewy arms. His striped shirt rode up and she could see the bare flesh of his waist, shining and soft and white where it had eluded the sun.

She dressed and went into the *sala*. Johnnie had on his white suit, a black silk cravat, and a waistcoat. He was freshly shaved around the contours of his beard, his cheeks pale from his morning toilette, his red hair brushed back from his high forehead, his curls damp.

The maid was clearing his plate.

Seeing her, he stood up immediately. "Ah!" he cried, full of high spirits again. "Be-a-tri-che!" The ridiculously extravagant name he'd given her last summer at Witley when they were reading Dante.

"Please." She nodded at the girl, a stranger who spoke Italian and might understand the reference.

The maid curtsied. "I hope Madame sleep well."

"Thank you, my dear. I did."

Johnnie stepped toward her and took her hand. He drew it up to his lips and covered it with his own as if it were something precious. He kissed her on each cheek and enfolded her in his large frame. She felt small against his tall body. Out of the corner of her eye, she saw the maid look away as if discomfited at the sight of the young husband kissing his old wife; or a son kissing his mother like this. The girl bent her head over the teapot, refilling it with hot water from the cart.

"You? Did you sleep well?" she asked him.

"A little bit. I didn't fall asleep until four a.m."

"You should rest this afternoon."

"If I nap, I won't be able to sleep tonight. I'm perfectly all right. Not tired in the least. Come," he said. His voice was too loud. "Have your breakfast to give you strength, and then let's be off. We've got lots to do. Let's go to the Piazza first."

After she'd eaten, she took up her parasol and they made their way along the Calle del Ridotto to San Marco.

As they came out onto the great Piazza, the pigeons flew up from the ground in a cloud, frantically beating their wings, then swooped down again, scattering the tourists and picking at the crumbs they'd thrown for them.

On the other side of the Piazza was the marble-clad Basilica with its campanile and domes and spires, gold and blue, and its mosaics of many colors, the four horses, and at its pinnacle, the statue of Saint Mark. Next to it was the Doge's Palace, Ruskin's "perfect" building, with its double tiers of columns and arches. And standing over it all, atop his great pillar, the lion.

Johnnie strode eagerly toward the palace. She had always thought the architecture of the place lacking, its friezes trivial, its Gothic windows too small for the building's scale. Johnnie went into the courtyard and leapt up the Scala dei Giganti to the main floor. She climbed after him, stopping every few feet to catch her breath. "Johnnie!"

"Sorry. I'm too eager," he said, and stepped back to give her his arm.

When they got to the top, Johnnie rushed through the rooms, exclaiming at everything in raptures, Veronese's gorgeous *Apotheosis of Venice*, a miracle of color and composition, Venice personified on her throne in the sky, encircled by clouds, her celebrants gathered around her. Most of the other Veroneses and Tintorettos and Palmas left her indifferent.

Johnnie stopped, remembered she was there, and waited for her to catch up.

They crossed the Bridge of Sighs and peered down into the prison cells, too small surely to hold a human being. Then, back down to the Piazza again and into the Basilica. It was so dark inside you could hardly see the mosaics, the marble and wood sculptures and alabaster columns, the Madonna from Constantinople hung with jewels. The church's pavement, embedded with stars, was dull with grime. They ascended the campanile and gazed out over the sunlit city to the sea and the distant mountains.

Back down in the Piazza, "Look!" Johnnie cried. Across the Piazza was a wooden platform and atop it sat a man on a stool at an easel, painting. A group of people had surrounded the platform, looking up at the strange edifice, trying to see what he was doing, but he was ignoring them.

"That must be Mr. Bunney," Johnnie said. "Mr. Bunney!" He hurried over to the platform while she hung back in embarrassment.

He stood under the platform calling up to the man, then beckoned vigorously to her to come. Bunney lowered a ladder and descended from his perch.

"John Wharlton Bunney!" the painter said, introducing himself. He was white-haired with a white beard and wore a smock. "Miss Evans," he said. Then, correcting himself, "I'm sorry. Mrs. Cross. I've been expecting you. I got Mr. Ruskin's letter saying you'd be coming." He had a North of England accent. "He's very anxious that you see the work we're doing about the restoration. Sorry about this contraption but there have been incidents."

She knew what he meant. Three years ago, Ruskin had written an angry review of James McNeill Whistler's painting *Nocturne in Black and Gold.* He called Whistler a *"coxcomb"* and accused him of *"flinging a pot of paint in the public's face."* Whistler sued Ruskin for libel. Everyone in London followed the case in the newspapers. Whistler won, but went bankrupt from the court costs. Recently, Whistler had been going around saying that when he was in Venice, he'd spotted Ruskin's employee, John Bunney, in the Piazza working on his eternal Basilica painting. Whistler said he tore a page from his notebook and wrote, "I am totally blind!" on it, then went up behind Bunney and stuck it on his back. Whistler claimed Bunney was so intent on his work that he didn't notice it until some tourists pointed it out.

Now, in the Piazza, Johnnie ordered the crowd gathered around the platform, "Could you step aside please?" as if he were Mr. Bunney's personal guard.

The people began moving away. Bunney climbed up on his platform, gingerly handed his canvas down to Johnnie, and they stood looking at it. "Isn't it wonderful?" said Johnnie.

It showed the facade of the Basilica, each column carefully articulated, the mosaic figures above the entryways exactly rendered, even the planes and girders of the dome. Not wonderful, she thought, mechanical. No romance in the light, the sky dull, the whole thing devoid of life. Indeed, there wasn't a human being in sight.

"Very nice indeed," she said politely. She couldn't be unkind.

"Have you been at it long?" Johnnie asked Bunney eagerly. People were watching the curious scene from a distance now, afraid, because of Johnnie's peremptory manner, to come closer.

"I'm here every morning at five o'clock, weather permitting. I'm in my fourth year now," Bunney said. "I've done four hundred sessions so far."

"My goodness," she said. "Do you know when you'll finish?"

"Before I die, I hope. As I said, Mr. Ruskin is very exacting. Well, I better get back to work while the light's good." He turned to climb up his ladder. "Oh, before I do, I can't let you leave without giving me your promise you'll come to the studio. Mr. Ruskin has sworn me to give you his pamphlets about Venice. He wants you to see everything through his eyes. He's so obsessed with this restoration." Then he pulled the ladder up behind him and seated himself at his easel.

Taking up his brush again, he called down to them over the platform, "It's number 2413 San Biagio!"

They left him at his labors.

As they walked away, Johnnie began humming, "Mr. Bunney, Mr. Bunney, Mr. Bunney."

"It's a wonderful name, isn't it?" she said.

"Yes," he said, then resumed in a little song, "Oh, Mr. Bunney, Mr. Bunney…"

"Yes," she echoed, "'Mr. Bunney.' A fine name."

"Yes, indeed." He kept going, singing brightly now. "Oh, Mr. Bunney, Mr. Bunney," over and over again.

"I think perhaps that's enough," she said. "It's not fair to make fun of him because of his name."

He stopped. "Oh, I am fair!" he cried. "Fair, fair, fair," he said.

He looked out across the Piazza, his brow knit. "We should go to the Accademia," he said. "It closes at three. Better hurry." He laughed. "There I am, going too fast for you again. Take your time."

———

The heat was rising now from the stone, and inside the Accademia the coolness and silence were a relief.

When they reached the entrance to the Sala dell'Assunta, Johnnie cried, "Look! Look!" At the far end of the gallery was Titian's immense *Assumption*, covering the entire wall, the Virgin ascending toward God on a cloud supported by cherubs, the Apostles beneath her gazing up at her adoringly. The expression on the Madonna's face was rapturous, dazed, fearful, yet curious.

"The Virgin looks just like you," he said.

She laughed. "That's sacrilegious."

Titian's Virgin wasn't like the traditional Madonnas. She wasn't delicate and girlish. She was androgynous, square-jawed, with a thick neck, flat-chested with broad shoulders.

"No, no," he insisted. "You are 'the Madonna.' George called you that."

"He was joking," she said.

"But I mean it. Why can't I say it? I can say it."

"Don't be silly. I'm not the Madonna."

"Yes. You are. Pure and wise and—"

"Not so pure. And wise—I wish it were so..."

Just then, a man and woman entered the gallery carrying their guidebooks. She lowered her voice. "Please, Johnnie. Let's go back now. Here—" She took his arm. "Come."

"No. I want to stay and look at the Madonna."

"Come," she said again, pulling him away.

"Let me be," he said irritably. It was a tone she'd never heard from him before.

"I think we should go, Johnnie. I really do. I'm tired. I'd like to rest."

"I thought you were rested. I want to stay. I want to look. It's my wife."

The other two had noticed them.

She whispered urgently, "It's not your wife." She tried to drag him away, but he was bigger than she, immovable.

"Johnnie, let's go," she commanded, raising her voice.

He scowled and abruptly walked away across the gallery ahead of her.

———————

On the way back to the hotel, he was silent, his mouth clamped shut. He didn't look at her, his eyes were fixed ahead. She'd never seen him angry. It was new and startling.

"Johnnie, what's wrong with you?"

"Nothing."

She was afraid to speak.

When they reached the *appartement*, he sat down at the dining table and stared out the window, biting his nails.

"I'm going in to rest awhile," she said. He ignored her.

She went into her own room. It was quiet outside, all of Venice was cast into an afternoon torpor.

Suddenly, she felt the twinging sensation in her left side. She touched herself there. Please, no. She couldn't survive it. What would she do if she had an attack here? Her doctor, Sir James Paget, was so far away across the sea. There were no good doctors in this foreign place.

She rinsed a flannel in cold water, lay down on the bed, and pressed it to her head. There was a foul, bitter taste in her mouth. She prayed, Please don't let it happen. Not now. Relax, every part...

He'd never spoken angrily to her before. And she hadn't had to raise her voice in years. She almost never exchanged cross words with anyone. No one ever challenged her. People were afraid of her. George had shielded her, babied her. For so many years, she'd been a loved woman, by George, by Charley, by all their friends and her admirers and followers. With all the fame, she thought, she'd become spoiled, everyone around her trying to anticipate her needs, everyone in awe of The Great Talent. That was the price of celebrity, she knew.

No one told you the truth.

Chapter 5

After a brief nap she felt better. The sensation in her side had abated.

They were going to a concert at the Teatro Malibran. It was to be the highlight of their stay.

She began to get ready. She put on the green silk dress she'd bought at Madame La France's in Battle Square just for this occasion and spread powder on her face. It gave her skin a thick, flat color, but it was better than having her naked wrinkles visible to the world. She dabbed on the Parfum Violette Johnnie had given her as a gift in Paris, and draped the mantilla over her head and shoulders.

She drew on her long, white kid gloves, took her gold lace fan with the mother-of-pearl handle from its silk-lined box, straightened her shoulders, and prepared to go out into the *sala*. At the bedroom door, she hesitated. What would she find?

She pushed open the double doors.

There he was, standing tall in the middle of the room, waiting for her, dressed in full evening regalia, black morning coat, black silk foulard, pearl stickpin, holding his top hat.

"Bella, bella," he said. He smiled broadly. "You look lovely. The dress is lovely."

For a moment, she believed him. Perhaps the dress made him see her in a new way.

They descended the stairs to the lobby, he smiling proudly with her on his arm, and she, queenly, almost pretty.

———————

The gondolier, Corradini, was there on the *riva*. She noticed again his pale blue eyes. They stood out against his tanned and oiled skin, his seamed face and sinewy arms. Again she noticed that his costume fit him too tightly. He was trying to look younger, showing off his body.

Once they were seated, he pulled the boat efficiently away from shore, working easily, unsmilingly, saying nothing, distant and skilled, his skin weathered by years in the sun rowing tourists around.

It was early evening, the night beginning. As they passed along the banks of the canal, the gaslights glowed, and the *riva* was filled with tourists out in all their finery for their evening promenade.

She gave Johnnie a little lecture on Vivaldi to prepare him for the concert. "He wrote *The Four Seasons* in Mantua at the court of Philip of Hesse-Darmstadt. There are four cantos representing each of the four seasons, sonnets that go with them which Vivaldi probably wrote himself—"

In the middle of her explanation, he bent forward, took her hands exuberantly between his own, and kissed them through her gloves. Then he squeezed them so tightly her knuckles ground together.

"Ouch! You hurt me!" She winced and pulled her hands away.

"Sorry. I'm too enthusiastic, I'm afraid," he said, patting them.

She flexed her fingers. "You've got a powerful grip."

He sat back in the gondola, smiling in anticipation of the concert.

The gondolier curved to the right and made his way through the maze of canals. The buildings loomed close together, a crack of dark blue sky just visible between the rooftops.

They came to a stop, and Johnnie told Corradini to wait for them. The man nodded, once again, she noted, just verging on rudeness.

Making their way along a dark *calle*, they came upon the Corte Sabbionera and the tiny, jewel-like Teatro Malibran, its warm lights beaming from the windows and the door, the concertgoers assembled on the *campo* waiting to go in.

Inside, everything was trimmed with gold. The boxes were held up by caryatids, the parapets decorated with crowns. There were two men already in their box, one older and gray-haired, the other much younger, clean-shaven, perhaps his son.

She scanned the program. The rustling around them quieted, and the curtain lifted to reveal the musicians and the conductor. The conductor lifted his arms, the musicians lifted their instruments, and the heraldic notes of "Spring" sounded. Immediately, the tight notes of the first violin, playing the *allegro*, possessed her. Then the other instruments joined in. In the excitement of the music, she forgot everything—Johnnie sitting beside her, the theater around her. There was the sweet call of a single violin, a spring bird, rising then calming into a *diminuendo*. The goatherd dozing on the meadow, an intimation of love to come; nymphs and shepherds dancing. It flowed through her body, lifted her.

And now, "Summer." In the last movement of the "Summer" concerto, the *presto*, the storm came. She noticed Johnnie moving from side to side in his seat, his torso quivering and shaking like the rain itself as the violins reached their peak, the thunder and lightning split the heavens, and hail rained down. Next to her, she heard a droning sound. He was humming. She glanced over at the men in the box to see if they'd heard him, but they were sitting at an angle slightly in front of them, absorbed in the concert.

She leaned over and pinched his arm. He looked at her sideways and grinned, lurching and swaying to the music with a strange, rigid posture. "Johnnie..."

He began lifting each shoulder one by one—left, right, left, jerkily, like a tin soldier, a mad puppet. "What?" he asked innocently, his eyes fixed on her as if daring her to stop him.

She inclined her head toward their neighbors in the box and whispered, "You're disturbing them."

He looked at them. "I love the music, that's all." He laughed. "What's wrong with that?"

He shifted back toward the stage and continued, shoulder up, down, up, with no relation to the music now at all.

She could no longer pay attention to the concert.

With the fierce, final drama of "Winter," he swayed, eyes glowing, rotating his body in a circular motion.

Then, thank God, it was over. He gave a final shiver.

The applause began, spreading out and lingering in the air of the hall. She stood up and smiled anxiously at the men in the box. The older one nodded at her. She wondered if he recognized her. She prayed to God, no—then hurried ahead of Johnnie to exit before the crowd.

Outside, on the *campo*, Johnnie was still smiling euphorically. She led the way back to the boat, he droning out of tune, lingering behind her, his attention wandering. A dog skulked along the edges of the *calle*. "Look," he said. "See, the window." Above them were geraniums in a box. Two women walked past, black shawls covering bent heads.

At the end of the *calle*, the gondola bobbed in the shadows. The gondolier, Corradini, was standing by it. As they approached, he scrutinized them with cold eyes.

"To the hotel," Johnnie ordered.

As the boat made its way slowly along the narrow *rio*, Johnnie still hummed, loudly, an approximation of the music from the concert. She sat in the gondola as if she were alone.

She noticed that the boatman kept glancing at Johnnie, with a calculating look on his face.

They reached the Grand Canal and in a few minutes they were at the hotel.

Johnnie stood up to get out and she saw the gondolier look directly at him, then boldly up and down his body. The man seemed to take in every part of him, his lips curled in a faint, mocking smile.

"*Forse potrei mostrarvi alcuni luoghi?*" he asked. "*Conosco un posto vicino al Rialto.*" Would Johnnie like to go out again this evening? he was saying. He was offering to take him to a place near the Rialto.

Johnnie glared at him. "*Non mi interessa!*" he barked. "My wife and I are retiring for the evening now."

The gondolier shrugged and smiled again. He reached out to Johnnie to help him onto shore, but Johnnie wrenched away from him.

As they walked to the hotel entrance, she glanced behind her. The horrible gondolier was standing there by the boat, his eyes fixed on Johnnie, a strange, knowing half-smile on his face.

"Why did he want you to go with him at this time of night?"

"They just want to take you somewhere and then get more money out of you."

"You were very harsh with him."

"It was very irritating," he said.

Inside the *appartement*, he removed his jacket, folded it, and laid it over the chair. Still scowling, he untied his cravat and unbuttoned the neck of his shirt.

She waited, then said, "I think I'll go to bed now."

"I'll stay up a bit," he said. "If I go to bed now, I won't sleep."

"I can't bear to see you suffer," she said.

He didn't answer but walked out onto the balcony. She came up behind him.

But there was nothing more coming from him. He was waiting for her to leave.

"Well, then," she said, "good night." He remembered to kiss her on both cheeks. But before she could step away, he'd gone back to watching the water below, swaying and black and glittering.

In her room, the bed had been turned down, the carafe of orange water set down beside it. The maid had done it before she left for the evening.

She began to undress. With difficulty, she reached around and tried to unhook her gown—it was nearly impossible. There was no one to ask for help. Always before, George would have done it, or Brett, the maid. She struggled, twisted her body around, and at last managed to undo the dress. She removed her corset and petticoat and unrolled her stockings.

Putting on the nightgown, she lay down on the bed on top of the covers. She thought about the events at the concert, the way his body had become so rigid, his strange humming. And his anger at the gondolier? The man was only asking if he'd like to go out again.

At first, he'd noticed her new dress, her effort to look attractive for him, but then she seemed to vanish for him, and he'd gone tensely into himself.

The nightgown stuck to her flesh. There was a faint stirring of air from the window, a moment of relief from the heat. She felt a coolness on her arms and thighs, between her breasts and on her stomach.

"I will accept whatever terms you want," he'd said at the beginning. "However you wish it to be between us..." There had only been her fear, her shyness. And his eagerness to marry her.

She wondered again, had he loved another woman before her? He swore that she was the only woman he'd ever loved. But his answers to all such questions were sparse, he volunteered nothing. He'd look into her eyes and smile, telling her without words that she mustn't ask anymore. He'd never spoken of other women, though he'd talked about the years when he was a young man living in New York with his brother, all the parties and the social life. Had he ever made love before to anyone? This was a question that she'd never dared ask him, even in the intimacy of marriage. In some way, she realized, she didn't want to know the answer. He was such a fine-looking man, it was impossible to believe that...to believe that he'd been celibate all those years. She knew that young men went to certain women before they married. It was understood. But if he hadn't gone to those women, if he had never had any relationship with a woman, then what did that mean? Did that mean there was something wrong with him? That he wasn't..."natural"? He'd been silent about all that. The "terms" of their marriage...there'd been no understanding between them as to whether the terms were mutable, whether they could change.

As she lay there in the heat, the perspiration smoothed her skin, softened the dryness of age, made it feel youthful again. Gradually, the quiet and the breeze calmed her and the events of the concert faded from her mind. She was here in this magnificent and sensual city, in this palace.

And she remembered being young, the summer night, outside in the darkness the sound of crickets and cicadas, the desire to be touched. Here in the humid Venetian night those feelings that she'd almost forgotten were revived, feelings that had been taken from her by the long months of George's illness, by the urgency of caring for him, by the blow of his death, and by her own age, exhaustion, and illness.

Within this body, there'd once been such a need for love. Before George, the men to whom she'd revealed that pent-up yearning had been so surprised to discover it.

PART II
In a Dark Wood

Chapter 6

Charles Bray was the first. She was twenty-one when she and her father moved to Coventry. She'd been torn by the roots from everything she'd ever known. Isaac was married, Chrissey too.

Her father had taken a lease on a new house, Bird Grove, on Foleshill Road. It was white stucco, semidetached, on a hill above the squalor of Coventry, set amongst fields and meadows. "This lease will send me to the poorhouse," he said, "but if we're to find you a husband, it's best you be in a real town, in society." He didn't say it, but she knew what he meant. Until she married, he'd have to support her. Till then, at least he'd have his spinster daughter to take care of him.

As she walked about the house with its strange walls, she felt as if the boundaries of her selfhood had somehow melted, as if she no longer knew who she was. From her bedroom she could see the three spires of the city, the factories in the distance, and the tortured little cottages of the slums. Going to market, she saw groups of children streaming in through the gates of the ribbon factories, some but five or six years old, their breath steaming in the cold, carrying their little lunch pails. They worked as winders. Outside the almshouses there were long lines of women in ragged clothes, babies at their breasts, stomping their feet in the freezing air, queuing for bread. All those poor souls coming to the city from the countryside hoping for work. *"The prevalence of misery and want in this boasted nation of prosperity and glory is appalling,"* she wrote to Maria Lewis, her old teacher at Miss Wallington's school. Maria had taken a position as a governess in a clergyman's family in Northamptonshire. They still corresponded, but Marian felt increasingly distant from her. Maria could not possibly know her world now, the books and learning she had taught herself. She'd gone so far beyond that sad little girl that Maria had taken in her arms at Mrs. Wallington's.

The people of Coventry were cold and unfriendly. The only acquaintances they had were their next-door neighbors, Abijah and Elizabeth Pears, whom her father knew from conducting business in Coventry for the Arbury Estate. The Pearses were pious Evangelists. Marian and Elizabeth became friends. Elizabeth was impressed by all the books Marian had read. They discussed the shocking conditions in the city and decided to found a clothing club for the miners' families.

Elizabeth came from a family of ribbon manufacturers; her brother, Charles, ran the business, C. Bray & Co., and he and his wife, Cara, lived at the top of Radford Road. "They have all sorts of strange types visiting there," Elizabeth told Marian. "Rather disreputable sorts, I'm afraid, freethinkers, reformers, writers. Perhaps if I introduce you, you'll have a good influence on them."

So, one brisk November day, Elizabeth led her across the fields and along the canal to visit her brother and sister-in-law. Marian was nervous at the prospect of meeting these vaguely "dangerous" people, these supposed "radicals." She was afraid she'd fail completely in the company of such exotic types, that they'd find her dull and provincial.

They came to a Georgian mansion, Rosehill, surrounded by acres of grounds.

Elizabeth's brother, Charles, was at the front door to greet them. "Come in! Come in!" he cried. Charles seemed like a force of nature, with ruddy cheeks, a full, sensual mouth, unruly hair, a sturdy body. Behind him stood his wife, Cara, a tiny, pretty, gentle creature, with a vague sadness about her, Marian thought. She looked like a doll, with round blue eyes, lovely, long, blond ringlets around her face, and sloping shoulders.

Marian sat on the ottoman in the drawing room by the French window and Charles pulled a chair up next to her. He looked down at her intently.

"My sister, Elizabeth, says you are a most extraordinary young woman. She says you've read everything."

"I don't know about that," Marian said.

"Well, have you read Emerson's essays?"

"I have," she said.

"Have you read *Sartor Resartus*?"

"Of course."

"What about my brother-in-law Charles Hennell's book, *An Inquiry Concerning the Origin of Christianity*?"

"He's your brother-in-law?" she asked.

"Indeed, he's Cara's brother."

"I am amazed to be sitting here," she said with a smile. "The way he so carefully analyzed the Gospels, and was able to find the smallest discrepancies. He must be an extraordinary man."

"He is," Charles said. "But you, you don't talk at all like a country girl."

"Well, I am one," she said. "But people say I've lost the dialect."

His eyes seemed to burn into her. "And you're hardly a typical woman in your reading."

"I hardly know what a typical woman is. Do you?" she said, again smiling.

———

When she was leaving, he said, "You must come again. You must come all the time. We shall feast on you!"

She began to go regularly to see the Brays, often on her own, slipping out of the house so Elizabeth Pears wouldn't see her go and disapprove of her growing friendship with her radical brother and sister-in-law.

It seemed as if that winter she and Cara and Charles discussed everything under the sun, philosophy, politics, and especially religion. A light had suddenly penetrated her existence, her mind engaged with ideas, with people who'd read the same books she had. She'd never known anyone like the Brays.

Charles told her that he and Cara had ceased going to church. They'd both come from Unitarian families. Now, partly because of Cara's brother Charles Hennell's book, they no longer believed that God's will could even be divined through Scripture. "God is nature," Charles said, "and nature is utmost perfection. Freedom and happiness consist in understanding the laws of nature and what drives us. Prayer is just a distraction from knowing what those laws are." These were akin to the thoughts she'd long had herself. Until now, there'd been no one with whom she could discuss them.

The winter deepened, and her long talks with Charles coalesced the doubts swirling about in her. God was indefinable, He emanated from within oneself and enveloped everything. It was His spirit which made one want to hug a child, to kiss a dear friend, to soothe her tears, to clothe the poor and feed the hungry laborers of the city. What mattered was to pay close attention to one's inner instincts and not to be distracted by the old, empty words of Scripture and ritual.

At Christmas, Sarah and Isaac rode over from Griff for dinner, and Marian told them about her new friends.

"Best watch out for those types, Marian," Isaac said. Isaac was a country squire now, a man of affairs in his new job as manager of the Arbury Estate, a Church of England man, a conservative now, just like her father. "You'll never find yourself a husband with the likes of them. The whole reason Father's taken on this lease is so you'll meet the appropriate people. You're going to be a burden on this family forever."

"But...they're so nice," she said. "They've made me feel so welcome."

"There's plenty of other people around who would make you feel welcome too, if you just tried," Isaac said.

She held her ground. She couldn't ignore any longer the changes that had swept through her. She was transformed, for the first time she had an identity that was sure and certain. The world made sense. To ignore all this would be to lie.

On the next Sunday after Christmas, after breakfast, she stood by the front door watching as her father got ready for church. Outside, the snow was falling softly, steadily, weighing down the branches of the firs. He took up his walking stick, then noticed that she still hadn't put on her outdoor things.

"Best hurry up, Marian. The man's awaitin'."

"Papa, I'm afraid I'm not going to church today," she said quietly. "I've decided that I'm not going to go to church—ever again."

He stared at her. "What's that? Hurry up now. The carriage is outside."

She took a breath. "As I said, Papa, with utmost respect, I'm no longer going to church because I no longer believe in religion."

"That's the stupidest thing I ever heard from your lips! Get on with ya now."

"But I mean it, Papa."

"Is that what those Bray people's taught you?"

"No. It's entirely my decision."

"Them's Godless people! How dare they interfere with my daughter!"

"They're not Godless, Papa," she said. "And they've got nothing to do with this. I've been thinking about this for a very long time."

"You don't believe in God?" he said. "I never heard such a thing."

"I believe profoundly in God. I believe He's a bigger, more sacred presence than any we can ever know, but that He's ultimately mysterious to us. Our task in life is to discover His teaching. The Bible is a set of fables, it doesn't contain the real truth of God."

"Poppycock!"

She could see through the window the carriage waiting outside, the snow deepening. The man was trudging down the path toward the front door.

"I'm not going, Papa," she said. "For me to go to church is a lie."

The man was at the door now. "Mr. Evans?" he said. "The carriage is here."

Her father glared at her as if he couldn't think of what to say. She tried to keep her eyes levelly on his.

Then he put on his hat and stormed out of the house without speaking another word. She watched from the window as the carriage drove away through the whirling white.

Thus began the "Holy War." Two hours later, he came back from church, his face tight, lips sealed. He went immediately upstairs to his bedroom.

At five o'clock, the maid, Clare, rang the bell for supper. Marian went to his bedroom door and called out, "Papa, supper is ready."

Clare had laid out the mutton and pies. When at last he entered the dining room, Marian rose and served him his food. Throughout supper, the only sound was his slurping and chewing in the furious silence. When Clare brought in the cabinet pudding and custard, his favorite dessert, he said nothing.

The following afternoon, Isaac appeared at Bird Grove. Her father had sent for him to intervene. "You're just trying to call attention to yourself," Isaac said. "As usual. Always the center of attention."

Why did he say that? She always tried to be gray, to recede. Was it because she was cleverer than he?

"That's not true. I don't believe in the language and the rituals anymore. Only the God inside us."

"You always think you know more than the rest of us."

"No! It's just what I know for myself."

"Then why do you have to cause all this fuss? And make Papa angry? Just sit there and keep your mouth shut."

"I can't," she said. "I just can't."

Next came her neighbor, Elizabeth Pears. "I'm responsible for this," Elizabeth said. "Please don't let them corrupt you with their thinking."

"No," Marian said. "You've got to understand, this is my own conclusion."

Her father enlisted Rebecca Franklin from the Misses Franklin's school to change her mind, and even a professor of theology, the Reverend Francis Watts of Spring College, a young man who distracted her with his attractive looks even as he tried to argue with her. But every book they cited to refute her arguments, she'd read and knew better than they did.

Then her father told Isaac, who informed her, that he intended to leave Bird Grove, as the lease was too expensive, and to move to Meriden to live with Chrissey and Edward Clarke.

But where would she go? How could she support herself? Perhaps she could be a governess or a teacher? She made inquiries at the Binswood Hall School in Leamington, but there were no openings. Word of her apostasy had spread. No one wanted an irreligious woman around children.

Her father's cold rage, his silence, was unbearable. She loved him more than anything on earth, this great, strong man, she was beholden to him. When a smile of approval escaped his lips, his barely perceptible smile, warmth flowed through her body. How she loved to stroke his face when he kissed her, and his smell, of male hair and skin. His care was the center of her life, the focus of everything. His rage terrified her. It was like a hell, as if he'd killed her and she didn't exist for him anymore. She'd become invisible.

After four weeks of this, she sat down and wrote him a long, impassioned letter reiterating her position. *"My Dear father, All my efforts in conversation have hitherto failed,"* she wrote. *"I admire and cherish much of what I believe to have been the moral teaching of Jesus."* But the teachings of the Scriptures themselves, she had come to believe, were *"histories consisting of mingled truth and fiction."* To continue going to church would be a lie, *"dishonorable to God,"* she said. The truth of feeling was the only universal bond of union. She'd do anything, anything, to make him happy—short of attending church.

He was unmoved. He didn't answer. He told Isaac again, who again told her, that he was determined to leave and go and live with Chrissey and Edward Clarke.

At the end of February, Isaac suggested that for the sake of peace, she move back to Griff with him and Sarah. Initially, she was comforted, surrounded once again by the familiar rooms of her childhood, the rooms she knew like her own skin, the landscape that had been so much a part of her. Sarah was pregnant for the first time, and anxious, and preparing the room that Marian was sleeping in for the new baby. Sarah tried to be kind, but Marian could tell that they didn't want her there.

Then Sarah, obviously wanting Griff to herself, told her father and Isaac that they were going about things the wrong way. It was no good telling Marian that she had to go to church just because people would disapprove. She was far too stubborn to accede to that. Tell her that her father needed her to care for him, and that he missed her. Say to Marian that out of respect for him, she should at least go to church with him, but that she didn't have to renounce her beliefs. She should just keep them to herself.

An arrangement was made. In April she returned to the house. She went to Trinity Church with him and tried not to pay attention to the service. She stared up at the medieval painting of the Last Judgment above the tower arch, with its depiction of the poor souls being ushered by Christ to Paradise on the right or to Hell on the left; Hell's mouth, a roaring furnace, gaped to receive the agonized figures consigned there. She no longer believed in that Hell, that crude superstition.

She waited out the service for the promise of the outdoors, the sweet spring air, freedom.

Peace was restored and she cared for her father obediently in every way. At first there were no welcoming arms, only a few grudging thank-yous when she served him his supper. He wanted to make it clear that he was hanging on to his disapproval. But slowly, his words grew in number, a few smiles here and there escaped from his lips, and gradually he seemed to forget his anger. And as she played his favorite songs for him on the piano—he particularly liked "When the Swallows Homeward Fly"—he sighed with satisfaction. "Ah, that's a good gel," he said.

When she was not caring for him, she continued her pilgrimages to the Brays. He no longer tried to stop her, he merely ignored these visits.

And she and Charles continued their perpetual conversation, walking arm in arm through the streets of Coventry in deep discussion.

As they strolled through the cobblestone streets, passing the timbered buildings and the shopfronts filled with displays of ribbons, he told her about his life. "I was a very spoiled little boy," he said. "But then my mother died when I was nine and I was sent off to boarding school. I was very rebellious, always in hot water. The teachers tied my leg to a desk—"

"They tied your leg to a desk!"

"I managed to cut the cord. Then they tied my leg to a log and I just hefted the thing up onto my shoulders and walked around with it. I defied them and I was very proud. The schoolmaster was a Methodist minister, and that's where I learned the meaning of injustice."

"How horrible!" she said.

"And it was. They took me out of there when I was seventeen and I apprenticed at my father's warehouse. I spent my nights reading, and that's where I abandoned my faith. I realized that God is nature, and that nature is perfect, and our principal task in life is to understand the laws of nature, for they are inevitably just."

"I wish I could believe that," she said.

He continued, "I saw the misery of the workers. After my father died, I took on the management of the business, but business bores me to death. I'd discovered Robert Owen and I decided to adapt his ideas of cooperatives to help the employees of C. Bray & Co. Cara and I have started an Infants' School, and we've given the workers allotments so they can grow their own food and earn some extra cash.

We set up a Workingmen's Club where they can go instead of the pubs and getting drunk out of their minds."

"It sounds most extraordinary."

"Cara loves her little school. And you should see the allotments. They grow everything under the sun. And I bought the *Coventry Herald*, so now I can put forth all my grand ideas!" He laughed at himself. "You should write something for my newspaper," he added.

"I'm not sure I could. I—"

"Of course you could. Write something about religion. Nobody knows more about the subject than you."

She agreed to try. She labored for weeks reviewing three books on Christianity and finally produced the essay. He printed it immediately. Then he asked her to review another book, Gilbert à Becket's *Comic History of England*, and she wrote a satirical piece called "Vice and Sausages." There had been an article in the paper the previous week about unwholesome meat of dubious origin being sold to the citizens of Coventry. The person responsible for inspecting the meat was a man called John Vice. *"Every kind of animals, mice, rats, kittens, puppy dogs, up to a dead beast or body,"* she wrote, *"may all be made, by judicious seasonings, to taste like pork."*

"In addition to all else," Charles told her, "you're a wit."

When her pieces were published in the *Herald*, she stared at the words printed on paper, her words, her ideas woven together and boldly put forward as if they made sense. And, strangely, they did make sense. Her name wasn't on them, as was the custom, of course, but they were her ideas in print, the first time she'd seen that.

Meanwhile, gentle Cara taught health and the importance of kindness to animals at the Infants' School, and became her dearest friend. She came to love Cara and Cara loved her back. They alternated playing piano at musical evenings at Rosehill.

During that time, Cara insisted on painting her portrait. In it, Cara made her look pretty, with a girl-like delicacy. She colored her eyes a lovely blue, gave her hair gentle curls. Her complexion gleamed tenderly, with rosy touches on the cheeks. She wore a light-colored pinkish-purple dress with a delicate lace collar. Her arms were crossed in their typical attitude, hiding her body. The pose was impatient, as if she'd been compelled to sit still, which she had, to humor Cara.

"That doesn't look a bit like me," she told Cara.

"Are you implying I have no skill as a painter?" Cara said. "I'm rather aggrieved."

Despite the picture's lyricism, she had had to admit it did bear some resemblance. There was the faint suggestion of her large brow, her big, curved nose, her upper lip shorter than her lower lip, her strong chin.

"You're just being kind," she told Cara.

"Nonsense, it's completely you."

The French windows at Rosehill opened onto a broad terrace, and from there to a long, sloping lawn. The house was always filled with callers. On summer days, a bearskin rug was spread among the roots of the immense acacia tree, and some of the most interesting people she'd ever met gathered there. "Everyone who comes to Coventry with a queer mission, or who's a little cracked, is sent to Rosehill," Charles said, laughing.

Charles's latest enthusiasm was phrenology, the belief that human character and faculties are indicated by the dimensions and bumps of the skull. His prize guest was the leading phrenologist George Combe, a tiny, hump-backed man with a big head who wore black swallowtails. He was married to the wealthy daughter of the actress Mrs. Siddons. "We must have a cast made of this noble skull," Charles declared, pointing at Marian's head and making a tapping motion. "Perhaps it'll reveal the source of her brilliance."

"I'll have no such thing," she insisted. "I will never submit to having my head shaved so someone can make a plaster cast of it."

But Charles buoyed her, he made her laugh with his silly enthusiasms.

Then, one spring day, like a gust of wind, the writer Harriet Martineau appeared, carrying a huge brass ear trumpet, for she was very deaf. Martineau was already famous. She suffered from chronic illness, but she was like an engine, incredibly prolific, the author of a nine-volume work, *Illustrations of Political Economy*, and an article opposing slavery for the *Westminster Review*, "The Martyr of the United States," which had attracted enormous attention. Martineau was a true radical, in favor of Parliamentary rule over the monarchy and expanding the right to vote. She seemed never to let the fact that she was a woman stand in her way and had no hesitation writing about subjects such as politics that were usually the province of male writers. And she also wrote novels.

"You must meet our very brilliant friend, Miss Evans," Charles Bray said.

Martineau cast the beam of her attention on Marian. "Really," she said, holding her ear trumpet toward Marian like an antenna. Marian was awed by her. This was the first woman writer she'd ever met. Martineau was in her forties, rapidly graying, and somewhat manly, even ugly, a robust figure who wore the plainest of clothes. In order for a woman to succeed in a man's world, to have success as a writer, Marian thought, perhaps she couldn't be pretty. Must she be sexless and deep-voiced like Martineau, and not care about her appearance? Perhaps Charles so readily accepted *her*, Marian, because she too was ugly, because he didn't see her as a woman.

But she was a woman, with such a need for love, for tenderness, a longing to be held.

One day, the great American thinker, Ralph Waldo Emerson, the founder of transcendentalism, on a lecture tour of England and Scotland, came calling.

Emerson was forty years old, tall, spare, hooked-nosed, but his voice was surprisingly gentle and sweet. When Charles introduced them, he told her he'd been reading Indian philosophy and it had had a great effect on him. He asked what the most important book she had read was, and she said Rousseau's *Confessions*. "It was the same for me," he told her. Later, when she and Charles were alone, he mentioned that Emerson had praised her. "'Your friend has such a calm, serious soul,' he said."

Another visitor to Rosehill was Edward Noel, a cousin of Lord Byron's. Noel was a short-haired man with a wide, warm smile. He owned an estate on a Greek island where he was instituting the latest agricultural reforms and trying to improve relations between peasants and landowners. He'd built stone houses for his laborers to replace their hovels. Noel also had a home in Devonshire, in Bishops

Teignton. His wife, Fanny, had consumption. He came to Rosehill alone with his three children or by himself. Marian noticed that he seemed especially close to Cara, and when the children arrived she always ran to greet them and made a fuss over them. She also noticed Cara and Noel were often alone in a corner of the drawing room in intense conversation, or strolling together in the garden.

When the weather grew warmer, the guests gathered under the huge acacia tree, talking and debating and laughing, and Hannah, the cook, a full-breasted girl with a complexion as soft and pink as a peach, prepared delicious picnics for them all of salmon and cold chicken and champagne.

At the center of it all was Charles, the sun around whom the entire household revolved.

One day, none other than Charles Hennell himself arrived. He was frail, melancholy-looking, with long, corkscrew curls, heavy-lidded, sensual eyes, rimless glasses, and cupid lips. Marian sat down beside him. "Your book's been very important to me," she told him. "Especially your conclusion that just because the Scriptures are myths doesn't mean that they don't have a beneficial influence."

Hennell's face lit up. "I'm very flattered," he said. "I seldom meet anyone who's even read the thing. I'm afraid it hasn't sold very many copies, though a few of my coreligionists have taken me to task, saying it's better to abandon Jesus altogether than to question the authority of the Bible."

There was a swirl of young men around her now, young men unlike any she'd ever known, brilliant people, people who, like her, read different languages, and knew philosophy, mathematics, and science. They seemed fascinated by her learning, so unusual for a woman, and by the way she fearlessly challenged them. She was conscious that she made her voice low and musical. She felt herself opening up to them in a slow, almost painful way, as if she were a bud whose petals were being inexorably forced apart by sunlight and warmth. What did it mean that these men loved to talk to her? Were they drawn to her as a woman? Or was she simply like another man to them?

Charles Hennell came again to Rosehill and joined them in their musical evenings, playing the viola while she and Cara alternated on the piano. She was moved by him, by his delicate looks, his sensual eyes and mouth, and by the courage it must have taken him, an ordinary man, not a scholar, to question the Bible, and still to reaffirm Christian belief. She tried to make herself pretty for him, to comb her hair neatly, though it always escaped her efforts to tame it. She put on a little coral necklace that she'd inherited from her mother. Perhaps he liked her? She couldn't tell. He was always warm, and grateful to discuss his book. When they played music, his wan features flushed as he sawed away merrily on his viola.

Then, a young woman with astonishing long, red hair arrived at Rosehill. She entered the room filling it with her presence, a cynosure. Her name was Rufa Brabant.

Marian asked, politely, the natural question, "How did you come by your name, 'Rufa'?"

"My real name's Rebecca," she said. "But my father was a friend of Coleridge and he gave me the nickname because of my hair," she said, tossing her mane about her shoulders, perfectly aware, Marian thought, of her beauty. "I knew him when I was little. Actually, he used my name twice in his poems. She laughed. *"From Rufa's eye sly Cupid shot his dart,"* she recited. *"And left it sticking in Sangarado's heart. / No quiet from that moment has he known, / And peaceful sleep has from his eyelids flown."*

This Rufa was not only stunning and had known Coleridge himself, but she was obviously learned too. "I'm translating Strauss's *Das Leben Jesu* for Mr. Hennell," she told Marian. David Friedrich Strauss was one of a group of German theologians who, like Charles Hennell, had begun questioning the historical truth of the Bible and the divinity of Jesus. "Mr. Hennell doesn't read German but he's heard about the book and asked me to do it."

Marian could feel herself disliking this beautiful creature.

Later Cara told her, "My poor brother, Charles, is completely in love with Rufa, but her father's forbidden the marriage. He's a doctor and he insisted on giving him a physical examination and discovered he's got weak lungs."

Then, the next day, Charles Hennell himself drove up to the house. He walked right past Marian and went immediately to Rufa, took both her hands in his, and they went outside into the garden. Marian, watching them from the French window, saw them walking down the hill, their heads bent closely together.

Disappointment settled over her like a dull wave.

Meanwhile, Charles Bray told her enthusiastically, "You've got the temperament of genius. You're the most delightful companion I've ever known." She'd utter an idea and Charles would praise it as if it were the most brilliant thing in the world. He was writing a book about religion, he said, and he'd been reading Spinoza, about his ideas on the

nature of God. But he didn't know enough Latin to translate it properly. "I have a little Latin," she told him. "From
church. Perhaps I could help you." And she rendered some
of Spinoza's Latin phrases into readable English for him.

Sometimes they argued violently. Charles insisted that
all religion was simply superstition.

"But you can't say that!" she insisted, even though she
herself had given up on organized religion. "People would
just kill each other if it weren't for religion."

As they argued, Charles would look deep into her face
and smile amusedly, infuriating her. But then the next day,
they'd make up.

They talked constantly about the turmoil in the city
below, the devastating effect on the workers of the constant
fluctuation in ribbon prices. In the winter months, work
was at a virtual standstill, families were cold and hungry,
and parents couldn't afford to send their children to school.
Charles believed in the necessity of a fundamental change
in the very nature of society.

But she'd seen what change could do when it came too
quickly, that time, when she was thirteen and had ridden
into Nuneaton that day with her father and seen the workingmen rioting over the Reform Act, and the Scots Greys
riding through the crowd and bludgeoning them. She was
still her father's daughter, she realized; the conservative
ways of the countryside had their hold on her. "Change can't
be too abrupt," she said to Charles. "All those old rural virtues, people's sense of obligation toward one another, the
rhythms of the harvest and tenancy, those are ancient ties
that bind people."

"That's called serfdom," Charles said.

As they walked arm in arm, she could feel his elbow pressed against the side of her breast. He made no attempt to pull it away, and she didn't move away either, because if she did, it would be an acknowledgment that his arm shouldn't be there, and that she'd noticed it. And besides, she liked it there, his closeness to her.

One summer evening, as they sat apart in the darkness of the garden, Charles told her, "Cara and I have a special arrangement. We believe our marriage bond is so strong that nothing can break it. From the beginning, we've said that if we were drawn to other people, our love could withstand it."

"Drawn to other people?" What did he mean? Did he mean sexually?

She could feel him, in the darkness, scrutinizing her for her reaction.

"You mean—" she said, but she couldn't bring herself to say it.

"We're free to be intimate with other people."

"That's awful!" she said.

"Not at all. Cara's developed an attachment to Edward Noel."

She remembered Cara's solicitousness toward Noel and his children. Noel's wife, Fanny, was increasingly ill, and Cara had been going to Bishops Teignton for days at a time to help Noel nurse her.

But how could Charles bear the thought of Cara intimate with someone else? And did he have someone for himself?

She found herself watching Cara and Charles in a new way, trying to understand. How could they love each other if they were taking other people as lovers? How could they not be jealous of each other? Why would they be married if not because they'd committed themselves wholly to each other?

She sensed there was significance in Charles's telling her about his and Cara's "arrangement." But could it really be that he was saying he wanted her? Not possible. He wasn't attracted to her at all, except that he loved to talk to her.

A week later, it was a stiflingly hot day, the height of the summer heat in July, the intense heat that came only once or twice each year. Her father was resting in his room at Bird Grove and Marian made her way through the fields to Rosehill, the meadows dry, the grass golden brown, the insects buzzing around her.

As she rang the bell of the house, it seemed unusually quiet. The maid said that Mrs. Bray had gone to Bishops Teignton to see Mr. Noel, and the servants had retired to their quarters, driven in by the heat. Mr. Bray was in his study.

She knocked on the study door and from within came his answering call. As she entered, the room was dark, the curtains drawn against the afternoon sun. He was sitting in the shadows behind his desk. There was a green velvet divan on which he took his afternoon rest, an oriental rug thrown over it, and great, soft pillows piled upon it. His books were stacked untidily on the shelves and newspapers piled on the floor around him. Behind the desk, a great, stuffed owl was mounted on a pedestal, and there was a marble bust of a Greek maiden, the tip of her nose broken off, her neck long and graceful, her hair curling in tendrils about her face.

"Ah—there she is!" cried Charles, rising to greet her. "My soul mate. Do you know, I believe I have an affinity with you unlike any I have ever had with another person."

She felt a sudden danger in the rush of his words, in his naked declaration in the isolation of the room, at this new closeness to him. "Thank you," she said warily. It was true that it sometimes seemed, in the excitement of their mutual understanding and in the intensity of their conversation, as if there were no boundaries between them.

She stood across the room from him, dwarfed by the high ceiling. He came closer. They were several feet apart. He studied her, taking her in from head to foot in a way he never had before. Then he came forward, reached out suddenly, took her in his arms, embraced her, and kissed her.

His full lips were on hers, his body against hers, and she felt a fierce sensation shoot up through her from her legs to her breast.

She tried to extricate herself, but he said, "No," and kissed her again.

At first when he made love to her, it hurt, and she cried out and he withdrew. "I'm so sorry," he whispered. "I don't want to hurt you." But she let him enter her again.

What happened next occurred so quickly that there was no thought involved, only urgency. It was her first taste of this pleasure, and once that taste had been taken and that boundary crossed, there was no going back.

Afterward she cried with shame at what she'd done, and he held her. "It's your first time," he said, and she nodded through her tears. "Thank you," he said, "for that gift."

As he pulled on his clothes, she asked, "But what will we tell Cara? She and I, we're so close. I love Cara. She's like my sister."

He sat down beside her on the divan and put his arm around her shoulder. "You don't have to tell Cara. She already knows."

"But how could she know? This is the first—"

"Cara sees everything. And you know that I have her permission. It's the same for her with Edward."

Cara was scheduled to return that evening from Bishops Teignton. The next day and the day after, Marian didn't go to Rosehill.

Then a note came to Bird Grove from Cara. *I miss you, dear friend. Where have you been? Why have you deserted us? We are having a party with music on Saturday and we want you to play the piano.* Cara missed her! She was inviting her to play the piano. Marian was afraid to face her, but by not going she would be bringing out into the open what had happened.

On Saturday, she walked slowly through the summer evening to Rosehill. She walked along the canal, across the bridge, the night sounds of frogs and crickets vivid around her. She could see the house ahead of her all lit up. From the open windows came voices and music and the tinkling of glass. As she entered the drawing room amidst the other arriving guests, Cara caught sight of her and looked at her for a long moment. Then she smiled and moved to greet her. Standing before Marian, she looked into her face. Cara's eyes were the warmest, deepest blue, so full of wisdom and kindness. In them was a look of reassurance and acceptance, a pledge not to censure her, a promise communicated that their own love couldn't be broken.

Perhaps Cara countenanced her new ties to Charles because it gave her permission to love Edward Noel. Now that Cara knew about herself and Charles, she could continue with Edward without doubt, without guilt.

Cara reached out her arms, embraced Marian, and held her. She could feel Cara's tiny body warm against her, her curls brushing her face.

And so the darkened study with its soft privacy, the green velvet divan, the door quietly latched against the servants, became the place where she and Charles met, discreetly, when Cara was out, as if to observe the formalities, the appearances, so as not to challenge too obviously the rules of others. And Cara was still her beloved "sister," and Charles was now her lover, and she and Cara never spoke of it.

Charles was tender and kind, but afterward the guilt and shame overwhelmed her. Still, she always came back. No matter how often she resolved not to, she couldn't give him up, the affection that came from him, this new pleasure that expanded and grew each time.

And Charles, though loving toward her, was still the husband of Cara. He loved Cara, he said, with all his heart, though he loved her, Marian, as well. And, she wondered again, did he have others? And who could they be? Was he still intimate with Cara? As these questions arose in her mind, she banished them.

She knew that he could never be hers alone. No man would ever give himself entirely to her, neither Charles Bray nor Charles Hennell, who had been so sweetly grateful to her for her appreciation of his book, but who loved only Rufa Brabant. She must take what was given.

In July Charles and Cara invited her to go on holiday with them to Tenby in Wales. Charles Hennell and Rufa Brabant were to come. Rufa's father, Dr. Brabant, no longer opposed their marriage. Rufa had inherited a small sum and Charles Hennell had found a job as manager of an iron company. Perhaps Dr. Brabant realized he couldn't stop them. Marian asked her father's permission to go with them; she would be carefully chaperoned, she pointed out. He grumpily assented.

In Tenby, they took long walks to Moonstone Point and bathed in the bathing machines, wooden carts with canvas awnings that rolled into the sea and enabled ladies, especially, to change and bathe modestly in the water without being seen. At low tide in the evening, they walked out to St. Catherine's Island and explored the caves, stirring the tidal pools into phosphorescence with pieces of driftwood. Charles and Cara had separate bedrooms, and Charles came to Marian's room at night. No one spoke of it. It was as if no one knew about it, or, if they did, they accepted the arrangement. She tried not to think about it, the possibility that Charles and Cara might still be together too. Charles belonged to everyone, in his warmth, his outgoingness, but she had no sense that he was with anyone but her, Marian.

As they played and laughed together, she came to like the vivacious Rufa Brabant. Pale, ethereal Charles Hennell loved Rufa, but Marian had her own lover to hold her now at night.

The party traveled on to Swansea. Rufa's father, Dr. Brabant, joined them. He was a small, ebullient figure with a corona of white hair around his well-shaped head, clean shaven, with muttonchop sideburns, high cheekbones, thin-lipped. He had watchful light blue eyes, taking everything in, observing everything, and when he looked at you it was as if he had a special relationship, a secret, with you.

On one of their rambles on the beach, he walked alongside Marian apart from the rest of the group, and he told her about his friendship with Coleridge, who'd just died. He and Coleridge were quite close, he said, with a modest smile, and Coleridge had sent him an excerpt of his revised *Biographia Literaria*, asking for his opinion. Coleridge had also confided to him, he said, his awful struggles with opium. He'd tried to help him but had failed and the great man had died, profoundly depressed, his life in ruins.

Dr. Brabant was no longer practicing medicine, he said, but was writing a book on theology. It would be a very long work, he said. He was friends with the theologian David Friedrich Strauss. His book would be on the same lines as Strauss and his future son-in-law Charles Hennell's work, questioning the facts of Jesus's life as presented in the Gospels. "I think it will be epoch-making," he said, "the final destroyer of all theological dogma." She'd read some Strauss herself, she told him, as her German was quite good now. She was looking forward very much to reading his work.

A few weeks after they returned from Tenby, one autumn morning, when the first frost covered the ground, she arrived at Rosehill to find Charles looking unusually serious. "I've got some news, Marian," he said. He drew her into his study and shut the door behind them.

He stood there, his hair hanging roughly over his forehead, his face florid with excitement.

"Cara and I are going to have a child," he said.

She was dumbfounded. All along—what she hardly dared to imagine—he and Cara had still been intimate.

"We're going to adopt a baby girl." So it wasn't what it seemed.

"But...how wonderful," she said. "I'm so happy for you."

He didn't smile, but continued watching her face, as if collecting himself before he delivered the next words. "The child is mine," he said. He was silent, pausing for her response.

"Yours?" So there *were* others. That possibility had remained unspoken between them, something she wanted to ignore because of her need for him, the gaiety he brought to her life, the distraction, the kindness.

"Yes, mine," he said.

Her voice faltered. "But who is its mother?"

"Hannah is the mother. Hannah Steane."

Her face burned with anger. Hannah, the cook, full-breasted, round-bodied Hannah, with her high color and dimpled wrists, who smiled sweetly and brought them their meals and lived with her mother and sister nearby on Radford Road. But right under her nose? And she hadn't noticed it. She thought back. Hannah had grown plumper recently, her eyes were somehow deeper and shining. And, she realized, she hadn't seen her at Rosehill for several weeks.

"You knew," Charles said, warning her as if to forestall her anger. "You knew that we'd agreed, Cara and I. I told you from the beginning. We had an agreement."

"But somehow I thought that I—"

"Marian, I never told you you were the only one," he said flatly.

She felt tears threatening to burst through her. He was right. And she had chosen to ignore it. She couldn't answer.

"Oh, Marian. I was honest with you. I made it a point of honor." He came around and sat beside her on the green velvet divan, the place where it had all begun. He drew her to him and kissed the top of her head. "You knew that Cara and I have given each other the freedom to love other people…"

Her head was swirling. All this time she'd so needed his love and affection that she'd chosen not to think about the fact that he could still share a bed with Cara, and…with others.

"Cara and I are going to adopt Hannah's baby. We'll have a little girl of our own, Marian. We're rejoicing."

"But Hannah will give up her baby?"

"No. Hannah's agreed to come and live with us as her nursemaid."

"I see." She tried to control her anger, to have some pride.

"She's a precious thing, Marian. She looks just like me. Cara has seen her and has fallen in love with her. We've named her Elinor. We'll call her Nelly for short."

He was watching her, waiting for an answer. "Well," he said, "what do you think? Isn't it wonderful?"

"I'm going home," she said. "Papa's waiting for me."

He went to take her in his arms. But she pushed him away.

"Please, don't go away from us," he said. "Will you still come? We both love you, Cara loves you, I love you."

She left the house. An icy rain had begun, little spikes of cold on her skin. She pulled her scarf tight around her. A fog lay over Coventry, obscuring the low-lying areas, the timber-faced workers' houses. Halfway down the hill, her face suddenly crumpled, like a struck child's.

———————

She stayed away from Rosehill. She was angry, angry at him and at herself for her willful blindness, her need. As the days passed, any residual desire she'd felt for him vanished within her. Her response to him, her enjoyment of him, had been dependent on the illusion of trust, the illusion she'd created for herself, and that had been broken now.

Again a note came from Cara. "Please come. Our baby is here, and we want your blessing. We have missed you so much. Please don't stay away. I need you."

Perhaps he had told Cara about her reaction? But to stay away would convey that she'd been hurt by his revelation. She must meet him on his own terms, as if she too had somehow been indifferent enough to him not to mind that she wasn't the only woman he slept with. And he had on his side the fact that he had told her the truth from the beginning.

She relented, and went to the house. There stood Cara, holding the little bundle tightly in her arms, radiant, Charles beside her, stroking the baby's cheek with his finger. "Would you like to hold her?" Cara said. She took the infant and gazed down at her heart-shaped lips, a tiny blister at the tip from nursing so hard. She was making little sucking sounds. Marian bent over her soft scalp and smelled its warmth. The wonder of the baby filled the air, and for now, at least, there was no echo in the room of what had happened with her and Charles.

"There," said Cara. "See how peaceful she is in your arms. She loves you already. Hannah will sleep in her room at first," Cara said, "so she can be her wet nurse."

Gradually, she began going back to the house. When Cara went to see Edward Noel in Bishops Teignton, she asked Marian to go to Rosehill and see that little Nelly was well.

At first she ignored Charles. As he stood there in front of her, there was an acknowledgment in his eyes, a pleading, hidden from the others. He was still saying that he wanted her. But she refused to return the look.

One afternoon in the study, he reached out for her again, but she put up her hands and refused him.

"No," she said. "That's finished. Forever."

He stepped back. "I understand," he said. "If that's the only way we can have you in our lives. But know that I will always love you, in every way, as a sister too. We both love you, and we will always take care of you."

She couldn't help herself. "Why?" she asked bitterly.

"Because neither one of us has ever known anyone like you, anyone as brilliant and good and kind. There is no one quite like you. One day, Marian, you will be a very important person in this world. Mark my words."

"As if that were enough," she said ruefully, and turned and left.

———

And that was the quandary. Rosehill was the center of her existence now, these were the only real friends she had. All life was there, parties and music, people forever broadening her horizons, giving her a glimpse of the world beyond and its possibilities, challenging her. Without them, she would be a prisoner in her father's house, she would have to retreat to her fate as his spinster daughter and caretaker. But she couldn't retreat now that the world had opened up before her.

She and Charles resumed their conversations. They never mentioned that they'd been lovers. It was easier that way. He still came eagerly to greet her when she arrived, put his arm around her and kissed her cheek.

But there was a wall between them, a wall that she had raised, and he respected it and didn't attempt to bridge it.

———————

November came, and once again she was a bridesmaid at someone else's wedding, this time Charles Hennell and Rufa Brabant's at Finsbury Square Chapel. As she listened to the marriage blessing, she realized that this was now the third time she'd stood behind two people at a wedding, she, dressed up and awkward, stooping to hide herself.

After the wedding, at the reception, Dr. Brabant spotted her and approached her. He studied her with his shrewd blue eyes. "Marian," he said. "I've thought of you often."

"It must be very difficult for you to lose your daughter," she said. "I know you'll miss her terribly."

"She's the apple of my eye." A look of sadness crossed his face. She was his only child, and now he was bereft.

Then, as if seized by an impulse, he asked brightly, "I wonder, if your father would permit it, if you'd like to come to Devizes for a few weeks to stay with myself and Mrs. Brabant? It would help us so much to fill the gap left by Rufa's going. My wife, Elizabeth, is blind, and her sister, Miss Hughes, lives with us and helps us."

She had never been to Devizes. She'd heard it was a pretty town, the streets laid out in medieval fashion, a famous system of locks that went up the canal. Winter was coming and perhaps it would be a little warmer there. It would be good to get away from Rosehill, to put a punctuation point to what had happened.

Her father was irritable because she was leaving him yet again, and so soon. But he said, "Well, go if you must."

A week later she was there. The Brabants lived in a large stone-faced house, Sandcliff, on Northgate Street. Mrs. Brabant's eyes were surrounded by the dark shadows of blindness, and when Dr. Brabant introduced them, she searched the air for Marian. Her sister, Miss Hughes, guided her toward her and she ran her fingers delicately across Marian's face while Miss Hughes stood there, a thin-smiling, watchful presence.

After supper—the roast beef and Yorkshire pudding were excellent—Dr. Brabant showed her his library, which was filled to the brim with books, the kind dear to her heart, books on theology and science and medical texts, mostly in German.

"Now, I want you to think of this as your own room," he told her. "You can spend as much time here as you want. No one will disturb you. Except myself," he said with a smile. He took her hand and kissed it. "May I call you 'Deutera'?" he asked her. "As if you are my second daughter?"

"How very sweet," she told him. "I'm touched."

She lingered among the books, her fingertips moving along the rows of titles. She was conscious of his standing there, watching her, still smiling.

When it was time for bed, she found that warm water had been set out for her bath. She was being spoiled, cherished by a kindly man who was like a father to her.

The next morning, she and Dr. Brabant took a walk through the old market town and along the canal and climbed up along the locks on Caen Hill.

She asked Dr. Brabant about his book on the myths of the Gospels, and he sighed. "It's a great sorrow to me," he confessed. "It goes so slowly. I've been at it for over two years now. I find myself constantly writing, then rewriting. I'm too much of a perfectionist and I can't bear to let anything go."

After lunch, he told her, "I have a surprise for you in the library." Eagerly she followed him there. He closed the door behind them, went to his desk, and picked up a manuscript. "This is it," he said. The whole thing was less than a half-inch thick.

"How wonderful."

"If you're a good child," he said, almost coyly, "I'll let you read some."

"Of course," she said. "I'd be pleased to."

"Very well." He handed it to her. "Sit here, by the light. I'll leave you alone with it."

"This is all?" she asked. Immediately she regretted her words.

"I'm afraid so," he said. "At the moment, I'm completely stuck. I just can't seem to go any further. Perhaps you can give me your thoughts."

It didn't take her long to read the twenty-eight pages he'd completed. But it was totally unoriginal, simply a recapitulation of the arguments of Strauss and Hennell. She already knew it all from her own reading.

When she'd finished, she went out into the parlor where she found him seated tensely forward in his chair, waiting for her response. Seeing her, he sprang up.

"Yes?" he asked, hopefully.

"It's brilliant," she said. Well, not quite brilliant, she added to herself. He seemed so eager for her approval. She couldn't bear to hurt him. "Such a succinct summary, so smoothly put, an important summary."

"Do you really think so?" he asked brightly, like an uncertain child.

"Of course. It's so difficult to do, to link them all, but you've done it."

She handed him back the pages and he clutched them to his chest. His face was filled with gratitude, he, a sixty-three-year-old man, old enough to be her father, and she but a twenty-four-year-old woman. "I—I can't thank you enough," he said. "Your words heal me, they give me hope."

"You must continue," she said. "You're synthesizing things, and explaining it to the world. The world needs your book." She was exaggerating again, but he seemed so vulnerable.

"Thank you, dear child. Thank you with all my heart. You're such a sweet, brilliant girl," he said. "I've found a beloved friend in you."

He was almost forty years older than she, infinitely warm, and he paid such close attention to her every word. And because Mrs. Brabant was rarely with them, except at meals, it was as if they were always alone.

As the days passed, she read to him aloud in German, and they read Greek together. She was happier than she'd ever been, adored by the little man, given nourishing meals, and left alone with him to expand the reaches of her mind. She felt suffused by a warm glow in his presence. For the first time, next to him she felt almost beautiful, perhaps because she was so much younger. Her skin seemed fresh and glowing, her hair soft, her figure lithe, her eyes shining. When she spoke, he gazed upon her with a kind of rapture. It was as if every word she uttered was a silvery thing. She was drawn to him, lit by his adoring eyes. Never had she felt so loved and cosseted, cherished for everything she was, for her youth as well as her intellect.

In the library after supper, when Mrs. Brabant and Miss Hughes had retired for the night, they read Archilocus together side by side on the couch in the candlelight, the fire glowing warm in the grate. *"A slender, lovely, graceful girl,"* they read, *"Just budding into subtle line—"* He looked up and said, "Like you, my dear girl."

He touched her breast and kissed her. Then he made love to her, and when it was finished, he stroked her hair and peered into her eyes as if he were awed by her. "You are such a sweet girl," he said. It wasn't the passionate coupling she'd had with Charles, it was gentler, as if she were a sacred object to be cherished, and his gratitude toward her was unending.

The next evening, they read Sappho exultantly in unison, alternating the lines between them and then finishing together in triumph. Suddenly, she stopped and found herself on her knees before him. "Please, let me stay with you forever," she said. "I've never been so happy. I'll help you with your book—"

Just then, behind her, the library door opened. Abruptly, he stood up from the couch and looked past her at the person who'd interrupted them. "My dear—" he said, addressing not her but someone beyond. She turned and there was Mrs. Brabant, so happy at the sound of his voice, but blind. And behind her, Miss Hughes. Miss Hughes had seen it all. She stepped in front of her sister.

"Robert!" Miss Hughes said. "Miss Evans, my God—" Her eyes were bright with anger. "Elizabeth," she said to her sister, "go to the parlor. I will attend to this."

Elizabeth Brabant stumbled from the room, groping along the furniture to find her way out. Miss Hughes stood before them. "Robert! What's going on here? How could you allow this? Miss Evans, you'd best leave at once."

Marian stood up. "But I—"

"Don't try to explain," Miss Hughes said. "I can see for myself."

Dr. Brabant's voice came to her. "Susan, I'm very sorry about this. The young lady suddenly, quite unexpectedly…I think she was a little overcome by her feelings. I'll go to Elizabeth at once."

He was transformed. He looked at her now as if he too was appalled. "Really, Miss Evans. I must say, I'm afraid you've let your emotions get quite out of hand in the past few days." He turned to Miss Hughes. "I've tried to stop her. I've explained that this just can't be. It's completely improper—"

"But, Robert—" Marian said, "Dr. Brabant, you—" She couldn't find the words. "I thought—" She left the thought unfinished.

Miss Hughes interjected, "Go to Elizabeth, Robert. Leave this to me."

Tight-lipped, she faced Marian in a fury. "You'll leave tomorrow morning on the first train."

Marian pushed past her, up the stairs to her room, and began throwing her clothes pell-mell into her trunk.

The next morning on the way to the station through the streets of Devizes, she wept. The coachman pretended not to notice. He had lied, lied! But why? Had she meant so little to him? The way he'd stood there as if made of stone, after all the love and praise he'd lavished on her. The betrayal was greater than any she'd ever known. He'd cared nothing for her.

She returned to Coventry, wounded. Hurt turned to anger at him, and contempt. He was a pathetic, selfish old fool. What had she done? Once again, need had overtaken her, smothered her judgment, all awareness. She hated herself for it, for giving in. Why wasn't she stronger? Why didn't she have a solid core that would enable her to survive without the love of a man?

———

Rufa Hennell, now married, announced that she couldn't finish her translation of Strauss's, *Das Leben Jesu*. She had already translated two volumes of it, but simply didn't have time to devote to it anymore. The only person whose German was possibly good enough to finish it was Marian. Rufa apparently did not know of the scene between Marian and her father, Dr. Brabant. If Marian would undertake it, Rufa promised to help her. And besides, Joseph Parkes, a wealthy radical politician from Birmingham, had promised to underwrite the costs of publication to the tune of three hundred pounds.

Yes, Marian said, she would do it. It would be her first book, though only a translation of somebody else's work. But she'd earn a little money at it, twenty pounds out of the three hundred—very little indeed, but something. It could be the beginning of a way to earn a living.

The Brays offered her a place of her own to work, a room on the second floor of Rosehill, with a little mahogany desk where she could retreat when she wasn't caring for her father at Bird Grove and running the household. "I will do everything to help you do it," Charles said. "It's a vitally important document, and only you have the learning to do it justice."

And so she began. Like Hennell, Strauss delved into the core of Christian belief, denying the divinity of Christ, saying that the supposed miracles of the Bible were merely tendentious fabrications by the early Christians, influenced by Jewish traditions, to show that Christ was the Messiah.

Snatching time from her household duties, she struggled over it. What was the proper translation of *materiell*? And *formell*? And the word *Abendmahl*? Was that simply "sacrament" or was it "*the* sacrament"? In addition to the German, Strauss quoted heavily in Latin and Greek. She had to try and teach herself Hebrew as well, to understand his arguments. But she took pride when she got it right, and the difficulty of it energized her. She realized she was good at translation. Perhaps she could somehow make a profession out of this, and it would be at the same time engaging and challenging.

Still, she found she could only translate about six pages a day, and the manuscript was 1,500 pages long.

———

At home, her father was aging and becoming more dependent on her. He'd never liked her going up to Rosehill, but it was part of their unspoken agreement that she could. Now he wanted her with him at all times. Dozing in his chair by the fire, his shawl wrapped around his shoulders, he'd wake up when she came into the room and realize that she hadn't been there with him all along. "Where have you been?" he asked querulously. "What are you wasting your time on now?"

"I'm translating a book, Papa," she said. "Remember, I told you? Don't worry. I'm here now. I'm going to make your toddy and read to you."

Every Sunday, she continued dutifully to take him to church, gripping the arm of the man who had once been strong as a tree and was now shrunken and bent.

But his need for her, his demands for her time, gave her intense happiness. He truly loved her. He made her read him his favorite passages of Walter Scott—the description of Luckie Mucklebackit's cottage and *The Two Drovers*—over and over again, just as she'd made him read *The Linnet's Life* to her over and over again when she was a child.

As she continued on with the Strauss, her headaches grew more frequent. She became so immersed in it that she began to live within it. She no longer believed in Christ's divinity. But he was still someone who had lived, a real figure to her, in his goodness and his sacrifice, and when she came to Strauss's discussion of the Crucifixion and the soldiers piercing his flesh—*"the habitual custom was to nail once only the feet as well as the hands"*—she could feel the nails piercing her own flesh, and in her mind, she could hear his cry, *"I thirst!,"* as vividly as if he were there with her. As the sponge was raised to his poor, parched lips, she tasted the vinegar on her own tongue. And then, his final words, *"It is finished!"*

After months of this, she collapsed in tears in front of Cara and Charles. "I just cannot do this anymore. Why did I take it on?"

"Of course you can do it," Cara said, putting her arms around her. Charles agreed. "You must finish it. We'll get Mr. Bury, the surgeon, to come in and see you." Mr. Bury examined her and said her "subconjunctivial vessels" were congested. He applied leeches to her temples. After he left, she fell asleep. For a while she was relieved of the headaches, but they always came back.

Sometimes, when she was completely "Strauss sick," she helped Cara in the Infants' School, happy to be distracted by the little children. Or she'd climb the road to Rosehill to see Nelly, just to see her laugh when she bounced her, and hold her little hands while she took her first steps. The child seemed to know her and always smiled in recognition when she saw her. Would she ever have a child of her own? She was twenty-five. There was still time. But first she must have a husband. And there was no one.

Exhausted by Strauss, she found herself one day sketching out the first few lines of a story. She saw pictures in her mind of Griff and being with her father in the gig and she was back again in that lost world. There was a village, she wrote, *"sleeping on a hill, like a quiet old place as it was, in the late afternoon sunlight. Opposite it, below the hills, was the purplish blackness of woods, and the pale front of an Abbey, looking out from among the oaks. A road wound under the shelter of the woods, of upswelling hills."* As she wrote the words, she felt an intense joy in imagining the town—the word "upswelling," so perfect, conveying the gentle-seeming softness of the hills, like a woman's breast. And the woods, "purplish black." They *were* that. Not many would use those blended colors to describe woods, the way the blackness was given warmth by the late afternoon sunlight, a special sweetness and mystery. She loved finding that color, imagining it, daring to describe it in not the usual language, but finding new words to make her impressions more real and live on the page.

How wonderful to be in the world of words, removed from Rosehill and all its complications, and most important, a world private to her alone, one that she owned and governed.

But the dream was interrupted. She rubbed her eyes and swung around in the chair to gaze out the window. Down below, on the lawn, she saw Charles and Cara sitting with a group of friends under the acacia. She was weary. And Strauss awaited her, pages and pages of it.

She bundled the pages of her "novel" together and put them aside.

―――――

At last the Strauss was finished, and in June it was published, *The Life of Jesus, Critically Examined,* by David Friedrich Strauss, *Translated from the fourth German Edition, in three volumes by Mr. John Chapman of 121, Newgate Street, London.* Marian's name wasn't on the title page, but that was the usual way. And she didn't mind the anonymity in the least. The book had already caused an uproar in

Germany for challenging prevailing Christian authority, and it would no doubt have the same effect in England. She was happy to be shielded from the criticism. And she got her twenty pounds for the work. It was the first real money she'd ever made. She was now an author—of sorts. It had given her a taste of what could be.

Still, when she looked around her, she saw no way to earn a sufficient living as a writer, no future project she could undertake that would pay her anything. For now, her job was to care for her father.

When the book was published, Charles took her up to London to visit her publisher, John Chapman. Chapman had recently moved his business to the Strand. Catching sight of him for the first time, she was overcome by his looks. He was in his twenties, a bit younger than she, very tall, with an erect carriage and dark, curly hair, a peaked brow, finely arched eyebrows, and a cleft chin. His eyes were dark and full, keen and inscrutable and closely set. He bent down to take her hand. "I'm very honored," he said, "to meet the translator of Strauss, the person who's done more than anyone to present his important ideas to the English-speaking world." This was her publisher, the man who had brought her words to light, and bound them between the hard covers of a book. And he was so fine-looking, overwhelming in his height. She was so intimidated she could barely answer him.

Later, Charles took her to visit the studio of the phrenologist James Deville, who was also nearby on the Strand. "I promise you," Charles said, "a cast can be made without shaving your head."

Deville's studio was filled with shelf after shelf of white plaster casts of people's heads. They were eerily still, looking blindly out, and covered with lines and inscriptions. Charles watched enthusiastically while Deville made Marian recline on a special seat. He divided her head with strings and applied a light coating of almond oil to her eyebrows and hair. Then he brushed on the plaster, leaving holes at the nostrils so she could breathe. He inserted two quills into the nostrils, which made her sneeze at first. But the plaster soon dried and Deville removed it in pieces. It was unpleasant but bearable.

Charles undertook to analyze the results himself, and later he showed her what he had written. *"In her brain development the Intellect greatly predominates,"* he said. *"She was of the most affectionate disposition, always requiring someone to lean upon...She is not fitted to stand alone."*

She had thought phrenology was silly, but oh, how true those words were. "Not fitted to stand alone."

Charles sent his report on to George Combe, who did his own analysis. Her head was so big, 22¼ inches around, that Combe wrote to Charles that at first he'd thought it was the head of a man. *"She has a very large brain,"* Combe wrote, *"the anterior lobe is remarkable for length, breadth & height...Love of approb[ation] and concentrativeness are large...She is extremely feminine & gentle; & the great strength of her intellect combined with this quality renders her very interesting."*

"As I have always said," Charles told her, when he read Combe's notes to her.

———

Her father was wasting away, skeletally thin, coughing up phlegm, his legs swelling. His arms and legs ached so much that he couldn't sleep. She tended to him fervently, and laid mustard plasters between his shoulders to try and draw out the illness and the phlegm.

Spring came, soft rain, new green on the garden's gray soil, the branches of the trees swollen with buds. His heart beat so rapidly, he coughed so uncontrollably at times, that she was terrified he was having a stroke. He couldn't climb the stairs to his bedroom anymore, so she made a bed for him in the dining room and slept by his side on the sofa. He became strangely peaceable, all his irascibility suddenly gone.

"Thank you, dear girl," he said to her now, whenever she washed his poor withered body or gently shaved his grizzled face. "You are a dear girl," he said. He smiled up at her feebly now, as if he were a child and she was his mother.

Finally, he lapsed into unconsciousness, his breath rattling in his chest. She held his hand and stroked his head as he died.

She wept in Cara's and Charles's comforting arms. "You have us," Cara said. "You always have us."

And then they swept her up and took her on a holiday to the Continent. Strange brother and sister, but always there for her.

Chapter 7

A lone now in her bed in the Hotel Europa, she said the word "Papa" softly aloud into the dark air. It was a name she could never call anyone again. But it was always there, the memory of saying it, even here in Venice, of being a little girl carried along in his strong arms, born aloft by him over all the harm and dangers of the world, in those moments when he wasn't stern and rough, his secret favorite, his "clever gel."

After he died and the Brays took her away, what a weight she must have been on them in her grief at her father's death, spoiling their adventures.

They crossed the Alps on horseback, the women riding sidesaddle through the Simplon Pass, thousands of feet above sea level, amid the splendid, jagged peaks. As she looked down from her horse at the plunging ravines and the icy torrents roaring below, she became giddy and cried out hysterically, "My saddle's slipping. Help!" The group came to a stop, the guide clipped a lead rope to her halter, and Charles led her behind him till they reached the safety and warmth of the hostel.

In Geneva, she announced she wasn't going back to England. Geneva, the home of Calvin and Rousseau, was so clean after Coventry. Her father's will hadn't been probated yet—he'd left her a tiny inheritance, £100 in cash and £2,000 in trust, which would yield only about £90 a year, hardly enough to support her. But she could live here more cheaply. "I'd be pleased to advance you the money," Charles said. He and Cara were anxious to get rid of her, she thought, because she was such a burden to them.

The Brays returned to England and she found rooms at a pension just outside the city, the Campagne Plongeon, a large, gleaming white house with a meadow sloping down to the blue Lake Geneva. The place was filled with people, refugees from all the revolutions sweeping through Europe, most of whom seemed to spend their days playing whist in the parlor.

She spent her days alone, sitting on the terrace of the pension, overlooking the vivid blue lake, watching the sailboats, and reading. She read more Rousseau, and Voltaire. She'd discovered the novels of George Sand and was transfixed by them. She knew of Sand's scandalous reputation, leaving her husband, taking lovers, dressing like a man, smoking tobacco—her affairs with Chopin and Alfred de Musset. But that was no reason not to read her novels. She was compelled by their passion and tragic power, by Sand's compassion for ordinary people, for the underdog—Consuelo, the Gypsy singer, a *zingarella* who rises from nothing to become a great diva. Sand refused to write simplistic moral maxims, but embedded them in the delineation of her complex characters.

Sometimes, to occupy her mind, she worked on mathematical theorems. One night, she attended a lecture on experimental physics at the Athenée by Professor de la Rive, who had been one of the inventors of the electromagnetic theory of batteries.

But the summer ended. The snows came, and the cold swept in off the lake, bitter and wet. It was daylight now for only a few short hours. She noticed clumps of hair in her brush—her hair was falling out. In November she passed her twenty-ninth birthday. It was obvious she'd be a spinster all her life. There was nothing here for her to do for her life's work. What was her future to be?

She was homesick for Chrissey, and for Charles and Cara, for their comfort and the brightness they brought to her life. Inevitably, she'd have to return to England, to face the future, whatever it was.

In March she journeyed home. She felt obliged to visit Isaac and Sarah at Griff, but they were busy with two children now, and Isaac was relishing his role as manager of the estate, giving out orders, confident in his importance and authority. As she sat to the side while they went about their days, she felt like an outsider. She couldn't stay in Meriden with Chrissey and Edward. They were mourning the loss of another child, Clara, seven years old, dead the past year from scarlet fever. And Chrissey had a brood of six other children to manage. Edward was still struggling to set up his practice. The Clarkes were near bankruptcy.

Marian was rootless; all she had was her portmanteau and her carpetbag. She was destined to be a stranger on the earth.

Again, Charles and Cara came to the rescue. They invited her to live at Rosehill, and refused to accept rent. It would do for the time, though there was no work for her in Coventry. The only skills she had came from her learning and her writing—and these weren't just skills, she thought, but what she wanted to do. The only place to deploy those skills, to find some meager way in which she could use them, was London. But she hardly had the funds to live in London, and how would she go about finding work in that distant city?

In October, John Chapman, the publisher of her Strauss book, arrived at Rosehill to visit Charles and Cara. As before when she'd met him in London, she was awed by his presence, his vigor and good looks, his intensity.

They sat outside on the bear rug under the acacia. It was a lovely autumn day, the sun bright in the sky, the leaves falling in golden spirals to the ground, the air rich with the fragrance of moldering vegetation, ripe apples, and smoke from the fireplaces in the houses below in the valley. Chapman's energy and curiosity made her forget her shyness. He drew her out. They had a lively discussion about French and German philosophy, subjects she knew well.

"This is marvelous!" Chapman said. "I do wish we could continue the discussion. I could use someone like you in London to help me with the firm and stop me from making mistakes."

She was conscious as they reclined there of his dark curls, the cleft in his chin, his long thin legs.

He'd brought with him a copy of a new book he was publishing, *The Progress of the Intellect as Exemplified in the Religious Development of the Greeks and Hebrews,* by Robert William Mackay. Mackay was a philosopher and theologian and his book carried on the arguments of Hennell and Strauss. Mackay went further, arguing that as human beings developed, so too would their intellects and their ability to understand the basic moral laws embedded in religion.

"I've arranged to place an article about the book in the *Westminster Review*," Chapman said. "Perhaps you'd agree to write it?"

"I'd very much like to do that, " she said diffidently. "I'd like to make something of a living writing reviews, and this would be a good start."

She would have an essay in the *Westminster Review*! All the great thinkers had been published there, John Stuart Mill, who'd also been the editor, and Carlyle. She was so pleased at the thought that she dared say nothing more lest he realize how unworthy she was, and how inexperienced.

She remarked to Charles and Cara that Chapman reminded her a bit of Byron. "Oh, Byron!" mocked Charles.

But he did indeed look like Byron.

The review of Mackay took her over a month to write. She quarreled with some of Mackay's analyses of the Greek myths, but his arguments, she wrote, were *"admirable, both from their panoramic breadth and their richness in illustrative details."*

In November the review was ready and she wrote Chapman offering to bring it to London. She was thinking of taking lodgings in town, she said. She'd heard he was renting out rooms in his house at 142 Strand to visitors and inquired about his rates. A first-class room was £2.10s. per week. But a second-class room could be had for five shillings less. A fire cost an extra three shillings and sixpence. This she could just manage because meals were included. She could perhaps supplement her income by writing reviews.

"We'd be delighted to have someone of your brilliant character among us," Chapman told her.

———

Number 142 Strand was in a tall building which had once housed a coffeehouse and tavern, next to Somerset House, on the bank of the Thames.

Chapman lived there with his wife, Susanna, who was fourteen years older than he, a plump, dour woman from a wealthy family of Nottingham lacemakers. She'd spent her own money to set Chapman up in his business.

The Chapmans lived with two children and their governess, Elisabeth Tilley, a pretty girl with a tiny waist, porcelain skin, and dark, wavy hair. The children, a boy and a girl, seemed a bit wild, racing through the hallways up and down the stairs, stopping only for a second when introduced to the new lodger.

Chapman showed her to her bedroom on the third floor. It was at the end of a long, dark passageway, with a dim little window. "It's quieter here, away from everything," he said. She went to the window and glanced down into the street below. She was aware of him standing close behind her, his clothing touching hers.

That first night she couldn't sleep with all the excitement, the hustle and bustle and noise coming from the street below.

The next morning, Chapman pronounced himself thrilled with her essay on the Mackay book. He was delivering it at once. She was elated.

After breakfast, she went out to explore, pushing her way through the crowded street. The Strand was lined with newspaper offices, public houses, and shops. It smelled of rotting refuse and open sewers, but this was London, and she didn't mind it. She noticed a display of books in a shop window and stopped to look. There was a book called *The Lustful Turk*, and another, *The Mysteries of Verbena House*, with illustrations of ballet dancers and actresses in dishabille on the covers. She stared at them, but afraid of being seen, she quickly walked on.

The Chapman household seemed to be in chaos, the meals were always late, the children running around constantly fighting, streams of lodgers coming and going. Susanna Chapman helped her husband in the office downstairs. She moved slowly and seemed rather unintelligent, Marian thought, and totally unable to keep order in the house. Miss Tilley also seemed unhappy and always frowning.

Every Friday evening the Chapmans held a soiree. That first Friday, number 142 was packed with writers, many of whose works Marian had read. She spotted Carlyle standing among a group of admirers. They were chattering away at him; he looked quite fiercely out from underneath his bushy eyebrows, and she was afraid to approach him. And there was Emerson—Chapman was his English publisher. She went to greet him and he bowed kindly. "I remember you very well, Miss Evans," he said. "And our talks together." Dickens came too. They didn't speak; he looked rather undistinguished, given his fame. She admired Dickens's novels, but she thought his characters were depicted only superficially, they lacked interior lives; they were portrayed mostly through the way they spoke, dressed, and acted.

One-forty-two Strand seemed to be the center of all progressive London. The room was filled with exiles who'd fled the Continent after the 1848 revolutions, gathered there because of Chapman's reputation as a publisher of radical works. There was Giuseppe Mazzini, campaigning for a unified Italy. Chapman pointed out a dark figure with a full mustache and beard across the room, Karl Marx, who'd published *The Communist Manifesto* in Germany, advocating the rebellion of workers against their capitalist masters. Marx had been forced to flee Germany with his family and was trying to earn money writing for the American paper, the *New York Tribune*.

She sympathized with the exiles. But revolution could never work in England. The workingmen of England were too brutal, and so was the military. Any attempt at revolution would result in terrible bloodshed. She still believed that slow change was better, and it was possible in England because of the parliamentary system.

Chapman moved about the room doing business, occasionally looking up at her, smiling warmly across the room. Then his eyes would move on to the next person.

She noticed a young woman wearing glasses, which made her look very intelligent. "This is Miss Eliza Lynn," Chapman said. "I'm publishing her new novel, *Realities: A Tale of Modern Life*." She'd heard of Eliza Lynn. She was three years younger than Marian, and had already published a novel, *Azeth, the Egyptian*, when she was only twenty-six. Marian felt a surge of envy. Was she too old already, not only for marriage, but to become a real writer?

On Monday morning she passed Chapman striding along the hall, frowning, a manuscript in his hand. He looked at her for a moment as if he didn't know her.

"It's Miss Lynn's book," he said. "It's full of love scenes, completely indiscreet. The books I publish are so radical that any novel I publish has got to be above reproach." He thought for a second. "Could you just take a look and see what you think?"

Of course she could.

The novel was about the immoral doings of the London theater world. The actress heroine, Clara de Saumarez, goes with the stage manager, Vasty Vaughan, to a hotel, unaware that he's married. *"Vaughan flung his arms round her almost wildly. He strained her to his breast; he looked into her face with a painful mixture of sorrow and passion. His lips were warm against her own..."*

It was far too shocking to publish, she said to Chapman. Later, when he told Miss Lynn that the scene had to be cut, she was furious and announced she was taking the book to another publisher.

Two days later, Chapman asked for help again. "I'm frantic. Mrs. Chapman in her usual stupid way got into a fight with James Nisbett about making revisions to his book. He's taken umbrage and refused."

"Would you like me to read it for you and speak to him?" she offered.

"Would you?"

Up in her room, she read through the work. It was a novel called *The Siege of Damascus*. Damascus is under siege by the Saracens. Jonas and Eudocia are in love and want to marry, but her parents are against it. Jonas is captured and converts to Mohammedanism. Eudocia kills herself rather than marry an apostate.

Marian marked up the manuscript and wrote a note for Chapman suggesting some revisions, which Chapman then passed on as his own. A few days later, Nisbett replied, calmly saying that the suggestions were excellent and he was pleased to accept them all.

"Thank you, *thank* you!" Chapman told her.

She began going to Chapman's ground floor office every day, reading over proofs for him, editing his manuscripts. It was possible to become entirely absorbed in the work, to shut out the world around her completely. There was satisfaction in carving out sentences from dross, in making the prose more pointed, in having an occupation.

"You're making yourself indispensable," he said. It was as if she had an actual job, though he said, "I'm sorry I can't afford to pay you yet. But perhaps something will come up."

Perhaps she could make a life of this in some way. She was good at being an editor, she had an innate sense of how language worked, she was attuned to its musicalities. The process of refining it was a craft, like wielding a knife, carving wood into a sculpted piece so that it stood out, the angles sharp, the image powerful. She could live an independent life as a single woman here in London.

Then, one evening at supper—the potatoes were as usual undercooked, the mutton tough, the children bouncing around and interrupting—Miss Tilley, the governess, rapped her spoon on her glass. "I have an announcement to make," she said, sniffing. "I'm giving notice. I'm planning to leave my post this autumn."

"Elisabeth," Mrs. Chapman said. "Whatever is the matter?"

"Nothing's the matter."

"But Elisabeth, we can't live without you!" Mrs. Chapman said.

"That is my decision," she said. And then she ran from the room weeping, the two children looking after her, speechless, spoons in midair, mouths agape.

Chapman put down his serviette, hurried after her, and didn't return to finish his food.

Later that evening, there was a knock on Marian's door. Chapman stood there. "I'm so sorry to bother you," he said, though she didn't mind at all. He sat down in her chair, threw his long legs out in front him, and sighed miserably.

"You look rather upset too," he told her.

"Miss Tilley—why did she run out like that?"

"Oh, Elisabeth's just jealous of every woman who comes into the house."

She felt a ping of hope in her chest. Could Miss Tilley, who was so pretty, somehow be jealous of her? Did Miss Tilley think that he was attracted to her? And she hadn't sensed that at all.

"She sees you're helping me with the business," he said. He sighed again. "But we need her desperately. I don't know what we'd do without her. The children, everything. If she went, there'd be absolute chaos. Mrs. Chapman is incapable of managing things. You've no idea how difficult my life is with the business. All I do is scavenge for money, to get people to pay me so I can pay my creditors. I have no time to even edit my books. But—" He let out another deep breath. "—at least autumn is nine months away. "

"Perhaps I should leave?" she offered.

"You can't leave!" he insisted. "You've made things so I can't manage without you. Let me try to calm her."

And he left the room.

The next day, Miss Tilley returned to the table, albeit somewhat sullen and aggrieved. It seemed for now at least that it had been merely a threat.

He was insisting that Marian stay in the midst of this chaos, with people who disliked her. Perhaps she could rent a piano to play and so calm her mind. She found a small piano at Chappell's for her room, and on Sunday morning, Chapman came up to her and she played a transcription of Mozart's Kyrie in G. As the music filled the air with a sound like cascading church bells, Chapman half reclined on her bed and closed his eyes blissfully.

When she finished, he rose, took her in his arms and hugged her. She felt the press of his chest on her breast, the contours of his pelvis and thighs. It was if her legs would collapse beneath her.

Then he left the room.

At dinner that night, Mrs. Chapman herself seemed animated with barely repressed anger. "I heard Miss Evans's little recital from the stairs," she said. "John, I think we should have a piano too, in the living room. And then you can stage these performances downstairs for the benefit of everyone." She raised her wattled chin stubbornly. "I'm sure Miss Evans would be delighted to play for all of us."

Two days later, another piano was installed in the parlor and Mrs. Chapman seemed appeased, listening contentedly as Marian played a Beethoven sonata, Mrs. Chapman and Miss Tilley holding down the two squirming children till the end.

Chapman asked Marian, "I've always wanted to learn German. Do you think you could give me lessons? Who better to teach me than the translator of Strauss?"

No sooner had they begun their lessons than Miss Tilley asked for lessons too—from Mr. Chapman, though he hardly knew a word of German. At lunch and supper, Miss Tilley now refused to speak to Marian.

After just two weeks of this, she heard a soft knock on her door.

"May I come in?" Chapman whispered. He didn't even say his name, as if he intuited her receptivity to him. She put on her dressing gown and admitted him.

He stood, head down, distraught.

"Whatever's the matter?" she asked.

He sat down on her bed, his elbows on his knees, and rubbed his face. "I just had a huge argument with Susanna. She accused me of being too fond of Miss Tilley. Everything's a mess. She's getting old, she can't manage things. She's useless at the business."

"It must be difficult," she said softly.

"She wants me to share her bed," he said glumly. "But I find it unendurable."

He looked up at her. He held his arms out to her and she took his hands. Then he drew her to him and kissed her. Once again, need flowed through her body, drowning out everything else, all caution, all self-protection.

She let him make love to her, but forced herself to lie there passively, tried to be indifferent, in her fear of what she was doing, her knowledge of how dangerous it was. Again she was succumbing to a man who belonged to another woman.

He went fast, like a bee dipping its tongue into one flower before flying quickly off to another. But it pleased her, in spite of herself.

At the end, he kissed her on the lips, quickly dressed, left her, and went back to the bed he shared with his wife.

————

At breakfast, Marian came downstairs first, served herself from the kippers and eggs and biscuits set out on the buffet, and sat down at the table. She didn't look at the door, but she was conscious of waiting for him. Ten minutes later he arrived. "Oh, good morning, Miss Evans." He greeted her in the distant way he would any lodger. "I do hope you slept well?"

Her face flamed, the hurt bubbled up in her. "I did, indeed, thank you," she said, coldly. And then she walked out without finishing her breakfast.

All day long she was sunk in depression. She didn't go down to the office to help him with his work. She was alternately angry with him for embracing her and at herself for giving in to him. Then she panicked: she'd been so cold to him, she'd put him off, and now he would be angry at her and he'd no longer come to her, she thought, and she'd lose him. She hated herself for these thoughts alternating in her mind.

That night, encountering him in the hall, she stopped him. "I'm sorry," she said. "You were in a difficult position. I shouldn't have walked out on you like that."

"You're forgiven," he said wearily. "But I'm miserable with all this turmoil, and with the business."

She felt sorry for him, and put her hand on his shoulder to comfort him.

He leaned forward with a kiss. He came to her room and she let him make love to her again. He was tender, though again hurried. After he finished, he pulled away, lying on his back, his arm over his eyes, distracted, put out.

"Is something the matter?" she asked, keeping her voice cool and neutral, though she'd just given in to him again. Instead of answering, he leaned over, kissed her on the lips, and departed. Had she not been enough for him?

She had to earn some money. She'd had the idea of writing another essay for the *Westminster Review*, on W. R. Greg's *Creed of Christendom*. Greg was a Manchester cotton manufacturer, another of David Friedrich Strauss's increasing number of disciples, a critic of the established church who admitted nonetheless that he found solace in prayer. She wrote up the review. *"Among these pioneers of the New Reformation, Mr. Greg is likely to be one of the most effective. Without any pretension to striking originality or extensive learning, his work perhaps all the more exhibits that sound, practical judgement which discerns at once the hinge of a question."* The editor of the *Westminster* was then a man called William Hickson, and Chapman contacted him on her behalf, but Hickson didn't want the piece.

She was in despair. She couldn't earn a living in London.

He continued coming to her room, jamming the chair under the doorknob. "I need you so," he'd exclaim, seizing her with a ragged breath. Meanwhile, antagonism swirled all around them, Mrs. Chapman jealous of Miss Tilley and both Mrs. Chapman and Miss Tilley jealous of her. But the more indifferent she tried to pretend she was to his lovemaking, the greater pleasure it was—as if the mask of indifference satisfied her need for self-punishment, her guilt at once more surrendering to a man who belonged to someone else, who couldn't love her, who could only hurt her. It gave her permission to allow it—and to enjoy it.

But she couldn't stop herself from giving in to him, each time seeking to fill an unappeasable need, it seemed, for tenderness and devotion. *"Of the most affectionate disposition,"* Charles Bray had written of her. *"Always requiring someone to lean on."* Every time hoping for more than Chapman could give. And at the end of each encounter, she rested, disappointed. And he was always so grateful.

Once more she suggested to him, "I really should go back to Coventry. I'm afraid I can't earn a living here." She couldn't bear to live in a household where she was so disliked.

"I need you here," he cried, to her relief. "Perhaps you could write an essay on Martineau and Atkinson for Empson at the *Edinburgh Review*. Let me speak to him." Harriet Martineau had had an ovarian cyst and believed her friend, a man called Henry George Atkinson, had cured her through mesmerism. Chapman was publishing a book of their letters about it and he wanted to publicize the book.

"But if Empson knows my essay's written by a woman—?" Marian pointed out. "He'll never give it to me to do."

"We won't tell him, that's all."

Empson didn't want the article either. He said the subject didn't interest him.

The hopelessness dragged at her. Every step she took was heavy. Once again, she was a failure, trapped by her unmet need to be loved. It was the need of a wounded child, she thought, not that of a woman in the full bloom of adult-hood, a woman of talent and intellect.

That afternoon, in her room, she heard the sounds of shouting and crying coming through the floorboards. Miss Tilley, Mrs. Chapman, and Chapman were yelling back and forth at one another. She went out onto the landing. "I saw you holding her hand!" Miss Tilley shouted. Mrs. Chapman threatened, "If you ever go to her room again…"

She didn't hear the rest. After forty-five minutes, he climbed the stairs to her room, wiping his brow with his handkerchief.

"I must leave," she said, yet again. She waited for him to beg her to stay.

But this time he didn't. He sighed. "I suppose it's for the better. Susanna's ruining my life. Miss Tilley is mad with jealousy. I don't know how I'll manage without you."

On Monday morning he escorted her to Euston station. As they waited for the train, she couldn't help herself. "John, do you have—any feelings for me at all?"

He looked down at her, grimacing. "Please don't cry," he begged. "I love you, and Susanna and Elisabeth too, only—I love you all in different ways."

And then the train came and he kissed her goodbye.

———

Once again, she returned to Coventry ashamed and humiliated. Charles and Cara didn't ask questions; Cara held her silently in a welcoming embrace. Thank goodness the house was big enough to contain them all, and she could stay out of their way and the Brays could afford to feed her.

Within a few days, a letter came from Chapman saying 142 Strand was unspeakably lonely without her, and he missed her terribly. All through the spring, he wrote saying he couldn't manage the business himself and he needed an assistant.

Then he wrote to say he'd decided to expand his publishing empire and buy the *Westminster Review*. He had to find backers, write up a prospectus. How he wished she were there to help him. Would she mind if he came up to Coventry to discuss it with her? He badly needed her advice.

The night before he was to arrive, she went out into the garden to collect herself. She sat on the swing in the soft, dark air. She mustn't expect him to love her, she must somehow learn to survive. There must be some part of her that was worthwhile without the love of a man, some essence within her that wasn't dependent on a man's love, that would survive if she were alone. But perhaps he was coming to Coventry to beg her to return to the Strand? To tell her he didn't care any longer about Susanna Chapman's fits of temper and Elisabeth Tilley's histrionics? That he needed her too much to let her go?

———

He arrived on the noon train and there he stood in the doorway at Rosehill, tall and lanky, his dark, lustrous eyes looking past Charles and Cara with an intense gaze to where she stood behind them, trying to be invisible.

At supper he talked about his plans to buy the *Westminster*, to make it again an organ for the most radical thinking of the time. He hoped Charles would be an investor.

Afterward he told Marian, "I've written up a draft of my prospectus. I have such difficulty putting my thoughts into words. Do you think you could look at it?"

She went over it. He was a terrible writer, his thoughts were unfinished, there were dashes everywhere, triads and dyads of adjectives and verbs, all in one watery volume. She began laboriously to try to render his words into coherent sentences.

The next morning, he asked her to go with him to Leamington, to see Kenilworth Castle.

It was a lambent spring day. They sat on the grass. Before them was the great sweep of green leading up to the soaring ruins of the castle, the gift of Queen Elizabeth to her favorite, Dudley, the skeletons of its Tudor windows outlined starkly against the bright blue sky.

"They say the queen really loved Dudley," she remarked.

He chewed on a blade of grass, his long legs stretched out before him.

"He entertained her here for weeks on end," she went on, "with parties and masques. They say he had his wife, Amy Robsart, murdered, to keep the queen's love."

"Ah, love," he said, exhaling into the spring air. "Ah, beauty!..."

"The queen wasn't beautiful," she went on. "She had smallpox. They say she had so many teeth pulled that she put rags in her cheeks to fill them out. But they say that she did have pretty hands." Here she looked down at her own hands, slender and delicate, her only good feature. "Yet he wanted to marry her. I suppose for the power."

He lay back on the grass, resting his head on his arms. "Female beauty is such a mystery. It's witchery."

"Witchery?"

"I'm thinking of my own weakness, the way I'm so swayed by it."

She knew what he was saying. He was sexually beholden to Elisabeth Tilley. And Mrs. Chapman overlooked it because she knew that the governess fulfilled his needs, and otherwise he'd leave her. Susanna could tolerate Miss Tilley because she had the governess in her power, she was her employer and she couldn't manage the household by herself. But Marian was too much to bear. She was a different kind of threat. With her, he had a meeting of the minds as well, and he needed her if his firm was to survive.

But, why, why couldn't he be "entranced" by her too? Why hadn't nature made her attractive too?

She felt a burning behind her eyes. She couldn't help it, she began to cry. He was gazing at the sky, but he heard her sniffle. "Marian, what's the matter?"

Embarrassed to answer, she buried her face in her hands.

"You mustn't," he said. "This is terrible. Please..."

She shook her head, her sobs overtaking her.

"Tell me," he urged.

"I wish I were beautiful," she cried.

"No!" he said. "It's not that. We just can't go on. There's war in the house. I can't afford to lose Elisabeth. And Susanna won't give me any peace. It can't be like this between us anymore."

He reached into his breast pocket, found his handkerchief, and dabbed at her cheeks. She could hardly stand his touch, it only reminded her of what it was like to be held by him, the comfort of his arms.

Then he said brightly, "If I buy the *Westminster*, perhaps you could be the editor."

"The editor? Why not you?"

"Because you're a far better editor than I am. And I'll still have to run the publishing side of the firm. I couldn't pay you right away. But I could give you free room and board at 142."

He went on. "You could also write for the magazine. I could pay you a contributor's fee. You could do a regular column on foreign literature."

For a moment, a surge of happiness blotted out her misery. "I'd like that, very much. But...will Miss Tilley and Mrs. Chapman ever allow it?"

"I'll explain to them I need you for the firm, but only on the most proper terms, of course. They'll have nothing to be concerned about anymore, the firm is the most important thing."

"I see," she said. But what did he mean, "the most proper terms"? That he was willing to give up their intimacy so she could do his work for him?

"I'll tell them we've taken a solemn vow," he said.

At this she stood up and began walking away from him, her mouth tight, furious.

He caught up with her. "Will you do it, Marian? Then I can tell them? Then you can come back to London," he said, knowing that this, at the very least, was what she longed for.

Perhaps the scar from this wound would be a barrier defending her from doing the same thing again, from being wounded by someone else. She nodded. She would come.

He returned to London while she stayed in Coventry and continued rewriting his prospectus. The *Westminster* would carry on all the best traditions of its heyday, she wrote; it would be radical, but mindful that real change is *"the result only of a slow and peaceful development."* Her own belief exactly.

The magazine would question Christian dogma, but be respectful of the importance of religion to morality. It would be against religious discrimination, in favor of free trade, judicial reform, and the vote for women.

The first week in June, she finished the prospectus and Chapman sent it off under his own name to potential investors.

But if she was going to be the real editor of the *West-minster Review*, she told Chapman, it had to be a secret. No woman had ever been editor of a literary journal, investors would never stand for it. And she wanted to be hidden from view. In fact, she couldn't bear to be known. If there were mistakes, if the magazine failed, no one would know she was responsible. Why not simply tell investors, she suggested, that he had an editor whom he couldn't yet name, but in whom he had absolute confidence?

It was agreed that they'd keep it a secret.

He wrote to say that he'd told Susanna and Elisabeth about their "solemn vow," and that he couldn't run his company without her. They'd relented, and agreed to let her return to the Strand to help him keep it going.

By the way, Chapman added, the writer George Henry Lewes had called to express his high opinion of her article on Greg's *Creed of Christendom.* After it was turned down elsewhere, Chapman had sent it to Lewes, who had published it in the *Leader,* the radical weekly Lewes had cofounded with the journalist Thornton Hunt. She'd written it unsigned, but Chapman had revealed her name to Lewes.

Chapter 8

Marian Evans was now the secret editor of the *West-minster Review*. She moved back to London to the Strand and stayed away from Chapman as much as possible, up in her own room or in the office downstairs in the back of the house. They kept the door open to reassure Susanna and Elisabeth Tilley that all was proper. He never ventured upstairs to the third floor anymore.

So this would be her life. She'd be a working woman. There would be no man for her, and she would survive. She had her "job," and was good at it and it satisfied her, and with her allowance from her father's estate she could just manage. She didn't need a man or a family. There were other women like this, women of talent—Harriet Martineau, for instance—who were in charge of their own lives, who didn't need men to shape them. There was a life here for her in London, people around her who were brilliant and engaging, who could be her friends.

Perhaps she was capable of taking a lover without loving him, or thinking at least that she loved him. She thought of George Sand, who'd apparently made love to many men. Did Sand really love those men, did she really give herself to them completely? Or was she somehow removed from her own body, detaching herself from true and profound intimacy, so that ultimately, it didn't matter to her as deeply as it did to other women whom she was with? Marian realized that she could never do that, separate herself from her own body. The only way she could completely give herself was if the act was inextricably bound with her emotions. In the end, she didn't understand women like Sand. They were incomprehensible.

One Friday evening after her return, at the Chapmans' soiree, she looked up and saw a stooped, rumpled-looking young man standing uncomfortably over her, silently staring at her. He had a high, domed forehead and big sideburns. It was Herbert Spencer. He was a subeditor at the *Economist*, which had offices across the street from 142.

She tried to make conversation with him, but he answered only in monosyllables. She told him she'd read his book, *Social Statics*, which Chapman had just published. That brought a flicker of interest to his eyes. Spencer had a new theory, based on Linnaeus and Lamarck, called social evolution, that human beings were infinitely perfectible and would evolve progressively and that the state would eventually wither away.

He told her he was writing a new book on "the evolution of human psychology." Suddenly he became voluble. "I'm positing the theory that people's mental faculties, like their physical selves, evolve under the influence of the environment. And because of selection. Ultimately, I'm arguing, this will lead to the highest development of reason."

She suggested he read Mill's *System of Logic*, and also Comte, if he could read French. "I think you'll find them useful," she said. "Especially Comte. You've got quite a lot in common with him."

He looked at her strangely, no doubt surprised that she, a woman, knew these books.

"Perhaps," he said uncertainly. "My French is almost nonexistent."

Meanwhile, she and Chapman were preparing frantically for the first issue of the new *Westminster Review*. She suggested to Chapman that Francis Newman write an article on the extension of the franchise, and William Rathbone Greg on "Relations Between Employer and Employed." The Oxford professor Edward Forbes could do an essay on shellfish, and George Henry Lewes on the Baltic-German mystic, Julia von Krüdener, who had had such an effect on Tsar Alexander. Perhaps Carlyle could be persuaded to write on the hereditary peerage, she said. These were splendid ideas, Chapman thought.

One morning in early autumn, she stood in the pouring rain across the street from Carlyle's house on Cheyne Walk while Chapman went inside to try to get the great man to contribute to the magazine. She couldn't go in because they had to preserve the fiction that Chapman was the magazine's editor. After a half hour Chapman emerged from the house. "He doesn't seem very interested," he said gloomily.

They searched the shops for books to review in the magazine. At William Jeff's Bookshop in the Burlington Arcade looking for foreign works, they ran into George Henry Lewes, who'd published her Greg essay. Chapman introduced her. Lewes was a jack-of-all-trades, a journalist, critic, novelist, and playwright. He'd also written a *Biographical History of Philosophy*, intended for a popular audience, which had done very well. He was a little man with a big head; his wiry black hair stuck out all around a pockmarked face, and his bushy eyebrows nearly met across his forehead.

Lewes had given Spencer's *Social Statics* a very good review in his magazine, the *Leader*. "We are eternally grateful," Chapman said to him.

"One must always review one's friends' books well!" Lewes said, laughing. Marian thought he looked like a miniature Mirabeau. "And," he said to her, "thank you for your excellent review of the Greg for the *Leader*."

She thanked him and turned back to searching through the books on the table.

As they left, Chapman muttered under his breath, "Carlyle calls him the Ape. He's so shaggy and he never sits still."

"That's cruel," she said.

"And despite it all, he's rather a rake," Chapman said. "He and his wife have an arrangement, I believe." She thought no more of it.

––––––––––

At the next Friday soiree at the Strand, to her surprise, Herbert Spencer came up to her again. "I read the Mill. It was useful," he said, as if reluctantly granting her something. "I managed to get through some of your Comte. But I didn't think much of him."

"Oh dear, why? He's not *my* Comte, anyway."

"Too limited. He says we can only accept as evidence that which we can see in front of our eyes. How can you have any philosophy with that?"

"He isn't saying you can't intuit things. He's just reinforcing the validity of human perception."

"I suppose I sympathize with him there. I'm with him on natural law, but there are some things that are simply unknowable."

At ensuing gatherings, Spencer continued to seek her out. He'd stand there tongue-tied, but the moment she asked about his work, he became talkative and monopolized her attention. He had a strange, unconventional mind, unlike any she'd ever encountered. He was unmarried and her own age. He seemed to appreciate her intellect, but also to be drawn to her as a woman. Sometimes, at the Friday evenings, when she played the piano, she could get him to sing along with her. He would jolly up, as if relieved that someone had shown him how to be normal. She saw in him then the possibility of happiness and laughter.

On another Friday evening, she noticed a tall, full-bodied woman with full long golden hair and a proud carriage. The woman was with Bessie Parkes, whose father Joseph Parkes had funded Marian's Strauss translation. Bessie introduced Marian to her. The tall, golden-haired woman's name was Barbara Leigh Smith.

Marian had heard of the Smiths. They were a "tabooed" family, immensely rich merchant princes who'd made a fortune in the whiskey business, among other enterprises. Barbara's father, Ben Smith, had stood for Parliament and supported liberal causes. Her mother was Anne Longden, a milliner whom Ben had fallen in love with and impregnated five times. But he'd never married her. Perhaps he was against the marriage laws, perhaps the difference in social status mattered to him. Nonetheless he was devoted to her and his children. She had died when Barbara was seven, leaving Ben heartbroken. He lavished everything on his offspring. When Barbara was twenty-one he'd settled a generous allowance on her so she could be an independent woman and study art. Still, all the Smith children bore the stigma of illegitimacy.

Barbara and Bessie told her they had begun to devote all their efforts to the cause of women, the fact that women couldn't vote, their poor access to education, and the property laws—once women married their property belonged to their husbands. Among other things, the two of them told her, they were protesting long skirts and stays, which imprisoned women's bodies. They themselves had abandoned corsets altogether, they said.

They'd even composed a ditty about it, they said, which they proceeded to sing for her there and then at the party, arms linked, kicking up their legs. *"Oh! Isn't it jolly,"* they sang,

> *To cast away folly,*
> *And cut all one's clothes a peg shorter*
> *(A good many pegs),*
> *And rejoice in one's legs*
> *Like a free-minded Albion's daughter.*

The people at the party turned to look at them and laughed. She laughed too, though it was a bit much for her. She was embarrassed by their breaking into song in the middle of the party and talking about exposing their legs. If anything, she wanted to hide her body. She was afraid of showing herself, of being known.

She knew the condition of women was wrong, but Barbara and Bessie's pronouncements were so shrill and absolute. Both of them came from rich, radical, freethinking families that gave them the confidence to rebel and declare themselves, she thought. She found herself getting into a heated discussion with them about women's education. "If you open up education to women," Marian said, "they'll disdain their traditional work of taking care of children and their families."

"But *you're* educated," Barbara said. "How can you deny the same thing to other women?"

"I had to earn a living, I had to educate myself. I have no husband." And it was true.

She didn't say this to them then—but the mere idea that women might disdain their roles as mothers, that children could be deprived of mothering, pained her. All her life she'd longed for a mother who would love her, comfort her, allay her sorrows. How could she wish to do away with a mother's watchful protection, a mother's unconditional love? She knew all too well the pain of its absence.

"I can tell we've got some educating to do here," Barbara said to Bessie.

Marian smiled. "We'll see," she said.

From then on, the two young women attached themselves to her. They invited her to their parties and to their parents' grand houses, where, dressed in her one party dress, of black velvet, she met more of London's important writers and radical elites.

She drew close especially to Barbara, entranced by her bustling, take-charge nature, her animal spirits. Barbara was everything she wasn't—fearless, headstrong, proudly tenacious. Barbara was determined to found a college for women at Cambridge, and she wanted to establish a women's hospital with Bessie's cousin Elizabeth Blackwell, the first woman to qualify as a doctor in America. Barbara was especially adamant on the topic of "enforced feminine innocence." "This whole idea of 'protecting women,'" Barbara insisted, "means they forfeit their rights and duties as human beings."

Barbara never spoke of her illegitimacy, though everyone knew and talked about it. Perhaps that was what fueled her sympathy for the oppressed people of the world.

As their friendship deepened, Marian confessed to her that one day she would like to write books of her own, novels, but she wasn't sure she had any talent. Besides, she had no time because of her work at the *Westminster* and her need to churn out reviews and essays to earn money. When she told Barbara of her secret desire, Barbara leapt on it.

"But if that's what you want to do in life," Barbara cried, "then you're obligated to do it."

"Think of Scheherazade in *The Arabian Nights*," Barbara said. "My father hired a tutor to try to tame us, and he used to read it to us. I loved it! Scheherazade telling the sultan stories night after night, so he wouldn't have her killed, entrancing him with them. In the end, he falls in love with her and he spares her life. Storytelling set her free!" Barbara cried.

———

One evening, Herbert Spencer invited her to go to the theater with him. He had press orders for *The Merry Wives of Windsor* at the Princess.

Arriving at the theater, they found George Henry Lewes in their box, there to review the performance for the *Leader*.

When Lewes saw her, he smiled. "We met at Jeff's, if you remember?"

She did remember. As they were waiting for the curtain, she told him, for the sake of conversation, that she'd read some of his pieces in the *Leader*. He used a pseudonym in them, "Vivian." "Vivian" was a witty, mischievous character, a blistering critic, and a ladies' man. Lewes had just published a satire in the magazine called "The Beauty of Married Men." But he'd also written serious things, including an essay on George Sand in which he'd compared her to Balzac. He'd defended Sand's position against marriage: Sand wasn't against marriage itself, he argued, just unfair marriage laws.

She told him she'd just read his essay "A Gentle Hint to Writing Women" in the *Leader*.

"Yes!" he cried. "That's my idea of the perfect woman, the woman who can write but *doesn't*. Charlotte Brontë and Mrs. Gaskell should just get back to their knitting! They're so talented they're crowding us men entirely out of the field. Burn your pens and purchase wool! say I."

She noticed that he hardly kept still as he chattered on. Even Spencer smiled at his ebullience.

At last the audience was settling down, the curtain was going up. "*C'est la pire pièce de Shakespeare*," Lewes muttered. "My grandfather was a comic actor, you know," he whispered. "I've done some acting myself and written plays. Did you see my play *The Noble Heart*, by any chance?

"Sorry, I didn't," she said, sitting up and focusing on the stage.

At last the play began. It was awful, the actors overacted. Every time there was a joke, they nudged one another and laughed loudly in case the audience didn't get it.

Intermission came. Lewes hit himself on the head. *"Oh, mon Dieu, c'est terrible, n'est-ce pas?"*

All through the rest of the play, he kept up a commentary in a loud whisper. *"Consolez-vous, chère Madame. Il ne reste qu'une heure..."*

At the end she asked him, "Do you often speak French?"

"Sorry," he said. "I spent part of my childhood in Jersey and France. When I get excited, I tend to lapse."

When they reached the door of the theater and it was time to say goodbye, he bent over low and kissed her hand.

"Au revoir, Madame," he said. "I do hope we meet again." She didn't quite know what to think of the man, but he was rather amusing.

Lewes began coming to the Friday evenings at the Chapmans. He was usually surrounded by a group of people, telling silly jokes: "An Irishwoman goes to a lawyer because she wants a divorce... 'Is he violent?' the lawyer asks. 'Yes! Once he was so annoying I threw a tumbler at him and he locked me in my room.' The lawyer says, 'I'm afraid that's not enough. Is there any other evidence in favor of a divorce?' 'Yes,' she says, 'I'm not certain he's the father of my child...'"

In spite of herself, she laughed. He was also a flirt. Whenever a woman left the party, he'd always notice it, jump up, and insist on kissing her goodbye.

He was clearly not a man to be trusted. She'd had her time with married men.

———

She and Spencer began taking long walks together on the terrace of Somerset House, deep in discussion about his work. And as they leaned over the balustrade looking out at the brown waters of the Thames—upstream toward Westminster and Whitehall, downstream to St. Paul's and the factories and smokestacks—she managed to draw him out about his own life.

He told her he came from a family of religious Dissenters in Derby. His mother gave birth to seven children and six of them had died. Herbert was the only one who survived.

"That must have been so very terrible for your parents, and for you," she said.

"They died in infancy," he replied, without emotion. "Except for my sister, Louisa, who died when she was two and I was three."

"Do you remember her?"

"I remember vaguely playing with her in the garden." He said nothing more.

He told her that his parents were so afraid their one surviving child would get sick that they refused to send him away to school. Then, when he was thirteen, they finally sent him to boarding school. But he was so homesick that he ran away, walking over a hundred miles home by himself. "All I had were two shillings in my pocket, some bread, and some beer."

The story made her want to cry, imagining the brave, stalwart boy marching through the countryside, missing his parents so, determined to get home. "Did your parents punish you?"

"No. They embraced me. I'm afraid I cried rather a lot. Eventually, they persuaded me to go back. From then on it was all right."

She felt so sorry for him, that his early life was so marked by tragedy. Perhaps that explained his coldness and his inability to engage with others. She felt herself wanting to allay the sadness that must surely lurk in his soul with warmth and affection, to woo him into the comfort of human companionship. She wanted to make him laugh, or at least smile, to lift the burden of his shyness and isolation.

"You have no lines on your forehead," she joked.

"That's because I'm never puzzled." And he gave her a little, self-mocking smile.

He had many peculiarities. He had constructed a device, a circular spring with ear pads. If someone was boring him, he'd put it on over his head to block them out, explaining it was on the advice of his doctors. Naturally, the person would stop talking. "Please, do continue," he'd say. "I can't hear what you're saying anyway." She teased him about it, and sometimes elicited a sly smile from him, as if he were aware of how odd he was. He was also a hypochondriac, forever putting his hand uneasily to his stomach and complaining vaguely of digestive difficulties.

Perhaps she held a special place in his life, perhaps even...perhaps he was even falling in love with her? Could it be that here at last was someone for her alone?

———

As spring warmed the air, and the daffodils, then the tulips, blossomed in the park, the sweet fragrance of new life floating in the air made her feel old. She was thirty-two now, her complexion sallow, her skin felt dry.

In July, the next issue of the *Westminster Review* was closed and she was exhausted. London was blisteringly hot. She decided to take a holiday and rent a room in Broadstairs.

Perhaps the sea would heal her. She mentioned to Spencer that she was going, hoping he'd offer to accompany her. But he didn't, so she went alone.

When the boat arrived at the little town, she disembarked and made her way to the room she'd rented, across from the cliffs overlooking the sea. After she'd unpacked her things, she went out for a walk. It was high season, and the narrow beach on Viking Bay was packed, every inch of sand filled with families and children and bathing machines. She seemed to be the only unaccompanied woman in the whole place, and she wouldn't think of using one of the bathing machines by herself.

She went to the town library and read the *Times*, and looked through the books. She felt safer there, not as uncomfortable being a woman alone.

Later, she had supper in the ladies' dining room at the Broadstreet Arms. Even there, no other single women appeared, just women in couples or groups. So as not to seem too alone or unhappy, to show she wasn't seeking to meet anyone, she propped up Harriet Martineau's novel, *Deerbrook*, in front of her. It wasn't bad. Two sisters arrive in a village and become romantically involved with the apothecary. Thank God, she could become absorbed in the book and didn't betray herself to the other diners as lonely.

In the morning, she rented a deck chair and sat on the beach. For two days she occupied herself reading and sleeping while the families played around her, their cries mingling with the cries of the gulls. Beyond her the narrow bay was flecked with sailboats.

She read George Henry Lewes's novel *Rose, Blanche and Violet*—very melodramatic, with courtship, adultery, suicide, prostitution—and walked along the beach beneath the cliffs, fending off the smiles of strangers who guessed at her plight and seemed about to try to engage her.

At the post office, she asked if any letters had come for her—perhaps there would be something from Spencer. But it was too soon to expect anything.

After a few days letters began arriving from Chapman about magazine business. Everything was falling apart in her absence, he wrote. The *Westminster Review* was going bankrupt and George Combe, who was one of the investors, said he was pulling out his money because Chapman couldn't manage the finances. Chapman begged her to intercede with Combe—Combe was fond of her because his phrenological analysis of her skull had revealed that she had such great intelligence. She wrote to Combe, pleading with him on behalf of Chapman, and he softened.

At last a letter came from Spencer. She dashed through it, searching for some personal note, an expression of affection. But it was mostly about his progress on his book on human psychology. He did, however, complain about the heat in London. "*Dear Miss Evans, London is appallingly hot, and my room is on a high floor, which makes it worse. I do miss our conversations. I think of you with some envy there enjoying the cool sea air...*" She felt a rush of joy—he missed her.

She wrote back, trying to be playful and not too forward. "*No credit to me for my virtues as a refrigerant. I owe them all to a few lumps of ice which I carried away with me from that tremendous glacier of yours.*" Careful to keep a joking tone so that he wouldn't be frightened off, she continued, "*We will not inquire too curiously whether you long most for my society or for the sea breezes.*" So he wouldn't think she was flirting, she called herself *"a Medusa."* *"But seriousness and selfishness apart,"* she wrote, *"I should like you to have the enjoyment of this pleasant place."* She knew of a hotel where he might stay—of course she couldn't invite him to stay with her. *"Do come Saturday, if you would like."*

Five days later, she stood on the pier to meet him. As the boat pulled in, all around her children jumped up and down excitedly, calling out, "Papa! Papa!"

Catching sight of the familiar stooped figure in the shabby suit, happiness welled in her. A man of her own age, coming to visit her. A man who wasn't married, who had sought her out, who cared for her, a man whose mind she so admired.

He spotted her and took his hat off and waved. When he alighted on the pier, he stepped toward her as if he were going to kiss her. Then he hesitated, and a vaguely startled look came to his face. He looked almost frightened, as if he hadn't expected to see her. At length he gripped her arms as if both to greet her and to keep her at a distance. He didn't kiss her.

She'd booked a room for him at Ballard's on Albion Street, and they'd arranged to have supper there too. As they studied the menu, he said, "This place is really too expensive for me, I'm afraid."

She felt a moment of trepidation. Would he be angry with her for booking his room at such an expensive hotel? She'd written him the rates and he'd told her to go ahead. Was he going to leave early then?

"I'm afraid I got a bit seasick during the journey and I'm not that hungry," he said.

"Have some ale," she suggested, "that'll settle your stomach."

The meal came and they spoke, as usual, about his new book on cognition. "I'm afraid I've taken on more than I can manage," he said

"Why not publish something on it in the *Westminster* first, and see the response? Perhaps it'll help."

His lips pursed as he thought it over. "A good idea," he said.

When they'd finished their trifle, he said he was tired. "I'll walk with you to your cottage," he offered.

There were still people about, mostly couples, strolling arm in arm along the promenade, looking out to sea. The night air was warm and sensuous, suffused with the smell of the ocean and the gentle sound of breaking waves. The sky beyond was deep violet. Below, on the sand, the breakers were iridescent, cresting and foaming along the sand, their phosphorescence glowing eerily in the darkness.

At the door to her cottage, he stopped, took her hand, and kissed it. Then, gently, he let it drop. He took his hat off to her, a signal for her to enter the house. From the door she watched him walking down the path. There would be no more from him tonight.

In the morning, they walked on the beach, northward under the cliffs. They walked apart from each other, but it was difficult to talk anyway because of the wind. They stopped to explore the tunnels, supposedly dug by smugglers, and she scanned the beach for shards of sea glass and pocketed them as souvenirs.

On the way back to town, she hid behind a rock and removed her shoes and stockings so she could go barefoot. She continued on ahead of him, hoping that he'd be drawn by her few inches of bare flesh, her naked feet and ankles.

She turned around. He wasn't looking at her. He was bent over a tidal pool examining something.

The long hike left her languid, her limbs suffused with a sweet relaxation. At dinner, they drank ale again and it made her limbs feel heavy, her body feel ripe.

"Shall we walk on the beach one more time before we say good night?" she suggested.

"If you wish."

The night sky was clear, the stars glittering in the blackness. "Look!" she said. "Is that the Scorpion?"

"I can't see it," he said.

She traced the air with her fingertips. "Over there. See it?"

"Sort of," he said.

She inhaled the night air. "I don't think I've ever seen the sky this beautiful."

"Yes," he said distractedly.

For a moment he was caught in her glance, his face visible in the starlight. She held him with her eyes and refused to let him look away.

She asked him softly, "I hope you've liked it here. I very much wanted you to enjoy it."

"Why—yes...," he said, as if he didn't quite understand the question.

"We've been happy together, haven't we? We share so many interests, our work..."

"Yes." He began scraping the sand with the toe of his shoe.

"I feel that I've never quite had the same sympathy with anyone...as I've had with you."

And then suddenly, without even thinking, she found herself moving toward him. She put her arms around his neck, pulled his face toward her, and kissed him full on the lips. She felt her body rise up to him, expectantly, longingly. But his mouth was tight, his teeth hard beneath her lips.

He stepped back and pushed her away. She could see, in the light of the stars, alarm on his face. "I..." He struggled for words. "I—I'm sorry...," he said helplessly. "I think you misunderstand. You see, I don't feel...that sort of...attraction..." For the first time since she'd known him, he looked desperate, as if he were going to cry.

He took his hat off and wiped his brow. "I think, perhaps, I'm not made for this..., that I can't feel—" As if he expected her to come to his aid, to finish his sentence for him.

The beach was deserted now, the night air filled with the hush of the waves rushing in.

Then he said, "I think I'd best go back to London. On the morning boat. It's best I leave."

There was nothing she could say. All she knew was that she couldn't let him see her face. She hurried back across the sand and up the steps ahead of him, leaving him there on the beach.

He didn't say goodbye. She knew the boat left for Westminster at 7:30 a.m. She didn't go out that morning, but lay in bed awake. He'd pushed her away, her desire to love him, to comfort him, to help him become whom he was to be. The shame would be with her forever.

She had loved him, yes, loved his sweet, shy, peculiar self, the deep unhappy part of him, the frightened child beneath his eccentricities, the little boy whose brothers and sisters had all died, who was afraid that he himself would die prematurely, who was so strong and determined that he walked a hundred miles at the age of thirteen to get home to his mother and father, the man with his extraordinary ideas, ideas unique and peculiar to himself.

She couldn't rest, couldn't concentrate enough to go out, to walk about the town. All she could think of was that she was losing him, that it was like death, and now would come even greater, unendurable loneliness, without at least this one intimate friendship, this one closeness that she felt. She was sure that somewhere he felt it too, that he loved her in his own way. And now she'd driven him away and it was unbearable to her. She'd have no friend in London, no one approximating a beau in her life.

Sitting down at the little desk in her room, she wrote to him: *"I know this letter will make you very angry with me, but wait a little, and don't say anything to me while you are angry. I promise not to sin again in the same way."* She implored, *"I want to know if you can assure me that you will not forsake me, that you will always be with me as much as you can and share your thoughts and feelings with me. If you become attached to some one else,"* she wrote, *"then I must die..."*

Never had any woman written such a letter to a man.

———————

Two days later, she returned to London. Standing at the balustrade in the garden of Somerset House, she gazed down into the turbulent waters of the river.

As she watched the river flow by, she thought for a moment, how easy it would be just to jump. Drowning would take but minutes, if you didn't fight it. Then it would all be over, this loneliness...

First, the water would enter your body. Your eyes and throat would burn. Then you'd cough violently as your body tried to expel the water. But if you could just stay down underneath, in three or four minutes the water would fill your lungs and you'd sink. Blessed unconsciousness. Peace.

Why wasn't death seen as a comfort rather than as a horrifying end to life? Eternal rest, surcease from pain, at the realization that no man would ever love her. No more, this fruitless search.

But as she stood there, looking down into the thick, gray waters, so cold even in late summer, swirling violently beneath her, filthy and opaque and filled with debris, bits of rubbish and wood drifting by, fear overtook her. There would be those few moments before you actually lost consciousness, when you'd know that this was your end—what if you changed your mind?

The longing for the water passed.

Back at 142 Strand, her work awaited her, a pile of manuscripts for the October issue of the magazine. She would lose herself in it, have the satisfaction of shaping another person's language, of making it sing.

PART III

The Earthly Paradise

Chapter 9

In Venice, the morning after the concert at the Teatro Malibran, she got up, went into the *sala*, and found Johnnie still dressed in his evening clothes from the night before. His face was exhausted.

"Johnnie, didn't you go to bed?"

"I'm afraid not."

"You didn't sleep?"

"No."

"But—what did you do?"

"Just sat here."

"All night?"

"Yes."

"You look terrible." His hair was awry. There were deep circles under his eyes. He began walking around the room in a slow, rhythmic pace, ignoring Gerita, who was setting up the morning tea.

"You didn't even undress?"

"I was afraid to."

"Afraid to? What do you mean?"

"I was afraid to try to go to sleep because…what if I couldn't?"

"'What if you couldn't?'"

"Then I'd know for sure."

"You'd know—what?"

"I'd know that I couldn't."

She couldn't think what to say to this.

"Why don't you sit down and have some breakfast?"

"I don't need breakfast."

"To give you a good start to the day."

"I'm fine," he said, perambulating the room.

"I see," she said, sitting down at the table and trying to pretend that he wasn't walking restlessly about. Gerita poured her tea. "A roll, Madame?"

"Yes, thank you. Are they warm?"

"Yes, Signora. I make sure of it."

"And a little jam, please. You're exhausted," she said to Johnnie.

"I need exercise. I'm not getting enough exercise. That's the problem." She felt guilty now because she'd deprived him of his exercise. She was old and holding him back.

"Let's go to the Lido!" he said, smiling for the first time, as if to get her to agree with him.

"But it's already hot out, I think, and it's only nine-thirty. Won't it be much hotter on the beach?"

"It'll be cooler there. I've just got to get some exercise," he said. "That's the answer." His brow furrowed.

"Let's take the steamer," she said. "I don't much like that gondolier, do you? Perhaps we should try to get another one?"

"We could try," he said. "But I think they're all the same. They work for the hotel. I don't know if we can change."

"I think there's a boat every twenty minutes from the quay," she said. "We could go to the Hebrew cemetery," she said. "I've never been."

"Good," he said. "Then we'll have lunch. There's to be a big new hotel there, the Angleterre."

He made for the door.

"Just let me finish," she said. "Aren't you going to change?"

"I don't need to change," he said.

"But should you go like that?"

He looked down at himself, at his evening clothes from the night before, his formal shirt unbuttoned, his striped trousers creased. "This is all right."

He stood impatiently, waiting for her. She hurriedly sipped her tea and ate her roll. He watched her, his jaw tight, his fists clenched. "Coming, coming," she said. "Almost finished!" She was in a panic, pushed by his urgency.

In her own room, she completed her toilette and dressed. She put on the mantilla and off they walked to the Riva degli Schiavoni, where the ferry was docked and a long line of tourists and excited children with buckets and spades was waiting to board.

The boatman unhooked the rope, the crowd surged forward, and people jostled one another to get up the gangplank.

On board, she took a seat in the stern, on the bench under the canopy, but he stood apart from her at the railing, an odd figure in his formal trousers, disheveled, without a jacket, his shirt unbuttoned and half out, unkempt, his red curls uncombed.

The sun was already high. As the boat gained speed and vibrated beneath her, she felt the soft, briny mist of the water on her skin, and it cooled her. The engine was too loud to talk over it.

Nearby was a family of Germans, the father, sitting on the bench, legs crossed, absorbed in his newspaper, the mother with her white dress and bonnet, and two boys in identical blue sailor suits with white collars. The boys kept running up to the railings and looking down into the water, bouncing up and down and trying to climb up on them. The mother dragged them over to the bench and forced them to sit.

The boat crossed the Bacino. To their right was San Giorgio, to the left, the public gardens. Out on the water were boats with sails of different colors. On the misty horizon, the Euganean hills were visible. The silvery city, Venice, with its spires and campaniles, receded.

It was a twenty-minute journey. In front of them, the Lido drew closer, and they could begin to make out low buildings and hillocks.

The boat was approaching the landing at Santa Maria Elisabetta, where conveyances drawn by frayed-looking donkeys waited for the tourists.

They disembarked and Johnnie hailed a driver and instructed him in his crude Italian to take them to the cemetery on the north end of the island. The wagon ambled along a tree-lined dirt road past little houses and gardens, the lagoon on their left and the Adriatic over the rise on their right.

They came to an overgrown meadow, scattered with trees and bushes, filled with gravestones, crumbled and fallen. Just beyond was the church of San Nicolò and the fort, its cannons trained toward the sea, protecting Venice from its enemies.

The cemetery was neglected, but it was cool and shadowy here, the light filtering through the trees. They strolled along the overgrown paths among the faded monuments, the Hebrew lettering washed away by wind and water, the toppled gravestones lying half buried in the sand. On the far side of the cemetery, two young men were lounging on upended gravestones, having a picnic, a loaf of bread on a newspaper and a bottle of wine resting on one of the tablets.

"How could they eat here?" she asked. "It's desecrating it."

She stopped to decipher the melancholy letters on the graves. "'Rabbi Leone da Modena,' from 1648," she said, translating for him the Hebrew inscription. "'Words of the dead,' it says. 'Four arm's length of land in this enclosure, possessed for eternity, were acquired from above for Giuda Leone da Modena. Be gentle with him and give him peace.'"

As they strolled along the broken stones and thick-grown weeds, she thought how the history of the Jews is written in a minor key, in the key of loss and disappearance. She'd written *Daniel Deronda* in that key, Mirah searching for her lost brother.

He interrupted her, impatient. "We should get on to the beach."

They made their way back in the conveyance. It turned toward the Adriatic, jostling along the road, and the sea came into view, sluggish and gray and somnolent in the heat.

There was a big white stucco building on a rise overlooking the sea, with a columned portico and HOTEL D'ANGLE-TERRE engraved in gold letters on the pediment. It was one of the new, grand palaces being built along the Lido.

They made their way to the terrace above the sea and sat down at one of the tables under an umbrella. Johnnie ordered lunch from the waiter, who was in formal dress with white gloves. Below them a tunnel led to the beach, and beyond that were rows of cabanas and men in their striped bathing costumes and women in bathing dresses and bloomers.

"I'd like to swim," he said.

"But you don't have a bathing costume," she said.

"I'm boiling hot. Would you deny me that?" he asked.

"I'm not denying it to you. But you're still in your evening clothes from last night, Johnnie."

The sun had moved high in the sky, it was hot, and he squinted angrily out at the beach.

Suddenly, he sprang from his seat and strode down the steps into a tunnel. Before she could stop him, he'd disappeared.

She went to the balustrade. Below her, she could just make out amid the crowd of bathers Johnnie marching toward the shoreline.

She rushed down after him into the dark tunnel and then out into the blinding light of the beach, struggling through the crowds in her long dress, her feet sinking into the sand, to where he was standing with his back to her, looking out at the water.

When she was a few feet from him, she saw him begin to tear off his shirt. He pulled off his boots, then he unbuttoned his trousers. He was down to his combinations. It seemed at first in the heat and glare that nobody was noticing him.

Then he began wading into the waves.

"Johnnie," she shouted, "what on earth are you doing?" Her voice was muffled by the sea sounds, the wind, and the din of bathers shrieking and splashing. She ran after him into the water, soaking her boots and the hem of her dress.

He stepped away from her, farther into the water. "Leave me alone!" he cried.

"You can't undress here, Johnnie!"

"Why not! Everyone else is undressed. Look around you. Do you see anyone who's dressed? Why must you order me about all the time? Why can't I do as I wish?"

He pushed her shoulder and she almost fell backward into the water. She just managed to catch herself.

"Johnnie!" she cried. "You pushed me!" The realization of what he'd done seemed to penetrate his anger and he hesitated.

She stepped back, afraid to go nearer to him. Her boots were waterlogged, the hem of her dress hung limply. "What's happened to you, Johnnie?"

Looking bewildered, he moved toward the water's edge, where she stood.

She bent down and picked up his shirt and trousers lying sodden and pulsing in the waves, everything covered in wet sand. She tried to beat it off.

"Put these on," she commanded, holding them out. He stepped into his trousers, as if dazed.

"They're unbuttoned," she said. He made no move to button them himself, so she did it for him, conscious of the intimacy of it, of her hands on his middle there, only wanting to get him off the beach and away from the crowd.

Carrying his boots and shirt, she led him by the arm back through the tunnel. His jaws were clenched, his eyes afire. While she paid the bill for lunch, he stood there, a tall, wet, red-haired man in soaking clothes, barefoot.

She dragged him to a carriage parked in front and made him get in.

On the way back to the boat, he sat there unspeaking, an immovable object. At the dock while they waited for the steamer, he slouched sullenly. When the boat arrived, he followed her, obediently now.

As they crossed the lagoon, she persuaded him to put on his boots. When he made no move to tie the laces she knelt before him and tied them.

The steamer pulled up at the Riva degli Schiavoni and bumped to a stop. He followed her down the gangplank, furious and silent. She took his hand and led him, like a big, glowering child, back to the hotel. She prayed that they could just make it without his lashing out at her again in public.

Inside the *appartement*, he began to pace again.

She rang for the maid and asked her to prepare a bath.

"You must take a bath, Johnnie, the sea water's filthy and salty. You'll feel better." Mutely, he went into the bathroom.

While Gerita stood by, she pulled a chair up to the bathroom door and sat listening for him. She could hear the splash of water. He seemed to be bathing himself. "Have you finished?" she called.

"Yes," he answered curtly, through the door. She opened it a few inches and handed him his dressing gown. He emerged, clean and dry, his mouth still tight with resentment.

The thought flashed through her mind of sending a telegram to his brother, Willie, in England, telling him what was happening. But, no—that was impossible, she couldn't bear to let anyone know that something was wrong.

Instead, she took a piece of hotel stationery from the sleeve in the desk, wrote *"Laudano per dormire,"* and handed it to the maid. "Please go to the *farmacia* and show them this."

When Gerita had left, she said to him, "Johnnie, you pushed me."

"Oh, God." He squeezed his eyes shut, clutched his brow, and shook his head. "I am so sorry."

"I've never seen that in you. I was frightened, Johnnie. What is the matter with you?"

"I was so hot. I longed for the water." He looked up at her, his eyes red from the salt. He seemed as if he was going to cry. "I don't know what's the matter with me," he said. "I just can't help it. It comes over me..."

"The girl will be back in a minute. And then you'll sleep and you'll be all better. It's because you're exhausted; you must rest."

Gerita arrived with the medicine. Marian poured some of his whiskey into a glass and carefully put the drops of laudanum into it while he silently watched her.

She handed him the glass and he drank. Hopefully, sleep would come, and it would bring with it a miraculous cure—for whatever it was that had besieged him.

As he drank down the whiskey, she went up to him and stroked his hair, trying to soothe him. His stillness and regret had given her permission to touch him. She could feel his oily curls beneath her fingertips. He closed his eyes and leaned his head back.

Then, suddenly, he opened his eyes again and sat up. Deliberately, he took her hand in his, drew it away from his head, and placed it gently but firmly down at her side.

Chapter 10

That night she slept restlessly. At four in the morning, she sat up in bed. It was still dark out. There was someone in the room with her. What was it? Had she heard something? She listened. There was only the soft sound outside the windows of water lapping on stone.

But she wasn't alone.

There was a full moon in the window. In a few seconds her eyes adjusted to the gloom and she could make out the blue-gray forms of the furniture. The windows were open to let in the cool air. Venice was full of beggars and Gypsies. Had someone climbed up onto the balcony, and into the room?

Opposite the bed, the double doors leading into the *sala* were closed tight. To her left were two other doors, one to the water closet, which she could see was closed. Next to that, the door to the bathroom was open a crack.

Then she saw him. He was standing across the room, absolutely still, just as he used to be when he got up from bed at night. Unmistakable, the big head, the wiry hair sticking out messily on either side of his head, his mustache. He was naked. She saw his small body, his thin legs, the vague shape of his genitals. He was standing there as if he'd briefly left their bed and now he was coming back to her.

He was looking straight at her. She could see his features quite clearly now. But his expression—it wasn't his usual one. His eyes were solemn, there was no laughter in them, only a terrible seriousness she'd never seen before. They bored into her, as if her surface, her immediate self, didn't matter to him.

She opened her mouth to utter his name, but nothing came out, she couldn't speak. Fear, terror that he'd vanish, made her clamp her lips shut.

"George…is that you?" she said, forcing out the words. He didn't move. She pleaded, "George, how could you have left me?"

She put her legs over the side of the bed as if to stand up and go to him. "I'm going to die without you," she said. "I am…I am…" She stifled the rest, afraid he'd disappear.

Still, he said nothing, but watched her intently, his eyes piercing as if he were seeing through her to something beyond.

She was about to touch her toes to the floor, to go to him, but she held back. Instinctively, she knew that if she came too close he'd flee, and he would melt into the air.

A full minute must have passed. He hadn't moved, his eyes were still fixed on her. She said softly, "Don't go, darling. Please don't leave me." She saw his eyes move, shift. She might have blinked, she didn't know. And then there was only the wall, the flat gray wall, the silent portraits.

The room was empty. He was gone. The night was all clarity now, banality.

Outside the window, a faint gray-pink light was beginning to suffuse the sky, dawn was coming, the morning clangor would be starting soon.

She lay back in the bed, her senses quickened, alert. He was not her laughing man now. It was as if he had been transformed by his journey, that voyage that only happens once.

She couldn't go back to sleep.

Gradually, the morning light filled her eyes. He'd been there. She knew it and believed it.

But maybe it was just a vision, an aggregation of love and memory fueled by grief and desire. Someone, not the God in whom she did not believe, but her own God, the accumulation of some universal spirit and moral force, all the love she had inside her, had sent him. Just as he had been sent in those dark autumn months in London, after the awful ending with Spencer, when her life seemed fixed forever, when she had no hope left, only the drudgery of work.

Chapter 11

H e would come to the Strand in the relentless autumn rain, all wet, shaking himself off like a dog, and find her in the office in the back of the house, her legs over the armchair with her feet toward the fire as she worked through her manuscripts. He'd sit down opposite her and warm himself, steam rising from his damp coat. When she looked up, he was watching her.

"You really are the backbone of this place, aren't you?" he said.

"Well—the unpaid backbone."

His eyes drifted to the fire. His habitual gaiety seemed muted these days, his manic jokes. "You seem a bit sad," she remarked.

"Perhaps," he said. "But I'm very pleased with the Goethe article." He'd written a piece on "Goethe as a Man of Science" for the *Westminster*.

"Yes, it worked well," she said.

"Thanks to your editing. It was a bit disorganized, I'm afraid."

"A little. But I'm glad we published it," she told him. "I think you're right, people don't know about all of Goethe's scientific work, the botany and geology."

"He said he didn't take any pride in his poetry, that he was proudest of his work on the theory of color." Lewes had been trying for years to write a life of Goethe, but his efforts were constantly interrupted by his having to write articles for money.

She patted the pile of proofs in her lap and sighed. "Oh, dear. This is just endless."

"What about Chapman? Why isn't he doing any of this?"

"He spends every minute urging his creditors to pay him and soothing his investors."

He looked at her intently. "What say you to this?" he asked. "I have press orders for *Masks and Faces* tomorrow at the Haymarket. Would you go with me to cheer us both up?"

"But—" She hesitated. "Would Mrs. Lewes be with us?"

"She's got the children to take care of. I promise you, Mrs. Lewes won't mind in the slightest if we go to the theater together." She thought she detected a faint bitterness in his voice. "It'll be very funny."

That night, as they sat next to one another in the theater, she was conscious of his physicality, his masculinity, the vague scent of his wool jacket and his skin. At first she didn't look directly at him, and held herself nervously apart from him. But soon, they were laughing together, touching one another's arms at the silly jokes—the married squire Vane courting Mrs. Woffington; the main character, Triplet, frantically writing comedies in his garret to earn money to feed his starving family; and the two critics, Soaper, who praises everything, and Snarl, who hates it all.

The play over, they stepped out lightly from the theater, their spirits cleansed by laughter. They walked home along Haymarket, through the thick yellow fog and the damp cold coming in off the Thames. She shivered and tucked her scarf around her neck. He moved around her so he was nearer the river, to protect her from the cold, then he took her arm and moved closer to her.

"Shall we get a hansom?" he asked. "Is it too cold for you?" His body next to hers was warm, wiry, her own height, shielding her.

"It's too expensive," she said. "I'm so glad I came. Laughter does make one forget one's sorrows."

"Indeed."

He accompanied her to the door of 142 and followed her inside. It was late, the drawing room was deserted, the lights dimmed, the fire was down to its embers, the only sound the steady nighttime ticking of the grandfather clock. Standing in the entrance hall, before she'd removed her coat, she smiled at him. Then he kissed her on the lips. Instinctively, she wanted to pull back, but his lips were soft and full, the kiss unexpectedly enveloping.

He stepped away. "Pardon me," he said. "I'm afraid I couldn't help myself."

She looked about. "You really shouldn't be here."

"Could we just sit awhile in the drawing room? There's still a bit of a fire."

"I suppose so." She removed her coat and sat down on the settee opposite the fireplace, clutching her arms around her body for warmth. He crouched down and stoked the coals, threw a log on, and the embers burst into flame. He came around and sat beside her. The room grew warmer.

"You're married," she blurted out. "I don't think I could bear..." She left it unfinished. She didn't say, "another married man, a man who belongs to someone else."

"My marriage is dead," he said firmly. "I've got to move out of Bedford Place, as soon as I can do it. But I can't afford to at the moment. I have to support my family."

"How many children do you have?"

"I had..." He paused, as if this was difficult to say. "I have three boys, Charley, Thornie, and Bertie. We lost our littlest one, St. Vincent, a year and a half ago." His face dropped in an expression of inexpressible sadness.

"I'm so sorry."

"Twenty-two months old. Measles. We lost another one too, early on, a little girl. Only four days old."

"There must be nothing like it," she said. "I'm not a parent but surely, God, whoever He—or She—is, didn't mean this to be."

"And...in addition to my own three boys, there are two others now." He took a breath. "Or at least they bear my name."

He paused. "I feel I should explain." He hesitated. "You have a way of listening that makes one want to confide in you."

"Thank you," she said, smiling grimly. "Yes, that's been said. I have one attribute, at least."

At this bit of self-deprecation he looked at her sharply.

He went on. "In the beginning, Agnes and I were both believers in free love."

"'Free love,'" she echoed with bitterness. "I've seen the results of that—only pain."

He paused, looking at her as if thinking this through, but he didn't answer.

"We were happy," he said. "We had our little boys. But I'm afraid I left Agnes to manage by herself too much. I was always out and about, furthering my career, trying to earn money, at the theater. Then my play *The Noble Heart* went on at the Olympic. My friend Thornton Hunt and I were trying to raise money for the *Leader.* I admit that I—I foolishly strayed. Agnes sensed it, asked me about it. I told her the truth, perhaps I shouldn't have. To my surprise, perhaps stupidly, she was distraught.

"Then Agnes became pregnant."

He stopped. "She told me that the baby was Thornton's. I was—there's no other way to describe it—shattered. Our agreement hadn't included having children with other people. Thornton was my best friend. I'd even named my son, Thornie, after him. But as I admitted, I—strayed first. Agnes said she'd never get rid of the baby. We'd lost our little girl early on and she couldn't bear it. I couldn't punish her for it. Look what I'd done. The baby, Edmund, was born just three weeks after little St. Vincent died."

"But how did she know it wasn't yours?"

"He looks just like Thornton, very dark-skinned. The Hunts are from Barbados, you know."

"Did you confront Thornton?"

"No. In an odd way, I couldn't blame him either, though he's married with children himself. He's got seven with his wife, Kate."

"Seven? It can't be!"

"Yes. Then Agnes had Rose. She's Thornton's too. By then Agnes and I had ceased all intimacy.

"That's when I met you at Jeff's Book Shop," he said. "I noticed you at once. I'd heard about you, that you were the brilliance behind the throne at the magazine. You had a way of looking at a man, making him feel he was the most important person in the room. And you have such an enchanting voice."

He hesitated. "I think you should know, I allowed Agnes to put my name on the birth certificates of her first two children with Thornton."

"Why?"

"I'd acceded to our arrangement that we could each have other lovers to begin with. And the children were innocent. It wasn't their fault they'd been born. I couldn't let them be bastards. I never knew my own father. He abandoned my own poor mother when I was a baby. I never saw him again."

As he told her his story, she thought, he wasn't ugly at all. His eyes were dark and searching, he had full, red lips, a thin, tensile little body.

"That means that I can never divorce Agnes," he said, "because, by giving the children my name, under the law I condoned Agnes's adultery."

He waited, letting that sink in.

"And Thornton," she asked, "does he acknowledge them as his?"

"He and I, we haven't ever discussed it. Some things are better left unsaid. He knew that I'd been unfaithful to Agnes. As I said, we were all freethinkers..." He gave a grim little laugh. "Free to be miserable would be a better way of putting it."

"Does he give Agnes money for them?" She knew that Lewes wasn't rich, he was always foraging for money by selling articles.

"How well do you know Thornton?" he asked. "He's always begging for loans, saying he's got all his children to support. If anything, he's poorer than even I am."

"You support Thornton's children, too?"

"How can I feed some of the children in the house and not the others? Yes, I feed them."

He drew back. "I'll go now," he said. He stood up and waited a moment. Then he said, "But I'm never going to let you be alone again."

He took his hat and coat and umbrella from the rack and was gone.

She sat there, contemplating what he'd said. Here was another man who believed in "free love." And yet he seemed so worn down by despair, broken. She believed, or she *wanted* to believe, she thought, the truthfulness of his regret, his sorrow. In spite of herself she was moved, that he refused to let Agnes's children with another man suffer, that he took the full blame for what had happened between them, that he refused to condemn his wife. He didn't ask for sympathy or praise for his decision not to abandon his family.

———

He came the next day and once more took her to the theater. And that evening, in the darkness of the house, everyone out or asleep, they crept up the stairs to her room, conscious of the treads squeaking, giggling like two naughty children. They didn't have to speak about their intention. In the peace and darkness of her room on the third floor, it was their first time.

After they had finished, she quickly drew the sheet up to her chin to hide herself. But he reached over, lit the candle by the bed, and firmly pulled the sheet down again. He held the sheet back away from her body. "No," she said, and tried to grab it from him.

"Yes," he said. He moved the candle slowly up and down her naked flesh, studying her.

"It's cold," she protested.

But he continued silently contemplating her body, and she allowed it, wordless and frightened.

"Your body is so beautiful," he said. Then he pulled the covers over both of them and wrapped her in his arms. "And I'll never let you be cold again," he told her, drawing her to him and rubbing her hands and feet to warm them.

He made love to her once more, and this time she wasn't afraid. Her desire was at first baffling, unexpected in its intensity and freedom, for this was desire mingled for the first time in her life with reciprocated love, desire reflected in the love of another person. No need to question it, to wonder about it. It was far stronger than her capacity to stop herself.

On November 22, her thirty-third birthday, he came bearing red roses, out of season, seizing a kiss in the back office when they were alone. "You shouldn't have," she said. "They're much too expensive!"

"It doesn't matter. I need far more money than those cost. You deserve them."

She put the roses on the windowsill of the dark room so she could look at them while she worked, at the deep, dusky red emerging from the winter gloom, a glamorous gift no man had ever offered her before, a gift of romance and honor.

When Chapman came in to consult with her, he asked, "Who're those from?"

"A friend," she said curtly.

He raised his eyebrows. But she didn't offer more.

Christmas was approaching. A letter came saying that Chrissey's husband, Edward Clarke, had died, bankrupt, leaving Chrissey with six children to feed.

She dropped her work immediately and took the next train to Meriden.

Isaac was there when she arrived, standing strong and bearded with his big, hooked Evans nose. Relishing his own success in the midst of the crisis, she thought.

Chrissey sat clutching her youngest child, Katie, only fourteen months old, while her other five children stood forlornly around her, brave young Edward, her oldest, and Robert and Emily and Christopher and Fanny. Chrissey's youthful prettiness had vanished. She was only thirty-eight, but her teeth had fallen out from all her pregnancies, and her hair had turned gray. She was worn to the bone from Edward's bankruptcy and the deaths of two of her children.

"I'm willing to let her live in the Attleborough house rent-free," Isaac said. The house was a broken-down hovel on the estate, not big enough for seven people. Isaac continued in his inimitable way. "And Katie and Fanny can go to the Infant Orphan Asylum."

From where she sat, holding dirty-faced little Katie to her breast, Chrissie shrieked "No!"

"They'll get food and a bed," he said impassively. He was always so sure of his rightness.

"Never!" Chrissey cried. She buried her face in the baby's neck.

Marian interrupted. "Isaac, please. I'll help Chrissey. I'll change my situation and earn some money."

She tried to make a Christmas for the children by filling a sock for each with an orange and some nuts. The day after Christmas, as she was gathering her things for the journey back to London, Isaac appeared again at the house. "Where're you going?" he demanded.

"Back to London to try to earn some money to help Chrissey."

"I'm the head of this family now," he said angrily. "I am trying to ensure our sister's survival, and now you're leaving without telling me. In future, don't ask me for anything." He stormed out.

"What have I ever done to make him hate me so?" she asked Chrissey.

Chrissey shook her head. "Perhaps he's jealous of your mind, your intelligence. You were always the clever one. Or perhaps it's that he once loved you so," she ventured, "and now you're independent of him."

When she got back to the cold, bleak streets of London, she arranged with the solicitor for their father's estate, Mr. Holbeche, to have a portion of her allowance sent to Chrissey.

In her brief absence, the finances of the *Westminster* had slipped further into arrears. George Combe had agreed not to be paid for his article on phrenology and education in return for advertising for his books. But Chapman had inadvertently left the advertisement out of the issue and Combe was again threatening to pull his money out.

Charles Bray offered to give Chapman funds to pay Marian her wages, but she wouldn't allow it. She wrote to Charles in Coventry thanking him: "*You are the dearest, oldest, stupidest, tiresomest, delightfullest and never-to-be-forgotten-est of friends to me,"* she teased.

She was working so hard now that she developed an intense pain in her shoulder from the writing and editing. She could hardly hold her pen. George came daily now to see her. He'd find his way to the back office, and if no one was about, he'd lay his hand on her cheek. "Poor soul," he said, "your worries are great, aren't they?"

"But so are yours," she said.

At night she let him into the house and he followed her upstairs to her room, and there he held her, kissed her, and warmed her with his body. Somewhere, Chapman and Susanna and Miss Tilley must know, she thought. Perhaps they were relieved that she had someone of her own now.

Once, at midnight, Chapman came in the front door just as George was arriving. Chapman looked askance at them, said "Good evening," and went upstairs.

The next day in the back office, he told her, "You should watch yourself with Lewes. He's a scoundrel."

"Well, you should know," she said, letting the anger out as she never had before. He daren't say anything to that. He had no idea who George really was. He only cared that she had shifted her allegiance to someone else and might leave him stranded at his magazine.

Every night that George didn't come was a void of loneliness, an unnatural state. There was now between them an attachment, profound and inevitable. He buoyed her with visits to the theater, tried to make her laugh when her spirits were down about Chrissey. His existence was woven into the fabric of her own, their separations unnecessary, a needless interruption in the inevitable continuity of their love.

Then, one February day, George arrived at 142 with his usual ebullience dampened. "Agnes is pregnant again," he said flatly.

He could endure it no more. His friend, Frederick Ward, was in Brussels and said George could live rent-free at his house on Cork Street while he was gone.

And she could endure it no more at the Strand. By the following autumn she had found rooms for herself on Cambridge Street, nine pounds a month for rent and food. Somehow she'd find the money. The rooms were on the ground floor, noisy and drafty, but it was only fifteen minutes from Cork Street and she and George could go back and forth unobserved.

On the day she moved into her new home, Barbara Smith arrived, her golden hair streaming around her, her face flushed with the autumn air. "This is so sweet!" she cried with her usual enthusiasm. "You'll be so happy here."

"It's a bit dark," Marian said.

"We'll fix that. I've brought some things to decorate with." From her bag she took two watercolors she'd painted, already framed: a delightful little beach scene from Hastings where the Smiths had an estate, and blue and white irises. She tacked them up on the wall, then helped Marian unpack and rearrange the furniture. And together they made the place cozy.

George came too, without supervision, without interruption.

Still, she couldn't escape the *Review*. Chapman brought manuscripts to Cambridge Street for her to work on.

Combe had written ninety-six pages on "Criminal Legislation and Prison Reform," with once again phrenology being the answer to everything. He was demanding the article be published whole. She toiled over it and persuaded Combe to cut it down to thirty-six pages, without offending him.

In an effort to keep her at the magazine, Chapman offered her thirty pounds to do a new translation of Feuerbach's *Essence of Christianity*. He'd put her name on it too, he said. Ludwig Feuerbach was another German critic of established religion, a philosopher and disciple of Hegel. Hegel had charted the evolutionary path by which humanity achieves a universal spirit, full freedom, absolute knowledge of itself. Feuerbach took Hegel one step further, arguing that Christianity itself would inevitably be superseded. God, Feuerbach said, was merely the outward projection of man's own nature, his innate disposition to do good.

All winter, she and George worked together in their little nest. He was editing a book on Comte. He'd met Comte in Paris several years before and had become interested in his philosophy of positivism, his belief that all we can know is that which we can see and hear ourselves. Now he was collecting his various essays into one volume, *Comte's Philosophy of the Sciences*, in an effort to popularize the philosopher with English-speaking audiences, and she helped him correct his manuscript.

To give him time to do his own work, she read proofs for the *Leader* as well. She even wrote some of his "Vivian" columns for him—she'd learned to imitate his style perfectly.

In between she translated Feuerbach. *"Love is God himself,"* Feuerbach said, *"and apart from it, there is no God...not a visionary, imaginary love—no! a real love, a love which has flesh and blood.*" It was just what she herself had come to believe. The essence of Christianity was not dogma, not the trappings of ritual, but human beings' love for one another. Even when Chapman couldn't pay her the full amount he'd promised, she kept on with the work. *"Marriage as the free bond of love, that alone is a religious marriage,"* Feuerbach had written. Furthermore, a marriage bond *"which is merely an external restriction, not the voluntary, contented self-restriction of love"* is neither a true marriage nor a moral one.

She began deliberately to pepper her letters with references to "Mr. Lewes," so her friends would grow accustomed to his constant presence in her life. When Barbara came to tea, Marian confessed to her that she loved him. Barbara had been aware of her growing affection for him. Sometimes, when she arrived to visit, she found George ensconced with his book or even working on his manuscripts at the dining room table, and he would rise up and greet her in his usual cheery manner. Barbara had looked at Marian, her eyebrows raised in a question, but Marian had refused to explain.

Then, one day, when Barbara came, he wasn't there. Marian made tea for her. "Where's Mr. Lewes today?" she asked.

"The doctor's ordered him to go to the country for a few days. He made himself ill with headache finishing the Comte book."

Barbara, as usual, got straight to the point. "Do you love him?"

"Yes," Marian said, her face flushed.

Barbara frowned. Marian could feel her doubt and disapproval. Barbara had known him only by his public face, always joking and flirtatious.

"I know you think he is simply a jokester," Marian said. "But you don't really know him. He wears a mask of flippancy. Underneath it all, he's so kind, and he's very sad about the way his marriage has turned out, and so worried for the children."

Barbara smiled, but her face was serious. "All I care is that he loves you and takes care of you."

"He loves me, Barbara. He does. And he wants to take care of me."

"Then as long as that's true, he has my support."

————

As it grew colder outside, they were snug inside. They began to dream—of saving their money and running away together to Germany, where they'd live as man and wife, where George could finish his biography of Goethe.

In January, she resigned from the magazine, though she told Chapman she'd continue to write for it. She had labored for four whole years as the editor. In early summer, they booked passage on the channel steamer to the Continent.

Then, one day in June, just before they were to leave, Charles Bray appeared at her door, brisk and rosy-cheeked, hair askew, but now grown broad and rather fat. "I came up to London and I thought I'd drop by," he said.

He was her dear friend, but looking at him now, thirteen years after she had first met him when she and her father had moved to Coventry, she couldn't even imagine why she'd ever been his lover. She knew that feeling had vanished for him too. He'd found more pleasing fare. He'd had three more children with Hannah Steane and he'd set up a home for them on Howard Street.

His admiration for Marian had superseded whatever it was he'd wanted from her physically. She was a flower in the garden of all his interests, part of the landscape of his energies, and he was still constantly dazzled and excited by her responsive mind. He was determined to support her, to be there for her like a brother. It was strange of him, and she didn't quite know why she had been singled out, but she was lucky, so lucky, to have him and Cara.

His face was serious. "Cara and I," he said, "we're very worried about Lewes."

She stiffened, warily. "What about him?"

"Everyone knows, now, Marian. He's a married man."

"Yes. He is married. But as you well know, that doesn't always matter." She said this cruelly, but he didn't flinch. He still believed without question in the rightness of his arrangement with Cara.

She stood firmly in front of him. "I've never been so happy."

"But...he's a rake. Everybody knows that."

"He may have been that once. But he's no longer a rake. He's a deeply unhappy man. He's paid the price. He supports Agnes and Thornton's children because Thornton is totally irresponsible. He gave them his name because it was the honorable thing to do. And he can never get a divorce because of that."

Charles sat down and let out a deep breath. "Marian, we can't bear to see you hurt again. You give your heart away too easily. He'll shame you."

"You have no understanding of him. You don't know him."

"But he can't marry you!"

"A legal bond isn't a real bond. As we both know."

He ignored this reference to their shared history, to his marriage to Cara and his family with Hannah Steane. "I can't change your decision?" he asked.

"No. You can't."

"We love you, Marian, you know that, Cara and myself."

She softened. "I know. You saved me. And I'm grateful for all you've done for me." She looked at him, measuring his reaction. "We've decided to go away together. We're going to Weimar so he can research his book on Goethe. We're going as man and wife."

Charles shook his head.

"Please," she said. "Promise me. Don't tell Cara that I'm going. I can't bear her disapproval." If George humiliated her, their sympathy for her would make it all the more awful. If he backed out...she'd die. The fear rose in her body.

Charles sighed, but she could tell from that that he was agreeing to keep her secret.

She went on. "I'd like to ask a favor of you. I can't let my brother, Isaac, know I'm going. May I arrange with Mr. Holbeche to send my allowance to you at Rosehill? And then you can forward it to me at the poste restante?"

"Yes," he said. "I'll be glad to do that." He looked at her worriedly. "But if I recall, the next payment from the estate isn't due to you till next December."

"Yes," she said.

"How will you manage?"

"Somehow."

"I'll advance you December's payment."

"Even though you disapprove?"

"I can't let you go hungry."

"Dear Charles, you are a brother!" She squeezed his hand.

"And I've got yet another favor to ask you," she said. "Will you go and see Chrissey sometime? Make sure she's all right and let me know if she needs money. Things are terrible for her."

"I will," he said. He picked up his hat to leave. "Dear Marian, I wish you great happiness. We all do." She embraced him farewell.

All that night she lay awake. She wasn't tired at all, her eyes burned, her thoughts raced. The things to do: leave instructions for the landlady, Mrs. Pitt, on where to forward her mail; put the cash she'd withdrawn from her account safely in an envelope; pack enough clothing; books, because it wouldn't always be possible to get English-language reading matter; paper, pen, and ink for letters, all the more expensive abroad at tourist prices.

It was still dark when she rose. She bathed and washed her hair so that it buoyed out softly and fragrantly around her head. She wanted to be as beautiful for him as she could be. She rummaged through her case, unpacked and repacked it to be sure everything was there, to make more room for another book or two.

The boat was scheduled to leave at noon from St. Katherine's Wharf, but she'd allowed two whole hours to get to the dock. It only sailed once a week, on Thursdays, and if she was late—

At ten o'clock Mrs. Pitt's boy whistled for a hansom. One stopped for her. The driver was coarse-faced, with a thick, heavy brow. Scowlingly, he hoisted her trunk into the cab as if he were doing her a favor. "I'm in a hurry!" she said. "I'll give you extra if you can get me there in time."

He didn't reply. Had he heard her? Should she say it again? But then he might be angry.

And off they went. It was only ten o'clock, but the sun was high. The hansom turned down Belgrave Road, across London, along Milbank and the Embankment. Oh, hurry, please hurry! The streets were packed, businessmen and shoppers, people up to London for the season. Would he be there when she arrived? They'd been so happy all these months, not a single moment of doubt spoken of. But now the old buried pain, of Chapman and Spencer and Dr. Brabant suddenly, at this moment of risk, resurfaced. The possibilities were before her again. Would this be the great disappointment of her life, the final hurt?

Suddenly their way was blocked by a knot of cabs, horses jostling each other and rearing up, drivers swearing. The thick smell of dung and horse sweat and leather rose up sickeningly to her. She lifted the trapdoor. "Should we take another route, perhaps?"

"Ahm doin' me bloomin' best!" the man snarled.

Then, at last they were free, picking up speed, barreling through the streets.

The Tower came into view, the noble tower, and the Bridge, and she could see the cranes and masts of St. Katherine's. She leaned forward in her seat, as if to propel the hansom faster with her body.

They reached the docks and she paid the man the extra shilling, ridiculous, because she was frightened that he'd ride off with her luggage. He threw the trunk to the ground.

Amid the warehouses and ships' masts glittering in the sun, the giant boat loomed, its name, *Ravensbourne*, emblazoned on the bow. The steam was rising from the funnel, it was about to leave. The horn blasted through the air, a warning. People were up on deck waving down to their friends and relatives below.

But no sign of George. She searched the crowd. No face, no figure that would fill her vision, obliterate all else. It would kill her.

Perhaps he was already on board, waiting. Another blast from the horn. She'd better board then. She hurried up the gangplank. From the railing, she searched for him amid the hordes below.

A porter was coming toward her, shoving his cart loaded to the top with teetering bags.

And then just over his shoulder—the small, familiar, jaunty figure bouncing along. He spotted her and waved and called out her name. "Ma-a-rian!" It came to her over the rumble of traffic, the clanking of cranes, the cries below. Heedless of all else, she pushed past the porter and ran toward him.

"You came!"

"Did you think I wouldn't?" He seemed surprised. She buried her face in his shoulder and he wrapped his arms around her, gripping her with certainty.

And she knew that he would never leave her.

The horn blasted a final warning, and at first almost imperceptibly, the boat began pulling away. It moved out onto the river, away, away from England. It bore them along through the forests of masts, the ships of all nations, the colliers and steamers, past the docks, the wharfs and granaries. His arm was around her waist, his body close to hers. They passed the Greenwich Observatory, Gravesend, Tilbury Fort. And now, out to sea.

They didn't sleep their first night together, open to the world, officially declaring themselves as man and wife. They were too excited, had too much to talk about and plan. Instead, they strolled the deck looking out at the calm, summer sea, the sun going down, the waves stippled with moonlight.

As darkness came, they lay on their deck chairs side by side, hands joined in the balmy night. She felt the rough skin of his knuckles, the little hairs on top of his hand, a small hand, but a hand the mere touch of which infused her with comfort, with safety. They could link their hands in public now and no one would care.

There was a crescent moon that night, and the stars were clear. Just before dawn, they entered the Scheldt, its black waters flat and calm. They drifted past low-lying islands, the outlines of poplar trees, farmhouses.

Quietly, the river wound its way. Ahead, there was a gathering of black clouds and the sky was lit up by flashes of lightning. Somewhere far away, a summer storm was brewing. It would not affect them. A faint pink emerged in the black sky, dawn.

And slowly, calmly, the great ship proceeded, winding its way along, then at last making the great curve, and they could see ahead of them the spires of Antwerp. From there they would go by train to Cologne, to Coblenz and Frankfurt, and on to Weimar.

Chapter 12

They drifted across Europe, her body humming, a sweet new soreness in her flesh, in a continual state of excitement, seeing the world anew. Far from home, they were safe from censure; she was no longer afraid.

In Weimar, George set about researching his Goethe book. They'd been there only a few days when Franz Liszt came calling on them in their rooms on the Kaufgasse. George had met Liszt before in Vienna and written a "letter" from "Vivian" about him for the *Leader*.

When Liszt walked in the door, the sight of him struck her with physical force. Here was the man for whom women wore bracelets made from the pianoforte strings he broke in the intensity of his playing. He reminded her for a moment of Chapman, in his height, his angularity, his penetrating gaze. But Chapman was a second-rater, and this—this man was a god. He sat and chatted with them in a warm, free manner. She couldn't quite believe that he was sitting there, in his black frock coat with his long hair flowing to his shoulders, on a chair in their sitting room, in human time and space. He joked about *Nélida*, the novel written about him a few years before, by his former mistress Madame D'Agoult, the mother of his three children, who had pilloried him for his philandering. It had caused a scandal, but Liszt just laughed at it.

Liszt was living with the Princess Carolyne zu Sayn-Wittgenstein now, in a house she'd rented for them on the outskirts of the city. "My poor princess," he said, "she's trying day and night to obtain an annulment of her marriage to Prince Nikolaus, so we can marry in the church—we're both devout Catholics. Fortunately, people here in Weimar are very open-minded and they accept us. They don't have these stupid prejudices."

Then, suddenly, he threw aside his gloom and smiled again. "You must come at once, this morning, to the Villa Altenburg. The princess is dying to meet you."

An hour later, as their carriage pulled into the circular driveway of the yellow mansion on Jenaer Strasse, the air was thick with the threat of rain. It was a rather plainly drawn, beige-and-yellow building, standing by itself on a hill at the edge of a pine forest with a view overlooking Weimar.

The butler, Heinrich, greeted them and showed them to the garden, where other guests were waiting for the Maestro at a long table under a canopy of trees, set with bread and smoked meats and cheese. There was a Herr Hoffman von Fallersleben, a poet, and a Dr. Schade, who'd written something about Saint Ursula and the eleven thousand virgins, and Liszt and the princess's secretary, Herr Cornelius, and Joachim Raff, a musician and expert on Richard Wagner, who was Liszt's main preoccupation at the moment.

As they waited for Liszt to appear, the guests chatted among themselves. Marian kept glancing up at the thick sky, praying it wouldn't rain and spoil the party.

Liszt made his grand entrance. On his arm was the teenage Princess Marie, the Princess Wittgenstein's daughter, dressed in white, an ethereal, wraithlike girl. Behind him trotted his Scotch terrier, Rappo. A few moments later, the princess appeared.

"I'm delighted!" the princess said warmly, extending her hand to Marian and making a little curtsy. Marian was taken aback. She'd expected that Liszt's mistress would be a great beauty, but the princess was a short, fat little thing, wearing a white morning robe of a semitransparent material. When she smiled, Marian saw that her teeth were black. Well, she did have a rather exotic profile and bright, dark hair, and very dark eyes.

Heinrich brought out pastries. Liszt passed around cigars. The princess took one—perhaps that accounted for her black teeth. Cigars gave Marian a terrible headache and she hoped she could endure the smoke filling the air. Liszt asked Herr von Fallersleben to recite some of his poetry and the poet, a big man, began declaiming some sort of bacchanalian piece in a gusty voice, but she couldn't concentrate on it. All of them, she realized, were hanging on the unanswered question: would Liszt play for them? Nobody said anything for fear perhaps of disrupting some plan that the Maestro had made. George was telling the princess about his Goethe biography and Marian heard her cry, "But Goethe was such an egoist!"

All she could do was stare at Liszt, who was sitting back in his chair, legs crossed, enjoying Herr von Fallersleben's recital and benevolently surveying his guests. The little dog cavorted among them. Liszt fed him scraps from the table. "He completely spoils that animal!" the princess said. "When he's upstairs composing, Rappo stands down in the garden barking up at him."

"He's my harshest critic," Liszt said, smiling and giving the dog a pat.

"So much for genius," said the princess.

Marian felt a drop of rain on her cheek, then another. They all glanced at one another. Soon the rain was pelting down on them and the princess was hurrying them up a flight of stairs at the rear of the house. Liszt and the princess led the way into a drawing room, which opened into the music salon, in which stood two grand pianos. "Please, sit," Liszt said, indicating chairs placed around the edges of the room.

He sat himself down at one of the pianos. "This is a piece I wrote during my first winter at Woronince, the princess's estate in the Ukraine," he said. "It's called 'Bénédiction de Dieu dans la Solitude.' It's inspired by Lamartine's poem of the same name."

The only sound now was the rain pouring down outside the windows. Then, just as Liszt was settling himself on the bench, Marian quickly, fearfully, stood up and dared to move her chair forward closer to his piano. She wanted to see his hands. He didn't seem to notice, thank goodness, and wasn't annoyed.

The beginning of the piece was slow, almost naive, like a child's song. There was a clear melody underneath it, the undercurrent of a gently trilling stream, lyrical and melodic, repeated in a minor key, the themes earnest and supplicating. Gradually, though, the music rose to an ecstatic pitch as Liszt played, his long hair flew around his shoulders, he threw back his head, compressed his lips, his nostrils dilated. His hands were a blur.

There were pauses, contemplative and thoughtful. And it was done. Liszt lifted his hands from the keys and held them in midair, on his face an expression of transcendence.

———————

Returning to their rooms in their carriage, she and George sat in a stunned state. They didn't speak.

Then she broke the silence. "I think that's the first time in my life that I've beheld true inspiration," she said, "the perfect fusion of inspiration and execution."

"You've got it in you," George said. "You have that gift in your writing."

"You have no evidence of that."

"I have complete and utter confidence in you." He grasped her hand and held it tightly the rest of the way back to the city, as they gazed out at the pine woods and the meadows glittering green and washed fresh by the rain.

For the rest of their stay in Weimar, George ran about the city doing his research on Goethe's life, inflamed with purpose, so happy to be immersed in it.

They went on to Berlin. The weather was bitingly cold, snow alternating with rain. George had friends in Berlin from previous visits, the art historian Adolf Stahr and his mistress, the novelist Fanny Lewald, another champion of the women's cause. They had lived together as man and wife for nine years while Stahr tried to get a divorce from his wife. In Berlin, the couple's union was accepted and they went about freely.

At night in their rooms on the Dorotheenstrasse, as the wind howled and the snow built up outside their window, she and George sat cozily while she translated Goethe for him for his book.

Meanwhile, letters were coming from London with news of gossip about them. People were saying George had abandoned Agnes and seduced Marian and he would surely abandon Marian next. Carlyle wrote and reported that people were saying Marian had made him leave Agnes.

That night they lay together in bed in the darkness. She could tell by the silence and stillness of his breathing that he wasn't asleep either.

"I can't sleep," she told him.

"Neither can I," he said. "I'll write to him in the morning and set it right."

The next day he showed her the letter he had written: *"My separation was in no ways caused by the lady named. It has always been imminent, always threatened."*

She wrote to Chapman in an effort to get paid for an article she had written, and added at the end, *"I have counted the cost of the step that I have taken and am prepared to bear, without irritation or bitterness, renunciation of all my friends."*

Only Barbara Smith wrote to say how wonderful it was that she'd decided to live with George. Marian was so profoundly grateful to Barbara, always there when she needed courage, supporting her with an almost physical lift. Barbara was irresistible. She made her ashamed of being afraid. Marian wrote back at once that the letter was *"a manifestation of your strong, noble nature."*

Every day she loved him more, and the more she loved him, the more frightened she was that one day she could lose him. She knew now that she needed something, which, unlike love, unlike George himself, could never be taken from her: the indestructible attributes of talent and genius, the ability of intellect and imagination to forge a link between present and past, between the pain and the happiness she had known; the capacity to give coherence to her existence through language, through the music and the variability and the flexibility of words. She wanted to write from her imagination, but she was afraid that she lacked the talent to do so.

They stayed in Germany eight months. In early spring, they sailed back to England, husband and wife now, in their own eyes. They found rooms for "Mr. and Mrs. Lewes" on Park Shot in Richmond. It was an out-of-the-way place, where they were unlikely to run into any acquaintances. There was always the danger that the landlady, Mrs. Croft, would discover they weren't married and throw them out, so Marian warned those few friends who knew about them to be careful to address all letters to her as "Mrs. George Lewes."

That autumn, George's *Life and Works of Goethe* was published. The *British Quarterly* praised it for a felicity *"rare in the annals of biography."* It sold a thousand copies in the first three months, but it didn't make them rich. Still, it surrounded George with the warm glow of success.

At Park Shot, they established a beloved routine, up at half past eight, quiet reading until ten a.m., writing until half past one, a walk in the park, back for supper at five.

She plowed on, churning out articles to make money. She wrote a review of Ruskin's *Modern Painters* for the *Westminster*: *"The truth of infinite value he teaches is* realism," she said, *"the doctrine that all truth and beauty are to be attained by a humble and faithful study of nature, and not by substituting vague forms, bred by imagination on the mists of feeling."* If she ever became a real writer, she'd adopt these words as her code. She sent funds to Chrissey and gave part of her earnings to George for his boys and for Agnes and her other children with Thornton.

Amid the piles of books that arrived daily for review she came across a novel, *Compensation*, by an anonymous author—a woman, it was said. In it a four-year-old child supposedly says ridiculous things such as *"Oh, I am so happy, dear gran'mamma;—I have seen,—I have seen such a delightful person: he is like everything beautiful,—like the smell of sweet flowers, and the view from Ben Lomond..."* The silliness of these female authors, their fatuous dialogue.

She wrote an essay for the *Westminster* on "Silly Novels by Lady Novelists," novels of *"the mind and millinery species,"* she called them, with their frothy heroines, their manly heroes, their insipid curates. It wasn't as if women couldn't write great works. Look at Mrs. Gaskell, Harriet Martineau, and Currer Bell. Surely, even she could do better than these women who'd published such nonsense.

George, having published his Goethe biography, decided that he wanted to write a book on science, on marine biology. They went down to Devon so he could do research for it. She was thirty-six now and he was thirty-nine, but they were like two children that spring, clambering over the rocks in their fishermen's boots, she carrying the landing net and he the hamper with the specimen jars.

"Look!" he cried, spotting a sea anemone with long, swirling tentacles. "It's an *Anthea Cereus*, I think." There was such joy in naming things, defining them, categorizing them, creating order and meaning through language. *"Anthea,"* *"Cereus."* All things on God's earth could be given names and thereby made part of the larger whole.

At night, their room was stacked with jars filled with specimens of sea creatures. George read *Coriolanus* aloud to entertain her, in full voice with all dramatic emphasis, making her laugh. *"Thus we debase the nature of our seats!"* he declaimed, *"and make the rabble call our cares fears..."*

They fell asleep in one another's arms, lulled by the rustling of the waves below their window. In the morning they were awakened by the cries of the gulls.

They moved on to Tenby. On Saturday, Barbara Smith arrived to visit. She'd become increasingly active on "the woman question." That winter she'd persuaded Marian to sign a petition to Parliament demanding that married women be granted the right to own their own property. Despite Marian's worries about the radical emancipation of women, that it would come too fast and interfere with their roles as mothers, as keepers of their families, the laws on property rights were so unjust that she'd had no trouble joining Barbara's petition.

Barbara had written she wanted to discuss something important with her. Marian guessed it was something about John Chapman. While Marian and George were in Germany, Chapman had fixed his new attentions on Barbara. He proclaimed that he was in love with her. He wanted to set up a household with her, and have children. Chapman was sure her father, Ben Smith, would approve—after all, he hadn't been married to her mother. When Barbara told Marian, she'd snorted with disgust. Barbara had been one of the few people she'd confided in about her own relationship with Chapman, and she'd been appalled to hear that someone as strong and confident as Barbara had given in to him.

Barbara's father, Ben Smith, was outraged too, by Chapman's proposal; if she wanted to live in an unmarried state with a man, he said, she should go to America! It may be all right for a man to live this way, but not a woman. (He apparently didn't mention his own relationship with Barbara's mother.) Anyway, he said, Chapman was an irresponsible lout, just after her money. Barbara tore herself away from him, and he was devastated.

When Barbara arrived in Tenby, Marian noticed at once that she wasn't her usual ebullient self. But she was so glad to have her there. Barbara loved George now, and he her, and to share her love of him with someone else warmed Marian's heart.

They set out at once for the beach. Barbara settled herself with her easel and paints while she and George searched for specimens.

At noon, the inexhaustible George was still out on the far stretches of the sand hunting. Marian and Barbara walked along the shoreline, dipping their toes in the oncoming tide, watching the clear water spread over them. Barbara was silent and preoccupied. Marian said, "You must be very happy after Ruskin's praise."

Ruskin had seen Barbara's painting of a cornfield after a storm and called her one of the preeminent female artists of the times.

"I'm happy about it," Barbara said, without smiling.

"Dear heart, you're troubled, aren't you?" Marian said. "It's him, isn't it?"

Barbara didn't answer but continued looking down, frowning. "I can't give him up. I made my decision. And yet—I miss him. I—I love him. I keep wondering if I did the right thing. He kept describing you and George as an example of a love relationship without legal bonds—"

"An example!" cried Marian. "There is no parallel whatsoever between him and George. Whatsoever. That is insulting. George is a different man entirely. How dare he!" She stopped walking and turned to Barbara. "And by the way, he told *me* that George was a scoundrel and would surely leave me too."

Barbara shook her head. "I know. But...I can't help thinking...that I've given up something important....He's the only man I've ever met who believes as strongly in the things I believe in as I do, in the cause of women..."

"Important!" Marian said. "Oh, he is so awful."

Barbara said, "He's very worried about my health. He knows a great deal about women's health. He says he trained as a doctor and he insists the act of love would be beneficial...for my 'irregularities'..."

"Perhaps," Marian said grimly. "But not with him."

Barbara went on. "But do you mind if I ask? The act of love, 'the Master Passion,' if you will, it completely terrifies me." Her face was anguished.

"When there's true love," Marian said gently, "then it's a very different thing."

"You...and George..., is it as bad as I've heard?"

Marian clasped her hand and smiled. "No. It's beautiful because he's the kindest, most considerate of men." She gazed fondly at George's figure in the distance, swooping down over his specimens and sweeping them up into his net.

"Will you have children?" Barbara asked.

Marian felt the sorrow move over her. "We've discussed it. We don't want to bring an illegitimate child into the world. And George is already taking care of Agnes's children that aren't even his, and given them his name. I'm helping him provide for them. We both feel strongly that we must do that."

"That's so good of you."

"It isn't good of me. I love him—and his sons." She smiled, saying the names aloud, "Charley, Thornie, Bertie. I haven't met them yet but I already love them because they're his. He's sent them away to school in Switzerland to get away from Bedford Place and all the chaos there. As for the others, I agree with him. You can't let an innocent child suffer just because he was born by an accident that had nothing to do with him. And I'm thirty-six now anyway. There are ways to stop it, you know. Or you should know if you don't."

"I do know, I think. Do George's children know about you?"

"Not yet. But we hope, one day." She gripped Barbara's arms. "Don't punish yourself for giving up Chapman. He's relentless, but he's incapable of true love and commitment."

"But I feel he did love me. *Does* love me."

"I'm sure he *thinks* he does."

They walked along together. In the distance, George looked up, saw them, and waved. Then he began striding toward them. They waited. "Look!" he cried, when he'd caught up with them. "I got an *Aeolis* too!"

For the remainder of her stay, Barbara continued her painting, quietly concentrating on her work. Marian could feel her turning over the question of Chapman in her mind as she worked. But they didn't discuss him anymore.

———————

As Marian helped George collect his specimens, the idea for a story began to take form in her mind. Again, she saw images from her childhood, of the Chilvers Coton church, and of the Reverend Gwyther, and she remembered all the stories she'd heard about him. There'd be a young curate—"Amos Barton," she'd call him, with a sweet wife, "Milly." The church is poor. The Reverend Amos invites a rich countess to live with them, hoping she'll give money to it. But people think wrongly that she's Amos's mistress...

The window of their bedroom faced east. The early sun woke her. The room was flooded with white light, the curtain swaying softly in the morning breeze. She felt as if she were floating on the bed. From outside came the sound of the ineluctable back and forth of the waves, the cry of the gulls. George lay with his back to her, breathing steadily in his sleep, his thin, narrow shoulders naked, his dark hair on the pillow, his body warm with the pulse of his life. He liked to fall asleep as close to her as possible, then, in the night, he would turn away.

Looking at him, she thought, one day he wouldn't be there, to warm her when she was cold, his flesh solid and moist next to her. Then her life would be at an end too. There was no eternity, not of love, nor of the body. She had nothing of her own, except him. No reason to live should he ever leave her. She edged toward him and kissed his shoulder.

He woke up, turned over, smiled lazily and drew her to him.

"Darling?" she whispered. "What do you think of this for a title for a story? 'The Sad Fortunes of the Reverend Amos Barton.'"

He rose up on his elbow. "That's a capital title!"

She lay back. "I'm afraid."

He sat up excitedly, his bony chest covered with wiry hairs, his arms thin but strong, trying to seize her enthusiasm before it faded. "Think of it this way," he said. "It might be a failure, but it might also be a chef d'oeuvre!"

"A chef-d'oeuvre! I don't think there's much worry about that."

"You *can't* write a bad novel—you've got wit, description, philosophy. And those go a long way. Though you may lack the most important thing, drama. Try it as an experiment."

Then they rose into the glorious white morning, and breakfasted. Soon they were heading down Bridge Street to the South Sands, with their nets and their bottles and the hamper.

———————

That autumn, in London, she wrote the words *"Chapter I."* Then, *"Shepperton Church was a very different-looking building five-and-twenty years ago..."* Mrs. Hackit and the town doctor, Mr. Pilgrim, and some neighbors, are having tea and complaining about the Reverend Amos. *"'Rather a low-bred fellow, I think, Barton,' said Mr. Pilgrim."* *"(Reason to hate him: Reverend Amos had called in a new doctor who'd cured a patient of Mr. Pilgrim's.)"*

In the late afternoon, when George came home, she said, "Can I read you something?"

"I'd be delighted." He hung up his things and settled himself in the armchair.

"All right," she began, and read him the scene of Mrs. Hackit in the farmhouse.

"Yes?" she asked, when she'd finished

"You've got the very things I was doubtful about. You can write dialogue. But what happens next?"

"His parish is poor. He invites this countess to live with his family. He has a sweet wife but she takes ill." She tapered off, losing confidence.

She must have looked disappointed for he quickly interjected, "I no longer have any doubt about your ability to carry it out. Oh, Polly," he said, "just keep going. Please! You have it in you."

After a week, she'd come to the end of the story. Once again, she sat him down and read to him—her voice thin, her words rushed with nervousness—the scene of Milly's death. *"Amos drew her towards him and pressed her head gently to him, while Milly beckoned Fred and Sophy..."*

She looked up for his reaction. He was wiping tears from his eyes with his fist. She kept going. *"They watched her breathing becoming more and more difficult, until evening deepened into night, and until midnight was past. About half-past twelve she seemed to be trying to speak, and they leaned to catch her words.*

"'Music—music—didn't you hear it?'"

Her own eyes flooded with tears now. George kissed her. "I think your pathos is better than your fun," he said.

And so it began. George wrote to his publisher, John Blackwood, in Edinburgh, enclosing a story written, he said, by a very shy friend whom he couldn't name. Would Blackwood be interested in publishing it in his magazine?

A few days later came Blackwood's response. "Amos Barton" *"is unquestionably very pleasant reading,"* he wrote. However, he said, he'd have to see more of this unnamed writer's stories before he published anything. And he did worry that there wasn't enough action.

When George read Blackwood's letter back to her, she collapsed in disappointment. George wrote again to Blackwood defending her story, and Blackwood relented. *"I have so high an opinion of this first Tale,"* he wrote, *"that I will waive my objections."*

When George showed Marian the letter, she jumped up and down and clapped her hands.

In January, there it was in the magazine, her own words, in the ineradicable medium of print. Without her name on the story, of course, as was usual. A secret. That was the way it was done. But it had begun.

Chapter 13

All because of him. Without him there would have been nothing. He cosseted her, comforted her, shielded her, warning Blackwood that his anonymous writer friend was *"unusually sensitive"* and of a *"shy, shrinking, and ambitious nature."*

"He is so easily discouraged," warned George. Yet more stories followed: "Mr. Gilfil's Love-Story," a love triangle set against the backdrop of Cheverel Manor, based on Arbury Hall; and "Janet's Repentance," about an alcoholic lawyer who dreadfully abuses his wife, in a town similar to Nuneaton. Blackwood collected them all in one volume under the title *Scenes of Clerical Life.*

"I want it printed under a pseudonym," she insisted to George. "I can't bear to have my real name used. I can't bear the scrutiny."

"Probably it must be a man's name," he said. "If the critics know it's a woman it'll never be taken seriously."

"Yes," she said. "'George,'" she said, smiling mischievously. "I will be 'George'!"

"'George'?" he repeated.

"Yes. 'George.'"

"I'm very honored," he said, with a laugh. "But not 'George Lewes.' I can't take credit for your work."

"What about 'Eliot.' 'George Eliot'?" she said. "A nice, simple name, easy to say."

"Madame George Eliot, then," he said, bowing to her.

The publication date for *Scenes of Clerical Life* was January 8, 1858. A few days later, George came bounding up the stairs, tripping in his eagerness. "I've got some very pretty news for you." He reached into his coat and drew out a copy of the *Times*.

"Read it!" he commanded. He stood smiling, watching her. *"...a sobriety which is shown to be compatible with strength, clear and simple descriptions and a combination of humour with pathos in depicting ordinary situations..."* It was a review of her book.

She stood there limply. "Oh, God." And then, falteringly, "Maybe this means I can go on."

"Bollocks! It means you have no choice."

———

Blackwood had sent presentation copies of the book to prominent people. Charles Dickens wrote complimenting the author on his "marvels of description," but he swore that no man could have written it.

Blackwood was beginning to wonder who his author really was. One Sunday he was visiting London from Edinburgh, and he came to supper to discuss with George the business of "George Eliot's" publication.

Blackwood was about forty, with light, Celtic skin, thin lips, a twinkle in his eye, and a broad, Scottish accent. George, of course, introduced him to "Mrs. Lewes." As always, she attempted to stay in the background, not wanting to be noticed.

"Will I ever meet the real George Eliot?" Blackwood asked.

George looked at her. "Would you excuse us a moment?" he said. Blackwood nodded.

She left the room and George followed her into the hallway.

"Should I?" said George.

"Yes," she said, fearfully.

They reentered the parlor where Blackwood stood waiting.

"May I introduce George Eliot?" George said.

"My goodness!" Blackwood cried, with a broad smile. "I am delighted."

After a moment of laughter, in which he shook her hand vigorously at finally getting to meet his author, Blackwood said, "But I think we should keep the nom de plume. I like the mystery of it. It will spur sales." And so it was decided.

———

Always, George propped her up. He cut bad reviews out of the newspapers and handed them to her with holes in them. He even kept good reviews from her if they referred back to a negative one.

Success emboldened her, gave her courage. That May, she forced herself finally to tell Isaac that she was now living with George. *"I have changed my name,"* she wrote, *"and have someone to take care of me in the world."*

A week passed. Silence. Then, a letter from Mr. Holbeche, the solicitor: her brother, Isaac, was so *"hurt at your not having previously made some communication to him as to your intention and prospects that he cannot make up his mind to write."* When and where was she married? Isaac wanted to know. She could only write back the truth. *"Our marriage is not a legal one, though it is regarded by us both as a sacred bond. He is unable at present to contract a legal marriage..."* Within days came a letter from Chrissey saying that Isaac had forbidden her ever to speak to Marian again.

Holding the letter in her hand, she saw Isaac in her mind's eye, tight-lipped, vengeful, cold, once the bright little boy she'd adored beyond anyone in the world. He'd cut her off as if her love for him was meaningless, as if he'd never felt the warmth of her little arms around his neck, or heard her calling after him, "Wait for me, Isaac!"

She didn't understand. Was Chrissey right that he was punishing her simply because he was jealous of her intelligence, for being independent of him?

His anger had gone to that part of her that would always be within her, forged in her childhood: the gossipy ways of the little country town in which she'd been raised, its strict etiquettes of love and courtship, the shame of a woman unable to resist her sexuality and who succumbs to it out of wedlock. It was as if she were naked now, for all the world to see.

She remembered that terrible story Aunt Elizabeth, her father's sister, who was a Methodist minister, had once told her. Aunt Elizabeth worked in a prison where she met a young woman who'd given birth to a baby out of wedlock, and then in shame and terror had abandoned it. The woman realized what she'd done and she ran back to save it, but by then the baby was dead. She was accused of murder and sentenced to be hanged. Aunt Elizabeth had prayed with her for forgiveness and accompanied her to the scaffold.

She told George the story. "Do you think I might make a novel out of it?" she asked.

"I think that's a grand idea," he said.

"You always say that about everything I do!"

He took her in his arms. "I cannot help it if I live with genius," he said.

It would be a country story, filled with the scent of hay and the sweet breath of cows. She created a character, Adam Bede—like her father, tall and strong, a carpenter, a moral man. Adam falls in love with Hetty Sorel, but Hetty is in love with the local aristocrat, Arthur Donnithorne.

As she composed the story, she tried to remember everything about the minutiae of country life. When, exactly, did the foxgloves bloom? She looked it up—July 3. And when was the hay harvested? July 13.

Blackwood kept asking what she was writing, but she refused to tell him. "I can't bear him to say anything negative," she told George. "I'll be so disheartened I won't be able to go on."

She read parts of it aloud to George. "Adam's too passive," he said. So she wrote a scene where Adam gets into a fistfight with Squire Donnithorne in the woods.

Hetty becomes pregnant with Donnithorne's child. She has the baby, but, as in Aunt Elizabeth's story, she abandons it. She hears its cries and she too runs back to save it, but it's too late. She's tried for murder and comforted by the exquisite lay preacher, Dinah.

When *Adam Bede* was published, the *Times* wrote that the author *"takes rank at once among the masters."* The book sold ten thousand copies in one year; it was printed in America and translated into German, Dutch, Hungarian, French, and Russian. None other than Leo Tolstoy called it the *"highest art flowing from the love of God and man."* Rumor had it that Queen Victoria loved the novel so much she read it aloud to Prince Albert in bed at night.

But along with success must there always come some punishment? Only a month after *Adam Bede* was published, Chrissey wrote that she was ill with consumption. It had now been two years since she'd heard a word from Chrissey, on Isaac's orders. *"How very sorry I have been,"* Chrissey wrote, *"that I ceased to write and neglected one who, under all circumstances, was kind to me..."* Chrissey had lost two more of her children, Fanny from typhus, and Robert, making his way to Australia to find work, had drowned at sea.

Of course, she wrote back to Chrissey saying she still loved her and had forgiven her for everything.

A few days later Chrissey's daughter, Emily, wrote to say that her mother had died. Isaac had taken Chrissey from Marian long ago, but still she mourned. Gone was the sweet sister of her youth, her big sister, who had comforted her when she was a cold and frightened little girl at Miss Lathom's.

———

Because of *Adam Bede*, for the first time in their lives they had money. They leased a house of their own, Holly Lodge in South Fields. They bought new linens, crockery, and carpets from a wholesale store on Watling Street. The house was yellow brick, three stories tall, and airy, with bay windows, though it was semidetached, surrounded by other houses. There was only a low hedge of laurel and holly between it and the road. But she and George could each have a study now.

Few visitors came, and rarely any women because of their unmarried state. Marian wasn't sorry. She'd have preferred excommunication to having to sit through visits with frivolous women. Of course Barbara Smith came, but Barbara wasn't afraid of anything.

A miracle had occurred for Barbara. After she had visited them that summer in Tenby three years before and confessed her torment over John Chapman, her father, Ben Smith, had whisked her and her sisters away to Algiers to get her out of Chapman's reach. There, Barbara had met a French-Algerian doctor, Eugène Bodichon, and she, who had so loved *The Arabian Nights,* had fallen in love with the tall, dark-skinned man. The doctor proposed. Barbara eagerly accepted. Again, her father had protested the marriage, worried that the doctor was another fortune hunter. Barbara insisted that she was going to marry him anyway—she was over twenty-one now, twenty-seven in fact, and her father couldn't prevent the marriage. Ben Smith set up a trust protecting her money from the doctor and reluctantly gave the marriage his blessing.

They had a small wedding in London. One summer evening, after the wedding, Barbara had brought Eugène to meet Marian and George. The doctor was exotic-looking, with thick black hair, but his English was poor. During supper, Barbara, her cheeks flushed, had mostly talked for him, about his work treating the indigenous people of Algiers, about his book on how the French settlers were vulnerable to native diseases. All the while, the doctor had gazed at her with a smile on his face, watching her, but, Marian felt, anxious to be elsewhere. "Eugène says he can't bear to live in London," Barbara said, "so we've reached a compromise. We'll live in Algiers in winter, where I'll have a studio and paint, but we'll spend our summers here in London because of the heat."

After supper, they had taken a moonlight cruise on the Thames to Twickenham, and all the while, Barbara, who was tall herself, never took her eyes off Eugène. It was clear that she had succumbed at last to "the Master Passion."

Now, two years later, Barbara, off for her annual winter sojourn in Algiers, had come to Holly Lodge to say good-bye to Marian.

"This is an improvement over your old rooms in Richmond," Barbara said. "You used to complain you could hear each other's pens scratching when you worked."

"But the houses are so close together," Marian said, "and the windows are so big. I feel as if everyone can see into our lives here. They know everything about us."

Barbara intuited what she meant. "What if George tried to obtain a divorce on the Continent?" she asked, no doubt in the excitement of her own marriage and wishing the same for Marian. "Perhaps it would be legal in England. Then the problem would be solved."

Later, after Barbara had gone, Marian told George of Barbara's suggestion. "I'll get on it at once in the morning," he said. "I'll speak to the solicitor."

But when he came in the next afternoon, his face was downcast. "I'm so sorry, my darling."

"He said no!" she cried.

"Yes," he said, taking her hands. "He says there is no such thing as an international treaty about divorce. Wherever we might get one on the Continent, it wouldn't apply here."

She turned away angrily. "What does it matter?" she said. "We're more married than most people who were wed in a church."

He caught her wrist and spun her around. "And nothing," he said, fiercely and finally, "and no one, can ever rend us asunder."

———

Another of their visitors at Holly Lodge was Herbert Spencer. George loved Spencer, that brilliant, eccentric fellow. And what did she care anyway about the hurt Spencer had inflicted on her, she who was so bathed now in George's love? She had told George of the episode—she kept nothing from him. "If it hadn't been for him bringing you to the Princess that night," George said, "we wouldn't be together. That was the first time we really spoke." Spencer was such a sad, aggrieved person these days, he felt his genius was unrecognized. He was writing his autobiography, though he was a very young man still. She couldn't stay angry at the odd soul who simply lacked the human capacity for love. They asked him to dinner and he was grateful, though apparently totally unaware of the pain he'd once caused her.

———

Ever since the publication of *Adam Bede*, the public's curiosity to know the real George Eliot had intensified. Someone from Coventry said that Isaac had recognized their father in the character of Adam. And there was a madman from Nuneaton, one Joseph Liggins, who was going around insisting that *he* was actually George Eliot, and the author of both *Scenes of Clerical Life* and *Adam Bede.*

It was impossible to keep the secret up any longer. They began to tell friends that George Eliot was none other than Marian Evans, a country girl from Warwickshire who had educated herself to become one of the most famous authors in the land, and soon the word spread. But they decided she would retain the pseudonym "George Eliot" on future books, as that was the name on her first great success.

———

It had been two years now since Isaac had cut her out of his life. Sometimes the hurt and anger faded, and then it arose again without warning. How could Isaac keep away from her this long? He had inherited their father's terrible capacity for anger, the ability to separate himself from what he loved out of the principles ingrained in him by his little country world. And Chrissey was gone now. There was no one now whom she could call brother or sister, she had no real family.

She sat in the conservatory window at Holly Lodge in the bleak, winter silence, looking out, thinking about him. Before her was a wide view, it was almost countryside, not quite, all the way to Wimbledon. The leaves had gone from the trees, there was only the brown grass, the cold that she so hated. George was in his study, working on a series of essays he was calling *The Physiology of Common Life.* They were descriptions of the nervous, digestive, and respiratory systems of different species. He wanted it to be clearly written for the common reader, but also of interest to scientists.

As she sat there staring out the window of the conservatory, she began to imagine a woman such as herself sitting
in a window, thinking about the past.

She turned to her little table, and wrote the words
*"I have been pressing my elbows on the arms of my chair and
dreaming that I was standing on the bridge in front of—"* She
saw in her mind's eye the little mill at Arbury, the turning wheel, jets of water spurting out of it. *"Dorlcote Mill,"*
she'd call it. A girl was standing there. *"That little girl was
watching too,"* she wrote. But it was no small stream, as it
had been at Arbury, it was a mighty river, the River Floss,
she'd call it.

The little girl was Maggie Tulliver. She has a brother,
Tom, whom she adores. Like Isaac, Tom has "cheeks of
cream and roses." Tom is bossy and they squabble, as all
brothers and sisters do. Maggie is keenly intelligent, but
she can only go to school for a year because it's her job to
take care of their elderly father. Tom, however, gets a good
education and succeeds in business.

As always the writing, the process of creating a story
from the recesses of her mind, from her fragile memories,
went slowly.

George came in with the post. "Something from Barbara," he said. "I thought you'd want to see it." She had told
no one but George what she was writing, but Barbara knew
she was struggling with a new book. Barbara had written a
little note of encouragement to her, and enclosed a drawing
of Parizade, the princess from *The Arabian Nights*, Parizade,
who demanded to be educated like her brothers, to be
allowed to hunt like them. Barbara had evoked their mutual
love of *The Arabian Nights* to cheer her up.

Marian hung the drawing up above her desk for inspiration, and wrote to thank her. *"Parizade has a mysterious resemblance to the heroine of the book I am writing,"* she told her.

She went on with her work. There would be aunts in the novel, her mother's sisters, the Pearsons. She made Aunt Mary into Aunt Glegg, a sarcastic old bat, whom the children hate; Aunt Elizabeth became the weepy, valetudinarian Aunt Pullet; and Aunt Ann, thin, sallow, and rich, was Aunt Deane. Sweet revenge.

Young Maggie is attracted to wealthy Stephen Guest. They spend the night on a boat on the River Floss—but they do nothing wrong. Tom learns about it and disowns her, just as Isaac had disowned Marian.

At the end of the book, the river floods, swelling into an immense tide, moaning in restless sorrow like an angry god. Brother and sister are reconciled, but they drown together, locked in an unbroken embrace.

On the morning of March 21, she finished. In her journal she wrote, *"Magnificat anima mea!"*—"My soul doth magnify the Lord," from the Evening Prayer.

"George Eliot is as great as ever," wrote the *London Times* reviewer. *The Mill on the Floss* earned her twice as much as *Adam Bede.*

———————

Three days after she finished the book, they set out for the Continent. "It's time for you to know the boys," George said. He had sent his sons to the Hofwyl School in Berne to get them away from the chaos in Agnes's house. It was an idealistic place, with rich and poor pupils alike, in which they learned their lessons through farming, but George missed his boys sorely.

They were teenagers now, and he had explained the situation with Marian to them. He'd begun to mention Marian in his letters, and then gradually to refer to her as "Mother"—Agnes was always, respectfully, "Mama." It was decided that Marian should begin to write to them herself. She sent them little gifts: for Charley, the eldest, who was sixteen, a watch, and for Thornie, the middle boy, who was fourteen, a copy of *Adam Bede*. To Bertie, the youngest, at eleven, she sent a pocketknife with a corkscrew. She suggested to George that she sign her letters to them *Mutter*. "Perfect," George said. "It acknowledges that you are not quite their real mother, but you *are* a mother to them."

They wrote back to thank her for their gifts, charmingly. Charley signed his letter *"Yours affectionately, Charles Lewes."* Thornie began, *"For the first time do I seize the pen to begin a correspondence which is to be lasting which affords me much pleasure."* Little Bertie wrote poignantly, *"I long to come back to England again, it is 3 yearys that I have not seen England."* "Poor little fellow," George had said. "He was very ill as a child and I'm afraid he's a bit 'slow.'"

"Thornie's most like me," George told her. "He's a devil, very high-spirited, I'm afraid. I hope he won't be too much for you." And indeed, soon Thornie was revealing his true colors, entreating her in his letters to persuade his father, *"Schnurrbarttragende alte"* (whiskery old man), as he called him, to increase his allowance.

Now she was finally going to meet them. They traveled through Italy toward Switzerland. In Florence, George was reading the guidebook when he said, "You should write a novel about Savonarola."

The idea caught her—here was a chance to confront the evil of absolute morality, the pain it caused, what it had done to her, as manifested in the cruel rigidities of the country life of her childhood, in Isaac's pitiless judgment. "We'll research it together," he said.

The next morning they set out through the hot, narrow streets of Florence for the San Marco monastery, where Savonarola had lived. At the door, a monk, dressed in a cloak and hood, slightly bent over, stood guard. Seeing her, he addressed George, "I am sorry, Signor, but women are not allowed inside."

"As if there's anything going on under those skirts of his," George whispered.

"Not to worry," she told him. "I'll wait here." So she stayed in the outer cloister studying Fra Angelico's *Crucifixion* while George went inside and made notes for her on what he saw. *"From the refectory a spiral staircase leads to (room)...Savonarola's cell 5 paces long 4 broad..."* Then they went to the Magliabecchian Library, where they saw Savonarola's manuscripts, written in his tiny handwriting. But they could remain in Florence only a few days because they had to go on to Switzerland to see the boys. As they left, she said to George, "I have all these facts, but what is my story?"

"You will find it," he said, with certainty.

They arrived in Berne, and in the morning George hurried to the Hofwyl School to fetch his sons. She waited in the hotel lobby. What would they think of her? Would they dislike her because their first loyalty was to their real mother, Agnes? What did one say to teenaged boys?

When they entered the hotel, George led the way, followed by the three of them in descending order, Charley solemn and round-faced, Thornie with a quicker, bouncing stride, little Bertie lagging shyly behind.

"This is *Mutter*," Charley said, formally introducing them one by one. Each politely shook her hand.

Immediately, as she gazed upon them, she felt love surge through her. They were *his* flesh. She could see *him* in them, in Charley's dark eyes, in the shape of Thornton's face with his high cheekbones, in Bertie's full mouth. They had come from *him*.

"Perhaps we should show *Mutter* the school," George suggested.

The school occupied a group of structures built on a hillside in the shadow of the Alps.

"This is the classroom," Charley said in a most grown-up way. "In the summer we work mostly on the farm and have only one hour of class each day."

Thornie poked his brother. "Oh, Charley, this is so boring!" he said. "Let's go to the museum. I want to show her my stuffed birds."

Charley poked him back, annoyed, and soon they were jostling each other and it was becoming a shoving match. "Stop now, this minute!" George commanded. "Let's show *Mutter* our best selves." He added apologetically, "We call Thornie 'Caliban.'"

They followed Thornie to the school's museum, which was filled with specimens of plants and animals. "Those are my birds," Thornie said. "See, I stuffed them myself! It's my desire to be a naturalist."

Little Bertie said nothing, and as they stood there, Marian put her arm protectively around his narrow shoulders, and he let it rest there.

In the afternoon, like proper parents, she and George had tea with the headmaster Dr. Müller and his wife, to discuss the boys' future.

Charley was seventeen now. It was time for him to leave school and take up a profession. They would bring him back to London with them. Thornie wasn't a very good pupil at all, and could use additional instruction, would follow soon to London. Little Bertie was very slow indeed, and he would stay behind for now.

At home in London, away from the teasing influence of Thornie, Charley was sweet and solemn and carefully behaved, as if he were afraid they would send him back to Switzerland. He was so polite and grown up, trying not to disturb them when they worked. In the evenings, she and Charley played duets on the piano, and sometimes chess. Charley was one of those beings to whom goodness comes naturally, she thought. She was becoming a mother.

A month later, rambunctious Thornie followed. They needed a larger home to accommodate them all, and they found a house in Blandford Square. It was near the Smith mansion, though Barbara spent the cold months in Algiers with Eugène.

Marian was up to her ears in "Boydom" now. But she didn't mind.

The boys needed a profession. George knew Anthony Trollope, a stout, big-bearded, hearty soul, who worked at the Post Office, writing on trains as he traveled around the country as an inspector. George asked if he could help Charley find a position at the Post Office, and Trollope readily agreed. But Charley had to pass the civil service exam first.

His spelling and grammar were rather weak as a result of all his years in a Swiss school.

George and Marian tutored him every day, dictating aloud to him so he could perfect his English. He earned the top score in the exam and got a job as supplementary clerk, second class. Eighty pounds a year!

Dear Thornie was another matter. His desired career as a naturalist seemed impractical, given that he wasn't a very good student. There were jobs opening up now in the colonies, and George decided that the East Indian Civil Service would provide an opportunity for him. The civil service exam for India was very competitive, and it would take a year to prepare for it. It was decided that he would do his preparation at the Edinburgh High School, where George knew the headmaster, Dr. Schmitz.

Immediately upon hearing he was to go to Edinburgh, Thornie imagined his adventures there, "kicking up rows. Perhaps I'll run away to Sicily and make a glorious name as a fighter with Garibaldi." Dr. Schmitz announced that he didn't want the boy staying in his house, as he had two daughters. He was to board instead in the house of the classics master, Mr. Robinson.

———————

Marian, forty-one years old, was for the first time be a mother. The boys were teenagers, and it was different entirely, of course, from caring for a young child. But with Charley, especially, who lived with them, the love had been kindled within her. She called him "our son." She was so grateful that he accepted her, and, she felt, he loved her too. Perhaps he'd missed proper mothering, having spent so much time away from his own mother, who was no doubt preoccupied with her hordes of babies. What would it be like to have a baby now? To be older and suddenly have a child?

She imagined a man, her own age, suddenly having to care for a child. She remembered riding in the gig with her father and seeing that grim, stooped-over weaver walking on the side of the road, the boys taunting him while he ignored them. The sight had always stayed with her.

What if the man was, say, a member of a religious sect who'd been wrongly accused of a crime? Perhaps stealing funds from his congregation? He's engaged to marry but the woman rejects him. He's driven out of his sect, and settles in a little country village. There, he lives a lonely life, hoarding his money. Until...until, one winter night, in the middle of a snowstorm, a golden-haired child wanders out of the cold into his cottage. Instinctively, he knows what to do, feeds her some of his porridge, warms her by the fire, takes off her wet boots.

Silas Marner was the easiest of all her books to write. Before it was even published Blackwood had subscriptions for 5,500 copies.

———

They had developed a habit of fleeing England for the Continent now at the end of each book, to avoid the reviews, the possibility of poor sales. The Italian book was still brewing within her; they would go to Florence to do more research.

As soon as they reached the city, she came down with fever and headache. She lay in bed in the hotel room alternately burning up and freezing. George had a fire made but it did no good. He lifted her from the bed and took her in

his arms. "Here, dance. Dance with me, that'll warm you up."
And he held her whole weight and frantically tried to move
her about the room with him, but she couldn't stand up long
enough to dance. He laid her back on the bed and covered her
with yet more blankets. "A bit better now," she said.

He rubbed her arms through the blankets. "Sometimes I
think my principal task in life is to keep you warm," he said.

At length she recovered and resumed her research.
She studied ancient manuscripts, made notes on medieval
clothing, streetlights, barbers, observed a silk weaver.
George made pencil sketches of costumes the characters
would wear. She pored through Tuscan proverbs — what
was a *sajo*, the Tuscan tunic, like? How was the *scarella*, a
purse, worn?

"A romance can't be written from an encyclopedia,"
George warned. And he was right. She had no story. She
took to calling her notebooks her "quarries." "Perhaps if I
dig hard enough I'll come up with a diamond," she said.

They returned to England and she kept up her research,
reading biographies of Savonarola, histories of monastic
orders. But there was still no story. She had never felt so
depressed. She would never be able to write another novel.
To try to allay her depression, George took her for brisk
walks in Regent's Park to the Zoological Gardens; as they
walked they discussed the book.

There came a new crisis, a letter from Thornie saying
that one night he came home from the theater late, and Mr.
Robinson had locked him out of his room. *"I did what you
would have done in my place,"* he wrote to George, *"knocked
him down."* The landlord wanted to throw him out. Dr.
Schmitz intervened and somehow he was allowed to stay.

But Thornie did poorly in his exam, took it again, and failed. So he announced that he was going to Poland to join the guerrillas and fight the Russians. Barbara Bodichon came to the rescue. "I have friends in Natal," she told Thornie. "You know, they have big game hunting there? I will write to them for you." He agreed to go and they sent him off with a rifle and revolver and letters of recommendation from Barbara.

It was sweet Bertie's turn to leave Hofwyl. He was not the sort to be able to pass the civil service exam, and it was agreed that the best thing for him was to learn farming in Scotland for a while. Eventually, they would send him off to Natal to join his brother and perhaps farm there.

Depression dogged her, the inability to write her Italian novel. Then, one winter day in Regent's Park, in the Zoological Gardens, no snow on the ground yet, just gray and brown everywhere, the pathways deserted, it came to her. "I think I've found my character!" she told George. "I'll call her Romola, and I'll make her look like Barbara, tall and forceful, with wonderful red-gold hair." Romola would be the daughter of a blind scholar. She would fall in love with an ambitious philanderer, Tito—the whole story would be set against the background of Savonarola's fanaticism.

Romola, she thought, was her best novel—simply because it had been the hardest to write. *"I feel as if it was written in my blood,"* she said. *"I've finished it an old woman."* The publisher commissioned the artist Frederic Leighton to do illustrations for the book. The *Spectator* called it her *"greatest work."* Queen Victoria gave it to Disraeli as a present.

They were rich. It was a new, miraculous state. Would they wake up one morning and find themselves poor again?

They sent Agnes £250 a year now for her expenses, including her children with Thornton. With Agnes and his actual wife, Kate, Thornton Hunt had now fathered fourteen children. But he was always broke and hardly gave Agnes a penny.

They were able to acquire the forty-nine-year lease on the Priory at 21 North Bank. It was a fine house, with stained-glass windows up to the ceiling, a rose garden leading down to the Regent's Canal, and, importantly, a red-brick wall surrounding it for privacy. They hired Owen Jones, who'd designed the interiors for the Crystal Palace, to decorate it.

"We're going to have to gut the place," Jones said, "and throw out your old furniture."

"But we can't afford that," George objected.

"I promise, it will be a house fit for a great author," Jones said, and they let him go ahead. He created a double reception room, with dark paneling, crimson drapes, and deep velvet chairs. He hung the originals of Leighton's drawings for *Romola* on the walls. She allowed Sir Frederic Burton to do a chalk drawing of her. He softened everything about her with a pinkish glow. George was enchanted by it, and had it hung over the mantel in his study. To cap it all, they purchased a magnificent new Broadwood piano made of gleaming burred walnut, with great hexagonal legs with roses carved on them. It was like a throne to sit at.

They held a double party to celebrate, a housewarming and Charley's twenty-first birthday party. "Mrs. Lewes, may I suggest—away with the black!" Jones said. "You must have a new dress for the party." So she bought a dress of antique, moiré gray silk for the occasion.

It was a grand affair. Spencer came, and Trollope, his deep bellowing laugh audible all the way across the room. Leopold Jansa of the Beethoven Violin Quartet gave a violin recital, and Marian accompanied him on the piano. Then, "Happy Birthday dear Charley" rang out through the house.

After everyone had gone, she sank down exhausted in her reclining chair. "I am so happy. I'm afraid the gods will envy me."

George, sitting opposite her with his Scotch, could only laugh. "There *are* no gods, my darling."

They began holding regular "at-homes" in the new house, every Sunday afternoon from two to six. She'd sit in the low chair by the fire, wearing her black satin gown—he still couldn't break her habit of black entirely—the green-shaded lamp shedding a soft light on her face, a wall of books stacked on the table as if to protect her. George would lead the guests up to her, one by one. They'd sit on the footstool at her feet. From across the room he'd keep an eye on them, and when someone was taking up too much of her time, he'd hurry over and whisk him away. Some people, she knew, thought she was haughty. But it was caution, fear.

Still, mostly men came to the house, rarely women because of their unmarried state. There were lots of bachelors, seeking her wisdom as if she were a priestess, young men struggling with ideas, eager to learn from her, drawn by the famous intellect. She was in her forties now. Perhaps she was like a mother to them. She encouraged them, listened to them, held them captive with their worship of her.

All these young men, they could never hurt her. She could experience the world of men without heartbreak.

One July Sunday, a dapper little man with a beguiling smile and yellow gloves was brought out of the dimness to meet her. His name was Emanuel Deutsch.

"Your article was glorious," she told him. She had asked to see him. He was a Silesian Jew, a lowly assistant in the British Museum who had just published an article in the *Quarterly Review* on the Talmud and its similarities to the Christian Bible. In the Talmud, he wrote, could be found the foundations of all Christianity, the notions of a Messiah, of redemption, regeneration, and turning away from sin. He wrote about the rise of Jewish nationalism at the time of the Babylonian captivity and the Jewish longing for a homeland. Until Deutsch's article, for the most part, non-Jews had been ignorant of the Talmud, but Deutsch had revealed it to them. Although Marian had long given up on formal religion, the question of religion and faith still preoccupied her, especially the universality of belief. Deutsch was speaking to her own notions.

He smiled his sweet smile. "Praise from George Eliot means as much as anything in the world to me," he said in his German accent.

"You must speak many languages to be able to write this," she said.

"I can read Chaldaic," he said. "Sanskrit, Amharic, and the Phoenician language."

"I very much want to learn better Hebrew," she told him.

"I would be honored to be your tutor," he replied.

He began coming once a week to give her Hebrew lessons. Meanwhile, his article had become a best seller, of all things. The *Quarterly Review* had gone into no less than seven reprints. People were attacking him because they said he was belittling the Bible. The London Society for the Promotion of Christianity Among Jews called the essay "*blasphemy.*"

When Deutsch next appeared at the Priory, he was near tears. "I beseech you," Marian said, "try not to think of it. Make the effort. You've done the world an enormous service."

As they grew closer, she came to love him like a son. He told her that the greatest longing of his life was to see Jerusalem. He managed to get a commission from his employer, the British Museum, to go to Palestine to decipher some inscriptions that had been discovered there on ancient stone.

From Palestine, he wrote to her: "*The East...All my wild yearnings fulfilled at last.*"

When he returned and came to the Priory, he described to her how he'd prayed at the Western Wall of the Temple along with other Jews. As he was telling her, he broke into tears and couldn't go on. "I understand," she said, touching his shoulder. "I understand and I envy you the gift of faith."

After *Romola*, which had seemed to drain all her blood from her, she tried writing a play. It would be easier, she thought, than a novel. The characters would simply move across the stage and speak, and she wouldn't have to fill in the story with details. She called it *The Spanish Gypsy*. It was set during the Spanish Inquisition, about a Gypsy girl. She did her usual research, studied Spanish, but foundered in a swamp of misery. "Maybe I'm destined never to write anything good ever again," she told George.

All he could do was sigh and kiss her—he was used to her litany of worries and sorrow.

When she let him read it, he held the pages to his chest and said nothing.

"Tell me the truth, please," she said. "I'd rather hear it from you than others."

He sighed. "The problem is it lacks drama," he said. "I can't stand to see you suffer. I think this isn't the thing for you."

Never before had he said this, and she knew he must be right.

As she'd been struggling with it, an idea for an English story had kept intruding on her thoughts, about the events surrounding the Reform Act which had so marked her childhood. She had never forgotten riding with her father in the gig that election day when they went into Nuneaton to market and witnessed the laborers rioting.

She conceived of an idealistic young radical, Felix Holt, and an estate owner with radical ideas, Harold Transome. They fall in love with the same woman, Esther Lyon, and the story of *Felix Holt, the Radical*, went on from there.

After she finished it, she returned to her play about the Spanish Gypsy. She decided to write the whole thing in verse—poetry might free her imagination. Not so. Like everything she wrote, progress was slow and painful. It didn't sell as well as the novels, though the *Spectator* praised it as *"much the greatest poem of any wide scope and on a plan of any magnitude, which was ever proceeded from a woman."*

She'd also begun to conceive of a novel about medicine. It would be set in the provinces in a town named

Middlemarch, a fitting name for a place that was in the middle of the road. She sketched out the character of an idealistic doctor, based on Chrissey's husband, poor, wretched Edward Clarke. "Tertius Lydgate" wants to use the latest scientific research in his work, but is trapped in a marriage to pretty, grasping Rosamond Vincy. As always, she thoroughly researched the background and the setting. She ordered books on medicine, studied the details about provincial hospitals—she must have read two hundred books for that novel. She even observed an Oxford professor, Dr. George Rolleston, dissect a human brain.

Writing the new novel was, as usual, a torment, but as George reminded her, "You've felt this way about everything you've ever written. And it's always succeeded."

"Rosamond's so hard," she said. "She's all surfaces."

"Perhaps because she's so unlike you," he said.

———

Increasing numbers of people were coming to the "at homes" now—naughty George started referring to them as "Sunday Services for the People" and took to calling her "Madonna." Charles Darwin came. George had been one of the first to praise his *On the Origin of Species* in the *Cornhill Magazine*, and Darwin was grateful to him. He was a tall, stooped man, with red hair fading to gray, a seemingly deferential figure, yet filled with a kind of tension, a guilt and defensiveness, she thought, about his radical ideas. She and George had read *On the Origin of Species* together. She'd found the ideas interesting indeed, but Darwin wasn't a very good writer, and the book was quite disorganized.

They held an evening so Tennyson could read his poem "The Northern Farmer." "Wheer 'asta beän sawlong and meä liggin' 'ere aloän?" it went. Impossible to understand with that Lincolnshire dialect of his. After he finished, he read "Maud" and became so totally swept up in enthusiasm for his own words that he went on until they were all practically falling asleep, and his son, Hallam, tugged at his arm and cried, "Papa, it's after midnight!"

She was recognized now even when they were abroad. In Rome, they were getting money from a bank and the cashier looked up and said, "Aren't you the author George Eliot?"

"Oh dear," George said, "would you mind not telling any other English people that Mrs. Lewes is here? We're trying to have a peaceful holiday."

It was fortunate they didn't keep everyone away.

They were wandering through the maze in the Pamphili Gardens, following the serpentine green hedges trying to find the opening to the end, when they ran into a young woman, Zibbie Cross, on her honeymoon with her husband, Henry Bullock. George had met the Cross family two years before while he was on a walking tour in Surrey with Spencer.

The next night in Rome, Zibbie's mother, Anna, called on them at the Hotel Minerva, bringing two of her other grown children with her, her daughter Mary and her son Johnnie.

They sat in the faded lobby of the hotel with its wood-beamed ceilings and worn frescoes, a statue of Minerva in a niche, and George ordered tea for everyone. Anna Cross was a widow who'd borne ten children. She was small and plump, Mary and Johnnie Cross were both very tall. (Father Cross must have been tall.)

Mary was thin, austere, and quiet. At once, Marian noticed Johnnie Cross's good looks, his dark red curly hair, his elegant beard, his tall, strong, athletic body, his good cheer, his youthful health and radiance. He was twenty-nine.

As they sat and chatted, Johnnie told her he'd gone to Rugby. Then, at seventeen, he'd been sent to New York to work at a branch of the family banking business, Dennistoun & Cross. "I've been living with my brother, Richard," he said, "on a place called Washington Square." He had a faint Scottish-American accent, she noticed: soft, round *r*'s and long vowels.

She noticed that he was kind and deferential to his mother, pouring her tea and carefully handing it to her. "Johnnie, dear, can you fetch me my purse with my handkerchief?" And he sprung up at once to get it.

"He's a saint," Anna said in front of him, "my perfect one. He was so sickly as a child. He had rheumatic fever and I spent months nursing him and praying over him. I thought I'd lose him. I think because of that he's my special boy." As she spoke, Johnnie smiled sweetly at his adoring mother and didn't seem the least bit discomfited at the mention of being nursed by her. A bit under his mama's thumb, Marian thought.

"I read your novel, *Romola*," he told her. "I was quite dumfounded by the learning in it. I don't know how you could have made it all so real."

"Thank you," she replied. "You couldn't have said anything better." What a sweet boy he was.

———

Arriving back in London from Rome, they walked in the door of the Priory and saw a figure sitting in the darkness of

the parlor. On hearing the door opening, the person struggled up from his chair and stood before them. "Thornie!"
George cried.

He was unrecognizable, he looked like a skeleton.
George went to him, and he sank back down immediately
into the chair. "I'm in some pain," he said.

Thornie had written from Natal saying that he was
suffering from back pain because he'd been in a wrestling
match. He was losing weight, he wrote. George had urged
him to come back to England to get medical attention.

At once, George sent for Sir James Paget—he was the
queen's own doctor. They tried to carry Thornie up to a
bedroom, but he couldn't bear to be moved. Instead, he lay
on the floor writhing in agony. When Sir James arrived,
he examined him, and then shook his head. "I really don't
know what it is, but I will give him morphia."

For a few hours it helped, and he slept. But then the pain
returned. Sir James called in a surgeon, Henry Roberts.
Roberts told them, out of earshot, "I suspect it's tuberculo-
sis of the glands."

"Is there a cure?" she begged.

"I'm afraid not," he said. "We can continue with the morphia. And pray for a miracle."

They made him a bed on the couch. Sometimes, when
the pain faded, the old Thornie would return, and he'd sing
Zulu songs to amuse them and try and make them laugh.

She put aside her work on *Middlemarch* to take care of
him. At night, George dozed in a chair beside him, ready to
give him more morphia when he awoke. She played the piano
to try to soothe him, Beethoven and Schubert sonatas.

Barbara Bodichon bustled in one day, bringing fresh chicken and fruit from her estate in Hastings. "Please," she said, "let me sit with him and you go out for the day and rest."

She and George took the train down to Weybridge to have lunch with their new friends, the Crosses, who had a large house at the foot of St. George's Hill. It was full of family and youth. There were two tall brothers in residence, Johnnie and his older brother, Willie, both of them bachelors and living with their mother. Willie was not as handsome as Johnnie, he was dark-haired like his mother, Anna, with small, narrow eyes, somewhat quiet and withdrawn. Johnnie Cross was the outgoing one, always trying to please everyone and thinking up games. Some of the unmarried sisters were there, Mary, Eleanor, who was round and plump like her mother, and Emily, a pretty, demure girl. Zibbie was visiting with her husband, Henry Bullock. Zibbie was big with pregnancy, and Anna Cross was fussing over her, for she was bearing the first grandchild.

"I have something I'd like you to hear," Zibbie told Marian. She sat down at the piano. "Oh dear," she said, "I hope I can still reach the keys."

She stretched her arms across her swollen belly and began to play and sing: "*Oh through the pines! The pillared woods, where silence breathes sweet breath...*"

"*The Spanish Gypsy*," Marian cried.

"I made a song of it," Zibbie said. "The music's mine."

Marian got up and hugged her as best she could, gently, across Zibbie's big stomach.

———

Thornie became paralyzed from the waist down. As Marian sat by his bed hour after hour, all she could do was write poetry: *"Death was now Lord of Life,"* she wrote, *"And at his word / Time, vague as air before / new terror stirred."*

The end was near. They sent for Agnes, his mother, and Marian absented herself from the house so Agnes could sit alone with her son.

In October he died, only twenty-five years old. Marian was forty-nine now, George was fifty-two. She felt as if Thornie's death was the beginning of their own. A few nights after Thornie died, George was standing by the bed when suddenly he dropped to the floor. She ran to his side. He soon recovered consciousness. Was George himself ill as well? He'd been complaining of terrible headaches and a constant ringing in his ears.

They went away to Surrey and rented Park Farm, a supremely quiet place, and they mourned. They saw almost no one, though one day they rode over to Weybridge to visit the Crosses, to grieve together with them, for they'd suffered their own tragedy. Zibbie Cross had died giving birth to a baby boy, who survived her, and Johnnie Cross announced that he was retiring from Dennistoun & Cross and moving back to England to be with his mother.

———

It was not until the following spring that she and George had the strength once more to take up their work. George had embarked on a new project he was calling *Problems of*

Life and Mind. "I've spent my career popularizing other people's ideas," he said. "Now I want to make my own contribution." The book would be an attempt to reconcile his belief in science with metaphysics.

Again she took up her novel about the idealistic country doctor. To boost her spirits, she changed the color of her ink, from dark brown to purple—at least purple was a slightly more cheerful color.

She invented a new character, Dorothea, who wants to devote herself to a higher cause, and thinks she must do it through a man—just as Marian herself had done, she thought, through Charles Bray, and awful Dr. Brabant, and Chapman. Only she made Dorothea beautiful, "*high-colored but with a bloom like a Chiny rose,*" and a gemlike brightness to her hair.

Dorothea makes a terrible marriage with Edward Casaubon, whom she believes is engaged in a great intellectual work, "The Key to All Mythologies," he calls it. But she discovers he's unable to finish it and all he does is rewrite his few paltry pages. (Silly George, taking his break from laboring over his *Problems*, took to calling his own manuscript "The Key to all Psychologies.")

For Casaubon, she summoned up her memories of Brabant and his unfinished manuscript. She gave him the little white moles Brabant had on his face—with hairs sticking out of them, and made him slurp his soup.

As she wrote, she laughed out loud to herself. When *Middlemarch* was published and people asked her who the real Casaubon was, she'd reply primly, "I fear that the Casaubon-tints are not quite foreign to my own mental complexion."

She made Dorothea fall in love with Casaubon's nephew, Ladislaw, and then she killed Casaubon off. She had two main stories going at once now, one about the idealistic young doctor, Lydgate, and his wife, pretty, vain Rosamond Vincy, and the other about Dorothea and Ladislaw.

But she had to bring them together. "Why not have Dorothea suddenly come upon Rosamond and Ladislaw and think that they're lovers?" George suggested.

And she did just that. Of course Dorothea is completely wrong. Rosamond and Ladislaw are certainly not having an affair and Dorothea and Ladislaw marry and live happily ever after.

———

She wrote the last pages of the book in Germany, in Homburg. Afterward they traveled to Hamburg to take the waters and heal their various illnesses—headaches and general biliousness (both of them), and decaying teeth (hers).

They went to the Kursaal to watch the gamblers (as theater only). The gamblers were mostly old women with gaunt faces and wigs and crablike hands, and vaguely louche foreigners. The room was hot, the lights bright, the air filled with the desperate chink and rattle of the croupier's wheel, the exclamations of the losers.

One person among them seemed out of place, a young woman, purer-seeming than the rest, a sylphlike beauty in a sea-green dress, bent over the table intently. An older woman was teaching her how to gamble. Someone next to them whispered, "That's Lord Byron's grandniece, Lady Geraldine Leigh."

At first the young woman was winning. Then she began to lose. She still had a pile of louis in front of her. The old woman, her teacher, tried to get her to come away, but she ignored her.

"*Faites vos jeux,*" the croupier commanded. The sylph pushed her last louis forward, watching the wheel, biting her lower lip.

"*Jeu zéro!*" the croupier cried. She'd lost again. The girl turned to her companion, the old woman, terror on her face.

"Poor thing," Marian said to George. "What could her story be?"

She couldn't get the image of the young girl out of her head.

When *Middlemarch* was published, her celebrity lifted her like the crest of a wave. They called it her "*masterpiece.*" She was "*a great teacher,*" they said. Barbara Bodichon, her dear friend, so incapable of telling her anything but the truth, wrote to her that it was her best book ever.

She and George had been living together for almost eighteen years in defiance of the world. Now she was so important that women overcame their scruples and began to call on her. She was invited to dinner everywhere, with women now, with Dean Stanley of Westminster *and* his wife, Lady Augusta, and with Mrs. Henry Frederick Ponsonby, who'd been maid of honor to the queen. The queen's own daughters wanted to meet her. One of them, Princess Louise, heard that the banker George Goschen was giving a dinner for Marian and asked to be invited so she could meet her.

The moment the princess walked in the door, she caught sight of Marian and went up to her. The princess was tall and slim, with brown hair and blue eyes, the most attractive of the royal children. She sat down beside Marian and they talked all evening, about art and women's higher education. The princess said that her mother, the queen, had allowed her to go to art school, and she was a serious sculptor.

Next, her sister, the princess royal, and her husband, the crown prince of Prussia, wanted to meet Marian as well. Now she'd received the blessings of the royal family *and* the Church of England, in the person of Dean Stanley.

But as her fame grew, death stalked them. She learned that Emanuel Deutsch, her dear little Silesian Jew, was ill with cancer. He'd been taken in by a clergyman, the Reverend Haweis, who lived on Welbeck Street. She went to visit him there.

He was gaunt and in pain, all his roundness and ebullience gone. "I think the pain is God's punishment for revealing the secrets of the Talmud," he told her.

"You can't say that!" she told him. "You did the world an enormous favor with all your work."

He closed his eyes. "Sometimes I think I should just kill myself."

"Please, dear man, no!"

"I would like to die in the Holy Land," he said.

When she got home to the Priory, she wrote him a passionate letter begging him not to take his own life. "*Remember,*" she importuned, "*it has happened to many to be glad they did not commit suicide, though they once ran for the final leap.*"

Somehow, the Reverend Haweis and his wife were able to get him to a boat bound for Palestine.

Later, she learned that he had gotten as far as Alexandria when they had to take him off the boat. As he lay dying in the hospital, he asked to be placed on the floor after he was gone. It was apparently a Jewish custom, to go from this world humbly. They buried him in the Jewish cemetery there.

All around them, the young were dying—Thornie, Zibbie Cross. And now Emanuel Deutsch. Deutsch's death haunted her, his feverish enthusiasm, his learning, his vision.

On learning of Deutsch's death, they left for another holiday on the Continent. To help her recover from the loss, George suggested she write something about Judaism. She began reading everything she could get her hands on about the subject. One Friday at sunset in Frankfurt, they visited the main synagogue. There, under the great domed roof, in the candlelight, they listened to the ethereal sound of the cantor chanting the Sabbath prayer in his minor key: "*Yedid Nefesh av harachaman / Mesoch avdechah el retzonechah...*" "Beloved of the soul, compassionate Father, / Draw your servant to your will..." Because of Deutsch, she could understand the prayer.

It was while she was trying to write her Jewish novel, *Daniel Deronda*, that, one morning at dawn, she saw a drop of blood in her urine. A short time later she was struck with an excruciating pain in her left side. Was her own death coming now? The pain intensified, spread around the middle of her body, bombarded her in waves. She hadn't known such pain was possible. George summoned Dr. Paget, who said it was a kidney stone. They gave her laudanum, hot baths, and fermentations, and eventually she recovered.

Then it struck again—and again after that. George nursed her lovingly. Sometimes months would pass between attacks, but they continued and they weakened her. Somehow, though, she was able to keep working. George always said that the secret to her success was her signal ability to endure, through kidney pain and headache and toothache, and despite that, to write her long books and invent entire worlds out of her imagination. When she'd finished working for the day, she would walk with him for hours through the city and the country, and listen to music with intense, devouring concentration, and study paintings for hours on end. One had to have that strength, she thought, or one couldn't live through one's allotted time.

Deronda took over three years to write. Once again, she had two stories going at once. She kept seeing Byron's niece in the casino at the Kursaal. What if the girl was gambling to save her bankrupt family from ruin? In the story, she'd call her Gwendolen Harleth.

To get money for her family, Gwendolen marries the rich, cold, and immoral Henleigh Grandcourt. Marian was good at depicting cold men, wasn't she? Gwendolen falls in love with Daniel Deronda, who's noble and good, and Jewish, but he doesn't know it yet. Deronda doesn't love her. One summer night, while out rowing on the Thames, he rescues a girl, Mirah, from suicide. She's Jewish, a singer with a divine voice. She has a brother, Mordecai, from whom she's been separated.

Mordecai would be like Emanuel Deutsch, steeped in poverty, obscure, dying...but alive with the burning intensity of his dreams, living in the invisible past and his vision of the future. Deronda discovers he's Jewish, falls in love with Mirah, and reunites her with her brother. How many of her writings were filled with that longing, the reuniting of brother and sister? *The Mill on the Floss*, *Romola*. If it couldn't happen in life, she would make it happen in her books.

—252—

Chapter 14

During the years it took to write her Jewish novel, she and George often went down to Surrey to seek refuge in the country air and stay with the Crosses in Weybridge, that place of youth and hope. There were the two brothers, Johnnie and Willie, and the sisters, "the Doves," as George began to refer to them. Marian was particularly drawn to Mary Cross, with her plain looks and soft, gentle ways. Mary had literary ambitions and had published a story in *Macmillan's*, "Marie of Villefranche," about the Franco-Prussian War. She had gone to aid the refugees during the war and set up a soup kitchen for them. Marian told Mary that she thought the story was excellent, and that she'd wept over the plight of the starving mother. In gratitude, Mary gave her a present of a vase on which she'd painted scenes from Marian's novel *Romola*.

Marian was aging now, fifty-six in the year 1875. She began using powder to cover the lines in her face, and Dr. Liebreich prescribed glasses for her in the hopes of alleviating her headaches. But when she and George were at Weybridge, they became young again. The Crosses didn't discriminate against them because they were old. They drew them into all their games and charades and Johnnie Cross took them on delicious hikes amidst the pines on St.

George's Hill, from which they could see all the way over to Windsor.

They spent holidays with the family, and rented houses near them in summer. There were growing numbers of Cross grandchildren romping around, and little family intrigues and youthful romances to pay attention to. One sister, sweet, demure Emily, had a suitor, Francis Otter, a young barrister from Lincolnshire. Marian saw them one day out in the garden, under a tree, arguing. Frank was remonstrating with Emily about something and suddenly she started to cry. Marian didn't ask what the matter was, but she wondered.

She and George began calling Johnnie and Willie their "two tall nephews," and she, Marian, was their "Auntie."

Anna Cross had had ten children. There was the offhand mention of another brother, Alexander, who'd died. But no cause was given, no expression of sadness.

Once, when she was alone with Mary Cross, she asked, "You had another brother, didn't you? One who died—when was that? How old was he?"

She saw Mary tense. "It's really something we never discuss."

"I'm sorry," Marian quickly replied. "Please—forgive me. It's all right."

"Please, don't ask Mama about him," Mary said. "It always makes her cry."

"My goodness. I couldn't bear to hurt Anna."

Mary paused. Her lips parted, as if she wanted to tell her something else. But Marian, afraid to cause her more pain, didn't ask more. She rushed to fill the gap. "You're all so lucky to have one another," she cried. "I always wanted a big family, lots of brothers and sisters, always there for you, no matter what. But my sister's dead, and my brother—he hasn't spoken to me for twenty years."

"But why?"

They never spoke to anyone about their "irregular" marriage. It was too private, and to do so would be to admit it *was* irregular.

"I'm afraid he didn't approve of George," was all she said.

"But you have us," Mary said. "We're your family now."

Johnnie offered them financial advice. He knew about the new American markets that were opening up and he took the royalties from *Middlemarch* and invested them in railway stock. By year's end, the interest on it made up half their income. George was grateful to be relieved of the burden of managing their money.

It was a good thing they had Johnnie to look after their finances, because there were more people to provide funds for now. There were the regular payments to Agnes and to her children with Thornton—a hundred pounds to her son, Edmund, to establish a dental practice, money to her daughter, Mildred, to buy a Latin dictionary. They sent money to Chrissey's daughter, Emily, for school. Charles and Cara Bray were in a bad way too. The silk industry was declining and they'd had to give up Rosehill and move to smaller quarters. She and George didn't see much of the Brays anymore—George thought Charles's belief in phrenology was ridiculous. But she couldn't forget all they'd done for her. She knew they'd be too proud to take money directly, so she suggested to Cara that she write a children's story about kindness to animals, and she sent her a check for fifty pounds as if it were a contribution to the cause.

In July there came a letter from the colonies. Bertie had died of bronchitis. He'd left behind a wife and the two little ones.

George held the letter to his heart and sank down into a chair. His face was stone.

She put her arms around him to comfort him, but he couldn't speak. And he couldn't cry. There was silence. She asked, "Would you like me to inform people?"

"No. Don't tell them. I can't bear the letters of consolation coming in."

He stared out into the room, then he bent his head and covered his eyes.

She did tell Barbara Bodichon about Bertie's death though, because she had taken such an interest in the boys. And she also confided in Johnnie. Johnnie was only four years older than Bertie, the embodiment of youth and life. *"He was such a sweet-natured creature,"* she wrote to Johnnie, *"not clever, but diligent and well-judging about the things of daily life."*

Now they would support Bertie's wife, Liza, and the children. It was good to know they could. Johnnie, with his skill at managing money, made her feel safe.

He had officially retired from the family business now, at only thirty years old. "You're so young to be retired," she told him. "You're so good at business, you ought to do something with that brain of yours, something of use to the world."

"I hope I am useful," he said. "I try to be, taking care of mother."

"Of course, taking care of Anna comes first." Indeed, Anna Cross had been ill lately and they were worried about her.

Johnnie seemed to have few interests other than playing tennis with his brother-in-law, Albert Druce, and boating with him on the Thames. He'd published a piece of writing in *Macmillan's* about his days in New York society, and Anna had proudly sent it to her. It was about how much freer the young women in New York were than in London, how they mixed more naturally with the opposite sex. New York girls were better read than the men, who were unlikely to have heard of great works such as George Eliot's *Spanish Gypsy.* Marian wrote to Anna that she had found the essay quite instructive.

"Perhaps you should write more," she said to Johnnie.

"I'm afraid writing's very difficult for me. But I do try and stay active."

"Of course. You're a young man. You must."

"As you know," he laughed, "I do love games."

Johnnie became the ringmaster of their amusements, always arranging distractions for them. He took her to the Lord Mayor's Show and on a tour of the Bank of England, where she autographed a thousand-pound note. He invited her and George to lunch at the Dennistoun & Cross offices on Cannon Street, and organized trips to the Woolwich Arsenal and the National Gallery and to tennis matches.

He was very athletic. She liked to watch him play tennis with Albert, his best friend. Albert was as tall as Johnnie and had dark blond curly hair, fine features, an aristocratic but warm manner, and a mellifluous voice. The two of them together were like young gods, she sometimes thought, playing tennis at Weybridge, dressed in their whites, their long, slender forms taking flight as they served, like great white herons. They were in perpetual, affectionate competition, laughing and goading one another. But at the end of the match there was always a consolatory hug, the two of them sweating and playfully batting at each other.

"You should play!" Johnnie urged her.

"We're much too old and infirm," she said. Johnnie and Albert wanted her and George to go out with them on their boat on the Thames, but that she would not do.

She wondered why Johnnie was so fond of two such old people as her and George, frail writers, both of them so often sick. Was it her fame, or George's humor and charm and learning? To be sure, Johnnie seemed to be equally as fond of George as he was of her. He gave a lunch for George at the Devonshire Club to celebrate his work.

It was Johnnie who found them their estate, the Heights, at Witley, close enough to Weybridge so that they could visit the Crosses often. It was a great vine-covered red-brick house with timbered brackets and a gabled roof, far too big for them really, three reception rooms, a wide terrace with a view of heather-covered hills, all the way down to Blackdown, where Tennyson lived. There were nine acres of sculpted gardens, fields, and woods, a conservatory, and a coachman's house. Johnnie negotiated the whole thing for them and even got the price down.

And now they had their own special paradise.

"You should get a billiard table for guests so they can play on rainy days," Johnnie said. They bought one and he and George played. Johnnie bought them tennis equipment and insisted they learn the game; he was patient when they kept missing the ball, and he taught them how to serve. They played until they perspired. Tennis was impractical for London, so in autumn when they went back to the city, he gave them a badminton set. He set it up in the Priory garden, but it was too windy to play outdoors, so he installed it in the entrance hall for them.

How often she called herself "Aunt" to him. Was she careful to do that, she wondered, instinctively to reassure him that she saw him as a son, not as a handsome and sexual young man?

At the Crosses' parties at Weybridge, she'd never observed Johnnie in close conversation with a young woman of his own age, other than his sisters. He was usually in a group, standing out among them because he was the tallest, laughing and merry.

She ventured once to ask Mary Cross, "Do you think that Johnnie will ever marry?"

It was New Year's Eve, 1876, and there was a party at Weybridge with neighbors from across the county. She'd noticed that Johnnie had danced only with his mother and his sisters, not with any of the young women there. Mary scrutinized her brother across the room. "I'm not sure," Mary said. "I guess Johnnie and Willie and I just aren't the marrying sort. We're destined to live together—forever," she said with a smile.

One summer day at Witley, Marian and Johnnie were sitting on the terrace having tea. He'd brought Albert Druce's children, his nephew Eliot, whom the Druces had named in her honor, and Elsie, his niece, over for a visit. The children were attempting to play croquet on the lawn below. Elsie was older and ordering around little Eliot, who was toddling about carrying the heavy mallet.

George had gone upstairs to rest and she and Johnnie were alone watching them.

Then Elsie snatched the mallet from her little brother, and he burst into tears and began crying piteously.

Johnnie jumped up to intervene. "I'm afraid this was a bad idea. The mallet's much too heavy for him." She watched as he marched down, gently remonstrated with Elsie, and tenderly picked up little Eliot and patted him on the back till his tears subsided.

"You're so good with little children," Marian said when he returned. "It's a shame you don't have any of your own."

"Mama keeps asking me about that." He sighed. "But I don't seem to be able to find the right person. Perhaps I'm lacking. No one's seemed particularly interested in me, either."

"I don't believe that," she said. "A handsome, healthy young man like you who's done so well in life?"

He looked distractedly into the distance, as if this troubled him too. "Yes, it's strange. I must have some deficiency. Something I'm not aware of..." He stopped, considering this. "...that I can't find the right one."

PART IV

On the Shores of Acheron

Chapter 15

Following the incident at the Lido, Johnnie slept through the night with the aid of the laudanum. When he finally got up, he was sluggish and slow and unspeaking. She watched as he stumbled around the *sala*, tall and bent and painfully thin, like a stick figure, his hands shaking as he poured his morning coffee from the urn and then spilled it from the cup. Had he forgotten what had happened on the beach? That he'd pushed her? She was afraid to confront him, to make him angry. Perhaps it was better left forgotten. Perhaps he'd be all right now.

As he sat down with his coffee, in an effort to occupy him, to rouse him, to pretend that everything was normal, she suggested that they make the trip to Murano and Torcello, obligatory on any visit to Venice. He nodded assent, still stupefied with the aftereffects of the laudanum, but thankfully, calm now.

Outside, the sun had risen higher, a burning disk just visible behind the haze, spinning malevolently.

The gondolier, Corradini, rowed them out to Murano, past the cemetery island and the Church of San Michele. It was peaceful and quiet on the lagoon, the splashing of the water on the side of the boat rhythmic and restful. The gondolier, standing on the afterdeck, plowing the water

with his oar, kept his pale eyes ahead, aloof, as if wary of
annoying Johnnie again as he had the night of the Malibran. Though the man lacked all manners, she thought, he
had an animal sense of how far he could go without losing
his employment. Johnnie seemed hardly to notice him.

She noticed again the sinew of the gondolier's forearms,
the strength of the muscles. As she sank back into the shade
of the *tendalin,* she felt a kind of fear at the man's quiet, his
seemingly inhuman indifference to them. He had them in
his power. She had a sudden sense of being rowed to her
doom, of the gondolier, like Charon, unclean, with hollow
eyes, rowing them across the river to the land of the dead.
She felt a headache coming on from the heat and the jagged
reflection of the sunlight on the water.

At Murano, as she stood up to disembark, the boat
rocked under her feet and she was afraid she'd fall in the
water. Corradini reached out his hand and grasped her arm
to steady her. His hand was rough, like sandpaper. "Thank
you," she said. He didn't acknowledge her, even to nod his
head.

They set out on foot, leaving him behind, smoking his
cigarette on the dock, looking away from them out at the
water.

They toured the Church of San Donato and visited Sal-
viati's, the glassworks, where she bought gifts for his sisters. "Look, won't Mary love this?" she said, holding up a
vase of turquoise glass, hoping to excite him. It had a rim of
gold acanthus leaves and gold handles in the shape of dol-
phins. "I want to take Mary home something nice."

He smiled painfully, with effort, and nodded. "Very
nice."

"Good, we'll take it," she told the lady shopkeeper.

When they'd finished, Corradini rowed them onward to Torcello, which was bleak and windswept even in June. It was largely deserted of tourists, with a few fishermen's huts, muddy flats, the canal lined with ruined brickwork. They walked to the crumbling old Cathedral of Santa Maria Assunta. A boy brought them the key and they went inside. It smelled of death and mold.

"See," she said to Johnnie, "that's the bishop's throne." She was the one with the enthusiasm and energy now. Johnnie was subdued, dazed from his long sleep, saying little as she pointed out the sights, eager to cheer him. "Those mosaics are from the eleventh century. See the Virgin, all the gold on the apse there?" She hoped to wear him out so that he'd sleep again, to give him the exercise he said he needed and had been so deprived of because of his old wife.

That evening after supper, he refused to take any more of the laudanum. "I can't bear the way it makes me feel in the morning. It makes me feel sluggish. I'll be all right," he insisted. "I promise."

Chapter 16

The heat oppressed, the sky was thick, hazy, the atmosphere weighing down upon the city. There was no air in the *appartement*, and her face was covered with sweat. She tasted the salt on her skin. It was the sirocco coming, the great, humid wind all the way from the Sahara, bringing with it storms and high water.

In the afternoon, they made their way to the workers' quarters in San Biagio to see John Bunney.

Number 2413 was a factory building with rough wooden doors. They rang the bell, and after a minute the doors flung open. "Welcome!" said Bunney. "Welcome to my humble abode."

He led them up the stairs to the second floor, to a large, light-filled space with plank floors and big windows that looked out over the water. Waiting there in the background was a wan woman with protruding eyes, Mrs. Bunney.

The room had little furniture, and was strewn with canvases and easels. There was an iron bedstead, a long table and chairs, a wardrobe with its door hanging off, a woodstove, canvases leaning against the walls.

"Lizzie asks that you please pardon her," Mr. Bunney said, "but she's having one of her attacks of neuralgia today."

"I'm so sorry," Mrs. Bunney said, drawing her hand across her brow. "I'm rendered just incapacitated by these things."

"That's perfectly all right," Marian told her. "I have them myself. We won't stay long."

"But some tea..."

"Please, don't bother," Marian told her.

"Mr. Ruskin said that I was to show you some of my work," Bunney said.

In the middle of the room was a long carpenter's table with paints and jars of murky liquid and brushes and stacks of drawings on it. Bunney began sorting through it. "This is for Mr. Ruskin's project on Saint Ursula," he said, holding up a watercolor of an hourglass, and another of a chair. "He's in the process of copying Carpaccio's *Dream of Saint Ursula* in the Accademia, and he's asked me to work at his side. I'm just doing the secondary objects, the hourglass, the bookcase, the chair, and so on, and Mr. Ruskin's doing the main figure, of course. But," he said sadly, "Mr. Ruskin hasn't been back in Venice for three years now. He's been ill, I'm afraid." Tactfully, he didn't say what Ruskin's illness was, but it was generally known that he'd gone insane.

"He says the saint reminds him of Miss La Touche, the young lady he loved so much and who died." Rose La Touche had been Ruskin's fourteen-year-old pupil when he became infatuated with her. Eventually, the girl had starved herself to death. It was said she was insane herself. Her death had apparently precipitated Ruskin's own illness.

Mr. Bunney continued separating out his sketches for them. "Mr. Ruskin likes everything precisely as it really is, every line, every pediment, every shadow. He made me redo the bookcase and the table. Ay, he's a rough taskmaster. But he took me out of the Working Men's College and gave me work. I've got Lizzie and the children to feed."

Mrs. Bunney, in the background, spoke up sharply. "Mr. Ruskin is a harsh man. He drives him too hard. He looks so old," she said. "Mr. Ruskin has aged him."

"No, Lizzie," Mr. Bunney said, "he is a perfectionist, that's all."

Mrs. Bunney said bitterly, "I can't forgive him for not letting you come to Florence when little Frank died."

Mr. Bunney sighed. "Yes, that was cruel. I was in Verona and Lizzie and the children were in Florence. She wrote that our—" Here he stopped, sat down on a stool, and shook his head, unable to go on. Then he took a breath and continued. "Our darling boy had...passed away. But Mr. Ruskin wouldn't let me go to them. He said there was too much work to do."

He collected himself. "Oh," he said, "I almost forgot! These are Mr. Ruskin's pamphlets. He says it's very important that you see the things he's written about, so you understand his whole campaign against the restoration, how precious these old things are."

Johnnie took the pile of pamphlets. He smiled eagerly. He seemed suddenly to come alive. "Thank you. This is wonderful!"

When they were out on the *fondamenta*, he said brightly, "Let's make a project of seeing every single thing Ruskin describes in his pamphlets. Shall we do that?"

"But Johnnie, there are hundreds and hundreds of things he mentions."

"We can do it! In honor of the place."

"I don't think I have the strength in this heat."

"I'm determined," he said. "You can stay behind if you must. I'll go without you." He began paging through the pamphlets. "Off we go! Every single one! Santa Maria Formosa, that's right near here."

"We've already been there," she said dully.

"Yes, but we haven't seen it through *his* eyes."

He started walking northward, to the Campo Santa Maria Formosa, and she followed. He came to a stop in front of the church and read from one of the pamphlets. *"The third period of the Renaissance..."* Looking up at the building, he exclaimed, "He hates it!" He looked down again. *"The architecture raised at Venice during this period is among the worst and basest ever built by the hands of men..."*

"This is apparently the only church in Venice with two facades," he said. *"This façade whose architect is unknown, consists of a pediment, sustained on four Corinthian pilasters..."*

He stared down at the page. "He's talking about a hideous face. Where's that?"

"Above the bell tower."

"Look at it!" he cried, pointing to the bell tower. Above the door was the head of a gargoyle carved in stone. It had only one eye, its mouth was grotesquely distorted, its tongue bulging. *"Huge, inhuman and monstrous, leering in bestial degradation...,"* Johnnie read eagerly.

And so it went. Across the bridge to the Salute to see Tintoretto's *Marriage at Cana—"The most perfect example which human art has produced..."*

"I've got to sit down, Johnnie," she said. "I feel weak."

A look of irritation crossed his face. "Of course," he said.

She sat down on a ledge, in a tiny bit of shade, while he paced impatiently, sorting through the pamphlets. He was almost spectral now in his thinness. After a few moments, he cried, "On to the Carmine."

"But that's all the way across the Dorsoduro."

On they walked, into the heat. Her feet began to hurt. The air weighed down on her. She straggled behind him as he made long strides. A ridge on the inside of her boot was cutting into her ankle.

"My feet are swollen," she said. "There's something hurting my foot."

In the past, he would've stopped immediately and tended to her, but not now. "We'll soon be there!" he said.

At last, in the hard light of the midday sun, they were at the Carmine, a small, stark church, red brick and marble. Inside, he stood before Tintoretto's painting *The Circumcision*, the baby resting on the table, his head propped in the priest's hands, his infant neck slack, his peasant mother watching, calm and accepting. *"A picture of the moral power of gold and colour,"* he read. And read.

Across the Dorsoduro to San Polo, to San Cassiano. Not even Tintoretto's *Crucifixion*, *"among the finest in Europe,"* could move her now. She could hardly see it. His voice was going to make her scream.

"Johnnie, I can't go another step. I'm going to faint."

Furiously, he hailed a gondola, and she sank gratefully into the seat, her feet throbbing.

At the hotel, she hobbled up the stairs behind him to the *appartement*, he still reading as they went. *"The horizon is so low, that the spectator—"*

"Please," she begged. "Could you stop!"

He lowered his voice ostentatiously: *"the spectator must fancy himself lying at full length on the grass..."*

She sat on the other side of the room staring at him, part of her fascinated now to see how long he could keep it up. It was as if he were a great distance from her, small, an insect. His voice was like someone droning the rosary, repeating over and over again, *"Hail Mary, full of grace, the Lord is...,"* the words onrushing, a river of words, engulfing one another, unrelenting.

"Johnnie, I'm going to go mad." She stood up and tried to snatch the pamphlet away from him, but he was bigger than she was, and he held it tightly against his chest. *"This picture unites color as rich as Titian's with light and shade as forcible as Rembrandt's..."*

The air in the room was close and awful, but he still wore his jacket, oblivious to the heat.

Quickly, she slipped out of the *appartement*—he didn't notice her leave. She went down into the lobby. Behind the reception desk was a clerk. "I want to send a telegram," she told him.

She wrote out her message: *"To Mr. William Cross. From Mrs. Cross, Hotel de l'Europe, Calle del Ridotto, No. 1207. Johnnie ill. Come at once. Hurry."*

Chapter 17

Back in the *appartement*, she fled to her own room, leaving him in the *sala*, still reading aloud to his invisible audience, the candle sputtering. She closed the doors behind her. What if he...she could hardly form the thought—if he were to hurt her? She hesitated, then drew the bolt across the doors.

The room was stifling, no oxygen here. She threw open the windows to the balcony to let in what little air there was. Outside, the canal was still and silent in the heat.

He was there on the other side, behind the wall, and she was alone. He had become someone else, apart from her. She was no longer exhausted, sleep was impossible, she was afraid to leave the bedroom.

Her skin prickled with fear. She was an old woman, sixty years old, weak, too thin, she'd lost weight along with him. Her eyes stung with tiredness, but she had to stay awake. Be vigilant. All around her, the folds of the room, the curtains on the four-poster, the thick red velvet drapes suddenly seemed to conceal dangers.

But these double doors were thick. No one could get in at her. She was barricaded here. She was afraid to get into bed, so she sat down on the *fauteuil*, exhausted, emptied out.

Despite all her efforts to stay awake, to remain alert to him, now that the doors were shut against him, the need

DINITIA SMITH

to sleep, to escape into oblivion, came over her. Her eyelids began to dip. Her thoughts were a mad jumble. "An industrious bunny...oh, he is an industrious bunny." His voice swam through her head: *"color as rich as Titian's...light and shade as forcible as Rembrandt..."*

Where was George now, when she needed him?

PART V

The City of Sorrow

Chapter 18

He must have already been ill when they bought the Heights. But he was so busy taking care of her that he hardly took care of himself. He was always tired that summer, he had terrible stomach cramps and he was losing weight, though when he wasn't in pain, he was always laughing and joking in an attempt to keep her spirits up.

All the while he was suffering he was trying to write the third volume of *Problems of Life and Mind*. He was such a determined little man.

After she finished *Daniel Deronda*, she'd been thinking about a new book, perhaps a novel set during the Napoleonic Wars—that would provide the broad canvas she liked for her tales. She began jotting down notes in one of her "quarries," and ordered some books to do research.

But George was increasingly ill. Sir James Paget came and spent hours with him. It was most likely a thickening of the mucous membrane, he said, and prescribed castor oil. To no avail.

She was too exhausted from nursing him to write another novel. She started writing some essays. There were pieces about writing itself—on plagiarism, originality, and literary controversy. And an essay on consciousness. It was *"a futile cargo screeching irrelevantly, an idle parasite in the grand scheme of things."* There was a passionate piece on the necessity of a Jewish homeland. She named it "The Modern Hep! Hep! Hep!" after the brutal cry of the Crusaders as they chased down the Jews to slaughter them. Perhaps she could collect them all into a book—make them into the reminiscences of an eccentric clergyman, she thought. She'd call her clergyman Theophrastus, after Aristotle's pupil, who was a terrible writer and deservedly obscure, and she'd model him on Spencer—though he was so self-centered he'd never get the joke. (And she was making fun of herself too, uttering all these pronouncements.) *"The person I love best has never loved me,"* she wrote, as Theophrastus, *"or known that I love her."* A reversal of the truth during those sad days of her youth. She'd call the book *The Impressions of Theophrastus Such.*

All that summer, George kept up his good cheer, but in the night, the demons came. At dawn, he, who had always been so careful of her sleep, would awaken her. "Darling, I'm so sorry, but would you walk with me? It's the only thing that relieves the pain." They would get dressed and she would walk with him, holding his arm, through the early morning world of the garden, along the paths, the servants still sleeping, in the perfect quiet, the only sound the gradual awakening of the birds beginning their dawn song.

He always tried to cheer her. One evening, when Johnnie Cross came to dinner, he lay on the divan and sang through the entire tenor part of *The Barber of Seville* while she accompanied him on the piano. *"Se il mio nome saper voi bramate,"* he brayed, a little out of tune, singing it to her. *"Dal mio labbro il mio nome ascoltate, Io son Lindoro..."* He made everyone laugh and forget that he was ill.

They stayed at the Heights through the early autumn. He was able to find the strength to make the journey to Cambridgeshire to a dinner for Turgenev, who was in England for the partridge shooting. At the dinner, Turgenev gave a wonderful toast to her in fluent English. "I must say that I think of myself as a writer only second or third to your own great English writers," he said, nodding toward Marian, "after George Eliot." The toast made George so happy because he knew now that with Turgenev's praise, whatever happened to him, her reputation was secure.

As winter came on, his pain grew so intense that it became nearly impossible for him to work on his *Problems*. He would lie on the divan with his pen and notebook and try to write, and then a spasm of pain would overcome him. "If I can't finish it," he said, "will you?"

"Please, darling, don't even say that," she pleaded. "You'll get better. You'll finish it, you'll see."

"But," he insisted, with rare seriousness, "if I can't, do you promise?"

"Of course, I promise. But this is so unnecessary."

He sank back on the divan and closed his eyes, reassured.

He began to stay mostly in bed, a shrunken figure amidst the pillows. Barbara Bodichon, with a rush of energy and kindness, came to replace her for a few hours, and read aloud to him from Victor Hugo. "I'm so sorry," he said, "but I'm too tired to listen."

Charley moved into the guest room to help care for his Pater. Solid, bespectacled Charley was a married man now with three little girls of his own, and twenty men under him in the Post Office.

But when she finished *Theophrastus Such*, George somehow gathered his remaining strength, hooked his walking stick to the bed post, pulled himself up, and limped over to the desk, where he wrote a note to Blackwood.

"You don't have to do that," she said.

"I have to be sure about the typeface and the cover," he said, as he'd always done with every one of her books. Then he sent off the manuscript to Edinburgh.

"Could you send a boy over for Johnnie Cross?" he asked her. "I want to speak to him about the money." Johnnie's mother, Anna, was very ill, declining rapidly, and Johnnie was constantly at her bedside. Nonetheless, he came to them that afternoon.

"Johnnie, dear boy!" George said when he saw Johnnie's poor, wan, exhausted face. Johnnie, seeing him, was at a loss for words. "Yes, I am a pretty sight, aren't I?" George said, his voice hoarse and cracking. "Even prettier than usual. Now, Nephew, I want to talk to you about business. I want you to look after Polly when I'm gone—"

"Please," Johnnie said. "This is too painful."

"I'm very serious. I want your solemn promise." His expression was stern.

"Of course," Johnnie replied, his voice almost a whisper.

"I can't listen to this," she said, and left the room. She waited outside in the hall, leaning against the wall, hearing the murmur of their voices inside. "Her money is in safe hands with you," George was saying. "But I'd suggest continuing with the American securities for a while, the yield is so good..."

Then George called out, "Polly, you can come back in now. We're finished." Johnnie had gotten up to leave, his face grave. "One more thing, Nephew," George said from the depths of his pillows. "Take these cigars." He indicated his cigar caddy by the bed. "Give them to Brother Willie. The best Cubans from Melbourne Hart. He's the only good smoker among you. He'll appreciate them."

Then he lay back, his eyes closing. As the night wore on, he slept. He didn't wake in pain as he had before. She touched him, but he, who was always so quick to sense her every touch, if she even stirred beside him or cried out with a bad dream, didn't respond. She climbed into the bed with him and put her arms around him and drew his birdlike body to her. He weighed nothing. She held him close, trying to keep him back, to infuse him with the warmth and life of her own flesh. But he didn't know she was there anymore, didn't even move his fingers to find her hand.

Outside, the London sky darkened, evening here already. At a quarter to six, he took a sudden breath, there was a rattling in his throat. Then he was gone.

Sometimes her sobs were uncontrollable. She refused to get dressed or to eat. She saw only Charley and the maid, Brett. Mrs. Dowling, the cook, brewed a special broth to tempt her, and Brett would bring it in to her. "Just a little bit, my lady, one sip," she said. "You do need it for your strength." But she couldn't. Charley wrote the letters informing everyone about what had happened.

Four days later, they buried him in the Dissenters' section at Highgate. She couldn't bear to go to the funeral. Charley went in her stead, and Trollope, and Johnnie Cross—though Anna was now near death. Spencer, who never attended funerals, came to this one for his best friend. When Charley returned from the funeral, he said that the

Reverend Dr. Sadler had seemed quite apologetic when he suggested that perhaps there was such a thing as the immortality of the soul.

She moved out of their bedroom to the spare room, and sat in her nightgown, hair uncombed, writing down her memories of him. *"When I first met you at the Princess theater with Spencer you made me laugh...I fell in love with you...at the St. Katherine's dock I thought you wouldn't come. But you did, oh you did...That morning in Tenby when I told you my idea for my first story...without you, I would be nothing..."*

Downstairs, Charley and Brett kept the house together. As she manically scribbled down her memories of him, she was aware vaguely of the bell ringing at the gate, of people arriving to pay their respects. They told her that Johnnie Cross, Spencer, Barbara Bodichon, and total strangers had come, begging for news of her, but she ordered Charley and Brett not to let them in. Every now and then Brett appeared in the room, to make sure that she was still alive.

Letters of condolence poured in. Turgenev wrote from his estate in Bougival in France that *"All your friends, all learned Europe mourn with you."* Then came a letter from Isaac's wife, Sarah: *"My heart aches for you in your sad bereavement."* It was the first communication she'd had from either her or Isaac for twenty-six years. But nothing from Isaac himself. No sympathy from Isaac.

Barbara wrote again begging to be allowed to see her. Barbara had supported her in everything. She was a force of nature, and wouldn't be stopped. *"I bless you for all your goodness to me,"* Marian wrote to her. *"But I am a bruised creature and shrink from even the tenderest touch."*

Once more, Brett stood in front of her, tiny and mousy, in the blur of her black-and-white uniform. "Mr. Cross is here again to see you," she said. "He's very worried about you."

"Tell him, no thank you," she said again. "I send my love, but I can't see anyone now."

"Poor man, I feel so sorry for him, he so wanted to see you," Brett said.

After seven days, she was able to get dressed, and with Charley holding on to her arm, went downstairs for the first time. Stepping across the threshold of George's study, she saw on his desk the pile of notes for his *Problems of Life and Mind*. He'd begged her to finish it for him. She couldn't look at it now.

All winter she lived in a dark cocoon, oblivious to anything but her own sorrow. On New Year's Day, she braced herself and again went into his study. She sat down at the desk and stared at his notes.

She knew his handwriting by heart, the letters formed in sweeping strokes, hard to decipher, that distinctive slant of the lines upward to the right. A masculine hand, not the perfectly formed letters of a dutiful schoolgirl like herself. She had looked at this writing for more than a quarter century, at the little notes he wrote to her, attached to other people's letters: *"Polly, what do you think? Can we do this?"* about some invitation, or on a statement from Blackwood about royalties.

For a second, it was as if she were again in daily intimacy with him, experiencing his very existence in front of her. Then, within seconds, the brief sensation of his being there with her flickered out. He'd vanished, the air was empty. The walls grew up around her again, the desk in front of her, the vacant room, big and shadowed in winter.

———————

The snow began, driving with blizzard force outside the window. Brett came to tell her that the pipes had frozen. The plumber was so busy with all the broken pipes in the other houses on the street that he couldn't come till tomorrow. Brett knew she felt the cold terribly, and now, in this state, she felt it even more. Brett made a fire in every room of the house for her and brought her a blanket to put around her shoulders, then a pair of George's silk socks.

"Silk is very warm," Brett said, as she pulled them over her feet.

"My principal task in life is to keep you warm," he had always said. And now he was doing it again.

At the end of January, she saw the little drop of blood in her urine. She knew what would happen next, and terror seized her. Always, a few hours later, the pain came and exploded in her left side. "I'm going to fetch Sir James!" Charley said.

She lay there on the bed begging God to make Sir James come soon.

And then there he was, stooped and benign, standing over her with his hooded eyes and his keen, intelligent face.

"What have we here, dear lady?"

"I think I'm going to die," she said.

"Not yet. I promise you, you and I will grow old together. Just give me a moment." She heard the words "another attack of renal colic," and then glimpsed the wonderful hypodermic in his hand. He was pulling up the sleeve of her nightgown. "Don't move," he said. At last the longed-for prick of the needle, and almost immediately she was floating, the pain was dissipating.

She slept, and when she awoke, Sir James was there and gave her more morphine.

———

One day she woke up and the light in the room was different. The clock said four o'clock, but the sun was still out. It must be spring. The big elm branch outside the window had little green tips on it, buds to come.

On the windowsill was a bowl of crocuses, brilliant white and purple flowers with golden throats.

"What are those?" she asked Brett.

"From Mr. Cross. He sent them when he heard you were ill."

"How kind," she said. They were in a blue-and-white japonaise bowl with a delicate pattern of figures in kimonos and wispy trees on it.

"There's a note," Brett said.

"Could you read it?"

"Dear Marian, You know I share your grief. George was my dearest friend and I do hope you'll let me come and see you soon. He asked me to look after you. Until then, I hope these crocuses cheer you up. They're a harbinger of spring. (If you look out the window you'll see that they've already come up on the grass.) Meanwhile, I remain, Very Truly Yours, John Walter Cross."

She remembered Charley telling her that Anna Cross had died, only ten days after George. She'd been so selfish in her grief, she'd hardly paid attention to what Johnnie and his brothers and sisters must be suffering at the death of their mother.

A day later, when she was stronger, propped up in bed with her writing board, she wrote to thank him. She couldn't see him now, she said, but *"Some time, if I live, I shall be able to see you—perhaps sooner than any one else."*

She recovered, and went back to work on George's manuscript. He was trying to carry forward Spencer's efforts to forge a philosophy that would fuse science, the human mind, culture, and politics, all together. Usually, he was such a clear writer, a journalist who could make anything comprehensible to the intelligent reader—the life of Goethe, the principles of philosophy, marine biology. But as he tried to clarify these fundamental questions of metaphysics and verification, his sentences had grown tangled. She had no idea what he was trying to say: *"The analogy between the growth of an organism and the growth of knowledge is further recognizable in the inevitable mixture of materials unfit for assimilation..."* What on earth did he mean? She held the paper away from her. The glasses Dr. Liebreich had prescribed didn't do much good. Her head was aching.

The arrival of the proofs from Blackwood for *Theophrastus Such* interrupted her, but she paid no attention to them. She was too busy working on George's *Problems*.

She struggled on, crossing out and inserting words and phrases where he'd not completely made his point, consulting his other writings for clues as to what he intended. As she was immersed once more in the products of his mind, her suffering seemed to grow worse, as if a hard surface were pressing against her bruised heart.

—286—

Outside the window the canal bank was now covered with daffodils. The fragrance of spring drifted in through the window. There was new leaf flesh on the trees. Beyond, on the water, a barge passed languidly by, the horse pulling it along the towpath, the man guiding it with his long pole.

She couldn't stand it anymore. She told Brett to summon the landau so she could go for a ride.

Outside the house on the pavement, Abner, the coachman, was waiting. Noggin, the horse, was standing there patiently, all clean and white.

"I'm very sorry about the Master, Madame," Abner said, removing his cap, when she came down the steps.

"Thank you, Abner. I deeply appreciate it." She went up to Noggin and stroked his velvety black nose. "Hello, Noggin. It's been a long time since we've seen each other, hasn't it?" The animal gave her a flicker of a glance with his big, dark eyes.

Abner helped her up into the carriage. "Just drive," she said, "anywhere. Where there's green. Sunlight. I don't care."

Noggin clop-clopped along the North Bank in the sunlight, past the white stucco mansions, the flowering bushes peeking out over the tops of the high walls. Strange new world.

As they headed out toward Maida Vale it became more countrylike. There were little cottages and gardens, fresh green willows, lilacs blooming, their fragrance heavy in the air, the smell of the warmed loamy earth, the heat breaking down the old leaves and brush, and new cut grass, the full panoply of the English spring.

She ordered Abner to stop so she could get out and walk, and she set out along the road by herself.

As she went, a skylark lifted out of the field and, wings whirring, let out its complex trill of little syllables, the song of sunlight, and then it returned to the long grass where somewhere it had laid its nest. She spotted a flash of red and white in an oak tree, a woodpecker, and heard the dum-dum-dum of its drilling. A flock of yellow finches scattered through the air. She named the birds in her mind. The names of things. Words. Order in the universe, taking possession. Bringing things to life again. She'd escaped from prison. She raised her head to the sun and felt the warmth on her face. Delicious.

In the next few days, as she continued to work on George's *Problems*, she realized the best thing to do was just to put some of his thoughts into her own words. She wrote an introduction for the section called "The Affective States." *"A phenomenon may be accurately observed by us although we are incapable of explaining it."* There are mysteries that can never be fully understood—like death itself, its finality. We will never understand them because our minds don't have the ability, we lack the cognition. There are phenomena the meaning of which we can only imagine. In the end, she knew, he accepted that. And she too.

Chapter 19

They were circling her like vultures. Word had gotten out that she was getting better. They wanted to borrow money from her. Bertie's widow, Eliza, whom she was already supporting, wanted fifty pounds more. Bessie Parkes wanted a whole five hundred pounds—probably for some women's cause of hers. Bessie was rich in her own right. Why did she want Marian's money? The rich liked others to give money to their projects, it conferred stature and validity. But she'd already given money to Bessie and Barbara for their crusades, albeit not that much. The woman question was much more complicated than they made it out to be, and their noisy declarations unsettled her. She was frightened too that if she used her fame as a writer to proclaim on such subjects as women and marriage, it would draw the world's attention to the irregularity of her marriage to George, and she couldn't bear to be scrutinized and judged, to have the moral, and physical, condition of their relationship discussed.

And as for Eliza, she and George had been giving her two hundred pounds a year since Bertie died. Eliza was always asking for more. What should Marian do? How much money did she and George actually *have*? Where was it all? She hadn't been paying proper attention, she hadn't cared as long as there was enough of it.

Johnnie Cross would know what to do. She dashed off a note to him. *"I am in dreadful need of your counsel,"* she wrote, and signed it, *"Your much worried Aunt."*

He sent back an answer immediately. He'd be there tomorrow.

The next day, before he was to arrive, she realized that he'd be the first outsider allowed into the house. There would be an introduction of beauty and youth into the dismal place.

It was raining, a bitter London rain that always came and disappointed you just when you thought it was spring. She wondered if, given the weather, he'd still come.

But she mustn't be caught unawares in this disheveled state. After lunch, for the first time in weeks, she sat down at the dressing table and studied her face in the mirror. Since he'd died she'd avoided mirrors—the Jews always covered their mirrors when there was a death, an excellent custom.

There was even more gray in her auburn hair now, and strands of white too. His illness and death had made her hair turn white! There were new lines on her face, ridges down the sides of her mouth. Her eyes were close-set, dull, neither blue nor gray.

She rubbed her cheeks to give them some color and pinned her hair in loops on either side of her face to make it seem fuller. For the first time since he'd died, she rubbed powder on her face to try to soften the lines.

She put on her usual black silk dress with the lace collar, and the black mantilla over her head.

Just before four, when he was to arrive, she positioned herself by the fireplace in the drawing room, in the shadows, as she always did. She heard the bell ring and the sound of voices. Brett announced him, and then there he stood in the doorway.

He came toward her, tall and youthful. His face filled her vision. It was grave and worn after Anna's death. His red hair was damp from the rain. He was dressed in a black mourning suit, perfectly draped on his frame, obviously newly made. "Marian, I'm so glad you've let me come," he said softly, fervently, in his sweet, soft, Scottish-American tones.

He reached out for her and pulled her gently to her feet and kissed her on the cheek. As he drew her to him, she could smell the fresh spring air on his skin. She felt the dampness of the rain on his suit against her face, the mass of his body.

His blue eyes were shining with tears.

"I've been so selfish," she said. "I forgot about Anna. I've been so engrossed in my own troubles, I didn't even write. I couldn't say the words."

"Now I'm here to help you," he said. "We'll try to heal together. What can I do to help you?"

"I suddenly realized I don't know where our money is, or how much I even have, or how to get it!"

"Not to worry," he said. "I've got records of everything. We'll get it straightened out."

He was confident, serious. She felt her anxiety abating a little.

He took her hand. His was strong and very large, and it completely enveloped hers.

"Are you doing anything for yourself?" she asked him.

"You'll laugh," he said.

"Why would I do that?"

"I've started reading Dante. I'm trying to teach myself Italian. I'm using the Carlyle translation as a crutch."

"That sounds like a wonderful thing to do. Why should I laugh?"

"Well, I'm not exactly a man of letters, you know. I'm more of a games man."

"Everything's contained in Dante. Perhaps I'll read it with you."

"Would you?" he said, as if she were offering him a present. "Your Italian's so good. You could teach me."

"Let me think about it. I'm not ready yet."

"Please," he said. "I hope you will."

They chatted for a moment more. Then he kissed her hand. "I'll be back tomorrow at four," he said. "With everything you need."

He came at four o'clock precisely. Clicking open the locks on his briefcase, he undid the straps, all solemn business, and took out a pile of papers. He'd done a summary of all their finances.

"I went to see the solicitor this morning," he said. "He says that for the will to go through, to get at your money, you're going to have to change your name."

"Change my name?"

"You see, most of the money, and the two houses, the Priory and the Heights, are under the name Lewes."

"But I *am* Marian Lewes. I've always been Mrs. Lewes."

"Not legally." He saw her anguished face. "I know. It's terrible. Legally, there's no such person as Marian Lewes because the marriage wasn't—" He hesitated to say the crude word "legal," but she knew, of course, what he meant.

They never discussed with Johnnie, or anyone else, the fact that they weren't legally married. In the early days, they'd try to explain the legal issues to close friends. She'd tried to tell Isaac. But then they stopped out of pride. They refused to dignify their love with an explanation. As far as they were concerned, they were married.

Johnnie went on, tactfully, "You'll have to change your legal name from Evans to Lewes. Under the law, it's done by a legal document—it's called a deed poll. I can arrange that for you with the solicitor and all you'll have to do is sign it."

"I'm so weary," she said. "It's so cruel. Before I can have my *own money?* Well, now at least my marriage will be 'legal,' after the fact."

"I agree," Johnnie said now. "It's a travesty." He coughed with embarrassment. "Now, for the money…You've got a great deal of it."

"I don't care about being rich. I just want to know I'll be able to eat and have a roof over my head."

"That's certainly not going to be a problem." He picked up a piece of paper and read down a list. "By my calculations, you've made about £45,000 from all the books together. *Middlemarch* has brought in nearly £10,000. *Daniel Deronda*, £9,200 so far. Even the poetry's sold extraordinarily well."

She told him about Bessie Parkes and Eliza asking for money.

"I'd advise you to wait until the estate is settled before giving anything away."

"Thank you," she said. "I feel a bit better. I know you're partly responsible for helping George make so much out of all our money." Suddenly, tears welled in her eyes. "How am I going to manage without him?"

He took her hand. Once again she noticed his hand, big and manly and unblemished, even the nails were perfect, oval, their tips perfectly straight. "Don't worry," he said in his lovely, young, tenor voice. "You've got me to help you now."

He shuffled through his pile of papers and passed one to her. "Here, I've listed all your investments."

"I can't look at it. I don't understand it. I don't want to know about it."

"I realize that. But I do want to say that I think you should sell some of the American securities, the San Francisco Bank, and Continental Gas. They're too unstable. I'd say you should sell about five thousand pounds' worth. And then invest the money in London and Northwestern Debentures."

She waved her hand. "Please. Just do it. It bores me."

"Very well. I'll draw up the papers for your signature."

"Also, I'd like to arrange for the annual payments to Bertie's widow, Eliza, to continue..." She hesitated. "And to Agnes Lewes in Kensington."

At the mention of Agnes, he gave her a sharp look, knowing what this meant. He was familiar with their accounts.

At last, she returned to their bedroom, to the bed where he'd died. Brett had thoroughly cleaned the room, but she'd told her not to touch his things, to leave his clothes in his wardrobe, his silver brush and comb on his bureau. The thick, brittle strands of his black hair still clung to the bristles of the brush. She touched them with her fingertips. Here were the only remains of his flesh. Opening his wardrobe, she buried her face in his jacket: there was still his vague, indefinable smell in the cloth, a bit of sweat, his cigar. Beyond, the bed was freshly made up for her, sterile in its cleanliness.

The first night, the sheets were cold, the mattress seemed hard, the bed too big, and she couldn't sleep.

The next day, going through the drawers in his study, she found all the letters she'd ever written to him, not many, for they'd rarely been separated. He kept them in a tooled leather box with a brass clasp. She pulled the chair up to the fire and read each one over, then threw it into the flames and watched them lap at the pages, the paper shriveling and disintegrating into black. She thought of the Hindu rite of cremation, intended to release the soul from its mortal prison. His body had been put into the earth, encased in a coffin to stay its disintegration. They said it took a year for the flesh to vanish, except for the tendons clinging here and there to the skeleton. Then, in forty to fifty years the bones become dust...

Outside now, the London spring was in a blaze of glory, the ground was covered in pink azalea petals, there were masses of bluebells under the trees. Through the open window came the smell of water from the canal on the breeze.

Johnnie arrived at the house in a burst of color. He'd ceased wearing his mourning black and now he had on a different-colored suit each time he came, cream or beige or blue, with brightly colored silk waistcoats and cravats. He was always elegantly dressed, a young man who cared about clothes. Perhaps it wasn't really petty vanity; perhaps he was aware of his fine form and thought it should be dressed appropriately. He was a man at ease in his own body; all of its shapes and angles were perfectly, evenly balanced. Completely different from her own dear man, that scruffy little person with his hair all awry, wearing the same clothes year after year until she noticed the holes in them and made him get new ones. She'd loved that total lack of vanity in George. But in Johnnie, there was also something to admire his God-given beauty—and it came with kindness.

She wanted to create a memorial, a George Henry Lewes Studentship in Physiology, at Cambridge perhaps, to enable young men to get training in those subjects that George had been interested in. Johnnie helped her set it up.

"A brilliant idea," she said.

"All will be done," he said.

Another letter came from Blackwood, asking once more about her new book, *Theophrastus*. When might she get a chance to go over the proofs, he asked, so they could go ahead with publication?

She knew the book wasn't very good. It would never sell, her readers were expecting a novel—but George would have insisted on her publishing it. And he'd be reminding her that she was always worried and depressed about every new book, no matter how successful the last one had been.

It took only a week for her to go over the proofs. Finally, the thing was done.

At last she let Herbert Spencer in. He swept eagerly into the parlor, like a dog finally allowed back into the house after being banished for some misdeed. He was more stooped now, balder, with long, gray side-whiskers.

"Marian, I am so sorry," he said, bending down and kissing her awkwardly. He seldom looked at one directly. For a brief moment, he studied her and his face was uncharacteristically awakened into curiosity about her, the other person. His best friend had died and the man's widow was there before him. Hastily he looked around the room as if he didn't know what to do next.

She indicated the chair across from her. "Do sit," she said. He obeyed, crossing his long legs tightly, winding one calf around the other, then locking them together, hunched over, his arms wrapped around his body.

His eyes wandered around the room. His theories of "social evolution" had made him the most important philosopher of the age. He'd never married, giving the excuse that he was "too much given to fault finding" to find the right woman.

"Shall I have Brett bring us some tea?" she asked. "I could use some of Mrs. Dowling's lemon biscuits." Their tart sweetness would give her strength for this.

"Oh, no, no." He seemed, as always, rather miserable.

"I had a chance to read *The Data of Ethics.*" In the midst of her mourning, he had delivered a copy of the new book to the house with a note saying he'd like her opinion of it.

He looked directly at her. "Yes?" he asked, hopefully.

"I thought it was very commendable," she said. "But I disagree with you on one point. You say the best government is the least government, that human behavior will evolve naturally because maladaptive traits such as aggression won't be reinforced. But this so-called social evolution is a long way off. Until then, there has to be government, people have to have laws."

He seemed chagrined.

"I believe in the rule of law," she said. "I can't escape that. Turmoil frightens me." She was still, in so many ways, her father's daughter, a conservative, a child of the Tory Midlands.

"But if you have less rule," he said, "when people behave badly they're punished, and inevitably their behavior withers." He was animated now, since they were talking about his book.

She shrugged. "I've said my piece." A sudden exhaustion descended over her. She didn't care about his book. She'd made her stab at friendship. She had no energy for anything more.

Then, as if having dispensed with the proper condolences, he could get down to his real purpose. "I've actually been eager to speak to you. I was waiting until you were recovered. I wanted to ask your advice about my autobiography. You know I'm writing my autobiography, of course?" Indeed, he'd been writing it for years. He continued, "As I said, the book is supposed to be a sort of natural history of myself."

"As you said."

"I want to be candid about my faults."

"That's very courageous of you." She smiled—she couldn't help it. It was all you could do with him at times. He usually failed to notice the reactions of other people.

"Yes, I do have many faults," he said now. "And I think I owe it to the reader to own up to them."

"Why not?" she said. It was rather fun to egg him on a bit, a distraction.

"For instance, I'm writing a passage now about my tendency to criticize."

"I've seen that in you," she said.

"I thought I'd use my criticism of saltcellars as an example. I warrant I'm a bit silly on the subject. But, nonetheless..."

She let out a little giggle, but put her hand in front of her mouth just in time and he didn't notice it. She couldn't resist encouraging him. "And—?"

"Well, when I was a boy, saltcellars were made in the shape of either ellipses or parallelograms. Thus, the salt spoon always remained in place on the edge of the saltcellar."

"I see..."

"Nowadays," he said, "saltcellars are all circular, and the result is, the spoon falls onto the tablecloth." He said this with a straight face and no apparent self-consciousness.

In the past, she would have let him go on, amused by his eccentricities. But suddenly exhaustion was enveloping her. "I'm sorry," she said. "I'm still very tired—"

He looked up at her, startled. "Yes. Of course...," he said, again as if he'd realized, for a moment, that one wasn't supposed to go and on about one's own troubles to exhausted and grieving widows.

"I think that you should probably go," she said, as if he might miss the point. "No single night's sleep is ever enough."

"Of course." He stood up, shook himself off, and looked at her worriedly. Perhaps it occurred to him now that he should have talked about something else, perhaps about George and his great accomplishments, or asked if there was anything she needed. "I'll go then," he said. "But I'll come again."

On his way out of the parlor, he stopped and for a moment focused on her again. "I did want to say something. I wanted to say—" He hesitated. " I wanted to say that...I think that you are the most forgiving person I've ever met."

And with that, abashed, he quickly pulled on his coat and hurried out the front door, as if embarrassed by his own words.

So, she thought, he did remember that he'd once broken her heart.

After he left, she thought of what she and George would say now, how they would've laughed, but not unkindly, at the poor man, at his strangeness, his utter self-centeredness.

That evening, she wrote to Johnnie and invited him to tea the next day. He would bring relief from the gloom, from the musty, lingering presence of Spencer.

———

The following afternoon, when he came, she said, "I would like to read the Dante with you. I think it would help me too."

His face lit. "I'd love that. I've been struggling."

"Where are you up to?"

"Only the first ten lines. I'm having trouble concentrating. It would help so much to have someone else doing it with me."

"Why don't you come on Monday?" she said. "And then we'll start again from the beginning."

So he began coming to the Priory with his Dante and his Carlyle. They sat side by side on the settee, a foot or two apart, each with a copy of the Italian.

"Why don't you put away the Carlyle," she said, "and try it on your own?"

"*Nel mezzo del cammin di nostra vita...,*" he read, in his Scottish-American accent, with its flat *a*'s and round *r*'s. "*Mi ritrovai per una selva oscura.*" His accent was a travesty, but the earnestness of a big, grown man struggling like this was touching.

"'In the middle—'" he translated.

"Go on."

"'In the middle of our life...'" He stumbled along next to her like a beginning schoolboy, every now and then looking up for her approval. She smiled indulgently.

She prodded him. "Yes?"

"'I was in...I was in a...,'" looking up again for guidance.

"No," she said. "'I found myself in a dark wood...'"

"'I found myself in a dark wood...,'" he repeated.

"Very good. Now, continue." As she waited for him to come up with the words, she studied him. She realized that she was observing him more closely than she ever had. He wore his dark red curls slightly long, his hair was colored a deep red, rich and shining with health. His eyelashes were dark brown and unusually long and curly for a man. His skin was pale, still downy above the line of his beard.

She was in a familiar and reassuring position, as a teacher of young men, all those young men who came to their "Sundays," seeking her wisdom.

He was saying, "*Chè la diritta via era smarrita...,* 'I had lost...' something or other..."

"'I had lost the straight path,'" she told him, touching his hand to guide him. He went on, following the Italian with his fingertip.

She withdrew her hand.

The next day she told Charley, "Dear boy, really, there's no need for you to come so much." He had been coming nearly every day since November when George died. "Gertrude and the girls need you," she said. "Everything's in order now, everything's better with the spring. I can manage. Johnnie's got all the business things under control."

She thought Charley looked relieved. "I'm so grateful to Johnnie," he said. "I know the Pater would be too."

At last she visited his grave. The head gardener at Highgate led her along the gravel path to Number 84 and his headstone embedded in the bare earth. *George Henry Lewes, Born 18th April, 1817, Died 30th November, 1878,* the letters and numbers still sharp in the granite. The soil around it was packed, brown, dry, and sterile, crabgrass beginning to grow up.

She stood in the shade under the trees alongside the gardener in his cap. He leaned on his shovel and contemplated the grave with her, a wizened, bent-over old man, with dirt-stained hands and cracked nails. The Spirit of Dryness and Death, she thought, yet genial in his kingdom, at ease, not afraid of the dead bodies in their graves.

As they stood there, the birds chirped in the trees and bushes nearby, a stray cat sunned itself on a tombstone. Around them, the hushed voices of mourners and tourists could be heard, as if this were but a pleasant garden.

"It's so bare," she said. "I'd like to plant some ivy. What else, do you think?"

"Maybe jasmine?" the gardener said. "Blooms in the winter, nice little yeller flowers. They've got a nice scent, very delicate-like."

"Yes. That would be good. When everything else is gray and desolate."

He was beginning to live now in her mind as a shadow, in a one-dimensional plane. Sometimes she could summon the sound of his voice, his laughter, his exclamations—"Oh, bollocks!" and "Polly, where are you?"—the note rising at the end in his jovial way, promising relief from the hard work of the day. "Tell me where you are and I will tell you what I have in store for us today to cheer you up and make you laugh!" That voice would always be in her mind, wouldn't it? A form of aliveness. But the image was fading now.

———

In late spring, Sir James said that she was strong enough to go down to Witley for the summer. "You're fit as a fiddle, my lady," he said.

"But the little pain?" she asked. "It's still always there—on the left side. It never goes away. I know it's going to come back."

"You don't know. It won't necessarily."

"But what if it does and I'm in the country?"

"I'll rush down from London immediately. Country air is what you need," he said. He smiled down at her, kind and amusing. "I've got one prescription for you."

"What's that?" she asked.

He laughed. "One pint of champagne daily. Champagne chases away all sorrows. Best medicine in the world."

She ordered Brett and Mrs. Dowling to pack up. In the third week in May she left London. She arrived at the Heights amid the new green and the spring flowers, the pink phlox, the violets showing through the grass. The horse chestnut blossoms were already in bloom, outrageously full and luxuriant. Were the flowers more lovely in England than anywhere else in the world?

On her second day there, Johnnie drove the sixteen miles from Weybridge to see her.

Now that it was warm she had discarded her usual black for a white muslin dress and mantilla, white being the color of summer mourning, and lighter in the heat.

They continued with their Dante in the summerhouse, which was down a steep slope from the main house and the terrace, and built on flat ground. George had himself roughed out the design for it. It was a little fairy place, with a conical roof and a finial on top, shaded inside yet open to the breeze and with clematis climbing up the sides.

Sitting on the bench with her, Johnnie was physically close yet removed. As if he'd been made suddenly cautious by their new isolation. She could smell faintly his young man's perspiration, not unpleasant. He wore his shirt open at the neck, his red chest hairs escaping from it, his skin gleaming with health and youth.

She admired him as if he were a son. A mother loved her son for the purity and cleanliness of his young body. A son was the embodiment of maleness in its unthreatening form; masculinity was harmless in the sweetness and youth of a boy who was dependent on her. And ultimately, wasn't the love of a mother for her son in some way sexual too, the love of the female for the body of the male, but the love of an ideal? Nature's ideal, something young and pure. And untouchable.

She realized again that she'd never actually seen Johnnie with a woman his own age, other than courteously talking to some female guest in a group. "Perhaps he's just a man's man," George had said. "He just prefers the company of his friends. I ran into him the other night on Shaftesbury Avenue and he was with a group of young men and they were having a grand old time. Been drinking a bit. They were laughing and playing with one another. On their way to some club, they said."

"You don't think he's a—" She couldn't say it.

"A Nancy boy? I doubt it." He laughed. "Though, you never know." He thought about it a moment, then he shook it off. "He's just a late bloomer, that's all. He'll find someone eventually."

But in the ten years they'd known him, Johnnie hadn't found someone. Other than his mother, the person Johnnie seemed closest to was Albert Druce. "I shouldn't say this, but he's even more of a brother to me than Willie, I think," Johnnie said.

Albert's wife, Anna, looked just like a female version of Johnnie, she could have been his twin sister. Albert had taken for a wife a woman who looked just like his best male friend. Marian had seen a portrait of Anna from before she married Albert: she was very pretty, with long, curly red hair, blue eyes, and pale skin. After she married, her looks had faded. She had removed herself from her marriage, it seemed, and was completely preoccupied now with the children, Eliot and Elsie. She refused to let the nanny tend to them, and she hardly had time for adult conversation. Every time you tried to speak to her, she'd spot the children doing some mischief and hurry over to bring them to order. Of all Johnnie's myriad nephews and nieces, he was fondest of Albert and Anna's children, Eliot and Elsie, and he was their godfather.

Marian invited Johnnie to dinner with his brother, Willie, and his two sisters, Mary and Eleanor. Narrow-eyed Willie was quiet and watchful. Mary was worshipful as always, Eleanor small and bubbly like their mother.

After supper, Eleanor asked Marian if she'd play the piano for them. She hadn't touched the instrument since George died. "I don't think I could..."

"Mama so loved to hear you," Eleanor said. "Do it for us."

They followed her into the drawing room and she opened the piano bench. On top of the pile of music were the sheets for Liszt's "Bénédiction," the piece he'd played for her and George in Weimar years ago.

She put them up on the stand and stared at the first page, trying to remember how to read notes. They were just shapes and lines, dead before her eyes.

Finally, she summoned her memory. She took a deep breath. The notes and the old connections came clear. She began to play, but stumbled over the trills and stopped.

"I can't," she said.

"Go on," Johnnie said. "For us. Make us happy."

Johnnie and Willie and the two women sat very still, waiting to see if she'd go ahead. She tried again. She sensed them sitting back, but her energy flagged, and she stopped. "I'm so rusty," she said.

Mary, tall and kind, came over and kissed her cheek.

———

In the seclusion of the summerhouse, Johnnie's concentration on Dante was now total. The heavy scent of jasmine hanging in the air around them, and the prescribed champagne, which she took in small doses throughout the day, made her languorous. There was a swelling of her body in the heat.

They arrived at Canto II, and the first mention of Beatrice. She stopped to give him a brief explanation of what was to come: "Her real name was Beatrice Portinari. Dante saw her only a few times in his life and they probably never spoke or touched one another. She married Simone dei Bardi and died when she was only twenty-four. Yet her image haunted Dante all his life. She was the personification to him of spiritual and physical beauty, a holy figure, his guide, forever chaste."

"They never touched?" he asked.

"Probably not. But he held her up as his ideal always."

He read the passage "*E donna mi chiamò beata e bella...*"

She interrupted. "Not a long *e*. It's '*eh*,' a short *e*. Remember, you separate out the syllables..."

"'A—lady— called—to me...blessed and beautiful...I begged to serve at her command...'"

He continued, first the Italian, haltingly, then smoothly, better than ever, stopping every few lines to translate. "'For I am Beatrice who made you come...I come from a place where I long to return...Love moved me...which makes me speak—'"

Again he stopped. He faced her. His face was damp, his eyes glowed. "Be-a-tri-che," he said softly, pronouncing the syllables long and separate in the Italian way, the accent on the final *e*. Then, in a whisper, "You are my Be-a-tri-che."

She was embarrassed and averted her eyes. He said, "You've got the voice of an angel. I thought that the moment I met you. It was the first thing I noticed about you in Rome."

And then suddenly came the words, "Marian, will you marry me?"

"What!" She let out a laugh, then she hid her face in her hands and shook her head.

"I'm serious. George wanted me to take care of you. I want you to be my wife."

In spite of herself, she spluttered, "This is utterly ridiculous!"

But his face was stern, his voice hushed, intense. "I mean it."

"Johnnie," she said, suppressing another uncomfortable laugh. "I'm embarrassed. Perhaps you should go."

He must have gone mad. She touched his shoulder. She could feel the solidity and tautness of the muscle under the cloth of his shirt. "You're sweet, Johnnie. But this is silly. I don't know what's gotten into you. I think we'd better go back up to the house." She stood up.

"Promise you won't make me stop coming?" he pleaded.

"Yes," she said uncertainly. "I promise." Her hands were shaking. She put her arms down at her side to hide them. "But maybe you shouldn't stay for tea."

He paused, then rose. He began climbing the stone steps to the terrace. She watched his departing form, tall and elegant. He didn't know what he was doing. It was a lie, a chimera.

She waited in the summerhouse until he'd disappeared. The shadows lengthened. When she was sure he'd gone, she walked slowly back to the house. Was it possible that he could be physically attracted to her? That he saw something in her that was pretty?

Brett had set the supper table, as usual for her alone, with the gold-rimmed Royal Doulton and a white lace cloth.

Before she touched the food, she drank down the glass of champagne that Brett always put there to accompany the meal. These days, in accordance with Sir James's prescription. In seconds, its calming effect pervaded her body.

What had come over him? He was grieving for Anna, he wasn't himself. The sensuousness of summer, the glow on her skin from the heat, distorted her, made her seem young to him.

This man, with his long-stemmed body, his clear blue eyes...desiring her? The flight of fantasy disappeared as quickly as it had come on.

Brett poured another glass of champagne, wiping the mouth of the bottle with a linen towel. "What a lovely prescription, ma'am," Brett said, "that Sir James has given you."

"Yes, lovely." She drank down half of it at once. "But it's a shame to have it by myself. Would you have a glass too Brett?" She'd never asked Brett to sit down at table with her before. Brett had been with them since she was a fourteen-year-old girl, a tiny, boyish figure, totally devoted to her and George. Brett was the surest thing in her life now, steady, constant, a certainty. But who was Brett, she wondered suddenly? The only thing she knew about her was that every Sunday, on her half days, she dressed in her long black coat and hat and went out to Hackney to visit her mother. She lived in the servants' quarters upstairs, a place where Marian never ventured. She wanted to be respectful of the servants' privacy.

"Thank you, ma'am," Brett said. "But I'm a teetotaler." There was a boundary that Brett knew better than to cross, that made her ultimately unknowable to them and preserved her dignity. Servants forced themselves to love their masters to make their daily work tolerable.

"You're good to be a teetotaler," she told Brett. She picked up the glass, raised it to Brett, and took another sip. "Don't worry, Brett. It's only the second glass. Doctor's orders—remember?"

———————

That night, when she went up to bed, the second floor of the house was hot and airless. There was an immense orange moon in the bedroom window hanging over the land, seeming almost as big as the earth itself. A nightingale had recently taken up residence in the elm and, as if on cue at her presence, it began to sing. "Yup-yup-yup...tweet-tweet-tweet..."

It was so hot that she took off her chemise and drawers. She was about to put on her nightdress when she caught a glimpse of herself in the cheval mirror.

She stepped closer to the mirror. She'd lost weight. Her flesh seemed to hang in creases from her arms and thighs. Her breasts, once firm, were flattened and hollowed out. The woman's hair between her legs had thinned and become gray. She was an old woman, not to be seen by anyone. Did the same thing happen to other women when they aged? She had no sister living, no Chrissey, whom she might have seen undressed.

Outside, the nightingale continued its song, little trills going on and on, mysterious and lonely in the dark. *Light-winged Dryad of the trees...*

Its song drowned out all the other sounds of the night, the grasshoppers and the cicadas..."Yes-yes-yes," it seemed to say.

————

When he next came to call, carrying his Dante, he said not a word about their previous conversation, as if afraid she'd make him go away forever.

The summer had reached its apex, not even the shade of the summerhouse provided relief. Johnnie kept on with his translation, stuttering like a schoolboy, constantly looking up for approval as he plodded along, she smiling constantly with encouragement.

"You're making a noble effort," she teased.

"This is the most important thing in my life now."

"I would hope you have something better to do."

"No," he said.

In late August they arrived at Canto VII and the Fifth Circle of Hell, where the sullen and the perpetually self-pitying are mired in the banks of the river Styx.

"*Tristi fummo ne l'aere dolce che dal sol s'allegra,*" he read.

"Yes?" she prodded.

"'Sad'?" he asked. "'We were sad...'?"

"Yes?"

He stumbled along. "'We were sad in the sweet air...'"

"He's saying there is no virtue in gloom. It's only an excuse for idleness. He's telling us we must give up gloom." She paused and smiled. "Perhaps we should listen to him," she said. "Both of us. 'The sun makes the air sweet and we shouldn't use our sorrow to be idle here...'"

Suddenly he clasped her hands in his. "Let's take the lesson," he said. "Please, don't make me go away again. I want to marry you, Marian. I want to make you happy."

At once she wished she could disappear, that her body would shrink into itself. The thought of...what he would think if...if he actually embraced her, kissed her full on the lips...felt her body close to his own—smelled her, her breath?

"It's impossible. I can't," she said gently.

"But why?"

"I'm terrified...I couldn't bear another man ever to—to be a bride—the physical side—"

He put his arm around her shoulders. "Marian, if that's what you're worried about..."

She nodded blindly.

"Then," he said, "it's no impediment. We don't have to be that way...We can be—lovers in our hearts and minds, but not the other way, if that's what you insist on..."

An odd disappointment slid from the back of her throat down to her womb. She surprised herself. Was he willing to give that up?

"I can't think about it now," she said. "It's all too soon. It hasn't even been a year."

"Then," he said, "let me just take care of you. We'll put the subject aside. For now. All I want, more than anything in the world, is to see you healthy and happy. And perhaps to see you write another novel again."

She didn't answer him. They'd reached a détente. She hadn't refused him absolutely, though they'd agreed not to discuss it.

They began taking private walks through the woods, arm in arm along the dappled paths. He didn't mention his proposal, but he seemed at ease, grateful she hadn't cut him off entirely. He seemed resolved to abide by her admonition that there be no real physical contact between them, and he held his arm out stiffly for her to hold.

He never kissed her on the lips upon arrival and departure, only on the cheek.

As they walked along the paths, as she looked up at him at her side and admired his young man's beauty—he was thirty-nine years old, to her, young. She admired the damp flesh of his neck, his curls stuck to his forehead in the heat; she wondered, just for a moment, what it would be like if his lips did touch hers. But the thought lasted only a second. Then fear overcame her.

They began to ask each other questions, like typical young lovers exploring the contours of one another's souls.

"Have you ever been in love?" she dared to ask.

"I've never loved anyone but you," he said firmly.

"Please—don't say that."

"But it's true," he said calmly.

"You mean, you've never even had a—romance?"

"I never have," he said.

It had taken a lot to ask him that and she didn't pursue it.

Another time, he asked her, "Do you believe in God?"

"I believe in the religion of humanity," she told him. "I believe God is but a projection of our own best qualities. Religion is doing good, kindness, bringing a smile to someone's face, the smile on a father's face when he catches sight of his little girl."

"That's wonderful," he said. "What language did Jesus speak, anyway?" he asked.

"Didn't they teach you that at Rugby?"

He smiled, abashed. "Probably. I don't remember. As I've said, I wasn't much of a pupil, I'm afraid. Hebrew, or Greek, wasn't it?"

"Jesus was born in Bethlehem," she said, "but he spent most of his life in the Galilee in the North. They spoke an Aramaic dialect. He probably had a little Greek too, because that was the lingua franca of the day, and some Hebrew, because it's very like Aramaic."

"I should've known that," he said.

"Well, now you do," she told him.

———

A letter came from Blackwood, saying that, contrary to all expectations, *Theophrastus* had completely sold out, six thousand copies in four months. She had no interest in the reviews. They were probably bad.

The next morning, in a surge of new confidence, she took out the "quarry" in which, before George died, she'd started making notes for her new novel on the Napoleonic Wars, and she began to write again.

She'd conceived, dimly, of a central character for the story. He'd be a man wrongly accused of something. There was always someone wrongly accused in her books. The central character in her new book would be wrongly accused of selling weapons to the French enemy.

Now, what to name him? The naming of a character was so important, like christening a child. You had to live with it for years. Perhaps Cyril—from *Kyrillos*, "lordly, masterful," with its sacred undertones. Cyril Ambrose—"Ambrose," connotations of amber, something embedded within, hidden. *"Cyril Ambrose,"* she wrote, *"a man of inventive power in science as well as philosophy married young, is very poor, has a family to support..."*

But she didn't have a complete story yet. Perhaps if she did more research, she'd discover one. That was usually the case. She'd carted down some of her books on the Napoleonic Wars to Witley from London, hoping to get something from them. They were heavy tomes. *The Memoirs of the Life of Sir Samuel Romilly,* a solicitor general during the wars, and *The Principles of the Law of Evidence: With Elementary Rules for Conducting the Cross-Examination of Witnesses.*

Now, every morning, she got up, went to her desk, and read through the various books, jotting down notes. Her days started to assume something of their old, contented rhythm, work in the mornings, entertainment in the afternoons, only now with Johnnie at her side, encouraging her and propping her up.

———

In early September, the air was golden, dryer. The leaves began to turn, drifting softly to the ground. The flowers in the garden were mostly gone, except for the late-blooming purple asters.

Barbara Bodichon wrote to say that she was coming down to Witley for a visit. It had been so long since she'd seen her friend, with whom she'd shared so much—even John Chapman. She was coming alone because the good Dr. Bodichon was in Algeria.

It was a shock when Barbara got off the train. She was in her fifties now, her once golden hair was graying, and she'd had a stroke. Instead of her old self-confident stride, she dragged her foot. Seeing her, Marian couldn't speak. Was this what she, Marian, must look like now to her old friend Barbara, worn and gray?

She recovered, and rushed to hug and kiss Barbara and to help her with her things.

They arrived at the Heights, and suddenly it was filled with Barbara's energy. She brought out gifts, including a painting she'd done for Marian of the sere Algerian countryside. Barbara was quite well known now, her work had been exhibited at the Salon and the Royal Academy. "And here's Eugène's book, *Étude sur l'Algérie et l'Afrique.*"

Marian had invited Johnnie over from Weybridge to see Barbara. At supper he was charming, as if trying to win her old friend over to his cause. Barbara was full of news about Girton, the women's college she and her friend, Emily Davies, had founded at Cambridge, to which Marion had donated fifty pounds, a generous sum, more than Brett's annual wage. "The main building's complete," Barbara said. "We've got a new science laboratory for the women. Now we've got to raise more money...By the way, Marian, I assume you've made George's physiology studentship open to women?"

"At the moment, it does say 'male,'" she admitted.

"But you can't do that," Barbara said. "How can you?"

"You know how confused I am about the whole thing."

"Confused?" Barbara said. "How can you be confused about it, knowing me?"

"I signed the women's property rights petition because the law is so obviously unjust. And I did contribute money for Girton. But as I've said, I worry about the effects of all these changes." As they spoke, Johnnie looked from one to the other smiling, as if in awe of them. She felt self-conscious at his unreserved worship, his open adoration.

"But you have to change the studentship to allow women," Barbara said. "You know that George would have wanted it."

"I'll look into it. I promise," she said.

"You'd better," Barbara said. "I'm going to keep at you till you do."

"I know you will," Marian replied, with a smile.

The next day they went for a ride in the trap. "You're feeling better, aren't you?" Barbara said, smiling at her, as they drove along the Surrey lanes.

"I'm always better in the country."

"I'm so grateful you've got Johnnie Cross. It makes me happy to know he's watching over you."

"Yes." Her face reddened.

Barbara stared at her. "Are you actually blushing, Marian?"

"He's over twenty years younger than me."

"There're plenty of men who've fallen in love with older women. Look at Annie Thackeray and young Richmond Ritchie. By the way, I hear she's *enceinte* again too." Two years before, Thackeray's daughter, Annie, had married her cousin, a man who was eighteen years younger than she. And they'd had a child, a daughter.

"Obviously, Johnnie wants to look after you," Barbara said. "He could have plenty of other women. He's certainly good-looking enough. You're not holding him prisoner, are you?"

"Really, Barbara."

"Marian, I knew George. I'd swear with my full heart that he always wanted you to be taken care of. He loved Johnnie."

"But...I'm an old woman."

She groaned. "You've always said that sort of thing about yourself. No one who loves you agrees with you. You've got a lovely figure, the figure of a much younger woman."

"A figure that's aging rapidly...I'm ill all the time."

"You're ill because you're still grieving. When you give it up, then your life will be restored. Give the poor boy a chance." She went on. "Sometimes, young men want something more than just...physical satisfaction. They're searching for spiritual fulfillment too. They want something other than a stupid, pretty face. Marian, be kind to the poor man. You're going to lose him."

Lose him? And then what? Then she'd be alone. How would she manage? She had a vision of the coming winter in London, the cold, the silence of the Priory walls, no voices but the occasional sound of the servants, all those days to fill, trying to work, without love, without encouragement.

———

Johnnie announced that he was going up to London.

"Must you?" But she had no claim on his company.

"I've got business I simply have to attend to."

That night, after he left, for the first time, she was afraid here in the countryside, though Brett and Mrs. Dowling and the other servants were in their rooms. She saw herself, a small figure in the great dark space of the house, all those empty, unused rooms, the woods beyond. Who knew what lurked there?

She wondered what he was really doing in the city. He said he was staying at the Devonshire. But did he have some other life up there she didn't know about? That was silly.

While he was in London, she continued working on the new book. When she was finished for the day, she drifted restlessly about the huge house. She tried to read, but she could only read so much.

A kind of madness overtook her and she wrote to him at his club. *"Best loved and loving one,"* she said, *"the sun it shines so cold, so cold, when there are no eyes to look love on me..."*

He didn't know anything about Hebrew verbs, *"or the history of metaphysics or the position of Kepler in science, but thou knowest best things of another sort, such as belong to the manly heart— secrets of lovingness and rectitude—"* She hesitated, then signed it *"Beatrice."* "Beatrice"—that was what he called her, what he wanted her to be. As she sealed it, she realized it was a love letter.

At the beginning of November, in London for the season, he took her about to galleries and concerts and on long, brisk walks through Regent's Park. He came up with new ways to occupy and distract her, just as he'd done in the old days with her and George.

They went to the Grosvenor Gallery to see Whistler's scandalous *Nocturne in Black and Gold*, the subject of Ruskin's scathing review. It was a painting of a fireworks display in an industrial park, with a dense, foggy night sky, a mass of black and gray, and flashes of light, nearly indistinguishable from anything real except for a few crudely drawn human figures watching the festivities.

Johnnie asked, "Do you agree with Ruskin?"

"I rather venerate him. I've tried hard in my own work to follow his theories about truth and nobility in art." She nodded at the painting. "I think it's a dreadful mess."

As they went about, she was conscious of what they must look like to the world, the tall, striking young man with the older woman, her head bent, her face shaded by a mantilla.

Perhaps people thought he was just one of her many acolytes, escorting the widowed celebrity. Perhaps they thought he was her son. He seemed to have a kind of dazed, beaming pride at being with her, as if her fame gave importance and meaning to his life.

One evening, as they were leaving the theater, a young woman stopped her, went down on her knees in front of her, and clutched at her skirts. "George Eliot! Oh, the wisdom in your books!"

Embarrassed, Marian bent down to the woman and tried to extricate herself. "Oh, dear," she said. "I don't think we've met, have we?" She looked to Johnnie for help.

"What are you doing?" Johnnie said to the woman. "Please! Mrs. Lewes is in a hurry." He sounded a bit proprietary, she thought, guarding his exclusive access to her.

But she didn't begrudge him that. He'd made himself her protector, her encourager, and she needed him now. He was an ornament on her arm, he had such fine carriage, he walked with pride, conscious of his good looks and expensive clothes. He was at her beck and call. She, who'd been such a plain young woman and had never been sought after by any handsome man, now had the hand-somest man of all.

He came to supper almost every night. Afterward they sat in the drawing room by the fire, reading aloud, just as she and George would do. They finished Dante and went on to Shakespeare, Chaucer, Wordsworth, none of whose works he really knew. It was strange to be with someone who'd read so little, or remembered so little of what he'd read, but she was touched by his desire to learn. Again, it was like having a son. Brett would come in and say good night, and seeing them together, would smile benignly at them.

She read: *"There was a time when meadow, grove, and stream..."*

He: *"The earth, and every common sight / To me did seem / Apparelled in celestial light..."*

They read in rhythm, as if they were playing chamber music. Saying the words to each other was the romance, the basic declaration unspoken.

The days grew shorter, winter came, their walks through Regent's Park were curtailed by the cold. The rains began and the fog made the days even darker. The shop windows were lit even in the afternoon. There were reports of hansom cabs crashing into one another in the miasma.

She sensed the coming sorrow in her bones, the anniversary of George's death. She asked Johnnie not to visit that day.

The week before Christmas, Johnnie left London to see his sister, Emily. Emily and Frank Otter had resolved whatever their mysterious quarrel was that day long ago in

Weybridge, when Frank had seemed to be angry at Emily and made her cry. Marian had never discovered what their argument was about. But Emily and Frank had married now and were ensconced at their estate in Lincolnshire.

On Christmas Eve, Charley and Gertrude and little Blanche and Maud and Elinor came to lunch and she gave them their presents, including a big doll house, completely fitted out with furniture and miniature paintings and china. She played with them for an hour, lost in their little world. When Gertrude told the girls it was time to leave, Blanche, who was seven, asked politely, "Can we take it home with us?"

"I want to take it home!" Maud cried.

Baby Elinor, sensing her sisters' discontent, started to cry.

"I'll tell you what," Marian said. "I'll have it delivered to your house, but I'll get another one just like it for here so we can always play together when you come. Is that all right?" And the little girls nodded solemnly.

Outside the window the gaslights glowed faintly in the yellow darkness. She wrote to Johnnie, calling him her *Bester Man,* and told him that she'd be alone on Christmas Day, smelling the servants' goose cooking, but she was well and content. She didn't want him to think she was lonely for him so that he'd feel burdened by her.

But, she asked, could he come to supper on Tuesday if he was back in town? If not then, Wednesday?

He did come, and she played the piano for him, Schubert sonatas. He sat apart from her on the settee, watching her from afar with an elated expression on his face. And at the end of the evening, he drew her to him. She raised her face to him and instinctively closed her eyes, expecting him to kiss her on the lips. For a moment, she wanted him to, she was giving him permission. Instead, he pressed his lips to her forehead.

She felt a question, another moment of disappointment. But, of course, she'd been the one to insist she didn't want a physical relationship. He was observing her prohibition, respecting her fear. She was relieved it hadn't come to that, that he hadn't taken that further step. Who knew where it might have led? To a frightening place, to his realizing the truth of what she really was, the truth of her old body. Then he would flee and she would lose him forever.

He took up his coat and hat, went out into the foggy night, and left her in the empty house.

She was alone, and the sadness was renewed, like a rock in her heart, unyielding as ever, the incomprehensibility of George's absence.

When morning came, she continued on the new novel. The work was reassuring. She had her hero, her impoverished inventor, Cyril Ambrose, desperate for money to feed his family. He wants to sell a weapon he's invented to the government to earn money.

But how exactly to make that happen? Maybe Cyril could unwittingly sell the weapon to a double agent for the French? Who would the double agent be? *"We should presume the strongest case against him,"* she wrote. *"He travels in the interludes when war allows as an agent for a great Museum or other institution..."* She had to give the man a name. What about "Rastin"? Good name for a villain, echoes of "Rat."

How would she ever finish this without George to read every word and prop her up? She couldn't imagine asking

Johnnie for help, or showing it to him and asking his opinion. He had none of George's intellect and learning, his magical imagination, his scientific and legal knowledge. Johnnie had never written anything in his life, except for that essay in *Macmillan's* years ago about his days in New York.

But it didn't matter. Just to see his bright face, experience his kindness. He could help her in other ways. Her letter to him had said it all.

———

At last, spring broke through. Walking in Regent's Park, they were confronted with a scene of overwhelming beauty, cherry blossoms falling to the ground like pink snowflakes, the willows turning golden as they leafed out, flower beds filled with masses of red and yellow tulips.

One day in April, Johnnie took her hands. "Don't say anything. But please, at least give me some kind of an answer? I'll wait, but not for long."

She opened her mouth to object. But he touched his finger to her lips, the first time, she realized, that he'd touched her mouth. "Don't answer yet. Just think it over."

They walked on, admiring the lake, the boats floating on the water, the cricketers out on the fields. There was a peaceful smile on Johnnie's face. Every now and then, someone would stare at her, as if recognizing her, but he continued proudly with her on his arm, she bending forward slightly, as she always did, to hide her face.

———

She asked Sir James to call on her at the Priory.

He came in, small and thin, with those twinkling eyes of his, eyes full of knowledge and cheer, though he saw death every day, every terrible disease. He never talked about the royal family, who were his patients, but she knew that he had recently discovered another important disease, Paget's disease of the breast. His accomplishments were endless, he'd also discovered trichinosis, which came from the parasite found in pork, and when she was writing *Middlemarch* she'd pumped him for information about medicine for her doctor character, Lydgate, and he'd generously given her details about such things as the treatment of addiction. Everything always had to be exactly right, down to the smallest detail.

She was nervous. "It's so nice of you to come. I know you're very busy."

"Never too busy to see my friend," he said. "Are you well, my lady?" He answered his own question. "I see from your smile that you are. When will we resume our evenings? I'm eager to hear you play the piano again."

"No recurrence," she said, smiling. "Though I still have that constant sensation in my side."

"Don't worry about it. It may never develop into anything again."

"But how do you know?"

"It's a sign of a small narrowing in one of the ureters, that's all. But it won't necessarily lead to trouble. Try not to think about it."

"I've got something important to discuss with you," she said. She was smiling, but how could she not, seeing the dear man?

"Because you're smiling, I imagine it's good," he said.

"I don't know. That's what I want to ask you about."

"Ask ahead," he said. "I'm a man for all tasks."

"I feel rather…uncomfortable discussing this."

His voice lowered, but he still smiled. "We've been through a lot together, you and I. You should never feel worried about speaking to me about anything."

"Mr. Cross…," she began. "He's asked me to marry him. I said no, of course. I'm sixty years old, more than twenty years older than he is. I'm ill…and weak…and…he's asked again…I don't understand it." She looked at Sir James. He was smiling broadly now. "He does make me happy. The loneliness has been unbearable."

His face filled with sympathy. He took her hand.

"Madam, you're healthy now. And the care of someone like Johnnie Cross who loves you, who's young and strong, will only make you healthier and stronger. I believe happiness is the cure for many ailments."

"But happiness and love didn't cure George."

"No, sometimes we're defeated. But here, Madam, you've got a chance for life. To live a second time. You thought you'd never be happy again."

"Please don't say anything to anyone about this—"

"I am, you know, a person who keeps his counsel."

"I realize that. Forgive me. But I don't understand why he wants it. I'm not pretty."

"To many of us, you are very beautiful indeed. Your goodness, your brilliance, and your kindness shine in you."

"Thank you, dear Sir James. He's a young man, he could have any attractive young woman—"

"Why wouldn't he rather have you? There's no one more brilliant in this land. Youth, prettiness, they fade away. And far too often when there's only physical beauty, there's no meeting of the minds. I've seen a lot of unhappiness when that happens, believe me."

She pondered this while he searched her face with eager eyes.

She stumbled on. "I—I'm very afraid of the...the physical side of things...with anyone but my dear husband. The thought of it terrifies me." She was too timid to say more, to say that part of her wanted Johnnie's ardor to overcome her fear, that she did have the wish that he'd love that part of her and that it would all come back, what she'd known with George.

"Does Mr. Cross know about your worries?"

"I've told him...in so many words."

"And what does he say?"

"He says—I think he says—he'll accept me on whatever terms I want."

"Then there you have it, don't you? He's man enough to know his own mind. He'll take you under all circumstances. That's love, I'd say. A definition of love."

"Then, you think I'm well enough?"

Sir James threw back his head and laughed. "Madam, I'm looking forward to seeing you only happier and healthier from this day on."

Then he kissed both her hands vigorously and left her, smiling.

———

That night, she sent a boy with a note to Johnnie's club summoning him.

When he arrived, his face was bright with hope.

Softly, she said, looking up at him, "I've spoken to Sir James. He says my health is good enough to marry. He thinks it's a wonderful idea."

His face seemed to swell, then tears began to run down his cheeks.

"Are you sad about it?" she asked.

He sat down and hid his face, then took out his handkerchief and wiped his cheeks. She saw that his shoulders were shaking, and she touched his arm.

She drew his head close to her waist and cradled it. At last he ceased and looked up at her and smiled. Then he stood up and took her hands. "We've got to set the date!"

"Yes," she said. She was suddenly dazed, unable to think clearly, disbelieving that she'd accepted him.

"We'll have the ceremony at St. George's, Hanover Square," he pronounced jubilantly.

"The ceremony?" she echoed, still unable to process it all.

"Yes. It's the only place to marry." By this he meant St. George's was where the most fashionable people in London married. "I want to do it properly." His eyes still gleamed.

"But..." She, who'd disdained for all these years the legal ceremony of marriage, the need for religious sanction, who'd made a principle of marriage based only on true love, she hadn't thought this through, what a marriage ceremony would mean. Marriage in a church?

Johnnie asked worriedly, "You're not against it?"

"No, I suppose it would be all right—but if only a very few people, the people we really love, are invited."

"I'll make the arrangements immediately. We'll do it as soon as possible. I've waited long enough."

She marveled at herself—that she'd so readily agreed to this, to be like other women. To be the woman her father would have wanted her to be.

Then, excitement, relief, expectation burst out of her as if she were a young girl again. This meant he'd never leave her. "Shall I ask Albert to give me away?" she said. She sensed it would make him happy to have Albert standing there beside them at the altar.

"That would be wonderful," said Johnnie. "Then we'll all be standing at the altar together."

"Please," she said, "we must tell absolutely no one till it's done."

"But why?"

"Because—people will make fun of us. They'll try to talk us out of it. It'll get into the papers."

"I don't care. Let them."

"Can they publish the banns without my real name on them?"

"But we've got to tell my brothers and sisters," he said. "And Charley. You must tell Charley."

"Will you tell him for me?" she asked. "I'm too afraid."

"Of course. I'll go tomorrow and ask him for your hand like a proper gentleman. And I've got a surprise. I've already found us a house."

"A house?"

"Yes, we're going to have our own home. We can't live here with all the sad memories. We're going to start fresh."

"How did you—"

"I've been living on hope." He laughed. "I began looking around, so at least I could imagine it for myself. Discreetly, of course. I didn't tell anyone it was for you."

She asked, falteringly, "Where is it?"

"Cheyne Walk. By the river. It's absolutely perfect. We'll go over there in the morning. But I'd better go now," he said, "and start making arrangements."

And with this he drew her to him and kissed her on the forehead. Not on the lips.

Chapter 20

H e was seized with a feverish happiness, running about, attending to details, the ceremony, the new house. Sometimes, in the middle of his rush, he'd grab her hand and kiss it. "Polly!" he'd cry. (Occasionally he slipped into "Beatrice.") "I'm so happy." He was possessed, catapulted into pure joy, as though if he stopped for a single moment she'd change her mind.

The morning after she accepted him, in the kind, spring sunshine, they drove over to 4 Cheyne Walk. The house had belonged to William Sandys Wright, president of the Society of Antiquaries, and it was the prettiest one in the row, red brick, with a crenellated roof and a wrought iron gate with a crown on top.

As they toured the inside, they came to an L-shaped room on the upper floor overlooking the Thames. "This will be your room," Johnnie said. "It's got the best view of the river. I'll be right across the hall." Married people often had separate bedrooms, of course, though she and George never had. He was reassuring her that he'd keep to his end of their understanding.

On Tuesday they took the train down to Weybridge, and Willie, Mary, and Eleanor were there at the station to greet them. They looked puzzled at this unexpected visit in the middle of the week.

"I have wonderful news," Johnnie said. "Marian and I are going to be married!"

He stood there beaming, but the three siblings were silent. She saw a frown on Mary's face, as if somehow she didn't understand what he was saying. Willie was unsmiling. At last, Eleanor, round little Eleanor, flung herself on Marian and hugged her. "Sister! We can call you 'sister' now!"

Then Mary stepped forward, smiling gravely. "I've always wished you could be my sister," she said, uncertainly, and embraced Marian.

Willie said nothing, as if he were calculating something.

"Willie?" Johnnie asked. "Aren't you going to congratulate us?"

Willie hesitated. Then he said quietly, "It's a bit of a surprise."

"But aren't you happy for us?" Johnnie asked exultantly. "You never thought it would happen, did you?"

"No," said Willie. She wondered for a moment why Willie had never thought it would happen. Then he too came forward and kissed Marian on the cheek. "Marian," he said stiffly. "I wish you every joy."

They gave them lunch. Eleanor and Mary now seemed delighted by the news. Willie smiled, but was still muted and withdrawn. On the way back to London on the train, she said to Johnnie, "Willie didn't seem very happy about us."

"He's just a solemn fellow. He's got no sense of humor. He looks down on me as his younger brother. And I'm getting married before him. Hah!"

When they got back to the Priory, Charley was waiting, stalwart and kind. *"Mutter,* I'm so happy for you," he said, and gave her a vigorous hug. "But I'm not letting Albert Druce give you away. That's *my* honor."

———————

They set the wedding date for May 6, three weeks hence. There was a rush of things to do, new wills to be drawn up. Johnnie had no need for her money, he was very rich in his own right. She left five thousand pounds to her niece, Emily Clarke, Chrissey's daughter, and a hundred-pound annuity to Cara Bray. She provided for Bertie's widow, Eliza, and for the servants. The rest of her estate and her royalties would go to "my son, Charley Lewes," the only one of George's sons remaining. Johnnie's estate would go to Albert's children, Eliot and Elsie, since there'd be no children from this marriage.

Johnnie was consumed with the arrangements. They'd honeymoon in Europe and return to England in late summer to the Heights. There was the renovation of the house on Cheyne Walk to attend to. It all had to be completed and ready by December, when they'd move back to London from the country for good.

Johnnie decreed that the entire place had to be gutted and new plumbing installed. He hired the decorator George Faulkner Armitage from Manchester to redo it. "I'm happy to leave it to you," she told Johnnie. "I'm afraid that sort of thing bores me. I just like to enjoy the results." All she cared about was that it be finished and orderly so that when they returned from the honeymoon she could settle in and get to work. She could feel the new novel growing in her now, needing to be written. It made her happy and tense, as if there was a new being in her demanding to be born.

"I'm worried that the books be properly arranged," she said, "so I can get to them quickly." She'd begun to put them in the chronological order of her possible story, books on weaponry, domestic spying, military tribunals. If they were disarranged now, her new, fragile structure might collapse.

Mr. Armitage, a small, serious Scotsman, suggested bookcases with molded cornices. "I'll draw up some sketches," he said. "And designs for wallpaper, perhaps a flower motif, pink and pale cream."

"I want everything light and cheerful," Johnnie said. "With a Gothic theme, perhaps, but not dark and heavy."

Then there was the matter of her trousseau. Mary and Eleanor suggested Madame La France's on Battle Square, where their sister, Anna Druce, had gone for her trousseau. It was an elegant little shop with damask walls and gilded mirrors. They were served tea while Madame La France, who was actually Polish, a wizened little woman with a humpback and a tape measure around her neck, showed them sketches and had her girls model dresses for them.

First, the wedding dress. "Something quiet, I think," Marian said tentatively.

"But not black," Eleanor said. "You absolutely cannot wear your usual dreary old black, Marian." Eleanor was the most enthusiastic of the sisters about all these details. She wanted desperately to marry herself, but had no suitors yet. For now, these arrangements for Marian's wedding would have to suffice.

"Perhaps lavender?" Marian said. "After all, I'm a widow. It's a second marriage. It shouldn't be too celebratory."

"But it's a happy occasion," Mary reminded her quietly.

"Something with black lace, at least?" Marian said. "As a sign that I'm a widow."

Madame La France barked at her assistant, "Bring out that lavender satin, dear."

A young girl twirled around in front of them in a lavender satin gown trimmed with dark blue lace. The dress was dignified, the color muted, but not too solemn.

"I suppose it will do," Marian said.

Next, there must be a dress for special events. She chose the pale green silk with tiny flowers embroidered on it, trimmed with orange braid. The pale green was kind to her sallow skin and brought out whatever color there was in her cheeks. The little embroidered flowers fascinated her with their perfection and intricacy. She felt a surge of enjoyment at this women's stuff that had never engaged her before. She gave herself permission to indulge, to enjoy it.

On to Harrod's, to Heilbronner's, Bon Marché, and Harvey Nichols to buy hats, nightclothes, underthings. As she and the two sisters examined the nightgowns and the chemises and the muslin drawers with their little silk ribbons in the waist to tie them, she felt constrained. They were his sisters, and when she realized what they must be thinking, picturing their brother seeing her in these undergarments, she wilted. Still, the buying of new undergarments was part of the marriage rite, wasn't it?

The wedding night? She shouldn't wear a white nightgown—she was hardly a virgin. White would make it seem as if she were pretending to be one. There was a long nightgown of ecru satin, with a low neck and little sleeves trimmed with lace, and she chose that, with the negligee to match. Ecru was appropriate for a woman who'd already had a lover, but was coming to a man with a fresh, new love for him.

She must choose the most alluring things she could find, for there was always the possibility that he would catch sight of her by accident—or perhaps on purpose—and she should be prepared. And then perhaps the delicate ecrus and pinks clinging to her, with their promise of what was hidden beneath, would make him overlook her aging body.

Such moments of excitement crowded out her fears, but the excitement itself frightened her. She spent as much money as she wanted, giving herself for the first time, at the age of sixty, the gift of the rites and rituals of a bride, night-gowns and chemises trimmed with lace, new dresses. She did it blindly.

In those rare instances of quiet when there wasn't business to attend to, it all overwhelmed her—what was she doing, marrying a man twenty years younger than she? There had been no physical connection, no long kiss even. Why did he want this? Whom could she ever discuss it with? No one. To question it now would be embarrassing. And if she told someone, perhaps Barbara, one of the few people she could trust, simply articulating her worries out loud would make them more real to her, more powerful. Though Barbara had championed Johnnie at the beginning, now that the wedding was actually coming to pass, she might try to talk Marian out of it. Barbara was a force to be reckoned with, hard to disobey. She realized now she didn't want to be talked out of it.

As doubts played in her mind, she felt lonely. How could a virile young man accept the possibility of marriage without "the physical side"? And how could she go for the rest of her life without the comfort of someone's arms around her in the night?

There was always something to interrupt these thoughts, a detail about the ceremony, the honeymoon, their hotel accommodations, arranging the boat and trains, Johnnie asking her approval. Perhaps this was why weddings were such a deliberate frenzy, they provided distraction for the bride and groom who'd taken a momentous decision, a public one that couldn't be revoked without heartbreak and shame.

Sometimes during those three weeks before the wedding, she'd find Johnnie brooding, sitting back in his chair, and looking into the distance as if he hardly knew anyone else was in the room, and anxiety would seize her. Had he changed his mind? Did he regret the whole thing?

"Are you all right?" she'd ask him, and he'd come to, startled. "Yes, yes. Just a lot to do, that's all. Making sure everything's absolutely perfect."

A few days before the wedding, she wrote notes to her closest friends, to Barbara, and to Mr. Holbeche, the solicitor who administered her father's estate, telling them the news, but instructing Charley to post them only after she and Johnnie had left the country. She asked Mr. Holbeche to inform Isaac about the marriage. Isaac didn't deserve to be told by Marian herself that she was now doing the proper thing, but she wanted him to know that at last she was "an honest woman." She drew up a wedding announcement for the

Times and instructed Charley to deliver it to the newspaper after they'd embarked on their honeymoon. It was not to be published until two days following their departure, when they were safely away from all the gossip.

On Thursday, May 6, at 9:30 in the morning, they arrived at St. George's, Hanover Square. They made up a tiny party, Charley, Gertrude, Albert and Anna Druce, Willie, and the other sisters, gathered close to the altar, lost in the great church with its spacious nave and empty galleries and stone floors. All through the ceremony, she felt weightless, barely conscious of the proceedings. In the distance somewhere, the Reverend Capel Cure was saying, "I require and charge you both, as ye will answer at the dreadful day of judgment when the secrets of all hearts shall be disclosed, that if either of you know of any impediment, why you may not be lawfully joined together in Matrimony, ye do now confess it..." Such angry words, as if this were the beginning of something final and painful, of death itself. There was no joy in them.

Holding her breath, closing her eyes, and plunging into the deep water was the only way she could do it. On either side of her, Johnnie and Charley held her arms, held her up. Johnnie, tall and elegant in his claret frock coat and cream silk cravat and waistcoat, looked firmly ahead at Capel Cure. She saw that his lips were trembling.

"Wilt thou have this man to thy wedded husband?" the Reverend asked.

"I will," she uttered, in a bare whisper, her throat so dry she could hardly speak.

Finally, the blessing. "God the Father, God the son...that ye may so live together in this life..." She was in a trance, shutting it out, everyone embracing her now, Charley, and Eleanor, who longed so much to get married herself and who'd been excited by the whole process of the wedding more even than she had, austere Mary, and Anna Druce, and a vague hug from Willie. Albert, Johnnie's other and perhaps more important "brother," bent over her and kissed her. "Welcome to the family, Mrs. Cross," he said with a smile, his voice as always soft and musical. She was completely passive. The Crosses, Charley and Johnnie, were bearing her along.

It had taken place, her first legal marriage, and a church wedding at that. Marian Evans Lewes was now legally Mrs. John Walter Cross. All those years with George, she'd stubbornly called herself Mrs. Lewes, intransigent in her deviance from convention, insisting that their union was all the more sacred because it was based only on love. Still, when the first opportunity at a legal union presented itself to her, she'd seized it and reversed her principles. This young man had wanted her. And now, at sixty years old, George Eliot was, at last, like other women.

———

They went back to the Priory to sign their new wills. Then off to Victoria Station, everyone, Charley and Albert and the sisters and Willie, waving to them as if they were a young bride and groom setting forth in life.

They were exhausted. Once on the train, they sank with relief into their seats. She sat back, Johnnie took her hand. She felt its warmth and strength. No need to be afraid. His determination would carry them along.

On the way to Dover he slept. She watched him, marveling at her prize, his dark eyelashes resting on his cheeks. He was still in his wedding costume, wearing the white carnation she'd pinned to his lapel. She'd changed out of her lavender wedding dress into a black traveling dress, but he'd wanted to keep his wedding suit on. "It's my first and only marriage," he said. He'd loved that part of the procedure, being outfitted for his wedding costume at Henry Poole's, the best bespoke tailor on Savile Row.

As the train rattled peacefully toward Dover, she looked upon him with love. He slept innocently, a pure, clean youth, a work of art—a Renaissance painting or a sculpture. And he was hers. Poor thing, he was exhausted.

He'd booked rooms for them for their wedding night at the Lord Warden in Dover. She and George had stayed there twenty-five years before when they'd first sailed back to England from their "honeymoon" in Weimar as man and wife. Was it a mistake for her and Johnnie to stay at the Lord Warden too? But it was right next to the station and near the pier, the most convenient spot.

They had a quiet meal brought up to their rooms, smiling at each other over the candlelit table, not saying much. In the back of her mind was the question, what would happen next? Would he keep his end of the bargain? Or, now that they were actually married, would he beg her to break it? Overcome by his eagerness, would she give in? To be held and touched and know those sensations again that had been gone from her since George became ill...If he knew what was in her mind, what would he think of her? After she'd insisted, so adamantly. But these thoughts coming to light within her frightened her.

They finished supper. He wiped his mouth on his serviette. What would he do now? She was too nervous to speak.

He stood up. "Come, Polly, you look tired. I think you're ready for bed."

"I am. There's nothing like signing your will to exhaust you. Or getting married." She laughed.

"But it's done." He came around to her, gave her a hug, then smiled. "It's wonderful, isn't it?"

"The maid's unpacked my things." What she meant was that the maid has gone for the night, we are alone now, we can do whatever we want.

"But the man will be coming to clear away supper," he said. He was saying, no, they wouldn't really be alone yet. They'd be interrupted. "I'll wait up for him. You go to bed now. We've got a long day tomorrow."

She paused, about to say something else. "Very well."

He glanced through the door into her bedroom. "It looks like a very nice room." He didn't move to enter it. As if it were her sanctuary, and to cross the threshold would be rude, an improper intrusion of his male presence. "You can hear the waves while you're sleeping. It's very restful."

She was lingering. Wondering. There was an awkward silence. He looked away.

"I think I'll just sit here and have a whiskey," he said. "Till he comes. It'll help me sleep."

"But aren't you tired too?"

"I slept on the train. Night sleep's always hard for me." For a second, she thought of taking him in her arms, and stroking his hair and soothing him until he fell asleep. Making love—that would surely make him wonderfully tired, bring him a delicious slumber.

"See you in the morning," he said. He kissed her on the cheek and sat down decisively at the table.

She went into her bedroom. She reminded herself that this was what she'd insisted upon. She'd made it a condition and he'd had such a careful, earnest desire to comply with her wishes. He couldn't know her other desires because she'd never told him about them. Perhaps as they went along, got farther away from England, and relaxed, and were surrounded by beauty, with no one to interfere with them, he would seek her out.

Through the open window, she heard the pounding of the surf below on the beach. She undressed quickly, though she was by herself in the room and the door was closed. Still, he might burst in and see—what? The body of his bride.

She washed herself carefully. Eleanor and Mary had given her a jar of a rose-smelling unguent to rub on her skin. It made her legs and arms gleam. She unfolded the ecru nightgown she'd bought for the first night. When she slipped it on, it clung to her, showing her curves. In the low light, her flesh seemed soft and smooth.

Gently, she trimmed the oil lamp till there was only a faint flame. It was an unfamiliar place and the soft light made her feel secure. Then she lay down. She waited, eyes open, listening for the sound of him out there. It was the first of many times she would listen for him. She heard nothing.

———

The next morning, he was up before her, and had ordered her breakfast. When she walked into the main room, he was full of smiles. "Good morning, Mrs. Cross!" he said cheerfully.

"Mr. Cross," she said, inclining her head.

"Your breakfast awaits," he said.

"Ah, tea," she said. "You knew what I wanted."

"Of course. The ferry leaves at eleven. We should take a walk on the beach beforehand to get some exercise."

They went for a stroll along the sand, arm in arm, the white cliffs behind them, the wind blowing, the waves breaking nobly on the shore, France beyond, not far.

The steamer to Calais took only three hours. They had a good cabin right on deck.

From then on, every evening, after they finished supper, Johnnie kissed her good night. Then there was a momentary question in her mind—what would happen now? Would he follow her?

He didn't. And she didn't raise the issue with him. By not asking the question, she'd never have to know the answer. The mere statement from him of another reason for their celibacy, besides her insistence on it before the marriage, once uttered, would have a terrible finality. Better to leave things uncertain, unspoken.

As the days passed, in the excitement of seeing new places and the distraction of travel, she began to push the question down into the recesses of her mind. Who could be kinder, more loving than he? Only George. He was the best-looking young man, escorting this old woman with eyes only for her, guarding her. How lucky she was. Without him, she'd have retreated forever, seeing no one, bent over her desk struggling to work again with no energy, no hope, and failing.

When they reached Paris, Johnnie went immediately to the poste restante. People had read the wedding announcement in the *Times* and the letters were beginning to come in. Barbara had immediately dashed off a note: *"Tell Johnny Cross I should have done exactly what he had done if you would have let me and I had been a man."* Barbara, always so kind, always in favor of life, always on her side. Johnnie held up a letter from Albert, smiling. "Look," he said. "He's been going over to Cheyne Walk to check on the work for me. Isn't he kind? He says it's proceeding really well." Even Spencer had sent a warm note congratulating them.

They continued with their vigorous sightseeing. They visited the Louvre to see Veronese's *Marriage at Cana*, Christ's first miracle, the panoply of figures rendered in exquisite detail. Then on to the Sainte Chapelle and Notre Dame. And back again to the Louvre. Then a walk in the Champs-Élysées. Each day his pace accelerated as he made long strides through the streets, and she found herself lagging behind, puffing to keep up with him. "I want to see everything. I want to see the world through your eyes," he said.

"But your legs are so much longer."

"Then I'll hold you up," and he gripped her arm and bore her weight.

Now that they were at a distance from England, she started composing her own letters home. She seized on each happy moment, writing back the letters she'd always wanted to write about a honeymoon. She consciously infused them with joy. For that was what she knew how to do, make things more vivid and dramatic by giving them language. There was pride too, letting people know she'd done the right thing, that she was happy in marriage to this fine-looking young man. She wanted the word to spread all over London, to allay the gossips.

As the rhythms of the honeymoon continued, she was happy. Her doubts were reserved for the night, when she was alone. She couldn't believe Johnnie was truly hers. Other women noticed him wherever they went.

To his sister, Eleanor, she wrote, *"When we were walking by the sea-side at Dover we agreed either that wedding days had been much maligned or that ours was a marvelously exceptional one."*

"Marriage has seemed to restore to me my old self," she told Charley. *"I am very well—quite amazingly able to go through fatigue."*

They went from Paris to Sens, where Johnnie wanted to walk the old Roman roads, and to visit the cathedral, the oldest Gothic cathedral in France, dedicated to Saint Stephen. And then to the archbishop's palace, and the House of Abraham. He was relentless.

When did she begin to realize the change in him, to admit it to herself? In Dijon, when they arrived at the Hôtel de Jura, she was getting exhausted by it all, but he was energized, wound up, wanting to go out, to see things, the cathedral and the crypt of Saint Benignus. "It's supposed to be five hundred years old," he said.

"I can't do it," she said. "I think I'll just stay here and rest."

"Well, I'm going anyway."

Despite the energy he was expending, the days spent walking—running, almost—he only picked at his food. And then, in the mornings when she went into the drawing room for breakfast, he was already up, with dark circles beginning to appear under his eyes.

On they went to Mâcon, and to Lyons.

"You're losing weight, Johnnie," she said. "It's worrisome. Perhaps we should see a doctor?"

"I've never been better," he said, smiling.

"But you don't look better. You don't eat."

"I'm just not hungry."

"Then that's another reason to see a doctor. I'm sure we can find a good one here."

He laughed. "I don't have time for a doctor."

"I'm worried about you."

"Don't be. I'm a big man." He smiled. "I'm very good at taking care of myself. I'll have some whiskey before I go to sleep tonight. See if that helps."

"But you always have a whiskey."

"Then I'll have two whiskeys. Now," he said, "let's be off."

———————

At Grenoble, they took a carriage to the Grande Chartreuse. As they stood together looking across the vast valley, at the impossible green of it, and the monastery in the distance, the sorrow that had begun to lurk within her, that she'd been holding off, overcame her. George had never seen this place. She wished that it was he who was here with her, the way they'd always seen things together for the first time, their mutual joy, his excitement piercing her innate melancholy. She said nothing to Johnnie, of course. He was standing there open-mouthed, full of wonder at the sight, as if a spell had been cast over him. Well, let him love it in all its beauty, in whatever ecstatic way he wanted.

But when they got to Milan, she wrote to Barbara that she felt within herself a *"hidden river of sadness."*

As she read over her letter before posting it, she wondered, should she have confided her sorrow to Barbara? By admitting it, she was making it real. She added a sentence, leavening it. *"But this must always be with those who have lived long."*

In Milan, they toured the Brera Gallery, San Ambrogio, Santa Maria delle Grazie. Then Johnnie brought back to the hotel the most important letter of all. She glimpsed the familiar handwriting on the envelope and grabbed it from him.

"My dear Sister," Isaac wrote, *"I have much pleasure in availing myself of the present opportunity to break the long silence which has existed between us, by offering our united and sincere congratulations to you and Mr. Cross upon the happy event of which Mr. Holbeche has informed me... Your affectionate brother Isaac P. Evans."*

Even as she finished reading the words, the anger caught her by the throat. He'd managed to stay silent all this time. His stupid, rigid, country principles, his old-fashioned ignorance, his jealousy.

Politely, formally, she wrote back: *"It was a great joy to me to have your kind words of sympathy for our long silence has never broken the affection for you which began when we were little ones."*

She would never see him again, she knew that. Too many years had passed, over a quarter of a century, unrecoverable time. She was no longer the same little girl who had loved him. She envisioned him, aged now, retired, or soon to be retired, from his position as agent for the Arbury Estate, still living in Griff House, still with his strong posture and his big Evans nose, gray-haired, the rigid sureness of his authority.

No longer the impetuous little boy with the rosy cheeks who'd led her through the fields like Pan with his pipes. The pain of what he'd done had erased her love for him.

She thought of the lines she'd written about him when Thornie was dying, as she sat by his bed, trying to recover some happiness from the past:

We never found again
That childish world where our two spirits mingled
Like scents from varying roses that remain
One sweetness...

———

The next morning she and Johnnie took the train, their destination Venice.

PART VI

"A Proper Honeymoon"

Chapter 21

O n Wednesday morning in the Hotel Europa, she was
awakened by a loud crash. She rushed to the door of
her room, and in the gray light of the dawn, she saw him
stumbling around the *sala*. He'd knocked over a chair.

"Johnnie?" She entered the main room, and immediately
she was hit by the reek of alcohol.

He sat down hard at the dining table. His shirt was
unbuttoned, his cheeks stubbled.

"Where have you been?"

She went closer. She could smell vomit on him and filth.
The front of his shirt was stained yellow. "You've been sick?"

He looked down at himself as if not remembering that
he had vomited.

"Where did you go, Johnnie?"

"I went...to the Rialto," he said confusedly, "with
Corradini."

"You went out with that dreadful man? What did you do?"

"We went to...a place..."

"What place?"

He looked vague. "A *taverna*...by the bridge...I couldn't
sleep. I went out. He took me there..."

Images came to her, of figures in the shadows of the
bridge, furtive movements and shapes coming together,

fusing, pulling apart. She tried to blank them out. She didn't want to know. Something terrible, outside her ken. Something she didn't have a way to give meaning to. She squeezed her eyes shut, forced the images away.

"You're drunk," she said.

"Yes."

"You'd better go to your room. To bed."

He frowned. "I think I may be sick again."

"Well, don't be sick here, please."

He looked up at her and grimaced. "I'm sorry..."

"I don't know what you've done, Johnnie."

He stood up unsteadily, then he pitched forward and grasped the table with both hands to stop himself falling.

"Please, Johnnie..."

"What do you want from me?" He glared at her, his eyes big and wild and round, as if she were a monster who terrified him. "Don't touch me! Get away from me!"

He covered his face with his hands and backed away, trying to shield himself from her. Then he peeped around the edge of his hands, eyes darting from side to side.

"Johnnie, I think you should see a doctor!"

From behind his hands, he suddenly peeked at her coyly, grinning like a naughty child, as if to gauge her reaction, daring her, seeing how far he could go. He stepped back in exaggerated horror, hands still covering his face, but looking out at her through parted fingers. Then he twisted away and covered his face completely, his shoulders hunched.

When she could summon language, she said quietly, firmly, "Go to the bedroom, Johnnie. Please." She passed him fearfully, as far away from his body as possible, and opened the doors to the bedroom. "In there, Johnnie, I'm going to get help."

He snatched his pamphlets from the table and went inside. He stood in the middle of the bedroom with his head bent, his eyes darting sideways at her, grasping the pamphlets possessively to his chest as if he were afraid she was going to take them. Carefully, she approached the doors and shut him inside.

Where was Willie? How long would it take him to come? He'd have to get to Dover, and then take the boat, then the train, all the connections to Venice. It could take days.

She tugged at the bell cord. Within seconds, Gerita appeared. "We need a doctor," she told her. "Please. Go at once. My husband's ill. Go!" The girl turned to leave."Where does the doctor live?"

"The *dottore* is on the Ponte dei Conzorzi. On the other side of the Piazza, Madame."

"Go!" she ordered.

Twenty minutes passed. He was behind the door. What if he came out again? Would he hurt her? He'd pushed her on the beach. He hadn't cared if she fell.

She paced back and forth. From within the room, still there came the incessant murmur. "...*the figures of Adam and Eve, sculptured on either side...*"

There was a rap on the *appartement* door. It was Marseille, the manager, and behind him a tall man carrying a black bag.

"*Il Dottore* is here," Marseille said.

The man inclined his head. He had long, greasy, gray hair drooping in waves on the sides of his face, and wore a slightly soiled, shabby, gray linen suit. "Giacomo Ricchetti," he said. He looked around the room for the patient.

"He's there," she cried, pointing to the bedroom. "He's very ill. I don't know what's the matter."

The doctor crossed to Johnnie's bedroom doors, grasped the handle to open them, but they didn't yield.

"He's locked himself in," the doctor said.

He pushed his shoulder against the doors and tried to force them. She went up behind him and knocked. "Johnnie, can you let us in? We've got the doctor here to see you."

From within now came a bestial cry, a long, dry cry of agony, "No–o–o..."

"Get someone to open it!" the doctor commanded.

Just as Marseille moved to find help, there was a loud splash on the canal below, then shouts. Marseille and the doctor rushed to the balcony, looked down, then ran out of the room.

She hurried to the balcony. Below on the *riva*, there was a commotion, someone was thrashing wildly about in the canal, sinking and foaming and spluttering to the surface. She knew instantly it was Johnnie.

One of the gondoliers dove into the water and swam out toward him. "Let me die!" came Johnnie's voice from below. "I want to die!"

Three other men jumped in. He flailed at them, choking and sinking as they lunged at him.

A group of tourists had gathered to watch. On the canal, the gondolas had come to a halt. From the corner of her eye, she saw people standing on their balconies watching the spectacle.

At last they succeeded in grabbing him, his thrashing grew feebler. They began trying to pull him to shore. Was he dead? Was it too late? Then, from three stories above, she heard the words again, "I want to die!"

They dragged him up onto land, but his body went slack and they had to pull him across the stone. One of them, she saw, was the gondolier, Corradini.

Above, on the balcony, Gerita gripped her arm. "Oh, Madame." Marian couldn't bear to look. She buried her face in the girl's shoulder.

Minutes later, Corradini and the other gondoliers were at the door of the *appartement*, half carrying, half pulling the heavy body, followed by the doctor and Marseille. Johnnie refused to stand up, strands of kelp and filth hung in his hair and face, his clothes were half off, his trousers down around his knees. "No...no," he said. "I want to die."

"*Tenetelo giù sulla sedia!*" the doctor ordered.

They struggled to lift him up onto a chair. Corradini pushed him down and the chair clattered backward onto the floor. "Get a sheet," Ricchetti commanded.

While they grappled with him, Gerita ran into his bedroom and tore the sheet from his bed. They bound it around him and tied him to the chair. Kicking his legs out, he tried to free himself. Corradini pressed his weight down on them.

The doctor searched through his bag and took out a bottle of medicine and a spoon. He commanded the gondoliers, "*Ora tenetegli la bocca aperta.* His mouth! Hold his mouth open."

Corradini tried to pry open his jaws, but Johnnie bit down hard on his fingers. "*Cazzo!*" Corradini yelled.

"Fatelo!" the doctor said. *"Voi!* Do it! Hold the nose closed."

Corradini pinched his nose tight. Johnnie kicked and squirmed.

Ricchetti attempted to spoon the liquid into his mouth, but he spat it out and it dribbled down his face and neck. Ricchetti kept on trying to force it down his throat.

There was a crowd in the doorway now, Marseille, a footman, hotel guests attracted by the commotion. Thank God for the darkness of the girl's shoulders, her little arm holding Marian tight.

Johnnie, exhausted from battling them, began to submit to Ricchetti, taking in the spoonfuls of liquid. Gradually he grew limp, his eyelids began to droop. The medicine seemed to be taking effect.

"We must get him onto the bed. Take him in there," Ricchetti ordered. "Do not leave him alone. Clean him. *Provate a pulirlo."* They pulled Johnnie's big, sagging body up and into the bedroom, his head lolling, his mouth agape. The doctor followed and they slammed the door behind them.

Gerita drew Marian into her own bedroom and onto the divan, and sat down next to her still holding her hand.

There was a knock.

In the doorway stood Marseille again, next to a small, dark-bearded man in a black suit, with a group of uniformed policemen behind them.

"Madame," said Ricchetti, "it is the police inspector."

"No," she cried. "No police. Not the police!"

Marseille said something to the man in Italian. The Italian murmured back in a firm, low voice. He was standing his ground.

"The inspector say he must speak to you," Marseille insisted.

She sank back, and the man entered. "Inspector Basso," he said. Behind him she saw a pool of darkness, men in navy blue uniforms and white-banded caps, crowding him. He sat down and drew out a notebook and pencil from the inside of his jacket. In the semidarkness of the room, she couldn't see his face clearly, but he seemed youngish, perhaps in his mid-thirties, beginning to go a little bald, with a small, neat beard, trying to keep his face expressionless in the surrounding storm.

"I don't want the police," she said again.

"I am sorry, Madame, but I must ask you some questions." He spoke English. He must have some education.

Her heart beat hard, her head throbbed, her mouth was dry.

"You are Mrs. Cross?" He seemed nervous, perhaps newly promoted.

"Yes!" she said, as if he should know.

He lifted his pencil to write, then looked at her uncertainly. "You are the mother?"

"No! No! I'm his wife!"

He bent his head down and wrote. There was silence.

He looked up again. "Please to tell me his full name and age."

"John Walter Cross. He's forty years old."

"And you own age, Madame?"

"Why must I tell you?"

"It is the rule, Madame, for the police report."

"A police report?"

"Yes, Madame," he said patiently.

"I am—" The cruelty of his question. "I am...sixty."

"Both are English citizens?"

"Yes."

"Your address please?"

She told him and he wrote that down too. Thank God, he didn't seem to have any idea of her other identity, that she was also George Eliot, the English writer.

"Now, can you tell me please, what happened?" he asked.

She took a breath, still holding on to Gerita's hand.

"He jumped...," she said. "I don't know..."

"Did you see this? Were you in the room with him?"

"There with him? What do you mean? In the room? No. Of course not. I didn't see it! I would've stopped him!"

"What time did this happen?"

"You know when it happened! Just now."

He made more notes.

"How was it discovered he had done it?" the inspector asked.

"What do you mean? I heard it down below!"

He nodded, wrote. There was quiet in the room. Behind him, the men had not moved, but stared down at her, a pha-lanx guarding him. Strangers, hearing it all. Perhaps they didn't speak English. She could only hope.

The inspector looked up from his pad. "Had the signor been acting in any way oddly?"

"Oddly?" She couldn't bear to tell him, a stranger, who didn't care.

He prompted her. "Was this unexpected? Was the gen-tleman behaving in an unusual manner?"

She delayed. "He was agitated," she said slowly.

"The agitation. What was the agitation about?"

Was he going to blame her? Yes, she *must* be to blame. She'd agreed to marry him. She'd let him try to make her happy.

"He had trouble sleeping," she said dully. "He wasn't eating. He said he needed exercise."

"Hmm," the man said, as if he didn't believe her. He made a few more notes, then stood up and tucked his notebook back into his jacket. He sighed. "That will be all for now, Madame. I leave you in the doctor's care."

So, he wasn't going to—arrest her, blame her. He left, followed by his men.

The doctor, Ricchetti, had come quietly out of Johnnie's room.

The manager, Marseille, lingered. "Is there anything I can do for Madame?" he asked.

"No. Why must that gondolier be with him?" The man who had led him in the darkness to the Rialto, to the *taverna*, who'd gotten him drunk, who had started this.

Marseille looked surprised. "The man works for the hotel, Madame."

"I don't like him." It was not in character for her to say such a thing. She couldn't help it.

"I am sorry, Madame. There is no one else. The doctor instructs us we must not leave the gentleman alone."

This was the final, terrible punishment. That the one who had caused all this should now be with him at all times, visible to her as a reminder.

"Is there anything else, Madame, that we can do?"

"No. Please, leave us." Another unexpected rudeness from her.

DINITIA SMITH

"He will soon sleep," said Ricchetti. "The chloral works quickly. Madame, let us speak privately, if you will."

She clutched Gerita's hand, she could feel her nails digging into the girl's flesh. "God, I'm sorry," she said to her, releasing her grip. "Please, stay with me."

"Of course," the girl said.

Ricchetti, seated opposite her, bent forward, elbows on his knees, his long, greasy gray hair hanging around his face. "He will sleep now," he said. "For many hours. Someone must be with him at all times."

"What will happen now?" she asked. "What should we do?"

"We must see the course it takes," he said. "Is there someone you can send for?"

"I've sent for his brother, William, in England. I don't know how long he will take." She looked at Gerita helplessly, as if somehow *she* would know.

"How long will the medicine last?" she asked him. "Will he stay calm now?"

"Six to eight hours is the usual time." He looked at his watch. "I will return at seven. We will keep the chloral, three times daily, around the clock, until we are sure he is calmed."

At this, he too left.

She felt as if she were shrinking, fading, ceasing to exist, like a shriveled leaf a sudden wind could crumble.

For the rest of the day, she stayed there in her room, the curtains drawn tight against the heat. She couldn't bear the light, and the possibility that someone might see in. "Please, would you stay with me?" she asked Gerita. "I will pay you extra."

The girl looked shocked. "I not accept from you, Madame."

Through the door, from the *sala* came the sounds of people coming and going to Johnnie's room, their voices rapid, businesslike.

"How is he?" she asked Gerita. "Do you know?"

"They say he sleep. They are with him. They will not leave him."

"I am afraid," she confessed.

"Corradini is with him, and Corradini's nephew and others." Again, the thought of Corradini. What would they do to him? Would they try to bathe him, wash the filth from the canal off him? The thought of the gondolier's dirty hands touching Johnnie's flesh repulsed her. But there was nothing she could do.

"Does everyone in the hotel know?" she asked. "I think I want to die."

The girl looked alarmed. "No, Signora. No. Do not say that. Please."

"Why would I want to live?" she said. She put her face to the wall and closed her eyes.

Throughout the hours, from time to time Marseille appeared, to survey the chaos, to ask if she wanted anything. "I'll pay for it all," she said, madly. "The extra people. I'm rich!"

He nodded grimly, said nothing. He was becoming impatient with the chaos, the use of his men, the scandal in the hotel.

When she ventured briefly into the *sala*, she saw Corradini with his gold earring pass in and out of Johnnie's room, closing the doors behind him.

She went to the window and parted the curtains, but still fearing to be seen, stopped short of stepping out onto the balcony. The terrible heat still hung over the city, the sky was dense and white, the sun invisible behind it.

"You must go home," she told Gerita.

"I not leave you, Signora."

"You must," she said. "*Tua madre*—you must look after your mother. Go—for a little while, dear. Just to see her. It's all right."

"I come back soon?" the girl said.

"Yes, come back soon."

———

That evening, Ricchetti came again, accompanied by a small, olive-skinned man with large dark eyes and heavy yellow pouches under them. "Signora, this is Dr. Vigna. I have brought him for a consultation."

"I am honored to meet you," Vigna said. "I have read your books. I am a great admirer." Who she was must be known to everyone now.

Ricchetti said, "Dr. Vigna is the director of the new women's asylum at San Clemente. Before that, he was the director of the San Servolo home for the insane. He is our foremost expert on diseases of the mind, the author of *La Trasmissione Ereditaria Fisico-Moral* and a friend of Giuseppe Verdi's," he said, as if that would make a difference.

"Diseases of the mind?" she echoed.

Vigna wiped his brow with his handkerchief. "Perhaps Madame would like some air," he said. "There is no air in here."

"The light hurts my eyes," she said. "But can you help him?"

"You say to Dr. Ricchetti that, prior to this episode, he was very agitated?"

"He couldn't sleep. He wanted to go everywhere. I couldn't keep up with him. Then, he just seemed to become like a storm, without warning. He was possessed. I can't explain it...reading aloud from these pamphlets about art without stopping."

"Can you tell me," Vigna asked, "has there been any other illness like this in the family?"

"What sort of illness?" she asked.

"Cases such as this? Mania?"

There flashed in her mind, for a strange second, that moment long ago at Weybridge when she'd asked Mary about the mysterious brother, the one named Alexander, who'd died. Mary hadn't wanted to tell her what happened, and begged her not to ask their mother, Anna, about it. "I don't know of anything," she answered Vigna.

"There is no family history, then?"

"No. Nothing," she said. "Will he get better?"

"Some do get better."

"Some?"

"The course of this illness, it can be—very mysterious. We do not know. All we can do is to keep him sedated. Then gradually we withdraw the chloral to see how he reacts. We prescribe warm baths."

Dr. Ricchetti interrupted. "Dr. Vigna is a pioneer in the use of warm baths and music for the treatment of the insane. It has been used to great effect in his asylum—"

She interrupted, "He can't go to an asylum! That's impossible!"

Vigna fixed his grave, dark eyes on her. What was he seeing? Did he too think it was her fault? That she was so old, that her young husband had been so repelled by her that when he realized his awful mistake, he was driven to kill himself?

The little man leaned over and touched her hand. "We will hope for the best, Madame."

Looking back at those hours, she wondered if God, or nature, or whoever it was, granted humans a kind of mercy at terrible times by dulling their minds with exhaustion and blunting their perceptions. There was much about those days that she couldn't remember. She felt only numb terror that he would do it again, that he would die.

And then, as her heart settled, and as she lay on the bed, she realized—he was willing to leave her, to give up his life, he didn't love her. This was punishment for her vanity, to think that he could really have loved her.

Was it possible for a heart to be broken so totally, more than once in a single life?

Chapter 22

"I am here, Marian." Willie's tall figure was silhouetted in the bedroom door against the glaring lights of the *sala*, which was lit up so they could conduct the business of his illness.

"I came as quickly as I could," he said. "I got the boat at Dover and I was just in time for the next train to Brussels. I've been traveling for thirty-six hours. God, it's hot in here!"

"Have you seen him?"

He sat down wearily on the chair and placed his hat on the table.

"He's sleeping," he said. "I met Vigna and Ricchetti on their way out. They explained the situation."

"I don't understand," she said. "What's happened to him?"

"Frankly, I was a bit worried about something like this."

"What do you mean?"

He rubbed his head, frowning. She remembered that she disliked him, his withholding ways. "Once before—" he began.

"Once before—what?"

"He was ill."

"Ill? With what?"

"There was no untoward attempt. Nothing like this, just a sort of terrible agitation, pacing, talking to himself. We'd just found out Mama was ill herself, and Johnnie was beside himself with worry about her. The doctor advised rest. He was put in the Surrey County Asylum. They gave him baths and sedatives. Gradually he got better. He was there for three weeks and came home, and that was the end of it."

"When was this?"

He said, guardedly, "Three years ago."

"But George and I, we knew you then. Nobody told us."

"We were sure he was all right. He seemed perfectly well. And Mama was absolutely adamant, she insisted we not tell anyone. You see, when our sister, Emily, fell in love with Frank Otter, he found out that there had been...illness in the family, and he almost didn't marry her because he was afraid if they had children..." She remembered that time at Weybridge, and Emily and Frank walking together and arguing and Emily crying. So that must have been what they were quarreling about that day.

Why hadn't they told her? Mary—Mary had been her friend.

Willie hesitated. "Mama wouldn't have wanted *you* in particular to know. You see," he said, "there had been difficulties in the family before."

"Difficulties?"

"Illness," he said. "Our uncle William was in the asylum in Dumbartonshire. And our brother, Alexander."

"Your brother?"

"Yes. It was the tragedy of our mother's life. He never learned to talk. He was like a wild animal. They had to put him away. We never saw him again. Then we heard he died."

She was reeling.

"I'm sorry, Marian," he said. "But I'm here to help you now. I know Johnnie better than anyone. I won't leave you alone. I'm going to sleep in the room with him along with the other men. He'll be very well guarded, I promise you."

"But why didn't he tell me?" she asked again.

"I don't know. Because he was ashamed. Or he didn't remember."

"He didn't remember?"

"We don't know. You see, when he got out, he never spoke about it again. It was as if nothing had happened. The doctor said amnesia is common with that sort of thing."

Chapter 23

I n the late afternoon the sky darkened ominously, as if it were night. A clap of thunder shook the air, then came the wind and the rain, a blinding rain beating down onto the canal. The horizon was completely obscured. Below on the *riva*, the boatmen struggled to buckle blue coverings over the gondolas. The canal was empty. The sirocco was upon them.

After an hour, the rain ceased. Gradually the sky cleared and for the first time in days, the air was fresh and cool.

In the morning, Willie came in to her. "He went without the chloral last night. He's awake and calm."

"Awake?"

"Yes. But very tired."

"Did he say anything?"

"He asked what happened. I told Corradini, the gondolier, to bathe and dress him. Perhaps you'd like to see him?" Willie said.

"I don't want to see him." She felt a sudden anger at Johnnie, for what he'd put her through, for wanting to leave her, for ceasing to love her.

"I'll be with you," he said. "Ricchetti is with him."

Reluctantly, she rose and followed him into the *sala*.

Johnnie was slumped at the table, washed, in clean clothes, silent, staring straight ahead. Dr. Ricchetti and Corradini stood over him. Now that the crisis had passed, the gondolier had resumed his cold, contemptuous expression, an expression he was making little effort to hide, with the big Englishman reduced to a blubbering fool. He'd seen it all with these tourists, drunkenness, violence, madness. He'd taken other men to the Rialto.

Johnnie looked up at her, bewildered.

"Johnnie," Willie said. "It's Marian."

His brow knit as if he were trying to remember where he'd seen her before. "Yes?" he said, mystified. His voice was faint, slurred.

"You've been ill," she said stiffly.

"What happened?"

"You don't remember?" she said, looking to Willie for help. Johnnie shook his head.

"Mr. Cross," Ricchetti said. "You had a collapse."

"A collapse," Johnnie repeated.

"Is it normal for them not to remember?" she asked Ricchetti.

"Yes. Typical. Then it comes back later, usually."

She said coldly, "I'm glad you feel better, Johnnie."

He appeared to think about her remark. "Yes," he said vaguely. "Better," parroting her. Then, uncertainly, "I feel better."

Ricchetti said, as if Johnnie weren't there, "We will try again today and tonight without the chloral and see how he does."

"But you'll still be here?" she quickly asked.

"I have other patients to see. But we won't leave him alone. The gondolier will stay with him. The chloral remains in the body for many hours. It will continue to sedate him, even after we stop the dosage. We are going to take him out for a little walk today. It will be good for him."

She looked at Willie. "But people will see him? They know what happened."

Willie hesitated. "Yes, that may be."

"He must have exercise," Ricchetti said.

Willie said, "I spoke to Inspector Basso."

"The policeman?" she said.

"By law they've got to file a police report." Willie waited, letting it sink in. "The newspapers take it from the police report. There's something in *Il Tempo* and in *L'Adriatico*." He shook his head. "I'm afraid there's nothing I can do."

Her heart sank.

Willie said, "It's in Italian. I don't think the English read the Italian papers. I'm doing what I can. I've given Marseille a very large sum to keep him quiet and to forbid the hotel staff from discussing it." He nodded toward Corradini and lowered his voice. "And to him, of course." The awful man had made money out of this. More than his wages. More than the "tip" Johnnie had given him that first day.

"And Gerita—the maid—she took money?" she asked.

"No," Willie said, surprised. "She wouldn't take it. It was a large amount too."

The next morning, Vigna came again. "It has been twenty-four hours now without the chloral hydrate. He is quiet still." He studied her with his dark, pouched eyes. "The mania has abated," he said. "He is in the depressive phase of the illness now."

"Depressive?"

"Yes. We must still watch him carefully. This can be a dangerous time. Sometimes, after the mania, they sink into a profound melancholia."

"What is the name of it? What he has?"

"The French call it *la folie circulaire.* Around and around," he said. He smiled sadly and circled the air above his head with his finger, as if, after all these years of coping with the mad as a medical man, he still saw some humor in this. A form of self-preservation. And perhaps because he knew there was no cure.

She asked, "That means he'll...It could happen again?"

"The fact that he is responsive," he said, "and that he has remained calm for this many hours, without the chloral, is a good sign. He is drowsy, he is slow, but he is talking normally. I think he understands what is happening around him now."

"Is it safe for us to leave? To take him home?"

"We will see what happens in the next twenty-four hours."

"What caused it? Can you tell me?"

He shrugged. "We cannot know. You say there have been incidences in the family. And," he said, "then there is the sirocco. Thank goodness, it has broken." With this, he gave a little smile, as if he had nothing else to go on but the weather. "Sometimes, with the sirocco, the tourists, we see they go quite mad."

Chapter 24

A t last, on Tuesday evening, eight days after the attempt, the doctors deemed it safe to move him. She'd refused to consider an asylum for him—the notion of the word "asylum" getting back to London appalled her. Ricchetti and Vigna said that in light of that, they recommended that they go on to Wildbad, where he could take the cure, which might be of help.

She wrote to Charley saying only that Johnnie had *"taken ill"* without mentioning the nature of the illness, that Willie Cross had come to Venice to help, that Johnnie seemed to be improving. They were traveling slowly back to England, she wrote, giving him time to recover, and they hoped to be there by the end of July if all went well.

Gerita and Corradini accompanied them to Santa Lucia, the gondolier supporting Johnnie, nearly carrying him. Johnnie shuffled his feet like an old man, vacant-eyed, slack-mouthed, concentrating, as if he couldn't put one foot in front of the other without effort. It was as if by some awful twist of fate, the cold, strange, stale-smelling man who had precipitated this had now taken full possession of Johnnie's body.

Willie managed the luggage and the tickets, then he and Corradini loaded Johnnie, heavy with his drowsiness and silence, onto the train.

Marian hugged Gerita goodbye. "Thank you," Marian told her, dully.

"Good luck, Madame," Gerita said.

Marian dug into her purse and found some coins at the bottom which she wrapped in her lace handkerchief and gave to the girl. She gave nothing to the gondolier. She would never have to see him again.

"Oh, no, Madame," Gerita said. "I cannot take."

"This is for your sweet mother, to help care for her," Marian said.

The train to Verona had no first-class compartment, and there were other passengers in the carriage with them. But no one seemed, thank God, to know who they were. Willie sat between her and Johnnie as if to protect her from him.

They spent the night in Verona, Willie never leaving Johnnie's side, taking care of him. "Johnnie, you've got to eat," he said, and later, "Johnnie, you've got to bathe." He held out Johnnie's fork toward him and Johnnie took it and fed himself a bite of food.

She was exhausted with fear, the need to be alert at all times, lest he try to hurt himself again. This quiescence could be an illusion, he could suddenly spring up, run away from them, try to do it again.

The next morning they left for Trento, two hours north. This time they had a private compartment with wood paneling and luxurious, upholstered seats. There was no fear of being recognized.

As they headed into the Tyrol, the air grew clearer and cooler. The train chugged through the brilliant, snow-capped Dolomites and glided along the narrow ledges, Johnnie seldom uttering a word, and then only in answer to a direct question from Willie.

What would happen back in England? She would be alone again. Everyone would have realized her failure. All the London gossips who pretended to worship her, the sycophants secretly envious of her, the same people who'd laughed at her when they saw the wedding announcement in the *Times*—they'd have real fodder now.

As she sat in the train contemplating this, everything went black. They'd entered a tunnel, the carriage was enveloped in darkness. It went on and on, the thunder of the engine filled her ears. She was frightened. What would she find when the light came back? Would he be standing up and yelling over the noise of the engine and tugging at the carriage door, trying to open it and jump out?

Suddenly the carriage filled again with a blinding light. And there he was still, looking submissively out the window.

They arrived in Innsbruck, and for two days it rained unceasingly; the atmosphere was close, the mountains obscured by fog. One evening, Willie said, "I think that you should come. He's in rather a bad way. He wants to see you."

He was sitting with his face in his hands, his shoulders heaving. "What have I done?" he sobbed, his voice guttural with tears.

"You've been ill, Johnnie," she said. "You got ill in Venice."

"But I don't remember. I've done something awful." Then, "Polly, what have I done to you?"

From behind her came Willie's voice. "You tried to harm yourself, Johnnie."

He looked bewildered. Then, as if remembering, "Yes," he said. "Polly, please forgive me. Will you forgive me?"

"Yes. Of course I forgive you." What could she say now? She couldn't ask, why had he done this? Was it because he no longer loved her?

Willie muttered, "Perhaps we should call the doctor."

"Oh, God," she said. "I can't bear it." Another doctor, another scene in a hotel.

He began weeping anew, clutching his head in his hands.

She saw him there, her boy who'd been kind and loving, reduced to this. She reached out and touched his head. "Johnnie, Johnnie," she whispered. "I want you to get well. Please, just rest and eat and sleep. Will you?"

He looked up, his eyes red, his face still wet, mute.

———

The next morning, he got up and bathed and dressed himself. It had been ten days since the collapse. He came tentatively into the drawing room, pale and thin and fearful, as if taking baby steps.

He went up to her, took her hand, and kissed it, then looked around the room, wonderingly, as if seeing it for the first time. The breakfast things were set out on the table. Cautiously, he lifted the toast cover and went to pour his tea. She was suddenly afraid he'd scald himself with the boiling water, and she poured it for him. He watched her as if learning anew to perform this rudimentary task.

In Innsbruck, as the days passed, he began to smile— faintly. He listened and nodded in agreement as she and Willie carried on their stilted conversation, commenting on the view, a neutral topic.

He seemed slowly to improve. He struggled to learn again the activities of everyday life, to act "normally," to join tentatively in the conversation. With each moment of his recovery, as he began to talk, to remark upon the sights, she wondered if he was gearing up for another catastrophe. Willie, still silent and unsmiling, never took his eyes off him. He knew more than she did.

They journeyed on, to Wildbad on the border of the Black Forest. It was three weeks since they'd left Venice. They'd engaged rooms at the Hotel Klumpp. It was unlikely anyone would recognize them here. Wildbad was a town of the old and the sick and the dying, people in bath chairs pushed around by attendants, bent over their crutches, inward-looking, preoccupied with their illnesses.

They'd arranged for Johnnie to take the waters at the Curhaus, under the direction of the head of the spa, Dr. Von Burckhardt, himself. The Curhaus was the grandest building in town, a pink sandstone Moorish structure with arches and a colonnade.

After a few days of treatments, Johnnie's face began to glow with health, there were roses in his cheeks, and he was smiling. He was putting on weight.

"Dr. Von Burckhardt says I'm making absolutely splendid progress," he announced.

In the afternoons they sat in the Platz listening to the band play creaky German marches, Johnnie nodding his head enthusiastically as the tuba thumped.

They took their supper together in the immense dining room. All around them were the crippled and the palsied in their bath chairs, old people bent over their tables, concentrating with shaking hands on lifting fork to mouth, slurping their food. She sat uneasily, Willie was constrained and unsmiling. But Johnnie was cheerful now.

Their food finished, Johnnie pronounced it "Marvelous!"

On the third day, after his session at the Curhaus, Johnnie said to her, "Shall we go for a walk? Let's go and see the ornamental gardens. I'm sure Brother Willie won't mind some time without us."

She hesitated.

Willie muttered uncertainly, "I suppose it'd be all right." He wanted it to be all right, she knew. "I'll be here if you need me," he said.

For the first time since Venice, Johnnie took her arm, and they strolled across the wooden bridge over the River Enz, past a cluster of houses that gave way into the park. On either side of the narrow valley were steep hills covered in pines. A walkway along the river led into a forest.

They made their way up the path, shaded by trees on either side. The afternoon air was pleasant, the Alpine climate warm and mild. As they walked, Johnnie breathed in the pure air and beamed, as if he'd forgotten everything that had happened, his back perfectly straight, his shoulders broad in their usual fine attitude.

Other tourists passed them. Along the path, there were little statues and wooden shelters where people could rest. Below them, the Enz ran clear, more a brook than a river, taking its course over the big rocks.

Close to the top of the hill, they came to a bench overlooking Wildbad. The other walkers had disappeared or gone back down.

They sat quietly, looking out at the little town beneath, the two broad streets lined with oaks, the row of hotels, the Platz, and the Curhaus. He stopped and took both her hands in his. Was he going to have another outburst?

He said suddenly, "I know I've caused you terrible suffering." He went on, "I know that I'm well now. I'm not asking your forgiveness, only that you'll let me, for the rest of our lives, take care of you and make you happy. I've got no words to describe how sorry I am."

His voice was measured, no longer the desperate rush of illness in it. His blue eyes were clear, his skin soft and pale, there was pink in his cheeks. There was no trace of the haggard man of only weeks before. She saw the neatly trimmed beard, his straight posture, heard his voice with its faint Scottish notes, its American softness. His big, warm hands enveloped hers, protecting her again.

They proceeded arm in arm down the hill, she silent, leaving her response a mystery, he eagerly beside her.

———————

The next day she took the waters herself. She lay in the blessed silence of her private piscine, the clear, green waters gurgling up around her, the dim light reflected in the blue tile. Slowly, her limbs were infused with its magical properties. At the end, the attendant enveloped her in a huge warm towel.

That night she wrote a letter home. A friend, Elma Stuart, had written congratulating her on her marriage. She thanked Elma and mentioned that *"Mr. Cross had an attack of illness"* in Venice, due, she said lightheartedly, to *"lack of muscular exercise which the allurements of the gondola bring with them."* That's what she'd say — *"due to lack of exercise."* Or, if pressed, it would be *"typhus,"* not uncommon among tourists in Venice. *"He is,"* she wrote, *"a little more delicate than is usual with him."*

"*En revanche*," she lied, "*I am quite miraculously strong and equal to the little extra calls upon me.*"

The following morning, she and Willie waited for Johnnie to finish his toilette so they could go down to breakfast. "I think he's much better now," Willie ventured.

She didn't trust him. He'd kept the truth from her. "Do you really think so?"

"He's almost his old self."

"What *is* his old self?" she asked.

"I mean calm."

"If it ever happened again, I couldn't survive—"

"I understand."

She shook her head. "I don't know if I could take it—I'm too old."

"The family is always there for you."

And now it came. "You didn't tell me. You let us go ahead."

"As I said, we thought it was over. He'd been completely well for three years. If you'd known," he said, "would you have accepted him?"

"I don't know," she said. He'd made her happy after George's death, delighted her, taken care of her, given her a chance for life she'd thought she'd never have again.

"How long are you going to stay?" she asked him.

"As long as you want. Until you feel entirely safe. Would you like me to go? Then you can have a proper honeymoon."

She let out a little laugh. "A proper honeymoon? Very amusing."

Johnnie did seem like his old self now. He took over the details of the remainder of the journey, studying the railway timetables and guidebooks, planning everything in his capable way. In the mornings, he emerged from his and Willie's bedroom, beaming and fresh and smiling. "A very good sleep," he said. He ate his breakfast with relish.

She felt herself being drawn back in again by his sweetness, his good humor, his command of things. She smiled back at him. She took his arm and when he bent down to kiss her cheek, she accepted the kiss. Though, sometimes still, the fear and the realization of what he'd done overtook her and she held back. She knew herself that it was easier to believe all was well, that she could trust him now and he'd take care of her again. Easier, but not safe.

He wrote to his sisters, saying he was well after recovering from his "*illness.*" It was a miraculous recovery, he said, because of the pure mountain air and the waters.

On Tuesday night, Willie said, "I think it's all right now for me to go."

A spark of panic shot through her. "How do you know it's all right?"

"Look at him. You wouldn't know anything had ever happened to him. If anything goes wrong, I'll be back at Weybridge in only a few days. You can telegram if you need me."

The next day she accompanied him to the railway station, accepted his little hug, and said goodbye.

On their way north, Johnnie was all joy, as if he'd been released from captivity, reveling in his newfound health. "Look at the view, Polly"—at the mountains, the flowing rivers, the valleys scattered with red barns.

At Baden, he insisted on exploring the Alte Schloss, running up and down the stairs, through the secret passages, and into the dungeons. She stumbled after him, heart pounding and out of breath.

While he climbed the stairs to the lookout, she waited for him in the narrow passage on the dusty seat carved into the stone wall centuries before.

As he regained his strength, she could feel her own receding.

A month passed, then another week, the horror of Venice dimmed, and the reality of his love, his competence, and his solicitousness began to overcome the memories of it. The warmth filled her again, and yes, love for him, and pity for what he'd suffered.

Still, in quiet moments she continued to observe him, almost without realizing it, alert for any small signs of a change, holding herself apart, waiting for it all to come crashing back down on her.

PART VII

Paradiso

Chapter 25

O nce more, he was bearing her along, all his skills put toward making her comfortable, making sure that they made the best connections from Dover to London to Witley. "I'm so looking forward to being home," he said. "I can't wait to see the Druces and their new place. Let's go there as soon as possible."

She began to feel excited too, about the arrival home, at the prospect of the blessed peace and quiet of the Heights, the big red house, the flower gardens, the green lawns, the smell of early morning. Quiet and stability at last.

They arrived at Dover in late July, nearly six weeks since he'd "taken ill." The train was packed because of the bank holiday with noisy, jostling crowds, and people sneaking into the first-class compartments. But at the station, the minute they stepped from the train they were greeted by the profound and eternal silence of the country.

When the carriage pulled up at the Heights, Johnnie jumped down, raised his arms above his head, and spun around, crying, "Home! Home at last! Mrs. Dowling! Brett! We're here!" And there they were, Mrs. Dowling, plump and round-cheeked, just as one wanted one's cook to be, and Brett down from London to take care of them until the new house at Cheyne Walk was ready, scurrying to greet them.

As they helped Marian from the carriage, she breathed a sigh. Exhausted from the travel, she gave herself into their arms.

Mrs. Dowling had set out a light homecoming supper for them. They ate in the dining room with the French windows open to the gardens and the sounds of the night, the crickets and cicadas singing, an owl hooting in the big oak tree. Johnnie sat in the place that had been George's. But he was the master of the house now. And he took up a lot of space. His presence dominated.

She'd written ahead to Brett instructing her to prepare the bedroom at the end of the second floor hall for Mr. Cross. Brett would note the significance of it. She'd witnessed every privacy of Marian's marriage to George, silently observing, discreet and proper about everything, of course. She and George had shared a bedroom; Brett must have noticed the signs of their love, their rumpled sheets, their clothing scattered on the floor in the morning, when she came in with their breakfast trays. Brett might well think it normal that she wouldn't share a bedroom with a man other than George, her husband of so many years, whom all the servants had loved. George had been so jolly and kind to all the servants, so generous with their Christmas bonuses, never treating them like slaves. Brett might disapprove if she shared a room with this man who was young enough to be her son.

The next day, in the clear brightness of the summer morning, she watched Johnnie from her window, running around outside, seeing to everything as if he now owned the place. The lawns must be cut, the vegetable garden, which was beginning to burst, needed a proper weeding and additional mulching. And something must be done about that line of firs obscuring the view from the terrace.

The estate would be taken care of, by someone who knew what he was doing.

That afternoon, they drove out in the carriage to reacquaint themselves with the Surrey countryside. They drove to Thursley and to Elstead, dragonflies hovering and sparkling in the air as they went, the river flowing lushly beside them. "Sorry for this bouncing," he whispered, as always aware of her smallest discomfort.

"I'm just happy to see it all again," she said.

They passed the verdant fields, the crops growing, the roads edged with sprinklings of yellow and pink and purple flowers.

"What are those yellow flowers?" he asked, trying to engage her again, to draw her in once more to teach him, playing to her interest in the names of things.

"Butter-and-eggs, *Linaria vulgaris*."

"You know everything," he said.

"I wish that were true," she said.

In the evening, after supper, she set out her map of the stars on the table and showed him the constellations.

They went out into the garden. Above them, the stars were spread across the sky in a brilliant display. They stood together looking up, his arm around her waist, their feet wet with dew. She pointed. "See? Cassiopeia, the queen on her throne." A tiny star shot across the blackness. "Look, a meteor," she said. And, pointing south, "That's our Milky Way. See, the summer triangle—Altair, Vega, Deneb."

He gazed up, his mouth ajar. "You are the greatest teacher," he said again.

———————

They'd been home for only two days when Johnnie announced again that he wanted to go to the Druces and their new estate, Thornhill. He wanted to see Albert, he said, as a newly married man, and play some tennis.

As they rode in the carriage to Sevenoaks, he watched eagerly ahead at the road, his face tense as if he couldn't wait to get there. When they pulled up in front of the Tudor house, the Druces were waiting for them at the entrance. Johnnie gave his sister, Anna, looking pale and weary as always, a perfunctory kiss. Eliot and Elsie bounced up and down at the sight of them. "Uncle Johnnie! Uncle Johnnie!" And Johnnie picked them up and tossed them in the air in the daring way that only an uncle could.

Then he spotted Albert, standing quietly with his arms outstretched toward him, and Johnnie ran to him. Albert put his hands on Johnnie's shoulders and held him away from him, looking deeply into his eyes. He drew Johnnie's head to the crook of his neck, and patted his back for a long moment before releasing him.

For the rest of the weekend, with Albert, his best friend, the companion of his bachelorhood, Johnnie seemed happier than he'd been in months. They spent most of the visit joking and laughing and teasing each other, playing tennis, yelping at their missed serves, and hooting with their victories.

She didn't want to be apart from him, so she sat in a deck chair under the big elm by the court with her book, watching them. They seemed to belong with each other. But Johnnie belonged to her, an old woman, and to no one else! Sitting there, trying to read about the laws concerning traitors during the Napoleonic Wars, she couldn't concentrate, and was drawn back always to the two of them on either side of the net.

That afternoon, Johnnie and Albert went for a long walk across the fields. She saw their heads close together in conversation, and then they entered the woods and disappeared. They hadn't asked her to go with them—perhaps they thought she couldn't manage it. They were gone for two hours.

When they came back, she said, "You were gone for a long time."

"We had a lot to discuss, didn't we, Albert?" Johnnie said laughing. His face was flushed.

"Indeed," Albert said, smiling. His gaze lingered on Johnnie affectionately, kind and intimate. Then he said, "Let's put up the badminton net so Marian can have a game!"

"No, no," she said. "I'm too old."

"You are not," said Johnnie.

They set up the net on the lawn. Johnnie saw her holding back. "Come, you're going to play," he commanded.

"I can't. I'm too weak," she insisted.

"Yes, you can. And you're not weak."

First she played with Johnnie, while Albert watched. Then Albert said, "I want my own game with the lady," and they played for a good twenty minutes. He let her win.

"Not fair!" Albert cried. "She's got a right- and a left-hand serve."

"She's stronger than she thinks she is," Johnnie said.

"She is indeed," Albert said, and he put his arm protectively around her shoulder and led her into tea.

———

Johnnie decided to cut down the fir trees at the Heights himself, attacking them with his ax, then standing by as they crashed to the ground. He kept at it all day in the heat. She wondered, was this burst of energy a sign of his illness coming on again? At the end of the day, when he came in, his face was bright red and he was covered in sweat.

"Are you all right?" she asked him.

He smiled. "Never better," he said, and went to change for supper.

As he continued his repairs and seeing to the estate, she took out the "quarry" for the new novel. She'd written seven pages of notes. Poor Cyril, her impoverished inventor hero, had sold his weapon to Rastin, not realizing that he was a double agent.

At lunch, she asked Johnnie, "Would you like to see what I've done so far? I've somehow got to get my man accused of treason. I can't figure it out. Perhaps you'll have an idea?"

As he read through what she'd done, she sat next to him, waiting.

"Marvelous!" he said. "Marvelous. Another great work."

"But you see, I don't know how to get Cyril found out. I'm stumped."

"I'm afraid I'm useless at that sort of thing," he said. "What if Rastin just confesses to having sold the weapon to the enemy?"

"If he simply confesses, there's no drama." She took the pages away from him. He'd never be able to help her with her work. He didn't have that sort of mind. George would have suggested a solution. But Johnnie had other talents.

After supper, they read Goethe's *Hermann and Dorothea*, which she and George also used to read.

As summer went on, they ventured into more serious fare. She read aloud to him parts of Sayce's *Introduction to the Science of Language*: "*Comparative philology was the result of the study of Sanskrit, and the Sanskrit vocabulary has been ranged under a certain number of verbal roots...*" She looked up. He'd fallen asleep. She didn't wake him, but sat there simply gazing at him, without interruption, with relief that he was well now and whole again. She'd never again hope for more.

He'd been well now for two months. She leaned over and kissed him on the cheek. His eyelids fluttered open.

She laughed. "The Sayce is too much for you?"

"Sorry. It's all that outdoor work and the fresh air. But it penetrates, it really does, even when you doze."

He smiled and kissed her, a benediction, on the forehead.

She continued with her writing, and managed to solve the problem of getting her man, Cyril Ambrose, into trouble. She came up with the idea of a masked ball—enjoyable to write about too: "*Proposed scene at a masquerade, in which Rastin meets a female spy, who piques him by her wit—refuses to unmask—says she is old. They sup together; she denounces him after.*"

Perhaps she *could* write again without George. All along he'd insisted she had it in her and all he ever did was to pull it from her. The process of composing a book had become habituated in her, the growth of a story from seed, its gradual flowering into something larger, the insertion of lines between the gaps, the weaving and binding together of sentences, trusting the images that came to her. And then, that wonderful day, arriving at the point where the words became a melody, took on life, filled the page, became, finally, a symphony.

———

On Monday evening, Johnnie said he wanted to go up to town in the morning to attend to business and see about the new house. He was still managing her money—it was his one formal occupation that resembled a job.

"I wish you didn't have to go," she said. She was fearful of letting him out of her sight. Would he wander somewhere off course? Without her watching over him, would he have another attack?

"I'll be back in time for tea."

"I'll meet you at the station."

"That's not necessary. The walk does me good after the train ride."

"No," she said. "I insist."

And there she was, early for the 5:50 train, waiting in the trap for his tall, young figure to step down from the carriage, to see him, tousled and perspiring from the journey, smile and wave when he spotted her.

He began going up to London nearly every day now. She wondered what was really occupying him there but she put the question out of her mind, as he told her about supervising the decorator, Mr. Armitage, making sure that workers were on schedule, that the colors on the walls were suitable, dropping in at Dennistoun & Cross, and handling her investments in accordance with the way the markets were going.

Every day she met him with the trap. "Really," he said, hugging her, "I don't want you to trouble yourself."

"But I wanted to see you as soon as possible," she told him. "I miss you when you go."

He kissed her cheek. "That's very sweet."

————

At the end of August they went to Cambridgeshire to visit the estate of Johnnie's other brother-in-law, Henry Bullock, the husband of his late sister, Zibbie. Henry had remarried Berthe, a lovely Alsatian woman, and they had two daughters. Henry proudly showed them all the improvements he'd initiated on the estate, new cottages for his workers, a school for their children, a cooperative store.

There were other guests, the classicist, Richard Claverhouse-Jebb, from Glasgow, and his wife, Caroline. Claverhouse-Jebb was a rather mousy-looking man with a weak chin. Caroline Jebb was an American, the widow of a Civil War general—the story went that she'd persuaded President Lincoln to give her husband a promotion after he'd been denied it. She made Marian think of Rembrandt's painting of Bathsheba. She was sensual looking, with a full, round face and auburn hair. And she was a typical American, too outgoing, very loud, Marian thought. She flirted with Johnnie and he seemed to be responding to her, chatting away and laughing.

Johnnie was delighted by her. As the hours passed, Marian wondered, would this finally be the woman who pierced that invisible wall of his, who would reach that part of him that seemed never to have been touched by any woman? Perhaps at this late date, at the age of forty, it could happen to him, with someone so overtly sexual, so forceful and forward and fearless, bits of her auburn hair sticking to her cheeks, her breasts rising above the neckline of her dress, moist with sweat in the heat. Would she overcome his hidden reserve with her insistence?

Jealously, the next day Marian put on her walking dress that showed her ankles. Mrs. Jebb was still chattering away at Johnnie, and he was sitting back, laughing. Henry Bullock was saying something to Marian about the new well he'd dug for his workers, but she couldn't pay attention. Naturally, young women would be attracted to Johnnie. Perhaps he was attracted to young women after all, especially very pretty ones.

"Are you all right, Polly?" Johnnie asked, when he came back to her side.

"Just a little headache." Then, under her breath, she said, "That woman's rather a coquette, isn't she?"

He laughed.

"She was flirting with you."

"No! Anyway," he said, squeezing her hand and giving her his warmest smile, "I'm most definitely taken."

The shadow passed over her.

———

The autumn rains came, bringing with them damp and a chill wind. The leaves on the trees began to turn, the horse chestnuts first, then the sycamores. One morning when Johnnie was up in London seeing to the house, there was a rare, brisk sun, and Marian sat outside on the terrace with a blanket over her.

She heard the honking of geese and looked up and saw them flying in formation, following their valiant leader, scores of them, determined. The sound of geese echoed in the air, the sound of autumn, departure, death.

A few days later, she felt the ominous spasm, then saw the terrifying red in her urine. It had been months since this had happened. Please—let it not be true! Had the horror of what had happened in Venice weakened her? That night the pain came with a viciousness. She managed to reach over and ring the bell, and Johnnie came dashing in in his dressing gown. The bed became a rack upon which she tossed and writhed in agony. She drifted in and out of consciousness.

When she came alert, she saw an unfamiliar face, the local doctor, Mr. Parsons, bending over her, and Johnnie hovering behind him. There was the stab of the needle in her arm. Then, the waves of relief.

Again, recovery, but gradual. "She's lost half her body weight," Mr. Parsons said. "You must give her a diet of red meat and clotted cream and toddies with egg."

She was surrounded by love. Johnnie's sisters sent warm undergarments and a chamois dress. The dress was light gold, like silk. When finally she got out of bed and tried it on, it was too heavy for her frame to bear. The attack had gutted her.

She tried to take up her work. She had to decide on the exact date when the action of the novel would take place. Perhaps early March 1815, around the time of the Seventh Coalition, when the fighting between the French and the English and their allies was reaching its climax.

Now, the characters' ages? Cyril would be twenty-five. That would make him born in 1790. Rastin, about forty, born in—? She tried to do the math. But she was too weary. She lay down on the divan, pulled the throw over her, and fell asleep.

In the morning, when she was usually at her best for work, she felt herself starting to fall asleep again. And if she were never to wake, it mightn't be so bad. Death no longer frightened her. Then she'd never have to experience the pain of missing Johnnie when he went away. Would she be reunited with George? Was it possible there was such a thing as resurrection? That all along she'd been wrong in refusing to believe in it? What a gift it was to have faith. Foolish thought. She didn't believe in it. But—if she were buried next to him? As the years passed—the centuries!—inevitably their coffins would rot and crumble together in the earth and their remains would mingle. Perhaps there was a kind of eternity, when the flesh turned to dust and blended with the earth, an eternal, indestructible essence containing the spirit, a state that couldn't be clearly conceived of because the human brain didn't have the means to conceptualize it.

She imagined floating in the warm air, a celestial light like sunlight, the blue sky, and particles of gold sparkling and drifting on the breeze, the heightened sound of a choir, the music of the heavens, a harp, the soft touch of cymbals, then the golden dust falling gradually through the air to the ground.

Outside the window, the sky was colorless, the wind blew through the trees. Where Johnnie had cut down the firs there was a clear view now to the sky and the meadows and hills beyond. In late afternoon, the clouds were silvery. The days were shortening.

The house was getting chilly, the big rooms difficult to heat. They decided to move up to London early to a hotel so he could more easily supervise the last stages of the renovations.

Bailey's Hotel was warm, thank God, well equipped with its low ceilings for the London winter. While Johnnie was out attending to Cheyne Walk, she found a copy of *Cornhill Magazine* in the lobby with the old Scottish wedding song, "My Faithful Johnny," in it. That evening, she read it to him:

When will you come again, my faithful Johnny?
When the corn is gathered, when the leaves are withered,
I will come again, my sweet and bonnie, I will come again.

She looked up. He had tears in his eyes.

There was another kind of love. It was a love without a name, not the sexual love of a man and woman, or the love of brother and sister, or parent and child, but a deep love between a man and woman that was beyond the physical. It was admiration and kindness. The sexual kind of love, she could only remember it—George was a gift that God had bestowed on her, with the proviso that she'd only have it once in her life. That need had gone from her. Age and weakness had robbed her of it. Perhaps even with George it would be different now too.

She was enveloped now in Johnnie's special sort of love, sheltered and adored. George would have wanted this. It was hard to imagine this kindness coming from anyone else—except from George himself. She knew that whatever happened, Johnnie would always be there.

Chapter 26

At last moving day came, their new home all bright and sparkling. This was the first time she'd seen the house since it had been refurbished. It was filled with light, much lighter than the Priory, the paneling was warm and gleaming, "rosewood," Johnnie said. And Mr. Armitage had designed a special wallpaper for the drawing room, a lovely detailed print of birds and strawberries in shades of blue-green and pale pink.

"I've got a surprise for you, Polly." He led her into the library. There were the new bookcases, holding rows upon rows of her volumes neatly arranged. "They're in exactly the same order as you had them before at the Priory," he said. "I hired a man to help me do it properly. I didn't want you to have any trouble finding things."

"It's wonderful," she said. That he would have noticed so exactly the way she'd arranged her books, and worked so hard to please her.

"I can go to work immediately," she said.

The house smelled of fresh paint and varnish and polish. Brett and Mrs. Dowling had cleaned up the dust from the renovations, the floors and every piece of furniture shone. "It's the most wonderful house I've ever seen," she said. She felt new strength coursing through her body.

They had their first supper in the house, a fire crackling in the grate, the flames reflected in the silver and brass, the candles sending forth a lovely glow.

He raised his glass to her. "To you, Marian. And thank you for standing by me." They'd still never spoken directly about the exact nature of his illness, that he'd tried to kill himself, to end his life. She'd surmised he had no memory of it and she was afraid to remind him of the awfulness, to say the words, "Johnnie, why did you try to kill yourself on our honeymoon? Did you hate me that much? Did I repulse you?" It was as if they had an unspoken agreement not to confront it directly, or to acknowledge that he'd been ill. She was content now to try to forget, and to pretend all was well. And it was. The more time that passed, the more he'd grown back to health, the further the likelihood of a new outburst seemed.

She had accepted what had happened. She'd accepted quietly, within herself, that there would be no sexual union between them. Illness and exhaustion had robbed her of the memory of desire. It was an abstraction, now and then a pang of remembrance, the fullness of her desire for George.

Johnnie wasn't a man for women in that way. Whatever was in a man's makeup for that wasn't present in him. Perhaps it was a kind of purity. But as she contemplated it, her mind was shadowed, briefly, by the memory of the gondolier, by Johnnie's love for Albert. Whatever it was, she thought, it couldn't be a physical love. If it was, she couldn't bear to envision it. Thank God for ignorance. She recognized in herself that she didn't want to know. And what did it matter? After this last illness, Johnnie was always at her side, he rarely left her.

Finally, now she was able to ask the question, barely audibly, that she'd longed to ask him. "Did you want to get away from me that much?"

He looked shocked. He stood up, came around the table, sat down beside her, and put his arm around her shoulder.

"No!" He put his face close to hers. "It wasn't that."

Her voice was a whisper. "What was it then?"

He looked away, his arm still around her shoulder. Then he turned back to her. "I didn't want to get away from you. I wanted to get away from myself. I can't even bear to remember—"

"Don't," she said, afraid again.

He ignored her. "If I could only describe it, make someone understand. It was like—an awful jangling in my mind, everything speeding up, and all your thoughts are cascading over one another, and you've got no control, your body isn't your own. One has no volition…it's like a cancer, only a cancer of the spirit, not the body…it's that kind of agony." He shook his head at the memory.

"You were the only thing that was keeping me alive," he said. "You loved me. You'd agreed to marry me. Everything I'd ever wanted had come true. And then, it came over me, and there was nothing I could do. Except…" He looked at her again, trying to anticipate her reaction. "Except destroy myself."

She took his hand and held it tightly. For a moment, they said nothing as she searched his face and tried to communicate to him that she loved him and had forgiven him for wanting to leave her alone and helpless in the world. She knew he'd be well now.

He pulled her to him and kissed her gently. "Thank you. That's all I can say. Thank you."

———————

The next day she sat down at her desk and took out her quarry. Johnnie came in and saw that she was working. "You are a noble soul," he said. "I just want to tell Albert that we're definitely coming down for Christmas. He wrote to ask us about it a week ago."

"Do tell them yes," she said. "It'll be fun, as always." There'd be a family, children around them, games and charades. And most importantly, Johnnie would be happy with Albert.

"Are you sure it won't be too much?" he asked. "You're still not totally recovered, I think."

"I have tremendous will," she said with a laugh. "You underestimate me."

"I know," he said. "I always do. You're a very strong little thing."

"In mind, if not body," she said.

He kissed the top of her head. "I'll let you get to work."

She went back to her quarry. When Cyril is arrested, how exactly would that go? She took the weighty *Principles of the Law of Evidence* down from the shelf. When poor Cyril is brought to trial, she'd get it right, so when it was published no man of the law could quarrel with what she'd done.

———————

On Saturday morning, when she awoke, her throat was dry. It was as if there were a lump on one side of it. Then, as she was getting dressed, there was the twinge in her back, in her kidney. Not again. She couldn't stand it. This afternoon they were going to one of the Pop Concerts at St. James's Hall. The German pianist, Agnes Zimmerman, was playing Liszt.

She ignored the feeling in her back. As the day wore on, and she'd had some good hot tea, her throat seemed better. But she felt warm and it was cold out. Her brow was moist. If she told Johnnie about it, he wouldn't let her go and she was very eager to hear Zimmerman.

After lunch, she put on her mantilla and Johnnie bundled her up in her beaver mantle. "We don't want you catching cold." He stood over her and tied the black satin ribbon under her chin as if she were his child. They set out for Piccadilly.

As they entered the lobby of St. James's Hall, she kept her head down as always, to hide her face, and increasingly now, to watch her step. But soon she could feel the recognition spreading through the crowd, people stopping to stare at her, the eminent old woman on the arm of the tall, fresh-faced young man, Johnnie, in his frock coat with his top hat and cane—the cane a bit of an affectation, she thought, given his young age. Never mind, he was proud to look so elegant, she knew. Glancing up, she saw a few familiar faces, Dean Stanley of Westminster, a tottering old man now. She raised her hand in greeting.

They took their places in the pewlike seats close to the stage. Johnnie settled her in. It was much too warm in here. "Don't you think it's hot?" she asked Johnnie, letting the beaver slip from her shoulders.

"I feel a draft," he said. "Better keep the mantle on." He pulled the mantle up again around her. A few moments later, she was again too warm and she shrugged it off and let it fall to the seat.

She gazed around her. The place was a veritable temple to music, with its churchlike windows and Florentine ceiling.

Onstage, a hand appeared and drew aside the curtain. Miss Zimmermann entered. She walked across the stage, reached the piano, and gave a little bow. She was wearing a simple black dress. Marian examined her through the opera glasses. She had a small, gentle look, her wavy hair was piled on top of her head, her nose was straight, her eyes deeply shadowed, her lips thin.

Miss Zimmerman seated herself. The moment of drama.

She began playing Liszt's "Bénédiction," the slow beginning, the gentle notes, the themes repeated in variation, the heartbreaking warmth of it. The audience was motionless, following her.

Miss Zimmermann paused. During those seconds of quiet, the pain jabbed at Marian's side. Her throat was dry again. As Miss Zimmermann took up the flow once more, she forgot the pain. She concentrated on the music. She knew the piece by heart, loved anticipating where it would go. Again the theme returned, each time culminating slightly differently. Then the furious crescendo. At last, the water slowed into little wavelets. A moment of silence and then the clapping began.

They hurried out of the theater to beat the crowd, and into the cold. Johnnie got her up into the landau and tucked the fur rug around her.

The sun had already set, in the distance a yellowish light in the black sky. The carriage made its way along Regent Street through the crowd of hackneys and cabs and omnibuses. The music from the concert still reverberated within her.

"That was extraordinary," Johnnie said. "That's one of the gifts you've brought to me. The gift of music. I'll always be grateful to you for that."

She touched his hand. "Thank you."

People were hurrying along the pavement buried in their hats and scarves in the cold. It was foggy. The shop windows were lit up, the gaslights diffused. There was a faint, clouded moon, but no stars. The trees were barren and skeletal, bits of rubbish caught in the branches. A group of ragged boys huddled together in a doorway. A plume of smoke rose from a food stand selling baked potatoes. She still felt hot but the cold air on her face was good. The pain in her side was increasing, her throat was scratchy again. Never mind, the music was still in her.

They rode west along the Embankment. Below them were the forbidding waters of the Thames, roiling and dark and dangerous, the waves broken up in the lights, the buildings along the shore murky and obscured, the faint red glare of bonfires on the wharves. The memory came to her of that night when Spencer had broken her heart and she'd wanted to throw herself into those black waters and die. But in the end, she'd been too afraid. She'd given that moment to Mirah in *Daniel Deronda*, standing on the riverbank about to drown herself in despair at losing her brother, only to be rescued by a man who would come to love her. Rescue...by George, by Johnnie, by a man who will love you.

Opposite her in the landau, Johnnie shivered. "Brr, it's cold. We'll soon be home, though. Are you freezing?"

"Not at all."

At Cheyne Walk, Mrs. Dowling had left supper for them, but Marian had no appetite. The pain in her side was definite now, from experience she knew that more would come. Her throat felt swollen. It hurt and it was hard to swallow. Never mind. She wouldn't let it ruin the evening. The fever somehow buoyed her.

She went into the drawing room and sat down at her grand old Broadwood. Johnnie followed, a smile of expectation on his face. He stretched himself out on the divan, preparing to listen. She could feel the fever rising, the ache beginning in her bones. She would play through it.

She settled her skirts and began playing the "Bénédiction" from the concert for him, the careful melody at the beginning, then the stretches of slow contemplation. *"D'où me vient, ô Mon Dieu! Cette paix qui m'inonde?* Whence comes, O God, this peace which floods me?"

Softly…soft…but she could do that, quietly, in the spirit of what Liszt intended. "Whence comes this faith with which my heart overflows?" The music was saying, "I'm not afraid because You are blessing me." Not just a holy passion, but also romantic, a rising up to Him.

Her arms stretched wide across the keyboard. And now the crescendo…I am with you…What did it matter who "He" was?

The music soothed her. The water falling…drawing to a close…This will ease your pain…will make you believe that once again peace and joy will come. Don't be afraid—If there is no God, then at least there is this earthly comfort, even as now the pain in her side was more intense, beginning to move around her body.

She was ill again, the pain was worse than it had ever been, but she went on playing, hurtling toward the inevitable, whirling into the darkness of the cold winter London night. Playing above all pain, going forward against it, when her fingers touched the keys...she was within the music...

And there he was, sprawled on his chair, her beautiful man, enthralled by her...his eyes wide and blue. Adoring her. Nephew, husband, loving and protecting her, guardian, her long-limbed man...

She was aware next of Johnnie carrying her upstairs in his arms, calling out, "Brett! Brett! I need your help. Fetch Sir James! Send someone!"

Every bump on the stairs was agony. He laid her gently on the bed, but the jolt was excruciating and she lost consciousness.

She came to when Brett placed a cold cloth on her head. "Ow! No, Brett! No. The cold hurts...I can't stand it!"

Sir James hurried into the room, he didn't even take his hat and coat off. She could feel the cold from the outdoors coming from him. He was looking down at her. He wasn't smiling. As he felt her forehead and examined her, she saw a panicked look come into his eyes.

She heard Johnnie say, "I can't watch this."

There was the prick of the needle. Then the morphine took hold.

"Does it still hurt?" Johnnie asked.

"No," she said, in surprise. She was gasping for air, but she managed to smile up at him. "Isn't that wonderful? I don't feel any pain at all now."

He knelt down beside the bed and took her hands in his. She saw tears running down his cheeks. "Please, Marian," he said. "Please, don't leave me."

Then she was gone.

Magnificat Anima Mea

Acknowledgments

To Joseph Luzzi, professor of Comparative Literature at Bard College, thanks for looking over the section on Dante. All errors are mine—or Johnnie Cross's! My deep gratitude to Hilma Wolitzer, who read the manuscript, made acute comments, and suggested the novel's title, and to other friends, writers all, who read various drafts and made valuable suggestions: Brooke Allen, Katherine Bouton, Gioia Diliberto, Emily Eakin, Leslie Garis, and Judy Sternlight; also to Anna Fels, physician and author, for helping me wade through George Eliot and Johnnie Cross's medical histories. Thanks to Dr. Howard Markel for the same. My appreciation especially to John Burton, chairman of the George Eliot Fellowship in Coventry, England, and to Vivienne Wood, the vice chairman, for showing me Eliot's world, and for their valuable insights into her character; and in Venice, to Matteo Giannasi, who gave me a tour of the Palazzo Giustinian, now the headquarters of the Venice Biennale, where Eliot and Cross stayed on their honeymoon.

To Joy Harris, my dear agent, without whom this book would not have happened, my thanks. I have never known an agent so willing to work so hard for a writer. She has helped me make this novel what it is.

Marjorie DeWitt, editor at Other Press, and Amanda Glassman, the editorial assistant, did an absolutely outstanding job in going over the manuscript and making it better. I also want to thank Jessica Greer, publicity director; Terrie Akers, marketing director; Yvonne Cárdenas, managing editor; Iisha Stevens, production and operations manager; and Lauren Shekari, rights director, for their care, hard work, and attention to detail.

Above all, there is Judith Gurewich, publisher par excellence, with a mind like lightning, a devotion to her authors like no one else's, who came to this armed with the most formidable intellectual background I have ever encountered in any publisher.

Finally, I thank my husband, David Nasaw, who has stood by me for thirty-seven years. He is my love.

Fact into Fiction

A BIBLIOGRAPHICAL ESSAY
ON WRITING *THE HONEYMOON*

For many years, I had pondered the strange, late-life marriage of my literary heroine, George Eliot, to John Walter Cross, a handsome young man twenty years her junior, who attempted suicide on their honeymoon in Venice. The accounts of the event in Eliot's biographies were meager, and indeed, the couple seems to have lied, or deliberately misled people, about what had really happened. They did seem, on the surface, to have recovered from their traumatic honeymoon, but Eliot lived only a few months afterward. Was this a tragic ending to what was an essentially noble life, which encompassed not only the genius of Eliot's writings, but also her long and loving relationship, out of wedlock, with George Henry Lewes, who had given her the confidence to become a writer and then died leaving her shattered?

As I began to write about Eliot's marriage to Cross, I was drawn deeper into her life, and I became fascinated by her evolution as a woman and as an intellectual. Here was one of the most famous authors in England, almost universally kind and generous. She was a woman of contradictions: a proper Victorian lady, shy and reserved, and yet I believe also a passionate and sensual person. Her "illicit" relationship with Lewes made her even more afraid of public disclosure, as did her daring decision later to run away with Johnnie Cross.

What were Eliot's thoughts while all this was happening, thoughts that, for the most part, she kept hidden under the cloak of her nineteenth-century propriety? I decided to write a novel in which I would try to imagine them. It would be fiction, yes, but in writing fiction one is always searching for the truth.

Thus, writing the book was a little like writing a detective story, a search for clues, a piecing together of facts and inferences.

For inspiration, I first went to the many biographies of Eliot. I began with Gordon S. Haight's magnificent *George Eliot: A Biography*, and the seven volumes of her letters which he edited, and upon which all other biographies stand. There were her journals, collected by Margaret Harris and Judith Johnson, and John Walter Cross's highly sanctified but nonetheless revealing biography of his wife written after she died. Frederick R. Karl's finely detailed *George Eliot, Voice of a Century*, and Kathryn Hughes's *George Eliot: The Last Victorian*, a more contemporary interpretation of her life, were invaluable. *Those of Us Who Loved Her: The Men of George Eliot's Life*, by Kathleen Adams, offered many new facts. I was especially fortunate to find, in the Princeton University Library, Eliot's notes for her unfinished novel about the Napoleonic Wars. But I profited from scores of other books about Eliot, too numerous to mention.

Eliot once told John Cross that *The Mill on the Floss* was her most autobiographical novel, and indeed, it provided insights into her relationship with her parents and with her brother, Isaac, as did Eliot's poetry, particularly her *Brother and Sister Sonnets*. Many clues were contained in Eliot's autobiographical essays, such as "How I Came to Write Fiction," her essays on painting, and her accounts of her travels through Europe, particularly of meeting Franz Liszt in Weimar.

Perhaps the most important people in opening up the world to the young Marian Evans were Charles and Cara Bray of Coventry. Charles Bray's *Phases of Opinion and Experience During a Long Life: An Autobiography*, was especially helpful in understanding the new world that confronted the twenty-one-year-old Marian. As for Dr. Robert Brabant, who probably seduced Eliot and certainly betrayed her, letters to and from Eliot's friends, particularly Cara Hennell, were revealing in understanding the crisis that occurred at his house in Devizes, as were secondhand accounts given by Eliza Lynn Linton in *My Literary Life* and by Brabant's daughter, Rufa, in John Chapman's diaries. Those diaries, discovered rather dramatically in a secondhand bookshop in Nottingham in 1913, and collected by Gordon Haight in *George Eliot & John Chapman, with Chapman's Diaries*, also contributed to my account of Eliot's romance with Chapman, as did Rosemary Ashton's delightful *142 Strand: A Radical Address in Victorian London*.

Eliot's friendship with the beautiful and fascinating Barbara Smith Bodichon sustained her through much of her adult life. Pam Hirsch's excellent biography of Bodichon helped me to create a fictional portrait of the relationship.

As for Herbert Spencer, that strange man, whose early work Eliot nurtured and whom she came to love, and who went on to become the most famous philosopher of his time, his two-volume *Autobiography* provided me with an account of his life, and also moments of humor. (I have no doubt that Spencer himself was entirely conscious of this.) Selections from *The Life and Letters of Herbert Spencer*, edited by David Duncan, were of great use to me.

For the wonderful George Henry Lewes, I am indebted to Rosemary Ashton's *G. H. Lewes*, and to *The Letters of George Henry Lewes*, edited by William Baker. *Dramatic Essays*, by Lewes and John Forster, provided much information about Lewes's humanity and wit.

The most difficult character to track was John Walter Cross. I traced his family tree, information about the bank his family owned, and accounts of the Crosses in Scottish and New York newspapers. I discovered his own, tentative attempts at writing in the archives of *Macmillan's Magazine*, and those of his sister Mary, too. Contemporary descriptions of Cross were very useful, by Cross's friend, Lord Acton, and by Eliot's adoring acolyte Edith Simcox in her *Autobiography of a Shirtmaker*, edited by Constance M. Fulmer and Margaret Barfield as *A Monument to the Memory of George Eliot*.

In trying to fictionalize the story of Eliot's relationship with Emanuel Deutsch, I owe a debt to Beth-Zion Lask Abrahams for her paper "Emanuel Deutsch of 'The Talmud' Fame" (Jewish Historical Society of England, Transactions, Session 1969–70).

Researching life in nineteenth-century Venice was a particular joy, as I read the travel essays of Henry James, William Addington Symonds, and William Dean Howells. Augustus John Cuthbert Hare's *Venice* was a favorite. Sarah

Bunney's paper, "Mr. and Mrs. Cross with the Artist John Wharlton Bunney in 1880," in the *George Eliot Review* (2011), helped me to imagine Eliot and Cross's visit to the artist.

These are only a few of the sources I read as I constructed my fictional world. I studied the floor plans of Eliot's homes, nineteenth-century railway timetables, accounts of resorts of the period, John Ruskin's *Stones of Venice*, the programs of concerts Eliot would have attended, and old maps and photographs of London, Venice, and other European cities.

All this enabled me to try and imagine George Eliot's thoughts and feelings as she lived out her life, and then, on December 22, 1880, as she died, with John Walter Cross, who truly did love her, at her side.

Reading Group Guide

1. When Marian and Johnnie arrive in Venice for their honeymoon, Marian finds that she is "unable to give herself over to the surge of excitement she'd experienced sixteen years earlier" (p 5) when she'd visited Venice with George Lewes. How does her romance with George compare to what she has with Johnnie? Do you think it overshadows her marriage to Johnnie?

2. Describe Marian's relationship with her brother, Isaac. What causes the rift between them, and how does this rift affect Marian's life and writing?

3. What is the relationship between Marian's perception of her own appearance and her intellectual development?

4. Referring back to Marian's perception of herself, how does the way she sees herself affect her demeanor and her behavior toward other people?

5. On page 367, Willie describes Johnnie as being "ashamed" of his illness. Is Marian ashamed too? If so, how does she handle her shame?

6. What do you make of Marian's reaction to Johnnie's "illness" (p 363) considering she herself had faced the prospect of suicide?

7. Describe Marian's relationship to other women. What do you make of her estimation of "frivolous women" (p 221) and her belief that women should take "care of children and their families" (p 147)? What does she mean when she realizes that in marrying Johnnie she will finally be "like other women" (p 329)?

8. Why do you think Marian marries Johnnie, even though she is still very much in love with George? How would you describe her relationship with Johnnie? How do you think Marian herself would describe her relationship with Johnnie?

9. Marian had "always wanted to write about a honeymoon" (p 344), and she calls her time spent with George in Dover their "honeymoon" (p 340). What are the differences between the two honeymoons in Marian's life?

10. Have you read any of George Eliot's work? How has *The Honeymoon* changed your knowledge or understanding of the famous author and her work?

DINITIA SMITH is the author of four novels, including *The Illusionist*, which was a *New York Times* Notable Book of the Year. Her stories have appeared in numerous publications, and she has won a number of awards for her writing, including fellowships from the National Endowment for the Arts and the Ingram Merrill Foundation. For eleven years Smith was a cultural correspondent for the *New York Times* specializing in literature and the arts. She has taught at Columbia University, New York University, the Bread Loaf Writers Conference, and elsewhere. She lives in New York.

ᴨ OTHER PRESS

You might also enjoy these titles from our list:

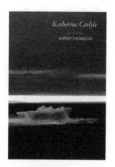

KATHERINE CARLYLE by Rupert Thomson

Unmoored by her mother's death, Katherine Carlyle abandons the set course of her life and starts out on a mysterious journey to the ends of the world.

"The strongest and most original novel I have read in a very long time…It's a masterpiece."
—Philip Pullman, author of the best-selling His Dark Materials trilogy

ALL DAYS ARE NIGHT by Peter Stamm

A novel about survival, self-reliance, and art, by Peter Stamm, finalist for the 2013 Man Booker International Prize

"A postmodern riff on *The Magic Mountain*… a page-turner." —*The Atlantic*

"*All Days Are Night* air[s] the psychological implications of our beauty obsession and the insidious ways in which it can obscure selfhood." —*New Republic*

THE DIG by John Preston

This fictional recreation of the famed Sutton Hoo dig tells the strange story of a priceless treasure discovered in East Anglia on the eve of World War II.

"A very fine, engrossing, and exquisitely original novel." —Ian McEwan, author of *Atonement*

"An enthralling story of love and loss, a real literary treasure. One of the most original novels of the year."
—Robert Harris, author of *An Officer and a Spy*

Also recommended:

COUPLE MECHANICS by Nelly Alard

At once sexy and feminist, this is a story of a woman who decides to fight for her marriage after her husband confesses to an affair with a notable politician.

"Nelly Alard delves into the core of infidelity with wry observation and subtlety. Riveting, beautifully detailed, and totally addictive. You won't be able to put this down." —Tatiana de Rosnay, *New York Times* best-selling author of *Sarah's Key*

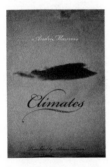

CLIMATES by André Maurois

First published in 1928, this magnificently written novel about a double conjugal failure is imbued with subtle yet profound psychological insights of a caliber that arguably rivals Tolstoy's.

"*Climates* is a delicious romantic bonbon that yanks the heartstrings." —*Wall Street Journal*

GALORE by Michael Crummey

A multigenerational epic set in the magical coastal town of Paradise Deep, full of feuds, love, and lore

"Crummey has created an unforgettable place of the imagination. Paradise Deep belongs on the same literary map as Faulkner's Yoknapatawpha and García Márquez's Macondo." —*Boston Globe*